Praise for

THE BLADE BETW

....

"The book is full of moments of slowly rising dread that end in shocking revelations, all of them building to a nightmarish town festival where the growing horror finally reveals its true face and intent."

—*Nightmare*

"[In] *The Blade Between*, the whole town of Hudson becomes a central character. . . . A sharp-edged novel. . . . Stunning." —*Locus*

"Miller's prose is phenomenal. . . . Miller has crafted a mature, thoughtful, and challenging novel that tackles the problem of *being ethical* in the world. . . . While *The Blade Between* is full of hurt people who are struggling, it's far from grim. The observational clarity Miller brings to the page is unflinching but, somehow, kind. He gives all these characters grace without erasing their flaws. . . . A discomfiting but vital story that throbs off of the page." —Tor.com

"The best horror is always timely. . . . Enter Sam J. Miller's *The Blade Between*, a supernatural thriller that hinges on an eviction crisis. Miller's novel, which also touches on homophobia, income inequality, and America's refusal to come to terms with its history, feels like the most 2020 novel imaginable." —*The Big Thrill*

"Miller expertly addresses the dark sides of gentrification. . . . All the characters in *The Blade Between* are three-dimensional (even the 'villain')." —*Alma*

"Sam J. Miller's *The Blade Between* stands out for its heroes' plan to raise sinister supernatural forces in defense of their city."

—CrimeReads

THE
BLADE
BETWEEN

ALSO BY SAM J. MILLER

The Art of Starving
Blackfish City
Destroy All Monsters

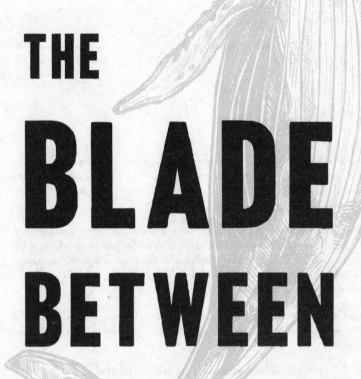

THE
BLADE
BETWEEN

A Novel

SAM J. MILLER

ecco

An Imprint of HarperCollinsPublishers

THE BLADE BETWEEN. Copyright © 2020 by Sam J. Miller. All rights reserved. Printed in the United States of America. No part of this book may be used or reproduced in any manner whatsoever without written permission except in the case of brief quotations embodied in critical articles and reviews. For information, address HarperCollins Publishers, 195 Broadway, New York, NY 10007.

HarperCollins books may be purchased for educational, business, or sales promotional use. For information, please email the Special Markets Department at SPsales@harpercollins.com.

Ecco® and HarperCollins® are trademarks of HarperCollins Publishers.

A hardcover edition of this book was published in 2020 by Ecco, an imprint of HarperCollins Publishers.

FIRST ECCO PAPERBACK EDITION PUBLISHED 2022

Designed by Michelle Crowe

Whale illustration by Alex Rockheart/Shutterstock, Inc.

Library of Congress Cataloging-in-Publication Data
Names: Miller, Sam J., author.
Title: The blade between: a novel / Sam J. Miller.
Identifiers: LCCN 2020014152 | ISBN 9780062969828 (hardcover) |
  ISBN 9780062969859 (ebook)
Subjects: GSAFD: Ghost stories. | Mystery fiction.
Classification: LCC PS3613.I55288 B58 2020 | DDC 813/.6—dc23

ISBN 978-0-06-296983-5 (pbk.)

22 23 24 25 26   cw   10 9 8 7 6 5 4 3 2 1

For my sister, Sarah C. Talent.
First friend; first reader; best critic.
A true child (and mother) of Hudson.

But it is not permissible that the authors of devastation should also be innocent. It is the innocence which constitutes the crime.

—JAMES BALDWIN

PART I

CHAPTER ONE

Welcome to Hudson: a whale of a town.

Bright raw wintertime, and Warren Street is a swathe of white and red. Blood-soaked men drag strips of whale flesh through the snow. Black smoke billows from man-size iron try-pots. Bones reach for the sky like irrational red fences; rib cages recently flensed. Hooks and knives and blades as long as swords slice and hack the air, a whole weird lexicon of specialized instruments: *mincing spade*; *monkey-belt*; *fire-pike*; *throat-chain*; *fin toggle*. The strips are sliced down into blocks; the blocks are fed to the bubbling pots. The whole city smells like blood and wood smoke and the thick meaty mammalian stink of melting blubber—marine and vaguely reminiscent of alcohol.

Blubber and skin and spermaceti are the engine of industry, the bloody gold that has powered Hudson's rise to power, boiled down and barreled and shipped off to light lanterns as far away as London—the baleen will become women's corsets, and the bones will be returned to the river—and the teeth will be scrimshawed and sent home to sweethearts, sold to collectors—but what will be done with the rest of these magnificent monsters, the livers as big as cows, the eyes the size of a human head? Intestines so long they could be stretched off to mark the extent of any one of Hudson's uphill streets. Brains bigger than any human's, and wiser, too, with the things they've seen, at depths that would crush a man like a baby chick in a fist. Sunken empires, sea monsters believed to be mere myth. The skeletons of a million drowned men and women.

What will happen to the rest of the whale?

Some will be fed to dogs and pigs. Some will be cooked and eaten by humans.

Most will be buried. Long trenches along the waterfront at first, then creeping up the streets as space runs out.

The hearts and brains of whales will feed Hudson's soil. Their blood ascends to the sky in oak tree branches, feeds its people in apples and corn. Seeps into the stone and cement of the foundations of its homes.

The sky darkens. The day's work is done. Men drink cheap cider. Tomorrow, maybe, more whale carcasses will come. The harbor stretches around into North Bay. You can count a couple dozen tall ship masts.

In twenty years the railroad will arrive, heading north from New York City, bound for Albany, for Canada, its path perfectly plotted to cut off Hudson's North Bay. Cripple the city's shipping trade. Start its slow decline into irrelevance.

Forty years after that, Hudson will have become the East Coast's largest center for prostitution, the Diamond Street whorehouses so notorious that they'll have to change the name of the street to Columbia after the governor personally sends a swarm of state troopers to bust up the brothels that local authorities have coddled—and patronized, and exploited for information—for decades.

Bootleggers will base their operations out of Hudson. So will crystal meth manufacturers, many years later. Movies will shoot here, ones that want somewhere that still looks like the Great Depression. Ones where Jack Nicholson is an alcoholic or Harry Belafonte is a broken-down gambler.

Hudson has been many cities, but it has always been this one. The one with soil steeped in blood; with a harbor full of bones.

CHAPTER TWO

*Easy, sailor—no need to take the stairs two at a time—she's not
gonna get any less dead, no matter how much you hurry.*

Dom slows down. Takes a deep breath.

These things happen. Town like Hudson, they happen all the
time.

Her neighbor found her. Came by to borrow a cup of sugar,
allegedly—more likely dropped by to buy weed—used the key Ossie
was entirely too free with giving away copies of—saw her lying on
her bed—checked for a pulse—found none—called the police.

Or, more accurately, called Dom.

Nothing unusual about that. Small town; she'd gone to school
with Dom, same as Ossie, same as everybody. The fact that she and
Dom and Ossie had smoked up together in this very same apart-
ment two nights before—the fact that she knew that Ossie and
Dom were sleeping together—none of that needed to go in a report.
Dom instructed her to call the actual police, who of course sent
him. Anything that happened downstreet, they sent him. The lone
Black cop on the force.

And now, here he is. In the sad sooty stairwell of Ossie's building.
Smelling cigarettes and spilled milk and cheap carpet cleaner—but
underneath it all, faint random atoms of the scent of some delicious

meat dish, something the nice Jewish lady on the second floor cooked every Friday for so many decades that you could still smell it six years after her death. Dom can't recall her name. Mrs. Kubiak? The ghost of the smell would never leave that building, not entirely. *That's all any of us leaves behind, sailor. If we're lucky. A smell in the air; a bunch of people who can't quite remember our name.*

Dom stands up straight. Gets himself together. Goes back into the apartment.

"Pills, probably," Louise says, looking at her with what seems to be anger but could be anything. "I won't tell anybody about you two."

"It'll be fine," Dom says. He takes the statement, lets Louise go, and goes in to sit with Ossie while they wait for the coroner.

She's on her back, arms crossed across her chest. He doesn't think he's ever seen her be still. Ossie was a live wire, a constant frenzy. It's what he'd always loved about her. As far back as middle school, she'd made bad decisions look magnificent. Even getting high couldn't make her chill—just unleashed a different kind of crazy: kinetic, compelling thoughts from her head, a new set of rambling theories and opinions.

And of course he'd never spent the night, so he'd never seen her sleep. When their time together was up, Dom went home. Ossie stayed here alone.

She looks alone, now. Dressed for bed, in a long T-shirt where a white and a black sperm whale made a yin-yang symbol. On top of the cluttered dresser, two empty pill bottles and a very minimalist suicide note. CREMATION, NO CEREMONY. And below that, standing in for a signature, a drawing of a cartoon whale. The one thing Ossie knew how to draw.

He didn't love her. They'd been friends. They were good together, in bed.

He doesn't feel guilty, either. This hurt is purer, harsher. She is gone. There will be no more late-night theories about Richard

Linklater movies, no more of the cookies she was forever baking but never mastering.

Dom sits down on the bed beside her. He feels so heavy.

"Ossie," he says, as close to a good-bye as he can come, and leans over so he can close her eyes. The pressure on the mattress causes her head to turn toward him slightly. Water dribbles out of the side of her mouth. Not spit: water. There is no glass by the bed, nothing nearby that she could have taken a sip from. Unless she swallowed the pills and then took a drink in the bathroom and then got into bed and somehow didn't swallow it or spit it up in the convulsions that almost certainly would have ensued? But even if that was possible—and it probably wasn't—why would she go to all that trouble?

He leans over. Sniffs her mouth. It smells like her—like cinnamon, chocolate—but like something else, too. *The sea at night*, Dom thinks, and whisks the thought away, and kisses her. The water is salty. Not like table salt. Dom recoils, stands up, suddenly eerily convinced that if he'd looked at her a second longer he'd have seen a hermit crab scuttle up out of her throat.

Someone downstairs is screaming. Someone always is, on State Street. Even though it's only a couple of blocks from Warren Street, where skyrocketing property values have replaced every poor family with a wealthy New York City transplant, State Street has stubbornly refused to be transformed. He knows exactly who is screaming, too. Because of course he does. He knows exactly who everyone is on State Street.

He hadn't closed Ossie's eyes, and now he can't.

CHAPTER THREE

RONAN

What new cage have I awakened in this time?

An old addict's trick, waking up wondering where you are and why without panicking. Being excited about it, even. Embracing the challenge of the moment.

I wasn't an addict anymore. I told myself that. Hadn't been high in a week and a half.

I was on a train, apparently. Engines churning. The wheel-thrum slowing as we drew near to the next stop. Lights arcing overhead—a bridge, an arm extended hopefully into the night. The Rip Van Winkle, to be precise.

So. I was going home. Huh.

Okay, cool, no problem. We can do this. We're grown-ups now. No one here can hurt us anymore.

"Hudson, sir," said the lanky child who collected tickets, and didn't he know that calling a forty-year-old gay man sir was like asking a chubby woman when she's due? The train smelled of hospital linen and cheap cherry-almond soap and blue gross Porta-Potty water from the open bathroom door at the end of the car and I was not ready to return to Hudson.

Twenty years, since the last time I made this trek up the river to the miserable grounds of my spawning. This shitty city full of terrible people. This place I swore never to see again. But, now, somehow—there I was, whole body aching, on a train I had no memory of boarding, pulling into the station.

It made you a pretty good detective, having a substance abuse problem. Piecing together the fragments of the moment, while trying to smile and look like you know what's going on. I took out my phone to check my calendar, but *Coffee with Katch* was the only thing marked down for the day. I smiled, remembering that lovely boy who'd shown up on my doorstep three days back wanting to model for me. I remembered making the appointment but couldn't recall whether it had happened. Come to think of it, I couldn't recall a goddamn thing, not even opening a bottle or unspooling a bag of crystal. I didn't feel any of the ordinary bliss or edginess of meth, so I was reasonably certain I hadn't relapsed. Between my legs lay my fully stocked camera bag, which I only ever trot out for an out-of-town shoot. Or a long trip. So which one was this?

The train blew its whistle. The lights of Hudson were sliding into place, a puzzle assembling itself against my will. Suddenly, I was having a hard time getting any air in my lungs. Suddenly my skin was on fire.

Shouts echoed in my head. Homophobic slurs. Hard fists to the face. Old wounds ached; faded bruises sprang to life. Unhealed scars. Shards of metal still stuck in me.

You can't be here.

I patted my pockets, plowed through my camera bag. No flask. No glass vial or plastic bag with sweet, sweet escape inside. So I had no choice but to turn to a lesser anesthetic. I switched on my phone, summoned up the soothing blitzkrieg of social media. Surfed the churning sea of my mentions. The fights I picked and the ones that picked me. Fallout from my latest photo shoot, which went live that week, all the predictable buzz and semi-scandal—an ad for some edgy new clothing line, starring that pretty boy from that big new movie, except in my photos he's naked on his knees surrounded by shadowy shapes, with a look on his face like he'd just been fucked into next Friday.

So I fought trolls for a little while. The guy who said I was an over-hyped pornographer, I called him an *underdeveloped hyena fetus*. Someone called me the six-letter F word and I told him to go suck a big bag of broken glass. And so on.

That got my blood going. Edged out the panic. Hate was reliable like that.

Smart money would have been to stay on the train. Wait one stop, get off at Albany, where there's an actual fully staffed station with stores and a platform, instead of getting off in Hudson, which is a ghost town after 10:00 P.M. But it was late—this had to be the last train of the day—and I didn't want to spend the night in any station. Or spring for a hotel. Success and money were still relatively recent developments, and anytime I could avoid spending it I did. My best bet was to disembark in Hudson, crawl home to Daddy no matter how much I was dreading it, sleep there, have a decent break-fast with the man, pat myself on the back for making him happy with a surprise visit, never mind that it was as much a surprise to me as it was to him, and then get the fuck back to Manhattan.

I stood up. Grabbed my stuff. Turned to step into the aisle.

But something was wrong. Hudson is a sleepy tiny town. The kind of stop you might sleep through. It had happened to me more than once, in college: dazed, exhausted, aching from drugs and sex in excess, heading home from my wild grown-up life to the weird mental limbo Hudson always put me in. Before I vowed to never re-turn. Back then, I was usually the only person getting off the train. And now—the aisle was full. A couple dozen people waited up ahead of me. Scruffy hipsters; impatient important women. Abun-dant piercings. A tiny dog peering out of a purse. A gay couple in pastel polos. Everyone looked expensive. Even the people who were obviously unemployed, who had come from overcrowded Brooklyn basements.

Was there some kind of arts festival that weekend, or secret religious retreat? Could that be why I had come? Was I here to photograph something? But no conceivable thread connected these inexplicable tourists. Only that they were all white, and they were all outsiders. And that an observer could not have known, by looking at us, that I was not one of them. Somehow, I was the last in line. Everyone else had been ready. They knew the stop; knew that when the train passed under the Rip Van Winkle Bridge it was only a matter of minutes before it pulled into the station. They came here often.

What the hell happened to Hudson?

"Hudson," called the conductor, sounding half asleep himself. Cold wind whipped down the length of the car. Autumn; I'd forgotten that, too. The city had felt like summer. My dizziness doubled. Impossible scenarios swamped me—what if I had been asleep for months? What if I'd been wandering the earth in an Ambien sleep-walk session, committing all kinds of irrational acts, and was only just now waking up?

That's what you get for trying to get sober, Ronan. Meth might have been a mean-ass bitch to you while you were doing it, but who's to say how much nastier it'll get now that you've quit cold turkey?

I took out my phone to try to call Katch, but I didn't have his number. He'd only ever shown up at my studio in person. I clicked onto the calendar event, even though I knew it didn't have any more information.

Except: now it did. I'd left the location blank, but now there was one: Hudson, New York. How the fuck had that happened?

Since stopping drugs, weirdness had abounded. Radio static when there was no radio around; shadows moving on the wall when there was nothing to cast them. Like the dark side was trying its damnedest to leak into the sunlight. This must just be one of those things. My brain had gone briefly on autopilot and piloted me here.

Just more evidence of how far gone you were—how close you came to destroying yourself—how broken you were, and how brave you are for fixing yourself.

I told myself that.

We shuffled down the aisle, them to their weekend escape and me to my doom.

No. You can do this. You're a big boy. They have no power over you.

That's who I was, after all. As an artist. Someone who sublimated his pain into art. Even when I was scared shitless, or shivering with rage, or sick with lust, or inexplicably sad to the point of collapsing to the floor in the fetal position.

Almost all of which, right then, I was.

Really? None of them have any power over you? Not even—your father?

I gulped cold air, my breaths ragged and desperate. There was only one way through this.

Hold tight to the razor edge of your hate, the blade that Hudson lodged ages ago between your ribs. Twist it just enough to keep you sharp. If it cuts your hands and you bleed, so much the better—catch the blood in a rectangle and call it a photograph.

CHAPTER FOUR

A bell rings, in Dom's pocket. Clear echoing bronze, sounding like the blue mountain sky above a temple. He'd listened to hundreds of bell sounds online, before he selected the one that would be his cell phone ringtone.

"Hello?" he says.

"Hey, hon," his wife says. "What time you coming home?"

"Soon," he says, looking down at Ossie, and feels so weary all of a sudden. "People still over?"

"Yeah, they're leaving soon," Attalah says.

Impromptu meetings have been happening in his living room a lot lately. Local businesses struggling with rent raises. Family friends—and then friends of friends—wondering what they could do about the eviction notice that had appeared on their apartment doors. His wife is a natural leader, fearless and well connected, and she always has something for everyone who calls her up or comes through the office of UPLIFT Hudson, the organization her mother founded. A lawyer who did favors, a social services agency that could help them access an obscure subsidy. But some things can't be stopped, not by all the wisdom and connections in the world.

The tide is rising, in Hudson, and Dominick wonders how long it will be before it swallows them all.

"You need me to make dinner?" he asks, grabbing a fistful of Ossie's sheet and sniffing it. She always went a little too long between changing the sheets on her bed. He'd given her shit for it, but now he is grateful. Her smell is strong on them. "I can swing by ShopRite on my way."

"Shiloh Baptist had a chicken dinner fundraiser," she says. "Joe brought enough for everyone."

"That was nice of him," Dom says.

Shiloh Baptist had been having a lot of fundraisers lately.

"You okay?" she asks.

"I'll tell you when I get home," he says.

"Somebody die?"

He chuckles. "Am I that predictable?"

"You are, and so is Hudson."

"I guess," he says. The town's crime rate is high, for it being as small as it is. So are its suicide numbers. "Let me finish up here and I'll see you soon."

"Okay, honey," she says.

"I love you," he says, and here the tears really do come.

He isn't in a hurry to share the details on this one. She's just lost someone to suicide herself, several months ago—Katch, a brilliant, beautiful troubled kid she'd mentored in her organization's after-school arts program. After graduation he'd spent a couple of messy years trying to be a model. Endlessly traveling down to New York City, "getting his face out there." Loading up his arms with ink. Making a lot of bad decisions in both places. He'd overdosed, but he'd also left a note.

And soon after that, Attalah's mother had had a stroke. A brilliant, incandescent woman, all rage and home cooking, who'd waged war on the newcomers from her public housing apartment when obesity compromised her mobility to the point where she could no longer visit the office of UPLIFT Hudson. Now unable to speak, barely able to move.

He looks back. Ossie is smaller than she'd ever been before. Already her corpse is replacing her in his head.

Dom goes downstairs, gets into his car. Sits for a while. Starts it up.

He isn't sure why he goes home the way he does. Something he sees out of the corner of his eye, maybe, or he just doesn't want to go right home. It's the long way around, looping down to Front Street and then up Warren. Hudson is like that. There are so many ways to go, but every one of them leads to the same place. So you change it up every time you drive. Maybe you turn left on Fifth instead of Third, or right on Columbia instead of State.

Dumb luck, sailor, or something else, that Dom drives by the butcher shop that night at all.

CHAPTER FIVE

RONAN

The train blew its whistle and pulled out of the station. Heading north. On to Albany, Niagara Falls, maybe even Montreal or Toronto. Sleepy people watched me from the windows, and then they were gone. One last whistle, a long and taunting sound, mocking me for being where I was, and then it was swallowed up in darkness and distance.

Across the street, a billboard sported a smiling blue sperm whale and the words: WELCOME TO HUDSON: A WHALE OF A TOWN! Loud hellos were being said. Pretty hip people were being picked up by their pretty hip friends. A boy turned to grin, walking past me, and that bare raw flash of gay lust was like another twist of the blade. To be so free and careless of such dangerous desire—here in Hudson, of all places.

Doors slammed. Cars scurried off. In three minutes, five tops, the station was as silent as it had always been.

So. Evidently Hudson had evolved. Become something new. The depressed postindustrial dead end I'd left behind was gone. That corpse had been resurrected, Lazarus-like, to be some kind of weekend haunt for the New Brooklyn's overflow. Vaguely, I recalled my father saying something about a story in the *New York Times*, the skyrocketing real estate market, "in a year or two we'll be able to sell the old butcher shop building for millions. Actual millions."

My father. Remembering his voice made my breath stop.

Idiotic, to have gotten off the train. To come here. To go see him. When I'd spent so long hiding from what was happening to him. When I'd ignored the desperate plea in his voice, the one he was too proud to put into words, begging me to come. Missing me. Wanting to tell me that things were serious. That whatever was going on in his brain, whatever was making him vanish into himself—he wasn't getting better. That he wouldn't.

Someone, hopefully human, howled from down by the boat launch. I turned onto Warren Street, scouring my phone for signs of why I was where I was. Still nothing but the calendar entry for coffee—but why couldn't I recall the actual encounter? Katch didn't have an email address. Not even a phone number. Our encounters had all been in person, since he first showed up at my studio a week ago. That hadn't seemed strange, before, but now it added to the uncanniness of my predicament.

Shadows danced in my peripheral vision. Dark shapes at the ends of side streets. Figures watching me from third-floor windows. A glass bottle broke, somewhere down the block. I felt stretched thin, pulled too tight. Like the Ronan I had been, that poor sad fuck I left behind so long ago, he was here. He'd been waiting for me. And now that I was back on his home turf, he could come clawing out of me at any moment.

The war between the two Hudsons was particularly acute on Warren Street. Old establishments like the West Indian grocery, with its beef patties and a cat asleep on the bread, or the sporting goods store that had been there since the fifties. But there weren't very many of those. Mostly it was antique shops. So many antique shops. Windows full of cow skulls. Empty bottles of laudanum or mercury. Campaign buttons for candidates long discredited. Gnarled statues that were probably racist once, but now the paint had peeled away. All of history was here, caught and carved up into tiny profitable pieces.

I passed Third Street. I stopped in front of one window, which boasted a bronze statue of three stacked life-size pigs. Capped with a weird sort of hat that I swiftly saw was a lampshade. A lamp. A fucking six-foot-tall, six-foot-wide bronze lamp. I took a step back, on outraged instinct. Raised my camera. And only when I looked through the wide-angle lens, taking in the entire storefront, and saw the precise shape of the darkness behind the pig lamp, did I know where I was.

My father's butcher shop. Fifteen years gone; died when Wal-Mart came to town. Vacant all this time, I'd imagined. I never knew he rented it out. I never knew so many things.

HUDSON BUTCHER, said the sign across the front. Where my father's name once was. An old-time, tongue-in-cheek typeface. Blue letters ribbed in red. So clever. So hip.

A phantom stepped forward from the darkness. Shaped like me—same height, same stoop—so that we each could have been looking at our own reflection—but this was not me. This was Narcissus's nightmare; Dorian Gray's portrait. His wrinkled face cracked into a curiosity that was a mirror for my own, but the pajamas he was wearing were a mockery of my own attempt to be sharp, to be fashion, to be somebody.

"Hey, Dad," I said, except that no sound came out.

With mild amusement, I saw that I wasn't breathing. The amusement evaporated when I saw that even when I tried my hardest, I still couldn't.

I dropped to my knees. That helped a little, but I still had to gasp and wriggle to get half a lungful of air. So I fell onto my side, and then lay on my back on the filthy sidewalk that smelled like dog pee. That was better. My father looked down on me from inside the shop. I crossed my arms over my chest and shut my eyes and what did it matter that tears were streaming out of them?

CHAPTER SIX

....

RONAN

The cop car pulled up, flashed lights, double-parked. A door opened.

Shit, I thought, pressing my cheek into the cold dirty sidewalk. *What kind of bullshit town has Hudson become, where a damaged addict can't even lie in the street anymore?*

"Sorry, Officer," I said, shutting my eyes, gathering my strength, my charm. "I fell."

"I thought that was you," the cop said, his voice strumming a chord deep in my belly. "Didn't quite believe my eyes."

Against my will, my eyes opened. It was him all right. Tears clouded my vision again.

"Dominick?"

"Hi, Ronan. Having some trouble?"

"You might say that."

I stared. Black bare tree branches spread out in a crown behind his head. Past that, the sky. Stars. I hadn't seen them in so long.

He held out one hand. I grabbed it, held tight. His touch unlocked something that had been locked up tight for a long, long time, except I wasn't sure what exactly it was.

He pulled. I pulled. Dom was trying to bring me back up to my feet, and I was trying to pull him down to the ground with me. Of course he won out. He'd always been the strongest man I knew. I rose up slowly, unwillingly, but when I was standing again he tugged me forward, into a hug.

"It's good to see you, Ro."

"You too," I said, and shut my eyes again, let myself collapse into the hug. He smelled the same. Same body oil he'd always worn, like the inside of a mosque, clean and sacred and earthy. Once, on 125th Street, I'd passed a street vendor with a table full of incense, burning a dozen different kinds at once, and one of them had been Dom's, except I couldn't separate it out from the panorama of over-lapping scents.

"You're a cop," I said, stupidly.

"Don't hold it against me. I try not to be one of the bad ones."

I laughed. It couldn't be easy for him, downstreet. Cops were right up there with cockroaches on the list of things people com-plained about. I got shit from the girl behind the counter at a store once because I have the same last name as an officer, someone I'm absolutely no relation to.

"So . . . my dad's in there," I said, pointing to the inside of the antique shop that had once been our butcher shop. "He doesn't . . . look well."

"No worries," Dom said, opening the door and calling my father's name. He stepped from the shadow, looking lost and little in his pajamas.

"Does this happen often?"

"Not often," Dom said, taking my father by the hand, leading him out into the streetlamp light.

"Hey, Dad," I said, trembling—startled at how much this hurt. After how hard I'd been trying to hide from him. From this. The tiny man he'd become. The damage that had clearly been done.

My father didn't answer. He looked in my direction like he could see me, but not like he recognized me.

Or he does, and he's too disappointed to know what to say to you.

"You're back," Dom said, the way you do when you want to distract a guest from something embarrassing. "For a day, or . . . ?"

"Not sure," I said, and then thought, *Wait, now we're not sure? Now it's not, you can bet your ass I'll be on the first train out of here tomorrow morning?*

"You're one of them, now," he said. "The hipster invaders."

"I'll try not to be one of the bad ones," I said.

"I set that up for you. You're welcome. Come on, I'll give you two a ride home. In the back like a perp, or in the front like my partner?"

"Your partner," I said, and wondered if he could hear the hunger in my voice.

He opened the door for me. "Some people get a thrill out of riding in the back, is all."

"Yeah, maybe some other time."

"Your dad gets to be the perp then," he said, opening the back door for him. Another twist of the blade, to see the childlike way he obeyed. Allowed himself to be seat-belted.

It smelled like Dom in there. Dom, and coffee, and leather. I got an instant erection and put my bag on my lap to hide it.

"My dad still lives in the same place," I said, pointing to the tippy top of Warren Street.

"I know," he said.

Of course he did. Hudson was small. Everyone knew everything about everyone else. "How's he . . . been?"

It was an idiotic question. The answer was right behind me, and it was *Not great.* Walking the chilly streets at night, barefoot and pajamaed, going to work at a job he hadn't done in ages. Living in a city that no longer was.

I felt skinned, stripped bare. Like I was the barefoot streetwalker. Exposed to Dom and everyone in Hudson as an utter failure of a human being, the selfish son who abandoned his father, ignored his descent into . . . whatever this was.

Dom shrugged, started up the car. "It's been hard on him, these last few years. The way the town is changing."

I nodded, like I knew.

"You know your dad," Dom continued. "This town is everything to him. Friends with everybody. So it's been rough, watching everybody suffer. Businesses closing. Folks getting evicted, struggling to pay their rising rents."

"Sounds like Brooklyn," I said. "I didn't realize it had gotten so bad."

"Some folks say your dad is the only thing standing between this town and total destruction," Dom said.

"How's that?"

"Refuses to sell the butcher shop building. Rents it, but won't sell. And it's the last piece they need, for this big proposed real estate development project. Pequod Arms, they're calling it. A bunch of big condo and rental developments that would fuck us all the way up."

"I'm glad to hear that he's holding out," I said, and wondered idly what kind of money was on the table. Like, buy a Brooklyn apartment money? Never have to worry about rent again money?

"But, yeah. It's messed him up a lot, the way this town has changed lately. My wife is the same way."

"Your wife," I said, and, yeah, I was vaguely aware he'd gotten married—had seen it on Facebook, maybe, or gotten an email?—to a classmate of ours, Attalah, a brilliant illustrator, in all my art classes, the only other person besides me who refused to say the Pledge of Allegiance. "Congratulations."

"Thanks," he said, with a chuckle. "Been ten years now. Have we really not seen each other in that long?"

"Been busy," I said. The streets went by slow, outside his window. The five-and-dime was gone; the family-owned restaurant. The toy store where my father got me a big plastic magenta allosaurus the day eight-year-old me crashed his bike and broke his wrist. Replaced by antique store after antique store. Each one throbbed like the socket of a long-gone tooth.

"Busy being a big-deal photographer," he said. "Your father is super proud."

"Thanks," I said, disturbed, to think of my father seeing my dirty sexy pictures. Somehow I imagined he'd be too squeamish to Google me, go to my website, follow the links I posted to new spreads and covers as they came out.

"You look exactly the same," he said. "How is that?"

"I'm a gay man, Dom. We're neurotic and obsessed with our appearance."

"Unlike straight guys like me who really let ourselves go, you mean."

I laughed. He laughed. It was a joke.

I mean, he *had* let himself go. But he was still every bit as beautiful as he had been in eleventh grade.

I started to say, *So now you're straight?* But there was no need. Because of course he'd always been straight. Even when he was my first boyfriend, his big secret, I'd known what was up. Why we could never be.

This was bad, that I'd been back such a short time and already I was feeling so many emotions. I had to get the fuck out of here. But first: I had to steer the conversation onto less raw ground.

"Stubb still around?" I asked, mock-nonchalant, like the boy I feared most was a matter of no importance to me at all. The most vicious of my high school bullies; the horriblest homophobe, the one who would punch me in the arm again and again in math class while the teacher pretended not to notice; the one who, one Saturday night while I was at the movie theater with my mom and dad, hollered from the back row, *Ronan Szepessy is a faggot!*

"Course he is," Dom said, shaking his head. "Where else is he gonna go? Nobody'd put up with his shit anywhere else, but here he's got his daddy the mayor to keep on shielding him from the consequences of his actions."

"His dad is *still* the mayor? How is that possible?"

"No term limits in Hudson. He's not running for reelection, though. Jark Trowse is running, and that's his handpicked successor."

"The internet guy?"

"Yup. Word is, mayor's stepping down 'cause his son's a liability. Sick in the head, or maybe an addict. Whatever it is, people say it's just a matter of time before he does something really cataclysmically bad, and Daddy Coffin doesn't want to have to be in the public eye when it happens."

"It's a little on the nose," I said, "the last name. *Coffin*."

"Historic," Dom said. "One of the founders of the town was named that. Also a whaling ship captain." At the next stoplight, he turned to me and smiled. "I probably shouldn't tell you this, because it's just gossip, but you remember Rich Trappan?"

"Of course," I said, "Stubb's little henchman and partner in crime. The two of them were practically joined at the hip." I grinned, excited for the gossip, but also—grateful to Dom, because of course he knew how feigned my nonchalance was, how much hate and fear I still had in my heart for Steve "Stubby" Coffin. *Funny how I probably haven't talked to this guy in like fifteen years and he still knows me better than anyone.*

"Well, word is—they actually did join at the hip on a couple of occasions. Buddy of mine who was on the baseball team said he saw them going at it in the gym showers once."

"No fucking way," I said.

"Fucking way."

"Those fucking hypocrites."

"Thought you'd like that."

"Thanks, Dom," I said.

"Anytime, Ro."

My knees throbbed, hearing my name in his mouth, his sweet deep voice.

"I always thought you were like the Prince of Hudson," he said, pulling up in front of my father's house. "The castle at the very top of Warren Street, looking down on all of us."

It *was* a great location. I'd always felt like somebody, perched where the main street became a dead end. "The place is a shithole," I said, and that was true, too.

"We know real shitholes downstreet," he said.

"Dom," I said, and put my hand on his. He pulled it away. So I didn't say what I'd been about to say. Which was good, because I didn't know what it was. And I was afraid of what could have come out of my mouth.

"Great to see you, Ronan," he said, and scribbled something on a piece of paper. "Here's my number. Call me up, if you're around for a little while. I know Attalah would love to see you, too."

"I'd like to see her, too," I said, and I meant it. I liked her a lot, even if I also harbored an abundance of impure thoughts about her husband. "Thanks for the ride, Dom."

"You need a hand with your dad?"

I did, but how could I ask anything further of him? So I smiled and said, "Nah, I got it," and went around to let my father out. I had to lean in close, to unbuckle his seat belt. I had to smell him. Cigarettes, Stetson cologne, stale linen, the faintest whiff of body odor.

Dom drove off. Left us standing there.

"Let's go inside, Dad," I said, and Dad came with me, up the steep steps—a docile child—*my* child.

I paused a moment at the front door. Let the wind sough through me. Pulled out the key that I'd never taken off my key ring.

It still fit. This was home, no matter how hard I had been hiding from it.

Back inside, safe in familiar surroundings, Dad seemed to come back to some semblance of life. Bolted the door behind us; pulled the blinds; went to the bathroom and started brushing his teeth.

"You gonna be okay, Dad?" I asked, but, again, the question deserved no answer. He was okay enough to have survived this long without me—and also he wasn't.

I didn't take out my phone and look up train times for tomorrow. New York City already felt flimsy, fading. Eyes shut, feeling my way in the familiar dark, I went down the hall to my room.

My Walkman was where I'd left it, beside my bed. Thick with dust. I plugged my headphones in, switched on the radio. Static filled my ears, and then, against all logic, music. How did the thing still have battery life after lying silently for so many years?

I got into bed fully dressed, my head still spinning with withdrawal and the general weirdness of the evening's chain of events. Stinking like sweat and booze and Hudson sidewalks. Scrolling through my mentions, letting the chatter of strangers distract me from the fresh hurt of my father's fallen state. It was working, still, but it wouldn't work for much longer. In the morning I'd have to find myself an actual drug.

"This is Ms. Jackson, here on the Graveyard Shift," came the scratchy familiar voice, the DJ who'd soothed all my lonely late nights. As baffling as my batteries, her still being alive all these years later. "It's coming up on eleven fifty-seven. So this will be the last song of today. Always a difficult challenge for a DJ. How best to sum up everything we've been through, and prepare us for doing it all again tomorrow? Tonight I feel like dedicating something to the lonely hearts, the people tucking themselves in tonight. One may be the loneliest number, but remember that we come into this world by ourselves and that's how we go out of it, and everything in between—all the love and togetherness that fills our hearts—that's all temporary. So if you find yourself by yourself tonight, just know that you have a leg up on the rest of us. An insight every happily coupled person lacks."

"One Is the Loneliest Number" came on and I wasn't mad at it, didn't feel sad about it. I appreciated her. Like she could see into my heart, just like she always had, and was speaking directly to me and me alone.

CHAPTER SEVEN

The meeting has mostly broken up by the time Dom gets home. A couple of people around the kitchen table with Attalah, drinking beer and laughing.

"Dom," says Joe Davoli, getting up. Shaking hands.

"Joe. What's the word?"

"Same old," Joe says, avoiding eye contact.

Joe's brother is an addict. Dom has never busted him, but sooner or later he probably will. The guy is dumb about the risks he takes, hawking stolen goods on Craigslist or saying on Facebook that he has Percocets for sale. Half the town, it seems, has a hard time looking Dom in the eye. Like they're afraid he can see their sins glinting there, or the guilt of their loved ones.

"Everything okay?" Dom asks, sitting down at the table. Attalah had baked. Whatever it was is gone, but the room smells like cinnamon. Their kitchen, like the rest of the house, is small but never feels that way. She makes it feel right.

"Planning a rent party for Susan," says Ohrena Shaw, who is several years younger than them but has a creative mind his wife admires. "Her rent went up in January and she's a couple months behind already."

"Awesome," Dom says, thinking, *That's not awesome.* A rent party might buy one, two months max. Not a sustainable business model. Especially not when half of Hudson is scrambling to pull together rent parties of their own. He listens as plans are put together, Attalah typing away on her tablet—who will cook, who will collect the cash, who can borrow a credit card swiper to take donations that way. Eventually Joe and Ohrena drift toward the door and depart.

"Sorry," Attalah says, returning. She wears a long red and black and green dashiki. Resplendent as always.

"Don't be," he says. "You know I appreciate the work you do. But what you *should* apologize for is not saving me any of whatever that was." He points to a baking sheet where droplets of watery white icing are splattered.

"Blame Joe," she says. "You know Becky never feeds him."

"I'm glad, actually. I need to not eat so much. I've let myself go."

She comes up behind him, puts her hands on his belly. "I think you're perfect."

"You're sweet to say so."

She goes to the sink. Dishes clatter. He shuts his eyes, savors the silence beyond their walls. There is space, now, between their lives and that of their neighbors. Three years in a house and he still hasn't gotten used to it, after spending his whole life in the ceaseless rumble of Bliss Towers.

"Who died?" Attalah asks, handing him an opened beer. Then she gets one for herself and sits down beside him. In the house she moves around as swiftly and gracefully as she had in high school, using its familiar surfaces to propel herself from point A to point B without the cane she needs to use outside of it.

"Ossie," he says.

"Oh, lord," she says. "That is so sad. How? Someone so young, there's no good answer."

"Suicide, seems like."

Attalah makes a small sound of pain and shuts her eyes. There's

Katch right there, on the fridge. Not five feet away. Huge smile, and the year he was born, and the year he died.

He almost mentions the salt water. He doesn't know why he doesn't. And then he doesn't know why he would.

"We were . . . me and Ossie . . ."

Dom doesn't need to finish the sentence. She knows how it ends. He feels like tears are imminent and wonders why they don't come.

"Oh, honey," Attalah says, and takes his hand.

"I'm sorry," he says. "I know you prefer not to know."

She laughs, a short, kind noise. "That's just when it's someone I might have to look in the eye," she says.

"You're not threatened by dead women?"

"Threatened differently," she says, and smiles.

He lowers his head to the table and kisses her hand, then rests his cheek against the cold Formica. It feels good.

"Ronan Szepessy is home," he says, when the silence has gone on long enough to give weight to the words, to communicate the nameless inexplicable fear he feels about Ronan's return. "I just picked him up off the sidewalk in front of where his father's shop used to be."

She curses softly, kindly. Of course she feels it, knows it. What this might mean. How it might disrupt the fragile status quo that has so far kept the Pequod Arms project at bay. Who knows how. Maybe Ronan will talk his father into selling. Or get a power of attorney, sell it himself. They sit there for a long time, and then they head to bed.

When Dom comes out of the bathroom, she has switched on the radio. Their favorite DJ is midway into her set.

"This is Ms. Jackson, here on the Graveyard Shift," comes the scratchy familiar voice. "It's coming up on eleven fifty-seven. So this will be the last song of today. Always a difficult challenge for a DJ. How best to sum up everything we've been through, and prepare us for doing it all again tomorrow? Tonight I feel like dedicating something to the lovers, the couples tucking themselves in tonight. The world is a cold, dead, sad, scary place, and love is the one thing that makes it livable. So cuddle closer, to the sound of Otis Redding, who knew love like nobody else before or since."

"These Arms of Mine." One of their favorites. Ms. Jackson has a knack for that, like she sees into their heart, and speaks directly to them and them alone. He gets into bed beside her. They cuddle closer, spooning together sexlessly, immaculate.

CHAPTER EIGHT

RONAN

lay in bed with my eyes closed for as long as I could, trying to convince myself I was safe at home in New York City and the night before had all been a dream.

But I knew from the second I woke up where I was. I could tell by the smell that I'd come home—old man and cigarettes, coffee and Stetson cologne and the muck of the river—and by the amber brilliance of the sunlight.

I lay still, taking stock of my body. Searching for the aches and woes of withdrawal, but came up with nothing.

Nothing, except abject emotional misery. And a head full of bizarrely vivid dreams (*black water; whales in the sky; drowning in the dreamsea*). And whatever the hell had happened to me the night before, to get me to Hudson.

One new piece the morning light illuminated: Katch called me, from a pay phone, and told me to meet him at Penn Station. And when I got to the station he'd called me again, from a different pay phone, telling me he was delayed but to get on the 9:30 train to Hudson, and he'd meet me there.

Why the hell would I have agreed to that?

More pieces were missing. I'd have to wait and hope they resurfaced.

I put clothes on, moved through the house. Taking stock of the situation. The fridge full of mismatched plastic containers; food brought by friends and neighbors. The line of empty beer cans beside the kitchen sink. Pabst Blue Ribbon; Dad hated the stuff. But Marge, the woman who'd worked the butcher shop cash register for as far back as I could remember, had loved it. Funny, how well I still knew the man, how certain I could be about this. That he would never be sleeping with Marge, any more than he would buy Pabst Blue Ribbon even if it was on sale. She was taking care of him. Cooking, cleaning. Wiping his ass for all I knew.

"Hey, Dad," I said, coming into the living room.

My father frightened me. Sitting in his ancient recliner, still in the same pajamas. Still not hearing me when I spoke. Still not seeing me.

Water dripped into a bucket in the corner. The bucket was overflowing. I picked it up, took it to the bathroom, dumped it into the toilet. Some splashed onto my hand. I lifted it to my face—smelled it—licked it. Sure enough: salt water.

"What's up with the ceiling, Dad?"

No facial hair. More forehead than I remembered. His curly hair cut shorter.

"Ro," he said, then opened his mouth, but nothing further emerged—which had always been his way, to say as little as possible, to make his sentences short if they happened at all. Back then I'd felt like it was a choice, a facet of his taciturn masculinity to keep his words mostly to himself. Now it was like there was nothing there, like a lifetime of holding back his words had caused him to lose them altogether.

I went back to my room and got dressed to go out. I had to get the fuck out of there.

Dad was waiting for me when I stepped out of my room. Standing in the hallway, mouth slack, eyes glazed.

"They'll be so glad you came home," he whispered.

"Who, Dad?"

He turned and padded softly back to his recliner.

"No one's happy to see me, Dad. Nobody in Hudson likes me."

"They finally got you here," he muttered as he went. "They've been trying for so long."

....

IT WAS WORSE BY DAYLIGHT, somehow. The night before it hadn't felt real, the spectacle of what had happened to Hudson. In the dark it had the same stillness of any normal American city that wasn't New York. The store signs were all updated, that was all. Now I could see it for the corpse that it was.

But not a corpse, or not just a corpse. The dead city had been infected with something, and reanimated. Doors opened and shut, cash registers clanged, pedestrians smiled; but the soul was gone.

Last night it had felt like the phantom ache of a long-gone tooth. Now each gap felt raw, fresh, like a hard fist to the face had just popped it clear out of my jaw.

A clothing boutique inhabited the body of what had once been Warren Street's best Italian restaurant, Mama Rosa's. My favorite toy store was now stocked with antiques. So was the bakery. So was the photography shop.

What did they do to you? I whispered, over and over again.

Barely ten A.M., and there I was. Awake. Dressed. Walking. When was the last time I'd done that?

Historical Materialism, one store was called. I went in looking for Karl Marx references, but of course it was only capitalism being clever—good old-fashioned materialism, the empty pursuit of material objects, as applied to old things—not historical, per se, but old, having been created during history.

"The theme this month is seafaring," said a sweet young woman with rectangular spectacles who I was probably wrong to instinctively hate. Harpoons hung from the ceiling. She held up a tray in which hooks and blades lay spread.

"That's so great," I said, staggering backward, fumbling for the doorknob in a blur of horror. "So great."

It slammed behind me.

I'd written a note. Left it on the butcher block in the kitchen. *Hey Marge! I'm back in town for a bit—give me a call when you get this? Ronan.* And I added my cell phone number.

The weirdest part of all: a coffee can ashtray on the front porch. Full of cigarettes. Unfiltered, though, and not Dad's brand. I'd picked one up, sniffed at it. Cloves. Katch's brand.

Marge made sense. Her beer cans could fit into a comprehensible narrative. Katch and his cigarette butts popping up on my father's porch could not.

Was he from Hudson? Was that why he showed up at my studio's doorstep? Was that why he'd had me come home?

They finally got you here, my father had said. *They've been trying for so long.*

I remembered the big real estate project Dom had mentioned. Maybe the people behind that were the *they*? But they'd have had a million ways to reach out that didn't involve a boy like Katch.

The next-best guess I could come up with was a homophobic conspiracy to get me home and murder me . . . but Katch was clearly queer himself, and probably wouldn't be a part of that . . . and why would my hometown bullies suddenly want me dead?

The familiar sooty chrome exterior of the Columbia Diner caught my eye, sucked me inside by awakened twenty-year-old instinct— an entire childhood's worth of Saturday-morning breakfasts with my dad, on our walk to work at the butcher shop—remembering the way I always wanted to sit on the stools along the counter, but Dad said those were for people who were by themselves, whereas we got to sit in the booths—and how I'd always imagined the counter to be for grown-ups, and dreamed of the day when I'd walk in the door on my own, miraculously an adult, and sit down on a stool and ask for my regular—

But there were no stools now. No counter. The booths remained, but their shredded pleather had been replaced with something shiny and stylish, in one of those of-the-moment shades I refused to know the name of. Puce, probably, or ecru. And there was no bowl of pee-flecked mints beside the cash register anymore. And there was no cash register. And the massive laminated diner menus I loved so dearly had been replaced by small squares of card stock. And instead of a heavy old Greek there was a young man with rectangular spectacles.

"Cup of coffee," I whispered, horrified as a recovering alcoholic would be to hear himself ordering a scotch on the rocks. "Black. No sugar."

He took me to a table. I sat. I drank my coffee when it came.

I never touched the stuff in New York City. My life was already high-strung enough without surplus caffeine. Part of my patented System for mind-altering substances. By exerting control in small ways, like skipping coffee or never smoking pot, I could ignore how I'd lost control in big ways. Like how I was spending five hundred dollars a week on crystal meth—Tina to her gay friends—and doing some increasingly unwise things while under her influence.

"Oh my god, my place is such a shithole," said a boy behind me. The girl he was with smiled understandingly. "The whole building smells like pork fat like *all* the time, from my neighbor downstairs cooking damn empanadas for the thirty-ish people who seem to live there."

"State Street is the Wild West," the girl said. "The new frontier."

"I know," he said, and here came the punch line, the self-congratulatory point to the story: "And it's totally worth it, for how much space I get for the money."

Unspoken: *unlike your place.*

I knew all the beats, because I'd been overhearing this conversation for years. Had had it myself on more than one occasion. But that had been in Brooklyn—Williamsburg, then Bed-Stuy, then Bushwick. That had been someone else's home being unraveled. Now it was mine.

State Street had been where the poor people lived, or one of the places, back in the day. Now it was the new frontier, the development that the gentrifiers were just beginning to dismantle.

I shut my eyes, blocked out everything but the words they said and the taste of my coffee. Hate and caffeine; each one exhilarating in its own way. On the wall beside me, a pig was painted in bright primary colors on a piece of plywood with splintered edges. It could have been the work of a child, except for the eye—which was entirely too human, and deeply disappointed in us.

Why did this hurt so bad? I hated Hudson. I'd hated everyone in it. For twenty years I'd hid from it.

But my father loved it. And losing it had broken him.

When the gentrifier larvae got up to go, I followed them. I barely thought about it. Hate had filled me up, was pressing the buttons that operated the machinery of me. We went down two blocks, then turned west and went one more. At Fourth and Columbia, they entered a long low industrial space that had been inactive for as long as I could recall but was now bustling with light and motion.

I walked inside and bile flooded my mouth. Light fixtures made of stag horns hung from the ceiling. So did human-size dream catchers. Hundreds of frames filled the walls, old photographs and obscene needlepoints and protest slogans in bright calligraphy. A woodworked banner placard ten feet tall and twenty feet long was behind a desk.

PENELOPE'S QUILT, it said.

"Help you?" a woman asked, smiling, because of course I did not look like a local. I had the knitted cap at an insouciant angle, the tight jeans, the short sweater. The beard that was eloquently tapered instead of unruly and lumberjacky. The leather jacket that was black and shiny instead of brown and scuffed from farm or shipping labor.

She thought I was One of Them.

And I hated her so much. With those vintage rhinestone cat-eye glasses—which were, admittedly, magnificent—and that proprietary smile.

"Not just this minute, thanks," I said, but did not depart immediately.

"I'm Lilly," she said. "You tell me if you need anything."

Of course I knew what Penelope's Quilt was. The internet's largest community of artists and makers. Headed by a quirky gay celebrity billionaire founder CEO, who was apparently running for mayor of Hudson. Hundreds of thousands of new artworks came on the site every week, but none of them could be bought with money. Barter only. Every maker started with a baseline score, and then the community assigned value to each new work, and then you could exchange that work for another artwork of equal or lesser value. Or you could trade twenty-five original lithographs for a fucking hand-sanded Tlingit canoe or whatever. It had been explained to me a hundred times before, by earnest artist friends who adored it, and it had always seemed proudly, unacceptably complicated.

What the fuck was it doing headquartered in Hudson?

"Here," Lilly said, putting a pamphlet in one caffeine-shaking hand. "Come to our potluck!"

"Thanks," I said, smiling, drowning, and stumbled out into the bright white day.

CHAPTER NINE

S ervice isn't 'til tomorrow," says Ossie's sister Lettie when she comes out of the funeral home and finds Dom waiting.

"I know," he says. "Wondered if I could talk to you."

"Hope you're not planning on wearing that," she says, heading down the walk and past him, tapping his uniform on the way. "Ossie's friends don't care much for cops."

"I don't care much for Ossie's friends," he says, following her. "But I won't be wearing it."

"Funny," she says. "Here I thought you *were* one of her friends."

So she knew that they'd been lovers. Of course Ossie would have told her sister. Not because they were close, but because Lettie was born-again now, and Ossie scandalized her whenever she could. Attalah won't like it, knowing that Lettie knows, but the two haven't talked since high school so it's unlikely to come up.

"I was," he says. "I am. But I'm not overly concerned about the opinions of her little wannabe gangbanger buddies."

"As if you were any better. A married man, stringing her along."

Dom frowns. *And what about you, Lettie? How good were you to her? How good are you to her now, putting together her funeral when she left a suicide note that explicitly said "No ceremony"?* But he bites back those words. He can't begrudge her her grief, or her anger, or even how she expresses it. To have lost someone she loved so much, to suicide—he feels certain he'd break forever from a pain like that. "That's not how it was and you know it. Did she or didn't she have a bunch of other guys to sleep with? Half of them, she was the one doing the stringing along."

Lettie nods. Looks at the ground. And just like that he watches her anger at him melt away—a flimsily constructed weapon, like her austere gray dress, against the grief that now rises to take its place. She shuts her eyes. Her cheeks redden.

"Hey," he says, reaching out a hand to touch her shoulder. She flinches, and then she hugs him. Her body is so much like Ossie's it hurts, small against his tall frame.

"I'm sorry," she says, the words hitching slightly. "I'm just—I've just . . ."

"Hey," he says. "Shhh."

They stand like that. Thick leaves shade them, but soon they will be falling.

"Don't take it personally," she says. "I'm mad at pretty much everyone in her life. Everybody who failed her. Including myself."

"Same," he says.

"Why'd you come here, anyway?"

"To talk to you. About Ossie. Find out if she said anything to you. Anything—" He doesn't know how to end the sentence—*that might explain why her mouth was full of seawater, 114 miles from the sea?*—so he just goes with "unusual."

"Things were bad," Lettie says. "Ossie was really messed up in the head, these past few weeks. Like, hearing voices, dreams she thought were going to come true, that kind of thing. She said she felt . . . threatened. Like someone was trying to kill her."

Hairs stand along Dom's spine. "What did she say, exactly?"

"Kept saying *they* were trying to silence her. Sounds like standard persecution fantasy stuff, right?"

"Yeah," he says. Dom knows that taking a sick person's fantasies seriously is a dangerous game—but what if they weren't fantasies? "Did she ever . . . say anything? About who they might be? Why they were trying to silence her?"

"No, but . . . the reddest red flag of all—she got religion."

Dom laughs, but doesn't say, *Ossie would never.*

"Got a kind of spiritual therapist, over at Grace Abounding. She said Pastor Thirza was the only one who could help her."

"That's excellent, Lettie, thanks. I'll go talk to her. And if someone really was trying to hurt your sister, you can be fucking certain that I'll make them pay."

Lettie smiles at first, and then frowns at the curse word.

. . . .

SOMETHING'S BEEN BOTHERING ATTALAH ALL DAY, making her jittery and unfocused at work and even afterward, volunteering at UPLIFT Hudson, and it isn't until she's home listening to the radio and Ms. Jackson plays "Happy Together" and she gets a vivid memory of Ronan Szepessy back in ninth-grade homeroom saying, *"I love this song because it's got 'Happy' in the title but it's like the saddest song ever,"* that she figures out the source. Ms. Jackson is spooky like that, somehow always able to choose a song that pierces straight to the heart of whatever's perplexing Attalah.

So she hauls out her high school yearbook and looks up Ronan.

His photo is goofy, an idiot smile on his face, but the Ronan she remembers wasn't goofy. And he never smiled. He's making fun of the photographer here. Shaved head. Awkward Adam's apple. Bright eyes and sharp cheekbones, but back then he hadn't known what to do with them.

He knows now. A short precise beard; professional haircuts. Practiced, skin-deep smile. In magazine pieces and glossy website profiles he looks stunning and sophisticated, in that way only gay men ever seem to be. She's watched his rise, taken pride in it. When *New*

York magazine named him one of the ten top photographers under forty, she'd posted the link to the 'You Know You're From Hudson When' group on Facebook . . . but then had to delete it when the *Hometown boy makes good!* comments got drowned out by a hundred variations of *Fuck that faggot.*

Remembering the slur twists tiny blades between her ribs. So many people she's loved have had it leveled against them. Katch's photo still hangs on her fridge: the program from his memorial service. Six months ago, now, but the hurt still so sharp. Such a radiant, special smile. The kind that went all the way to the core of who he was.

Unlike adolescent Ronan, teenage Katch had known exactly what to do with his beauty. He'd taken it to the streets, let it open doors for him, even if some of those doors opened onto exploitation. With his sights set on a modeling career, and a pretty shallow pool of self-esteem to draw on, damaged as he was by growing up trans and of color in a racist transphobic place like Hudson—like America—he'd trusted a whole lot of untrustworthy people and engaged in a whole lot of sketchy activities. Which had led him to heroin, and an overdose.

With difficulty, she snaps her focus away from grief.

Ronan's return could mean defeat. That's the most likely scenario. That's why she's been anxious all day. He gets hold of his father's building and sells it to Jark Trowse's Pequod Arms project.

But Ronan's return could also mean victory. It all depends on how she plays it.

Hudson had not been kind to Ronan. He'd talked a lot about how much he hated the town back in high school. But so had she. And here she was, still, trying to save it.

Because here's the thing she learned along the way—hate is a kind of attachment. To hate something is to cleave your soul to it. And sometimes love is the root of hate. Sometimes you say you hate something because you love it, love what it could be, but hate what it *is*, how flawed and broken. She feels that way about her country. Hates it, because of how much she loves it, and how much awful stuff it does, how far short it falls of its own professed ideals.

She texts Dom for Ronan's phone number, and when she gets it she texts him: A little bird told me you're back in town! Want to come catch up over cookies? I remember how much you liked my mom's peanut butter chocolate—I finally mastered the recipe. Let me know when works for you.—Attalah

She thinks a second, before sending another one:

Dom is so happy you're home, and so am I

······················

CHAPTER TEN

RONAN

Pure masochism brought me to the potluck dance party.
Masochism, and Katch. I'd been way up Columbia Street
when I saw him in the distance. Tiny in the twilight that smelled
like the sea, even though we were a hundred miles upriver from it.
Beautiful—proud posture, inked arms, clove smoke clouding the
air behind him—but stunted somehow, like the weight of Hudson
threatened to break him.

Sunset had made the sky spectacular, deep dark blue in contrast
to the amber cast the streetlights gave the city. The Catskill Mountains were black in the distance. Clouds shaped like whales drifted
high overhead. My breath caught, the scene was so lovely. Something throbbed through me. A feeling, for this place. This city. This
fucking city. Something a lot like love.

How the fuck is that possible?

I took out my camera.

But when I looked through my lens? They weren't clouds that
looked like whales. They were whales. Blue whales and black sperm
whales, big as zeppelins, swimming through the sky in hyper-slow
motion.

Good news, Ronan! You're going crazy!

Bile flooded my mouth. I stopped and spat it into the street; tried to shake off the shivers.

According to the internet—where I'd spent entirely too much time that morning—the most dangerous symptoms associated with methamphetamine withdrawal are severe depression and the potential to develop psychosis.

A laugh or a shriek tried to climb my throat, but I bit it back. I had the strangest feeling that if I laughed out loud I'd break every window on Warren Street.

I followed Katch down, too far away to call his name without sounding like a crazy person—but when he turned into the Penelope's Quilt warehouse I figured I'd have ample time to corner him in there.

And say what? What are you doing in my hometown? Did you show up for the photo shoot I had you scheduled for yesterday? And did you have anything to do with my ending up here? Did you smoke some cigarettes on my father's porch?

Anyway, the vast place was so packed I couldn't find him, with the lights down low and the music up high, and strobes and screens turning every person's face into a dozen different faces. So while I waited for him to emerge from the crowd, I indulged in masochism. The pain of looking at these laughing hipsters. Maggots consuming the corpse of my town. Filthy hyenas savaging the body of a magnificent elephant. Pretty much all I'd been doing, in the days since my arrival. Reveling in agony; hiding from my broken father.

Jark Trowse smiled down at us from a dozen giant campaign posters. Lilly stood beneath him, rhinestone glasses and all, handing out buttons and big sincere smiles.

I didn't venture far from the door. Katch might slip out once he'd had something to eat—and anyway I wanted an easy escape route myself, for the inevitable moment where I gripped the knife blade of my own hatred a little too hard and started bleeding. I wasn't standing there very long, but I was able to snag and drain champagne flutes off the trays of three separate waiters.

Cold wind caressed my face, but I didn't look at the opened door right away.

"Ronan," Dom said, startling me, and I turned to take him in. In uniform, gun at his hip, he looked like the latest avatar of some magnificent warrior god.

"Dom," I said, throat dry, struggling to clear my head of how the sight of him still hit me. So tall, so clean-shaven. "Don't tell me you're part of this scene."

"You blend in better than me," he said, but then grinned.

Attalah had texted me earlier in the day, and I'd meant to write her back. Now I felt guilty for ignoring her message, on top of my guilt for feeling such lust for her husband.

Thirty seconds of silence later, Dom asked, "Wanna get the fuck out of here?"

"Hell yeah, I do," I said. "But we didn't eat anything. Allegedly they spend a ton of money—"

"Don't you read? If you eat the food of the underworld, you're condemned to stay there."

"Of course," I said. "How silly of me to forget that."

Once we got outside I leaned against him as we walked. He let me.

"Those fucking assholes," I said.

"Yeah," he said. "You eat *anything* today?"

"Why?"

"Because you sound like maybe you're a little drunk."

"I'm fine," I said. "I had a lot of coffee, which is a stimulant, and a lot of alcohol, which is a depressant. So they cancel each other out."

"Come to my place," he said, and my heart leapt, and then quickly crashed down: "Attalah will get you fed."

"Sure," I said, because what was the alternative? Wandering the streets in a panic of hatred? Heading home to be swallowed up again by the sadness of my father's fallen state? To drown in the sea of words we'd never get to say to each other? So I went, to the home of the first man (*the only man*) I'd ever loved, to be fed by his wife.

"You moved out of the Towers," I said, when he steered us away from State Street.

"Yup. Bought our own place."

"I'm so happy for you guys," I said, dishonestly. Or rather—I *was* happy for them, but I was also desperately unhappy.

So maybe I *was* kind of a little drunk.

"Kids?" I asked, as we walked up to the front door.

"No kids," he said, ushering us in, and there had to be a story there.

Attalah was seated in a recliner, reading a book. I'd forgotten how impressive she was, how regal. How big, in so many senses of the word.

"Hello, Ronan," she said, smiling. "Welcome back to our fucked city."

She got up. It took her a minute.

"I'm sorry I didn't reply to your text," I said. "Figured showing up in person would be even better."

"You figured right," she said, and hugged me. And I felt so held. So found.

Our eyes locked. I could see it there, somehow. Her hate. Her anger. It mirrored mine. And I smiled, and so did she.

Where had it come from, this anger? This town hated me. My life in Hudson had been miserable. I still carried the scars. The broken-off blade between my ribs.

So why was I so angry? Why did I want to murder them all, these innocent, wide-eyed hipsters who were killing the thing I spent years dreaming of killing? Why save Hudson at all?

I couldn't answer. I didn't know. All I knew was: this rage, this hate—it felt a hell of a lot better than the hurt of how I failed my father. Hate was a drug, and if there was one skill I'd spent years cultivating, it was the knack for self-medicating.

"It's good to be back," I said. "I think."

"We don't get to choose our cages." She gave me one last squeeze before releasing me, and it felt so good (*so maternal*) I could feel my throat tighten. "For better or for worse, this is home."

And, *yes*. I knew. Even then, even there at the very start, I could see that they were a scapegoat, an oversimplification. That I hated the invaders, blamed them for my father's decline—because if I didn't have them, there'd be nowhere for this hate to go but back onto me. I'd have nothing to drive this harpoon blade into but my own barren, fucked-up heart. And that was unacceptable.

. . . .

"I WANT THEM GONE," I said, without planning to. Two hours had passed, drinking beer and eating cookies Attalah had baked. Talking shit about the new Hudson. Two hours of her anger seeping into me, a contact high that did for my rage what crystal did for lust—magnified, multiplied it; mutated it into something dark and disturbing and dangerous. "I want them all to run screaming from this town and never look back."

"Shhh," Dom said. He took another cookie.

"No," I said. "I don't just want them gone. I want them broken. I want them to hurt like we've been hurt. I want them evicted, displaced. I want them to lose everything."

Dom started to say something, but Attalah silenced him with one raised hand. "So do lots of us, Ronan. But there's nothing we can do."

I continued, feeling weirdly like I was watching myself from outside my body. I'd finally found a replacement drug, and I was well into the shoulder of the high by now—the sweet spot where you can feel your whole body and brain blossom. "I want to harrow them down to their very souls. I want them to know that they are hated, and to live the rest of their lives with the shadow of that hatred blocking out the sun on even the brightest days."

"There's nothing we can do," she repeated. Her dreadlocks went halfway down her back. In the time we'd been sitting there I'd fallen maybe a little bit in love with her. Back in high school we'd been buddies, but I'd never had a conversation anywhere near this long with her. She was compelling, dynamic. Enchanting. Sitting there, under her spell, eating her cookies, I could feel the boundaries of the possible begin to shift inside me.

"We've tried," she said. "For years, we've been trying. I've talked to every lawyer and community organizer and halfway-human politician I could get on the phone or whose office I could talk my way into, and there's nothing—"

"Nothing *legal*," I said. The words hung there. They got bigger the longer the silence went. I had never seen Dom so shocked, not even the first time I kissed him. "You've been doing, what? Petitions? Meetings with politicians? Church fundraisers? Nonviolent demonstrations? That won't work here, will it?"

Attalah's eyes locked onto mine. I didn't blink.

Dom laughed, but it failed to break the tension. "You can't be serious. What are you—"

Attalah raised her hand again, without breaking eye contact. Dom fell silent. "What are you saying, Ronan?"

"I'm saying that I want to destroy them," I said, and it felt so sweet to say it, like a hit of a drug that peeled back my inhibitions and let me see parts of myself so ugly and beautiful I'd spent a lifetime hiding them from myself. Even sweeter was seeing that it was true. I *did* want to destroy them. I could do it, too. I could do anything.

Fuck meth. This feeling was magnificent.

"I will break every law of man and God to do it," I said.

"That's a bold statement for someone who ran away from here

the first chance he got and never looked back," she said. "Where's all this town spirit coming from?"

"I failed my father," I said. "I abandoned him. All the hate and pain I felt here—I connected it with him. I may be too late to correct the damage that I did, but not to atone for it. And for so long, I was so focused on how much I hated this place that I never saw how much I also loved it. I see it now, though, walking Warren Street, seeing what they've done to it. I think we can do this, Attalah. You and me."

"Me," she said. "Why me?"

"Because you know this place and all these people. Who has power and who has secrets. And people love you and respect you. They'll listen to you. But mostly—because you're as angry as I am. Aren't you?"

She nodded.

"Between the two of us we could probably come up with a pretty solid plan. Couldn't we?"

She nodded again.

"Fuck," Dom said, standing up. "Y'all are serious. You are, aren't you? I can't be here for this. Whatever the hell you're doing, I don't want to know about it."

"Then go," Attalah said, scooting her chair closer to me. "And shut the door behind you."

PART II

ey, A," Zelda Outterson says, sliding into the well-worn seat across from Attalah's desk. They went to high school together, but the past ten years weigh like twenty on her face.

"How've you been, Zelda?"

"You know. Getting through it."

"That's all any of us can do."

Originally, Attalah had planned to use a client as her proxy. She'd ransacked her files, read deep into sordid stories. Assessing the parents she knows are terrible, versus the ones who ended up under the watchful eye of Child Protective Services only because of a messy divorce or a vengeful ex or a racist neighbor with CPS on speed dial. Attalah has access to so much information. For hundreds of parents, she knows precisely how they had failed their children. All their oversights and errors, whether due to ignorance or malice or addiction or sheer dumb blistering bad luck. And she knows the fault lines of hate and rancor between friends and neighbors—who snitched on who, who phoned in false reports. And she has a lot of leeway in the work she does. A huge amount of power over the outcomes of the cases under her purview.

In the end, she realized there was no ethical way to use a client.

And anyway the perfect person has been right under her nose all along.

Zelda Outterson has worked at CPS for five years. One of five people Attalah supervises. She is quiet, and kind, and hardworking. Attalah remembers hearing that she'd had a bit of a bad reputation back in high school, but who hadn't? All she needs to know about Zelda is, she loves her town and she's struggling to make ends meet.

"How's your downstairs neighbor been treating you?"

Zelda rolls her eyes at the perennially sore subject. "That fucking asshole. Every time I fucking watch TV or have one fucking friend over, he's banging on the ceiling or knocking on my door, asking, *Would I please please make less noise?* And he's some rich city fucker, paying three thousand dollars a month, and my rent is a thousand because I been there so long, so you know damn well which one of us the landlord sides with."

Shouting, from an adjacent office. Shannon Gallo, probably. One of the hottest of the many hot messes on Attalah's caseload. Three hours late for her appointment, and pitching a fit because they wouldn't let her in to see Attalah right away.

"And your sister? Where's she these days?"

"Philmont, like pretty much everybody else who got pushed the fuck out of downstreet."

Attalah nods and bites back a smile. She can smell it on Zelda: the hate. The anger. So palpable that she feels comfortable scrapping the long and roundabout map she'd charted, for how to bring the conversation around to the Ask. "What if I told you there was something you could do about them? The people jacking up the rents?"

"I'd say I'm not trying to go to jail for murder, and I'm not sure what the fuck you can do about it other than that."

"I'm working on something," Attalah says, and leaves it there.

Zelda looks out the window, onto Long Alley. Kids go by on bikes. Someone has spray-painted SATAN'S GOT YOUR NOSE on the door to Mitch Teator's garage. Eventually she leans forward and says, "'Something' sounds a hell of a lot better than the *nothing* that we've been doing."

CHAPTER TWELVE

RONAN

The Hudson River had risen.

All the way up Warren Street, to the tippy-top of the hill where our house sat. The whole town was underwater, and little waves lapped at the steps to our front porch. My father sat beside me on the top step, bare feet in the water, looking out at the river-sea that extended to the horizon. We cradled coffee mugs; two cigarettes smoldered in an ashtray between us. We watched whales swim through twilight thunderstorm skies.

He turned to me and opened his mouth to speak. No sounds came out. He kept trying, making heaving noises, gagging sounds. I scooted closer, leaned my head toward his.

A hermit crab scuttled up out of his throat.

My own screaming woke me up. Or anyway—brought me back to the here and now, the safe Hudson whose sloping main street wasn't underwater. Whose river glimmered safely in the distance. Whose sky was bright with sun coming through gray morning clouds. I was still sitting on the front porch. My father was asleep inside.

I looked in my lap: same mug, but full of water.

I took a sip. Salt. But not sterile like table salt mixed with tap water. Brackish and murky and full of flecks of things, like someone had scooped it out of the sea a moment before. I poured it out into the grass, and a little trail of sand was left along the inside of the cup.

I remembered now. This had been normal, once. This . . . bleed-through. All through my childhood, all through my adolescence. Dream leaking into reality; nightmare seizing hold of you in the middle of the street. Passing people in the high school hallway or the McDonald's parking lot who maybe weren't real, or maybe died a long time ago. As soon as I moved away I stopped thinking about it, the way you don't reflect on a headache when it's gone, but it occurred to me in that moment that I must have been craving un-reality pretty hard. Because right around then was when I started indulging in illicit substances to excess.

I started to text Dom, but what would I even say? *We need to talk about whatever fucking supernatural miasma hangs over this city? I finally figured out why I became a drug addict?*

I put my phone away. There was too much work to do.

. . . .

THREE TRIES WAS ALL IT TOOK to catch Treenie Lazzarra's eye and have it seem like happenstance. Twice I walked up to her storefront window and pretended to peruse the FOR SALE AND RENT postings, but both times the space was empty and I had to walk down the block and wait five minutes before attempting it again. According to Attalah, the girl we'd gone to high school with ran the city's busiest realty office. And according to her ads, which were up all over town, the *New York Times* had called her *"one of the prime architects of Hudson's renaissance."*

The third time I went by, she was sitting at her desk facing out. I saw her see me, out of the corner of my eye, saw her jump up out of her seat waving frantically while I fronted like I couldn't see her.

"Ronan?" she called, opening the door, her voice every bit as too-loud as it had been in high school. "Ronan Szepessy?!?"

"Treenie?!" I exclaimed, mock-shocked. "It *is* you! I saw your name on the sign and I just didn't believe it. 'Must be another Treenie Lazzarra,' I told myself, but of course there could only be one."

We hugged. I held on extra tight for extra long. Like I was just that happy to see her.

"Come *in*, come in," she said, ushering me over the threshold into a spare wide space that held only images. Giant flat-screen televisions. Picture frames for slideshows shuffling through images of houses. Silvery black and white; bright, clean, muted color. Hudson's history; Hudson's new moment. Her desk was tiny, minimalist; a white shelf built into a white wall. The place smelled like money, like a bank.

"Wow," I said, meaning it. "This is something."

"Isn't it though?" Her hair, wild and big and curly in high school, had been straightened into lifeless drapes down the side of her head. She looked older, in spite of the makeup. "Who would have thought shitty little Hudson would become such a happening place?"

"Not by accident, I'm sure," I said. "We owe all this to a small handful of hardworking people who made it happen. People like you."

"Oh, stop," she said. "There's just something about this place, you know? Something magical. Like Bruges. Have you ever been to Bruges?"

"Not yet."

"It feels frozen in time. Old buildings, untouched by modern development. I wanted to share Hudson with the rest of the world, but so did plenty of others. Have you seen Dom since you've been back? You two were inseparable. Made the oddest pair"—she paused, thought about how that sounded, then added—"Because he was so much taller than you."

"Right," I said, smiling, remembering how we must have looked when we left the potluck together: the tall, well-groomed cop beginning to fill out his uniform and the short skinny, scruffy haggard addict. We'd looked different back in high school, yes, but now we were worlds apart. "Yeah, I've seen him."

"I am *such* a fan of yours," she said. "I'm sorry, I know I come across like a total stalker with how I use that GIF of Michael Jackson eating popcorn every time you're tearing some new asshole a new . . . well, asshole." I smiled. I hadn't noticed. I had set my Twitter so I only ever saw notifications from blue-check accounts— famous people, fellow "influencers," whatever the fuck that meant on any given day. Small-town real estate agents didn't cut it, no matter what the *New York Times* said about them. "How long are you in town for?"

She sat. Treenie had always been formidable, a bundle of energy and enthusiasm that was unstoppable once she set her mind to something. In high school the something had always been related to cheerleading or the yearbook or something else I had no emotional stake in. But now, mere feet away from her, I could feel the radioactive intensity of her determination. Idle, now—a down moment—but a deadly engine once cranked up all the way. What a foe she would be, when she knew what I was up to. Why I was there.

"You here for your dad?" she asked.

"Yeah," I said, and didn't fight the sudden rush of sadness that bowed my head. Emotion was good. People understood emotion.

"We're all so sad for him," she said. "And for you. He was an amazing man, your dad. *Is* an amazing man."

Except that we're all salivating over the prospect of his death because he's the only thing standing in the way of our plan to transform this city into a playground for the very rich.

"Yeah," I said, and decided not to ask about the Pequod Arms just then. I knew she was involved—Attalah had said so, and there were images of the expensive artist renderings mixed in with the slideshows on her wall—but better to make it seem like I was clueless for as long as possible. "Such a different world now, it seems like. A whole different crowd of people."

"Oh my God, Ronan, you'd fucking love it here now. There's so much cool stuff happening! So many gay people, so many artists . . . you had a rough time of it in high school, but you wouldn't recognize the place now."

"I hear that guy—what's his name? The tech superstar?" And I pretended to wonder. "Jark Trowse? I hear he walks around town like it's nothing. Like he's not worth more than God." So casual.

Treenie laughed. "You have *got* to meet him. He is such a character. We've become quite close. Obsessed with this town. You know he's going to be our next mayor, right?"

Yes, I thought, pocketing the TROWSE FOR MAYOR button she handed me. *I have* got *to meet him.*

Word was, he'd offered my father five million, six times the building's assessed value. You couldn't stand long, against money like that. Sooner or later he'd take it off the table, offer it somewhere else. Bribe a mayor to engage eminent domain; launch a smear campaign. Hire a hit man.

"Let's set it up," I said, refraining from licking my lips. "The three of us, let's get drinks."

This, I could do. This was my skill set.

I was a photographer, sure, but the photo itself was only the icing on the cake of my art, the tip of the iceberg of me. My vision, my concepts—they took work to make real. They took plotting, and scheming, and manipulation. Finding bizarre locations; sweet-talking owners into offering them up for free or cheap. Reaching out to hungry Instagram thirst-traps, pretty tatted unemployed gym boys who would work dirt cheap for someone with a six-figure follower count. Props; stylists; catering; costuming. To say nothing of the concepts themselves, the smutty or gory story lines that got me called *a fucking sicko* on the regular, like the one I did for PETA where the reality-star-child-turned-clothing-empire-maven of the moment stood naked and blood-drenched over a very realistic-looking CGI skinned human corpse with a sign in her hands that said: FUR: HOW WOULD YOU LIKE IT?

"I'll text him right now," she said, and then her phone rang and she excused herself.

There were no documents to root through, and the computer on her desk was showing a password-locked log-in screen. But this was just a scouting run. An attempt to make contact. Form a relationship. Work a source. Already I'd wrangled an invite to hang out with a billionaire mastermind. I'd work my way into the inner circle of whatever the fuck this was in no time.

"Business calls," she said after hanging up. "Sorry to cut this reunion short, though, Ronan."

"No, no, do what you have to do," I said, and handed her a business card. "That's my cell phone number. Let's set something up with Jark."

"Will do," she said, and hugged me again. This time it was she who held on tight.

I followed her out onto the sidewalk, and she locked the door behind her.

"You don't want to turn off the screens?"

"No," she said. "They run twenty-four-seven. You never know who might walk by."

It was the old photos that infuriated me. Our history slid past, one image at a time. A worm to hook customers with. I don't know why it bothered me so much.

"Bye, Treenie," I said as she got into her car.

I didn't recognize any of the faces I saw on Warren Street. But they were still there, all the people I had known back then. All the people I had hated. Maybe one or two got out. A couple more were locked up, and probably an abnormally high number of them were dead. But mostly they were still there. Somewhere.

They never liked me. None of them. Because I was gay—because I didn't care about any of the things they cared about—because I couldn't wait to get the hell out of that shitty town.

Because you were an asshole all the time, prompted an unwelcome voice in my head.

I was an asshole all the time because they were assholes to me first. And because I was just generally miserable.

Because of your mother.

I flinched away from the topic, but that would not do. If I was going to be ruthless with them, I had to be ruthless with myself.

Yeah, because of my mother. Because she killed herself when I was sixteen. Because I didn't handle it well. Because who fucking could. Because my dad didn't, either, and who can fucking blame him . . . but I *had* blamed him, of course. I'd needed his help and he couldn't provide it, and so I hated him, and so I did stupid things and burned a lot of bridges and then as soon as I graduated I got the hell out of Hudson and didn't look back and didn't talk to him for a year, even though he called me once a month, and when we did resume communication it was a weird, desultory thing where we never really said anything of substance—and I could tell I hurt him—and I knew I could help him so much with a simple fucking visit—but I couldn't bring myself to do it—and I told myself there'd be time, there'd be so much time for us—

And now: there wasn't time. He was almost all the way gone.

I stopped myself short of the edge of that abyss. There was no time for self-pity or regret. I had work to do.

Hate had taken me this far. It was the blade between my ribs. It was the pain I grabbed hold of, to make my art.

I owed it everything.

CHAPTER THIRTEEN

A ttalah!"

Rick Edgley is mostly naked when he opens his door, wearing only cut-off jeans, and he's clearly mortified to have been discovered in such a state by someone he actually respects. Luckily for him, and for her, he still has the lean muscled body he'd had back when he had a serious shot at making it as a professional fighter. "Thought you were the Jehovah's Witnesses again. Was gonna just curse you out and slam the door in your face."

"It's fine, Edge," Attalah says, laughing. "Can I come in? Wanted to talk to you about something."

"Sure," he says, nodding nervously, now that his initial embarrassment has died down and he has time to wonder what this visit is all about. "Let me go get decent?"

"I'm plenty indecent," she says. "Don't put yourself out on my account. Looks like you were working on something."

"Basement's flooded," he says. "Again. Can't fucking figure it out."

She follows him down the hall, to an open door. He pulls a flannel shirt off the knob and puts it on, then descends. "You okay to come down with that cane?"

"I can do anything," she says, descending after him.

Her own home's basement floods sometimes. It means a slightly wet floor. This is serious—water comes up at least one step, maybe two.

"Cleaned it out, so there's nothing to be damaged, and I put the washer and dryer up on risers, but it's still fucking weird."

"You had someone look at it?"

Edgley takes the last couple of steps down. Water comes up to mid-calf. "Couple of plumbers. Nobody can figure it out. Or at least, they say they'd need to do a whole lot of work to figure out the problem—let alone fix it—and I just don't have that kind of money. The weirdest thing?" He sticks his finger in the water, and then sticks it in his mouth. "It's salt water."

"How is that possible?"

"Beats me. I thought maybe limestone in the foundation? Or natural sodium deposits in the ground? But I don't think that's actually a thing."

Now that he mentions it, the basement does have the very definite smell of the sea.

As nonchalantly as she can, she says, "Are you still the only locksmith in Hudson?"

"Pretty much," he says. "Gotten so busy in the last couple years that sometimes my wait time is too long, and guys from Kinderhook or Catskill come in instead. But mostly it's all me."

"Do you have the contract with the county to change locks after evictions?"

"Ah," he says, smiling. "There it is."

"Do you?"

"Yeah," he says. "Why?"

"I just want information," she says. "That's all. I promise. County won't give us numbers on how many evictions happen. But you could, couldn't you?"

"I guess I could, actually." He nods, relieved, thinking that this is all she wanted. "Offhand, approximately, I'd say about ten to twenty a month, depending. More so in spring and summer."

"But you could get me more detailed numbers, right? Look through old invoices, that kind of thing?"

"Yeah, but that'd take me a shit ton of time. What's this for, anyway?"

With great effort, letting the pain show in her face, she lowers herself to sit on the steps. "We've been talking behind the scenes about trying to get a bill introduced in the Common Council, to make Hudson a zero-eviction city."

Edgley frowns. "Zero evictions? How would that even work?"

"There's precedents for it working in other towns. Look," she says, her face all candor and vulnerability. So far she hasn't said anything untrue. "I'm not trying to take money out of your pocket. But these are your friends, your neighbors, right? How many times have you had to help throw somebody you care about out of their home?"

He just watches where the water laps against the wall and then nods.

"And the chances are good that this would never be introduced, let alone pass. And even if it *does*, we're talking three years *at the soonest* before it takes effect. It's really just an organizing tool, something to get folks riled up behind. See who's willing to stand on our side, who's against us. That kind of thing."

All of this is true. But it isn't why she is there. What she wants to do with that information.

Edgley kicks at the water. She respects him, for the pain he feels. The conflict between his money and his people. Access to his records is so close to being hers. The numbers will indeed be useful, facts and figures to show for sure what everyone already knows but pretends not to: that hundreds of people who have lived in Hudson for generations are losing their homes. And a disproportionate number of them are people of color.

But the numbers are just the beginning. If her hunch is right, the invoices will come with copies of the eviction notice, which will identify both the tenant and the landlord. She'll know exactly who has lost their homes, even the ones who are so ashamed that they never talk about it.

And she'll have the names and addresses of the people who threw them out onto the street.

"It's funny," Edgley says at last. "I love the beach. Dream about the ocean all the time. Haven't been able to make it there in a couple years now. Not enough time or money. Now the ocean came to me."

"I have that dream, too," Attalah says. "We both must be water signs."

"Something like that."

"I'll do the work," she says. "I'll come to your office, look through the invoices, figure out the numbers. Whatever it takes. And I promise no one but me will ever know you helped us. I wouldn't do anything to jeopardize your livelihood."

"Fine," he says. "Come by my office Thursday morning. Cool?"

"Cool." She reaches up for the banister and winces. "Is it okay if I just sit here for a second?"

"Of course."

In the beginning, the cane had been a prop. Or at least that's what she told herself. A way to make people underestimate her. It still serves that purpose, but now she also needs it for its actual purpose.

"What are you even doing down here?" she asks, watching him slosh around. "I wouldn't know what to do about it."

"Neither do I, really. Just . . . I don't know, looking for a leak or something."

They chat easily now. Favors do that. They bond you together. An old organizing trick—get someone to do something for you, and they're in your debt. Who knew why, what quirk of human psychology, when it should have been the other way around.

But favors that break the rules are even better. Because they give you leverage. What won't Edgley do, to keep his contract, if she threatens to reveal that he'd supplied them with information? And a man like Edgley, who had been a hell of a fighter once upon a time—he has a lot of potential uses.

. . . .

PASTORAL CARE, PROBABLY. That's all it was. Ossie was on the edge of dying, desperate for help.

Even hardened atheist Ossie had picked up the phone and called a church, when the push came to the shove. Despair was a hell of a thing.

Dom's gut doesn't buy it. Not 100 percent. There is still that little voice remembering Lettie's words: *she kept saying they were trying to silence her.*

Grace Abounding is a small wooden building in a town full of big brick-and-stone churches. St. Mary's Catholic, Shiloh Baptist, St. Michael's Ukrainian Orthodox. Grace Abounding has low ceilings, no stained glass, nothing fancy anywhere to be seen. A meeting is just ending when he walks in. Dom sits down at the back of the church and watches. Men and women move pews, clean up the coffee table. The mood in the room is tense, uncomfortable. None of the nervous chatty relief that follows an AA session or the happy, pleased hugging after a prayer meeting. Lights click off one by one, until the only illumination is on the pulpit. Pastor Thirza is a small woman, short-haired, bespectacled. Deep dark brown skin. Mid-forties, maybe early fifties.

"Officer," the pastor says, approaching him, once she's walked her last two congregants down the center aisle. She sees the name tag on Dom's chest and then says, "Officer Morrison," extending a hand and a smile. "Any relation to Earl Morrison?"

"My father."

"A good man. That laugh of his—you couldn't hear that without laughing yourself, no matter who you were or what you were going through."

"Thank you for saying so, Pastor," he says, smiling, hurting. "Any chance we can talk in private?"

"Of course," she says.

"Sorry to bother you so late in the evening," Dom says, once they are in the pastor's very small, very messy office. "Seemed like a difficult meeting just now."

"It's fine," the pastor says, and rubs her temples, and Dom sees it at once. This woman is exhausted. And stressed. And she has been for a very long time. "Several of my congregants are . . . unhappy with me. And they asked for a meeting about it. And it lasted four hours."

"Unhappy about what?"

The pastor winces. "Unhappy is the wrong word. I'm sorry. But the church has been planning an ambitious expansion for several years now, and they're frustrated at the slow rate of progress." She waves her hand.

Officially, there is no investigation into Ossie's death. A suicide, complete with note: case closed. No reason at all for him to be here. But Pastor Thirza doesn't need to know that. "A woman took her own life," he says. "Pretty open and shut. But there's evidence she was connected to some other things we're looking at, so I'm just asking some routine questions."

"Of course."

"Did you know a young woman named Ossie Travers?"

Pastor Thirza blinks and nods and does not answer right away. Instantly, Dom's antennae are up. Not for dishonesty, but for fear. Evasion. "Ossie. Yes. Of course. Is she the one who . . . passed away?"

"She was," Dom says.

"That's so, so sad. She came to me, sometimes. For pastoral care. Troubled, as I'm sure you can imagine."

"Of course," Dom says, his suspicion increasing. "It's interesting to me that she was a member of your congregation. According to people who knew her" (*including myself because I was carrying on an extramarital affair with her even though she was a drug dealer and I am a police officer and what does the good Lord have to say about that*) "she was not a religious person. An atheist, in fact."

Pastor Thirza smiles tolerantly. "You'd be surprised, the changes that come over people when they reach their lowest place."

"Of course. Did she ever mention to you that she felt . . . threatened?"

Again the tolerant smile—and again the evasion. "She never did. Although I did get the sense that she had . . . contact . . . with some unsavory characters. So many of us do; I'm certainly not one to judge."

"Indeed," Dom says, standing. "Thank you so much for your time."

And what are you hiding, Pastor?

She stands up and walks Dom out of her office. The nave is fully dark.

It doesn't play, no matter how many times Dom runs it through in his head. *No way in hell Ossie had been a parishioner here. No way she found religion in her final days.*

Are you sure about that, Dom? You don't know the first thing about despair like that. What it feels like; what it does to you. If it'd make her do something like kill herself, couldn't it also make her go to fucking church? Call a fucking priest, just to have someone to talk to?

And are you still so sure she killed herself at all?

The salt water still naggles at him. The brackish smell of it in her mouth hasn't fully left his nose. The eerie, shivery feeling down his spine, the one he only ever got reading ghost stories or watching horror movies.

If somebody had killed her, trying to make it look like a suicide, the salt water was an inexplicable (impossible) addition—the kind of thing that would rouse suspicions in cops who wouldn't otherwise be suspicious.

Unless the message wasn't for you. If she was in something over her head, the conspiracy Lettie suspected, there might be more to this story you're not seeing.

Maybe Ossie was just a pawn in someone else's war.

Pastor Thirza flips a switch, so Dom can find his way out. A door slams, somewhere.

"My son, probably," the pastor says. "He's sixteen, and therefore has made it his mission to make everyone in Hudson as miserable as he is."

Dom laughs. They shake hands one more time. Now that the nervousness is gone, Dom can see the sadness on her face again. The stress. Probably the same stress half of Hudson feels. Panic over what the future holds. Of course the church's expansion plans had been put on hold. No one local can afford to do anything big, not in a city where everything has suddenly gotten six times more expensive.

The cold startles Dom. He hurries to his car.

"Mister!" someone calls, whispering as loudly as they can. Dom turns around to see a young man running toward him—the pastor's son; he can see it at once.

"Hi," Dom says, extending a hand. "I'm Officer Morrison."

"Wick," the boy says. He has striking eyes. Because they are so big, and because they are so sad. "I was eavesdropping on you and my mom. I'm sorry," and he grinned like he wasn't. "I knew her. We were friends."

"Ossie?"

Wick nods. His stance is proud, unintimidated by the man in uniform. It makes Dom feel a rush of fondness for him. So many young people see the uniform and feel fear, hatred. If Wick feels any of those things, he hides them well.

"Was she just your friend, or was she your friend and your drug dealer? Mind you, I don't give a shit either way."

Wick grins. "Just my friend."

"Mine, too," Dom says, smiling. "You have any idea why your mom might be lying to me? Or at least, not telling me the whole truth?" Then he winces—most people don't want to hear their mom's a liar. "I could be wrong here. Just a cop's gut."

Wick says, "You're not wrong." Then he turns to look at the church behind them, as if it might be able to hear what he says, snitch to his mother.

"What's going on, Wick?"

Wick doesn't answer.

Dom says, "Can we talk tomorrow, maybe? Someplace else?"

"Yeah, thanks," the boy says, smiling gratefully. Something else Dom sees, at once—the kid is probably gay. Does his mother know? Is she okay with it? Where's his dad? The woman Dom just met with was kind, gentle, understanding, but one thing police work in a small town teaches you is that even the nicest people are capable of the foulest shit. Was Wick abused? Had he turned to Ossie for help? Dom hands Wick his business card, tells him to call him in the morning.

"She mentioned you," Wick says, shaking his hand again. "She said you were nice."

"Call me tomorrow," Dom says, and watches the kid run off. *Nice. Nice is what I am.*

Nice is all I am.

CHAPTER FOURTEEN

RONAN

We can't beat him," Attalah said. "Mabie Brabender is only running because the mayor asked her to—he wants Jark to win, but he needed an actual opponent to make it look good—she's polling at ten percent."

"Of course we can. A big-enough scandal, people will turn on him."

"I'm not so sure. Maybe that shit is true in the big leagues, but we're still Tammany Hall up here. Political machine in full effect. You could hand them Jark Trowse covered in blood standing over a dead grandma and people would cluck their tongues and step into the booth and vote for him."

"Come on," I said. "Let's go crazy, be bold, be ambitious, even if it seems impossible. We can make this happen."

I grinned. She grinned. Conspiracy is a very special kind of crazy, a manic contagious acid buzz that can eat away any obstacle.

"If anything, it's an opportunity," I said. "It raises the stakes. Jark has a spotlight on him, which means any damage we do to him will be magnified exponentially."

Blue corduroy couch. Cinnamon incense. Hammer crossed atop a roll of duct tape on the dining room table. I tried my best to root myself in the here-and-now of Attalah's apartment, to focus on the banal quotidian details . . . and not the head full of vivid filth that refused to quiet down. Flashes of dreams, so alive they felt like memories.

Stinking darkness; a rising and falling sensation like we were in a ship at sea. One lone hanging lantern burning clear and bright, its oil smelling like musk and alcohol. A beautiful brutal man doing beautiful brutal things to me. Jug-handled ears and a deep, dark beard visible in the lamplight.

"Even if we *could* defeat Jark," she said, "what's happening here is so much bigger than any election. So much money is sunk in the transformation of Hudson—so many people stand to benefit from it—that it's gonna take something really big to turn it around."

"We can do big," I said. "Just watch."

In the dream-or-memory I'd asked the beautiful demon man *What's your name?* and he'd hissed, *Tom. Tom Minniq,* before clamping one meaty hand over my mouth to prevent any further conversation.

Be cool, Ronan. Don't get an erection in the middle of describing your little plan for Jark Trowse.

Somehow, I got through it, telling Attalah all the sordid evil little details I'd been assembling for the past twenty-four hours.

"That's fucked up," she said at last, after a long silent time spent looking into my face and wondering what the hell was going on in there. "You might be even more messed up than I originally imagined. How did you get like this?"

"This town," I said, smiling—tingling—ecstatic with the high of hate. "It made me the monster that I am. How can I repay the favor, except by saving it from certain destruction?"

She breathed out, flexed pre-arthritic fingers. Looked into her hands, like she was wondering just how badly she could bloody them. Or like I'd taken something from her and transformed it into something horrifying. It felt good, her fear. It stirred something sweet and sharp inside. Hate was a wonderful weapon. A hell of a drug.

"Well?" I asked. "I was serious when I told you that I'd break whatever laws I had to, to do this. In the grand scheme of the depths we *could* descend to, framing someone isn't really such a big deal."

"It *is*," she said. "Mind you, I'm not saying we shouldn't do it. I just want you to be real about what you're saying."

"I am super real."

I stood and then jumped up and down a couple of times. Something filled me up and overflowed. I felt a giggle coming on and I didn't even try to stop it, even though I knew it made me sound crazy.

"We're dangerous," she said. "You and me, together."

"Damn right," I said. "I pity the fools who dare to stand against us." And it was Lilly I pictured, that earnest well-meaning young woman in the vintage rhinestone glasses, who had no idea how much she was blithely accidentally helping to destroy.

Attalah nodded.

"All we need to figure out now is—who to use? And what kind of leverage do we have over them?"

The floor in front of us was spread thick with paperwork. News clippings. Printouts from the internet. Legal documents. Binders of state and local legislation. Precedent projects. All arranged in a jagged spiral. Fifteen years of scrupulous research on her part.

Attalah said, "I got a list of everyone who's been evicted in the past few years. So I've been able to look up every landlord. And look for who might be susceptible to pressure."

We were in the basement of her house. An empty room they'd one day turn into a guest room or man cave. Not a play room. A speaker outside the door played loud music. The foundation made it soundproof; no one could eavesdrop from outside or sneak up and listen at the door. "And there's no place for Dom to hide a bug,"

Attalah had said, pointing to the blank walls and bare floor. She laughed, but I wondered how likely she thought that was. How far would Dom go to uphold the law? Would he entrap his own wife, abet the destruction of his town?

"The Pequod Arms project is complicated," she said. "There are five potential scenarios. The first one, the simplest: they could break ground on that tomorrow. A couple of renovations, one new building. No big thing. But Jark wants *big*. So he's been talking to tons of property owners, faith leaders, local stakeholders, trying to get them to commit their property or their support. Bribing them with all kinds of things. Getting politicians to issue zoning variances, so he can build bigger than current height restrictions. He wants the fifth level, the biggest and most complex. The one that would transform Hudson completely."

I nodded.

"Remember that we only consult here, in person," she said. "No phone calls, no fucking text messages. Even when we think we're being clever. Activists use an app called Signal, for double-encrypted correspondence. I sent you the link. Download it, and we'll use that."

A door creaked open.

"Hello?" Dom hollered down into the basement.

"Hey, honey," Attalah called, her voice suddenly startlingly loud. "Come on down!"

Dom entered the room, his smile as wide as the Hudson, and then he saw the floor and it slowly shrank down to nothing.

"What's going on, guys?"

"Nothing to worry your pretty little head about," she said, lurching forward on her cane to embrace him.

Somehow, it made me smile. The sight of them together. Rarely did two friends I respected and admired so much come together in a couple.

How many friends do you even have, Ronan? You have strangers you fuck, and strangers you photograph, and clients you schmooze with but don't respect—

That wasn't the point, not really. I was happy for Attalah and Dom. They stood there talking, catching each other up on their days, and something sort of like peace filled me up.

Even if a little part of me is still in love with Dominick. Will always be in love with him.

From pure force of habit I took out my phone, opened Grindr, saw the grid of nearby boys and men who had put their faces out in search of sex. Just a thing I did, several thousand times a day. From horniness mostly, but sometimes from boredom. From curiosity. From the little thrill of seeing how much sex surrounded me.

The night before, I'd replaced my face pic with a torso shot. Changed my profile name. No one would know who I really was. Not the local gays, the married closet cases, and tragic out ones— one of whom actually had the profile name *I'm Lonely*—and not the invading gays. There were a lot more of the latter. Hipster beards and curled mustaches. Old-timey-style tattoos done by twenty-somethings on twentysomethings.

The idea flashed into my head so fast and fully formed that I wondered if it didn't come from (*the dreamsea*) somewhere on high (*or down low*), like he was already a real person just waiting to be born.

Ronan Szepessy couldn't be on Grindr. But someone else could. Someone fictional. Manufactured. Engineered to be absolutely perfect. The broadest shoulders, the smallest waist, the biggest biceps. The biggest (*jug-handled ears*) dick. Twenty-nine years old—not too young or too old for almost anyone. As much a top as he was a bottom. A man absolutely everyone would tap back, if he tapped them.

I had all the raw materials already. In my backpack, at my father's house, was a laptop with hundreds of thousands of pictures of men in all sorts of stages of undress and degrees of flaccidity. Who was better than me at Photoshopping? I could construct a man for all seasons: smiling in full-color flannel squatted on the bed of a pickup truck; pouting in naked black-and-white; awkward-angle Pride parade selfies and hotel-mirror torso shots. Make a consistent face from two or three others. An elaborate catfishing experiment, chatting up dozens of boys and swiftly talking them into sharing their private albums, their most secret desires and fears.

But why? Just to mess with them? Get their hopes up for a man who never wants to meet?

Maybe.

*Or maybe there are a thousand uses for (*Tom*) this guy. Some of them far more exciting and more sinister than others.*

And not just the gay boys, either. It'd be easy, once I had the raw materials, to fashion a slight variant version of my Frankenstein sex bot and let him loose on the lonely Hudson transplant women of Tinder. Learn their wants and needs and weaknesses. Tell them hurtful little lies about each other. Talk them into running little errands. Play little jokes on people.

Being in Hudson was doing something to me. Feeding my hate. Feeding *on* my hate.

". . . huh, Ronan?"

Dom was looking at me with deep concern, so I figured whatever he'd said had had something to do with my dad. So I shrugged and said, "Fine, I guess." And Dom nodded, like that answer worked just fine for what he'd asked, and said, "I'd like to come see him."

"Yeah," I said. "We should make that happen."

"It looks like you two have a lot of work to do," Dom said. "I'll leave you to it. I'm going to head to Catskill, go bowling."

"Take Ronan with you," Attalah said. "We're mostly done here. And I get the impression he needs to have a little fun."

For the first time, I wondered: Did she know? What we had been to each other? What we had done together?

Dom looked at me nervously. Like he was afraid I'd say yes. Or worried I wouldn't. "I couldn't impose on you like that," I said. "I should be getting home."

"No imposition," he said. "You should come."

I did love bowling. And I did enjoy spending time with Dominick.

"Okay," I said. "If that's okay by you, that sounds like fun."

"Excellent," Attalah said.

"You don't get boat sick, do you, Ronan?"

"Fuck, Dom, I don't think I've even *been* in a boat since we took your dad's—" I stopped myself, but the damage was done. I could see the hurt in his face, at the thought of his father.

"It's my boat now," he said, blinking away the pain like it was nothing. "And we're taking it across the river to Catskill."

"That sounds fantastic," I said, remembering taking that beautiful little slip of a thing out on the river in the middle of the night, without his father's permission. How many stars were overhead. How good my hand felt in his.

Dom chuckled. "Work on your elaborate murder plot is done for the day?"

"Shush, you," she said. "We're nowhere *near* the murder part of the plan. We're barely to the arson."

I followed Dom upstairs. When we got there I was shocked to see bright sunlight streaming in the windows. It felt like hours and hours that Attalah and I had been down there. Like it ought to be night by now. Like the darkness inside us must have swollen to fill the sky.

CHAPTER FIFTEEN

"Hey, Mom," Attalah says, already regretting having come.

Hazel makes a noise of greeting. It sounds like a baby gargling. Ever since the stroke, seeing her mother makes her miserable.

"I'm going to make us some coffee," Attalah says. Her mother tries to answer, and the sound makes her want to scream in rage at whatever cruel god could do this to her mother. The apartment stinks of burned pork chops, of home. "Why don't you go sit down and watch the news?"

Hazel drags herself slowly, ponderously back to her couch.

The woman weighs well over four hundred pounds. She has lived in the same apartment on the top floor of Bliss Towers for forty-five years. Most of her time is spent in the impressive recliner that Dom and Attalah got her ten years ago. She sits there now, angry at the television and the world. Attalah hands her her coffee, with cream and six sugars, just how she likes it, with the same inward pang at participating in her mother's slow diet-based suicide. Once a week she comes through to cook something big, a casserole or stew to last the next several days, something the home health aide or her mother's friends can heat up for her.

It's only been a month since the stroke. At first Attalah tried to talk to her, keep up a stream of idle chatter. Problem with that was, her mom kept trying to answer. And then she'd get frustrated. And then she'd get angry. And then she'd start to break things.

The worst part is, as bad as these visits are, they're better than they were before the stroke.

"You're weak," Hazel used to hiss, when Attalah told her about UPLIFT Hudson's latest attempt to fight back against the invaders. *"That's what you are. You and your whole generation. Just look what you've let them do to this town."*

"Mom, I don't think—"

"Do you have any idea how hard it was, to protect our community from the Urban Renewal plan that came through here in the sixties?"

Attalah knew. Her mother had told her, many a time. Most of Black Hudson knows. There's a chapter in a book about it, naming her mom and everything. Among dozens of others, of course. Hazel never exaggerated her own role or downplayed that of the dozens of other leaders who helped. They'd seen the way Urban Renewal played out everywhere else. Paid attention, when James Baldwin called it a mispronunciation of *negro removal.* So when HUD came to Hudson, the city's Black community was not about to let the mostly white city government submit their own proposal. Everywhere else, that meant bulldozed slums and thruways slitting the belly of the South Bronx open.

Hazel went to a million meetings. She collected a thousand signatures. Made hundreds of phone calls. And, Attalah suspected, did a whole lot more besides.

Compared to all that, of course Attalah's own efforts look paltry.

Hazel is watching a PBS documentary, longtime Harlem residents discussing the destruction of their community by mass displacement. "Our big mistake was, when the white people started moving in, we treated them okay. Not all of us, of course, but by and large we treated them like we wanted to be treated. That was the problem. They got so comfortable. We should have let them know, right off the bat, how hard they were hated."

Disappointment used to roll off her mother like the smell of too-strong perfume. Attalah tried not to take it too personally. It was *life* that had disappointed Hazel Draven. Attalah was just one small piece of the massive machinery, made up of economics and racism and misogyny and geography and biology and God Himself.

But now, since the stroke, there's no disappointment. Or at least—she can't voice it anymore. And Attalah is happy about that, even if she also hates herself for being happy.

. . . .

"HOLY SHIT, THAT was fun," Ronan says, stumbling as he steps back onboard the boat.

He's had a few beers, Dominick thinks, *but then again so have I. Not so many I can't get the boat back across to Hudson.*

"You don't go bowling in the city?" Dom asks, untying the knots that hold them to the dock.

"Everywhere you go it's expensive and fancy," Ronan says. "Disco lights and fifteen-dollar fucking truffle fries. And bachelorette parties shrieking at like half the lanes."

"That sounds terrible."

There is so little space to sit in the boat. And they are bigger now than they had been when they last sat there. Their shoulders press together.

Ronan asks, "What's it like, being a cop in Hudson now?"

"It's fine," Dom says. "I mean, it fucking sucks, but not in a way that I can't handle. Most of what we do is about drugs. Opioids are really fucking people up. Since fentanyl started getting cut into the supply, overdoses have skyrocketed. Meth is still a huge problem.

There's this new stuff, spiderwebbing or whatever, coming up from the city. Domestic calls have been going up."

"Domestic calls, like, domestic violence?"

"Yeah," Dom says. "Fights, screaming matches, neighbors calling the cops or Child Protective Services on each other. Times are really tough, and people are stressed. The real test of any relationship, whether it's with your partner or a sibling or a parent or whoever, is how you act when you're two months behind on paying the rent."

"That's what happens when your town gets taken over," Ronan says.

"You're already sounding like Attalah," Dom says, with a laugh.

"You must see people at their worst," Ronan says. He lets one hand dip into the water of the Hudson. "That must take a toll on you."

"It does."

In the pregnant pause that follows, and perhaps abetted by the alcohol in his system, Ronan says, "Attalah told me about your father. I'm so sorry—I didn't know. I would have come to the funeral. I would have—"

"It's okay. He had a lot of respect for you, and I know you did for him."

"What's it . . . like? Losing your dad?" When Dom doesn't answer right away, he adds, "I'm sorry. We don't have to talk about this if you don't want to. It's just—I'm just . . ."

"I know, Ronan," Dom says softly, his voice as warm and kind as he can make it. "I wish I could tell you something other than . . . nothing in my life ever hurt like that."

Dom puts his arm around Ronan. Ronan leans gratefully into his heat. The engine chugs them slowly eastward, across the wide choppy river to the town that took its name.

. . . .

AHEAD OF THEM, the lights of Hudson are looming larger. Ronan doesn't want to arrive at their destination. He never wants to get out of the boat, or for Dom to lift his arm from around him. His hand feels frozen all the way through, from dragging in the cold water most of the way across the river. The wind whips right through them, stirs up the water in startlingly high waves.

"I never in my whole life felt safe the way I did in your arms," Ronan says, without intending to.

"Yeah," Dom says, and thinks—but does not say—*no one in my life ever needed me the way you did. Not Attalah, who is a thousand times stronger than me, and not my father, not even at the end, when he was so sick he*—"Yeah."

And then Dom also does something he did not intend do. Not consciously, anyway, but once it is done he has no desire to take it back.

With the arm that is around his best friend, he lifts his thumb and presses it to Ronan's cheek and turns it in his direction. And kisses him, full on the lips. Ronan kisses back, his hunger a perfect match for Dom's.

The boat sputters the rest of the way around Middle Ground Flats. Dom only pulls out of the kiss when it is necessary to turn his attention to the piloting of the vehicle, to ensure they do not crash into the boat launch.

"That was dumb," Ronan says.

"I guess it was."

"So why'd you do it?"

Dom shrugs. Ties the knots.

Ronan lifts Dom's shirt with his dry hand and presses his wet, frozen one against the warm skin of his friend's stomach. Dom yelps, and they both laugh.

"This is a terrible idea," Ronan says.

"It is."

"Attalah's your wife—my partner in crime . . ."

"She is."

The boat is fully docked, but still they sit there.

"I can't do this to her," Ronan says.

"Our marriage is open," Dom says. "We're both free to pursue other people. Only rule is, neither one of us ever wants to know anything about it."

"Really? That's the only rule?"

Dom laughs. "I guess there's other rules, but that's the main one."

"I'm sure one of them is: not forming emotional attachments."

"We've never really discussed that."

Ronan leans back, looking up at the city climbing uphill ahead of him. The low-income apartments of Hudson Terrace; the bright shadow of Bliss Towers. The statue of Saint Winifred, smiling down from Promenade Hill.

"This is a terrible idea," Ronan repeats, and leans over to kiss Dom on the warm throb of his neck.

....

CHAPTER SIXTEEN

RONAN

The morning's scheming completed, Attalah and I went upstairs for coffee.

We'd done well. Accomplished a lot. So much that I hadn't had to struggle to keep my mind free of filthy thoughts, or guilt over what I'd done with her husband the night before.

"You okay?" I asked, watching her wince as she struggled to climb the steps. "I can make the coffee and bring it down."

"I'll have to come upstairs eventually," she said, and I could hear the pain in her voice.

"Why not just set up our dungeon of schemes on the ground floor? We can keep the good stuff locked up . . ."

"I need this," she hissed. "I need to challenge myself as much as I can, for as long as I can."

For the first time, I wondered what exactly was wrong with her. Hip problem, knee issue? Bad back? The body was so full of pain waiting to inflict itself.

Skullduggery and shenanigans had no place in her bright beautiful kitchen. We talked about Dom, his job, and what a good man he was. We talked about her mother; how she, too, was gone . . . but not.

I helped her as much as possible with the making of the coffee.

Putting the milk away, a photo on the refrigerator caught my eye. "You know Katch!" I said.

"From when he was ten," Attalah said. "Even before he started transitioning."

"I had no idea Katch was trans."

"Yup. Did not have an easy time of it, here in Hudson, as I know you can imagine. Such a beautiful young man. And so sweet. It's a fucking shame."

"Shame?"

"I mean, suicide is always a tragedy. But someone so young— someone who had come so far . . ."

All the blood left my face. All the words left my mouth.

"You didn't know he died," she said. "I'm so sorry. It happened a couple of months ago. Did you meet him in New York City? I know he used to go down there a lot for modeling and stuff . . ."

I met Katch for the first time two weeks ago, I tried to say. *And I just saw him last week. Walking into the goddamn Penelope's Quilt potluck.*

No words came out, and I was glad of it. If I was fucking nuts, no sense letting Attalah know it. Who'd want to be co-conspirators with a crazy person? A crazy co-conspirator was a liability.

Her hand found mine, and she made a soothing noise. I had to bite down hard on my lip to keep from laughing. An irrational, full-body laugh, bubbling up from my most twisted hidden place. *He was dead the whole time!* I reached out to move two magnets and saw that the photo was part of the program from a funeral.

"I have to go," I said, startling myself by saying the words out loud.

"Of course," Attalah said, rubbing my shoulder. I waited very patiently for my body to be able to move itself toward the door.

om is watching the Bangladeshis play cricket. A cold October
Saturday morning, but here they are, and here they'll be until
the snow covers the vacant lot. Mill Street is just a couple of
blocks from Warren Street, but it's at the bottom of a steep hill and
the marshy land is ill-suited for anything but shabby multifamily
prefab homes. It might as well be on another planet. No one ever
comes here who doesn't have a reason to. Perfect for secret meetings out in the open. Most of the recent transplants aren't even
aware this street exists. Probably the hipsters wonder where they
live, the many South Asian immigrants they see on the street every
day. Hundreds of them came to Hudson to work at the Emsig Button Factory in the 1980s and '90s, and they're still here even if the
button factory's long gone.

"Officer," Wick says, sitting down beside him.

"Hey," Dom says, and slides the McDonald's bag in his direction. "Call me Dom."

"Oh shit," Wick says, eyes widening at the smell. He scoops
french fries out by the fistful. "Thanks!"

"Thank you for speaking with me. What did you—"

"My mom's a drug addict."

"Shit," Dom says, and suddenly Pastor Thirza's evasion made

a whole lot more sense. "I'm sorry, Wick. That must be hard on you."

"She's fine as long as she can get them. Functions normally."

"Painkillers?" Dom asks.

Wick nods. "Prescription, at first."

"Of course," Dom said. "That's always how it starts."

Still, he's missing something. Ossie selling drugs to Pastor Thirza supplied a piece of the puzzle, but it wasn't enough. Ossie was scared of someone, and probably not the pastor.

What if it wasn't someone human? he thinks, and bats the idiotic thought away.

"You eavesdrop on all your mom's meetings?"

"Not all of them," Wick says with a laugh.

"The other night when I came by, a meeting was just wrapping up. Seemed like people on her board were pretty mad at her. You know what that was about?"

Wick nodded. "Mom made a deal with Penelope's Quilt. Sold off a portion of the property for a ton of money, to be part of the Pequod Arms. Couple board members tried to get her fired for it, but they didn't have the votes."

But they would have, if people had known she was an addict.

And there it is, sailor. A very real (*very non-supernatural*) reason for powerful people to be after Ossie. For Ossie to be scared.

But the hairs on the back of his neck won't go down. Because the Ossie he knew—the Ossie he loved—the Ossie he missed so fucking much—she wouldn't have been driven to suicide over some damn real estate speculation.

"You're sad, too," Wick says, touching his shoulder softly.

"I am," he whispers, gut-punched by the kindness in Wick's voice.

"I don't have a lot of friends," Wick says. "She saw that, some-how. Went out of her way to be nice to me."

"Yeah," Dom says, and he gets it. Ossie would have taken one look at that awkward, lonely, little gay kid and decided it was her mission in life to love him. *For all of Hudson's sudden status as a gay mecca for artist transplants, that wouldn't have trickled down to the halls of Hudson High.*

Shouts from the cricket field: men hugged, whooped, clapped each other on the back.

"I'd love for you to meet my friend Ronan. I think the two of you—the three of us—would get along real well together."

CHAPTER EIGHTEEN

RONAN

Cold morning; the smell of the sea in the air. I walked all the way home from Attalah's house, my head on fire from what I'd just learned. And because fire wants nothing but to make more fire, I stole a cigarette from my father and went out onto the porch to smoke it.

Two fresh clove stubs lay in the coffee can ashtray I'd emptied the day before. Shivers started, and they wouldn't stop.

One of two things was true. Either I was completely crazy, or ghosts were real and one was haunting me. Actually both things could have been true.

But was this such new knowledge? Hadn't I felt it from the second I stepped off the train? Hadn't I known it in my heart, in my gut, the whole time I was living here? Something was wrong with Hudson. Always had been. The city was submerged in (*the dream-sea*) something, caught up in a spiritual membrane that rendered the normal rules of life and death inapplicable.

I had a choice. I wasn't helpless. I could choose to believe I was crazy and try to get help accordingly. Head back to Manhattan, check into rehab. Abandon my dad again, and Attalah and all our schemes. And Dom.

Or: I could proceed like ghosts were real.

Sometimes accepting the impossible is as easy as preferring it to the alternative.

I called out, "Katch?" but no one answered me. I went inside and put two hoodies on and walked down Warren Street, to the train tracks that split the city along Sixth Street—past grinning campaign volunteers in bright Jark blue—and took a left to follow the rails south.

My head still spun. My stomach was sick. But leaving the street behind and walking into the woods felt forbidden, delicious. I'd always imagined cops or wicked brakemen would descend upon me the instant I left behind the safety of the city street grid, but that was absurd. No one could see me. No one cared what I did.

A culvert ran alongside the rails. Dead blond cattails; a tricycle; standing water; in another week or so it would be edged with ice. Then the woods fell away, and a set of rusted black trestles carried the train tracks over Power Avenue. On my left, a sprawl of low yellow buildings surrounded by fences three stories high, capped with coils of razor wire: Hudson Correctional Facility.

"Ella Fitzgerald was incarcerated in Hudson," said Katch, who was squatting on the rails on my right.

"Shit," I said, startled.

"Sorry. I lose track of where and when I am, sometimes. Hudson exists outside of time and space as you understand them. Shit gets confusing. Anyway. She was fifteen. It was 1933. The House of Refuge for Women in Hudson was only the second gender-specific prison in American history."

"Hey, Katch."

"Hey, Ronan."

He got up and walked beside me. His posture was better. His face brighter, skin almost glowing. Hair sculpted, coiffed: spiky sea urchin couture.

"Are you really him?"

"I think so," he said, and looked down at his hands.

"How . . . why?"

"They brought me back. So I could bring you back. And we could save the town together."

We came around a bend, walking west now. We could see the river glimmer. "They who?"

"It's probably easier if I show you."

He put his hand on my shoulder. Wind hit me, sharp and cold, making me wince, making me blink.

And—we were on a ship. Standing in the crow's nest, looking down on slaughter. A whale thrashed. Tiny men shouted, screamed. Brandished blades. Swung ropes. Bright red foam churned. The sun was setting and it was bitter cold and we were thousands of miles and hundreds of years from home and something magnificent was being murdered. Katch took hold of my hand with his, and I was grateful for that human (*human?*) touch.

"Take me away," I whispered. "Please? Take me anywhere, just—"

Wind again, blistering, scorching my exposed skin until I had to cover my face with my hands to keep it from cracking open. When it died down and I dared to look, we were home. Except, not. Hudson; the waterfront; ages ago. Long wide wooden docks. Tall ships. Barrels and boys and crates and commerce. Still in the crow's-nest, I could see to the top of Promenade Hill, where no low-income housing or statue of Saint Winifred stood. No streetlights. A whale lashed to the side. Dead, at least. That was something. Its suffering had stopped.

"That," Katch said, pointing to the great mammal's corpse. "That's who *they* are."

Again his hand on my shoulder; again the icy blast. This time I was ready for it. Tried to keep my eyes open. But the wind kept up and my eyes watered and the world blurred, and when I blinked to clear it we were standing atop Cemetery Hill. Full night. Cloudless sky. So many stars. Because of course there were; because electricity hadn't been invented yet. The only light that humans could make in the dark was with candle or torch or bonfire, none of which could dent the light of the stars.

As if in response to my thoughts, stars darkened overhead. A huge patch of the sky went black. The patch moved. Something was flying (*swimming*) between me and the stars.

"Is that—"

"That's us," Katch said, and it came closer, and I could see its shape clearly. Long, streamlined. Massive tail propelling it. A whale, bigger than all the whales that ever were. My heart sang in my chest. My lungs filled up with helium. Knees weakened. I could have dropped down, pressed my face to the cold dirt, groveled, kowtowed, banged my forehead bloody, and it still wouldn't have been enough to convey the awe and the love and the rapture I felt. The gratitude, to get a glimpse of something like this. What I saw was majesty, power, of a sort I'd never dared hope or dream or believe could be.

This is what they talk about, the born-agains, the zealots, the faithful. The ones who have a lightbulb come-to-Jesus moment. This is what it's like to see God.

This wasn't God. It was just a god. But it was enough. Whatever Katch was, I believed.

So I surrendered to the wind. Let it batter me. Blind me. Whisk me from place to place and time to time.

Bright, cloudy wintertime, and Warren Street was a swathe of white and red. Blood-soaked men dragged strips of whale flesh through the snow. Black smoke billowed.

"This city was built on their blood," Katch said. "It's in the foundations of the buildings. The sap of the trees. The oxygen that mosses excrete."

All the ink was gone from his arms. Only one tattoo remained. A strange scribble, like an infinity sign crumpled in on itself.

More wind, and we were back. Train tracks firm beneath our feet. Much closer to the river now, as if we'd kept walking while we wandered through time. The bliss of what I'd seen remained. I never wanted it to end. Already I could feel that it was diminished, slightly. Already I knew that it could continue to shrink, and knowing it was almost more than I could bear.

"They made this town theirs. And their magic is powerful. Their wards have held for almost two centuries."

"Show me again," I said. "I want to see it. See you. That" (*sky whale*) "other you."

"No," Katch said. "Human beings can only stand so much bliss."

We walked in silence. I wanted to beg, to argue, but how could you debate a (*god*) (*ghost*) (*monster*) whale?

"They've kept this city safe. Kept its people safe. And now—"

I laughed out loud. "Safe? Are you serious? Hudson had *slavery*. Local chapters of the KKK later on. And what about those decades of economic decline? Depression, drug addiction, suicide—hate— Hudson seems to have way more than its fair share of all those things."

But it went deeper than that, I could see now. I thought of my father, his mind sucked dry long before its time. My mom, so damaged by dreams or visions that they broke her in the end. Was this how it went, here? Was this what it meant to be from Hudson? To never not have nightmares. A lifetime of waking up in cold sweats, weird dreams, voices in our heads—or was someone calling from the street, whispering in the next room? Surely life wounds all of us—surely plenty of people carried broken-off blades between their ribs, no matter where they grew up—but the wounds Hudson left bled a special kind of blood, sweet and rich to the great dead gods who swam through our skies.

Katch sighed. We crossed the intersection, where the westbound freight train tracks we'd been following bisected the passenger rails that ran north to south. "Humans take such a shortsighted view of things."

"Help me understand."

"I can't. For right now, all you need to understand is that they're losing. Their wards are being broken one by one. The hold they have on Hudson—the bonds they've built, between people—they're shattering. They're losing control. The tide is rising—the ocean (*dreamsea*) is intruding into the strangest places. They thought they were immortal—they never imagined anything could hurt them—but as people get pushed out—as buildings get rebuilt—they grow weaker. Smaller. And now they know they're losing."

We were almost to the water's edge. A willow's yellow arms were nearly empty.

"Do you get what I'm saying to you, Ronan?"

"So, after you died, they—the whales—they saved you? Sent you to bring me back?"

Katch nodded. "Their power flows through me. And now it flows through you. You can do . . . things."

Things. My spine tingled with ill-defined excitement. "Like what?"

"I don't know. The rules are very unclear, and they are not good communicators. I just know they've invested you with power, the same as me."

I thought of the feeling I'd gotten, in Attalah's living room. A replacement drug.

"Why me?" I asked.

A train whistle wailed. Katch shrugged. He may have been a ghost, in thrall to gods or monsters, but he was also still a confused kid trying to make sense of a whole ton of confusing, terrifying shit. Which, weren't we all.

CHAPTER NINETEEN

"ello?" Dom calls, stepping into Grace Abounding.

No answer, so he ventures deeper in. Down the nave, through the door, down the hallway—

"Officer Morrison," Pastor Thirza says, rising to hug him, when he arrives at the door to her office. "What can I do for you?"

"Please, call me Dominick."

She smells like his mother, rose perfume and Pink curl moisturizer. But she is much shorter. The wig she wears today is also short—*Joan of Arc short*, he thinks.

"Dominick, then. What can I do for you?"

"I wanted to follow up about Ossie," Dom says, real smooth like, but still, she stiffens. He's spent a long time thinking about how best to broach this and still has no idea. So he just does. "I want to put this as gently as possible, and to be clear that nothing I'm about to say is intended to be accusatory or to imply any kind of law enforcement action around you. But in speaking with one of Ossie's colleagues, I've learned that she was supplying you with unprescribed opioids."

Pastor Thirza smiles, and for the first time it occurs to Dom to be afraid. This woman is formidable. "Who told you that?"

"That's not important, but I give you my word that I have no intention of telling anyone about this or doing anything further. My only concern is with figuring out whether Ossie was dealing with any possible intimidation or pressure that could have been a factor in her decision to take her own life. Her sister believes she was being threatened. Do you understand what I'm saying?"

Thirza nods, skeptically.

"How many people know you're addicted to painkillers?"

The pastor winces. "I wouldn't characterize . . ." but there's no sense finishing the sentence.

"Again, I don't care and I'm not judging. I just need to know."

"Hazel," she says, after a second.

Dom doesn't know what he was expecting, but it sure as hell wasn't that. "Hazel as in my mother-in-law?"

Thirza nods. "She was kind of a mentor to me. We've always been close. But we're on opposite sides of this Pequod Arms project. Anyway, she came over, like she normally does, and my fool self had left all my pill bottles in the medicine cabinet, where she found them. None of the names on them were mine. She was going to . . . use that information."

Dom blinks. "If you two were friends, I can't believe she would have exposed you to so much shame and reproach."

"Same here," Thirza says. "But that's how much she loved her town. She knew I was facing significant opposition from my board. She could have gone to them, and they'd have given me the option to resign quietly, which I would have done. If she hadn't had that stroke when she had it, I'd already be out of a job and the Pequod Arms would have lost another big chunk."

An eerie shiver slides up Dom's spine.

What is it you're imagining? That they—whoever the fuck this they *is—gave your mother-in-law a stroke, right before they killed Ossie with salt water and made it look like a suicide?*

But the shiver does not subside, no matter how much ridicule he holds his fears up to.

Something's still missing. Something I'm not seeing.

Something

*(*supernatural*)*

unexplainable.

"Did you tell anyone that Hazel knew? That she was a threat?"

Pastor Thirza looks at him. "No one."

"Are you sure about that?"

"I'm sure." She flips through her daybook, then shuts it. Dom knows it's performative. His time here is up.

"I appreciate your time," he says. "I really do."

"She was a troubled woman, Officer Morrison. I wonder why you're so eager to believe that there's more to it than that."

Dom fully intends to answer but finds he can't. "Your sermon," he says, turning to go. "I saw it on the sign outside: *Love is harder than hate.* That's this Sunday?"

"Services start at nine."

"I'm going to try to make it."

"Please do," she says, and smiles—and he thinks, *She's furious*—and he shivers all the way out to State Street.

....

ATTALAH WIPES THE WORK PRINTER. Deletes its entire memory, after she's printed up five hundred address labels and five hundred copies of the flyer she designed.

Huddled homeless people, shivering on a sidewalk. Jark's face, stolen from his campaign poster but with blood-dripping vampire fangs added in, looming over Warren Street.

WANT HUDSON TO LOOK LIKE NEW YORK CITY?

A VOTE FOR JARK TROWSE IS A VOTE FOR HOMELESSNESS

For too long we've let outsiders take our city away from us, piece by piece. This election is our last chance to stop them in their tracks.

She and Ronan and Zelda split it up, keyboarding all the contact info on the eviction forms she got from Rick Edgley. Of course she's pretty sure most of the people on it aren't registered to vote, or don't plan to vote even if they are, but this is just the initial salvo in a broader election strategy.

Anyway that's what Attalah tells herself.

. . . .

DOM WAKES UP WET, from dreams of the sea, but the water persists across the wall of sleep—salt sweat fine as ocean spray across his body.

Blue light shows beneath his bedroom door. Attalah is awake, hard at work in her insomnia, down the hall with the computer on to keep from disturbing him. Her side of the bed is in shambles, from her tossing and turning before getting up and going back to work. He pulls her pillow close to suck in the scent of it.

With reality firmly reestablished, he can afford to reflect on his dreams. The sea at night—a storm, a ship, waves so tall they crashed across its high bow.

Ronan in danger. Dom standing over him, unable to help. Watching in horror as something . . . clawed its way out of him.

Shivers run through him, remembering.

The temple bell tolls. It's Ronan. The spooky coincidence of it doubles the shivers, then triples them. The ringtone's turned down far enough that Attalah probably didn't hear it, and anyway she usually works with headphones on and disco blasting. He keeps his voice low anyway.

"Bad dreams?"

"Yeah," Ronan says, after gasping. "How'd you know?"

"Me, too."

"You're not helping, Dom. I called for you to tell me I'm being ridiculous, not to reinforce my insane delusions."

"If it helps, you probably *are* being ridiculous. What's up?"

"I had a dream. A nightmare. And I think I might be going crazy. So I wanted you to help ground me."

"How can I, when I'm not grounded myself?" Dom asks.

"You and me," Ronan says, his voice small, rattled. "We used to have conversations in dreams, and then continue those conversations in the middle school cafeteria. Like it was nothing. Do you remember that?"

"Sort of," Dom says, and he sort of does.

"I convinced myself those memories couldn't have been real. My father and I, having the same dream on the same night. The vivid dreams I had in Hudson, and the fact that I'd never—not once— had a dream outside of Hudson. Not that I remembered in the morning, anyway."

All of this rings true for Dom. Has he ever discussed it with Attalah? His dad? He'd never needed to. It was just something everyone took for granted. Something best not spoken of. If he'd bothered to think about it at all, he'd probably have assumed it was normal. Something that happened everywhere.

"Get some sleep, Ronan. That's the best grounding I can give you right now."

He wants to ask what the dream was. Whether something was ripping Ronan open from the inside, killing him to come out. He decides not to. Because if Ronan *had* been having the same dream, he wouldn't want it validated. Given extra weight. Neither does Dom.

"Good night, Dom. Thanks. And I'm sorry for bothering you."

"Good night."

He watches the blue light beneath the door, hoping it will switch off and Attalah will come back to bed, and afraid that if she did come it would be because she'd heard his conversation. Heard something in his voice that shouldn't have been there.

CHAPTER TWENTY

RONAN

My magnificent Frankenstein sex bot was taking shape. *Tom Minniq*. Where the name came from, how it ended up in the filthy daydreams that had been plaguing me since my return to Hudson, I couldn't say. Just echoed into my head and demanded to be let out. But I liked it; the faint exotic whiff of the Other. A good guiding principle, as I stitched photo features together to make him. The man I assembled could have been Sicilian or Syrian, South American or some Southern California melting pot product. Half Asian; half Black; straight outta Ukraine. Whatever you were looking for—other than straight-up Aryan—you would see it when you saw Tom.

The work felt good. Safe; familiar. A thoroughly rational task to pour my energy into, while the world became completely irrational all around me.

I had so much material. Thousands of photos: the naked edgy stuff that was my stock and trade, the wholesome outdoorsy men's fashion shoots I'd shot. Grinning men in suits at weddings; leering men brandishing impressive erections. Men fishing. Mock-selfies of men on Ferris wheels.

Nor was I limited to photos that I'd taken myself. On Instagram, on Flickr, on a million sites there were scenes I could stick Tom into. Flop the settings, stretch them slightly, color-shift, and crop and pretty soon you had something no image search would be able to backtrack to. In a dozen different outfits, in a bright assortment of scenic situations, I assembled Tom's profile. Perfect for sex apps and online dating alike.

Dense, short, thick, black curly hair. Approachably average height. Lithe, catlike. Devastating.

"Meat is the universal language," one of the men on the television said, and I swear my father grunted. "Everywhere you go, people eat meat."

A montage showed a hundred men in a hundred countries, smiling, holding up pink flesh cupped in bloody hands.

I watched my father's face. He was one of them, part of the international brotherhood of butchers . . . but his back and his business had been broken by the inexorable unbeatable decline of small-town America.

Fifteen years, now, since the butcher shop went belly up. Bad enough spending his whole life watching his hometown die. The factories shutting down. His hardworking friends forced onto welfare. But everybody needed to eat (*and meat is the universal language*) and he'd held out for far longer than most of the other small businesses that lined Warren Street, but eventually even Szepessy's Meats couldn't stay in the black (*without his son to help him*) (*or even take his calls*).

"Dad?" I asked, and he blinked. "Did you ever—"

I didn't know what I wanted to ask, and he wouldn't have been able to answer me even if I did.

"You did your best," I said. "It's not your fault."

His eyes stayed on *Meat Men*. But was it just my imagination, or did he turn his head the tiniest bit toward me?

"And I'm sorry," I said. "I'm so sorry I stayed away so long."

Easy to say it now, when he probably couldn't even hear me. And that made it worse. Made me sicker. My cheeks burned; my mouth was full of sand. I stayed there stewing in the full knowledge of what a wretched man I was until the next commercial break.

Fifteen minutes later, my phone rang. An unknown number— the Ronan of a week before would have ignored it, but the Ronan of right now was Up To Something.

"Hello?"

"Ronan! Jark Trowse," he said, his voice effusive and chummy and enthusiastic.

"Hey," I said, looking over at my dad. Had he heard the man's loud, happy bark? Did he know I was chatting with The Enemy? "How are you?"

"I'm great, since Treenie said you wanted to meet. That sounds fantastic. Although I must admit I was surprised. I thought I'd be the last person you want to talk to."

"Why's that?" I asked, mentally rolling up my sleeves.

"I figured if your father hated me, so would you."

I got up swiftly, went out into the backyard. "My father hates you?"

"I can't think of another reason he'd turn down what I offered him."

"Really?" I asked. "You can't?"

"Enlighten me, Ronan."

Really? I thought. *You want to do this on the phone?* But, no. He wasn't challenging me. He was prodding. And his smug voice had come close to pushing me into saying something stupid, like, *How about he loves his city and he won't let you destroy it.* But I was better than that.

"My father's mind is mostly gone," I said. "I couldn't say what he's thinking. Or why he did what he did. I can't even ask him."

"I'm sorry to hear that," he said.

"Well," I said. "You might have an opportunity now."

"Really," he said.

Oh well, I thought. *Here goes nothing.* I had hoped to wine and woo him, but I could adapt. "It'd be pretty easy for me to get power of attorney over my father. And then I'd be in a position to take that offer he turned down. Or another one."

"Another one," he said. "You want more than the very large amount of money I offered your father?"

"Not more money," I said. "In fact, I might be willing to negotiate a lower dollar figure, in exchange for some other nonfinancial things."

I could practically hear him grin, shark-wide. He was a businessman first and foremost, however much he and his Wikipedia page went on about being an artist committed to creating a community of artists. "What were you thinking of?"

"To start with, I want full transparency. I want all the information you have. Who's behind the Pequod Arms project. The property owners. The architects you hired."

"Much of this is public record," he demurred.

"Much of it is not," I said. "And what *is* on the public record doesn't quite add up. I want to know the local union leaders you've bought off. Your contacts in New York State government who are helping facilitate this project, and what they're getting. Everything. This isn't just about money, for me. Not just about this project. I'm thinking of the future of my city. I want a say in what it looks like."

A train whistle wailed.

"Done," Jark said. "Is that all?"

"For now," I said.

He laughed. "I like you, Ronan." Of course he did. People always like people they can purchase. "You love this town as much as I do, I can tell. And you want the best possible future for it. We should meet, get drinks. Something."

"Sounds good," I said, and hung up, and went back inside. My father still stared into space.

"I'm going to make them sorry they ever set foot in this fucking city," I said to him, and swiftly finished putting up Tom Minniq's sex app profile.

CHAPTER TWENTY-ONE

Ronan is carrying on twenty-four conversations at once. He has been for days. Sometimes it gets as high as fifty. Mostly men, on Grindr, but plenty of women on Tinder, too.

Tom Minniq is a busy boy. Telling bottoms how hard he'll fuck them; telling tops all the things they can do to him. Telling women about his kids and his job and his therapist. Ronan recognizes he's falling into probably-problematic stereotypes about what women want to hear, but he has nothing else to base his heterosexual romance upon. It seems to be effective, mostly, although he suspects the photos do most of the work.

Tom is so busy, in fact, that he is never able to actually meet up. Sorry, working late. Got friends over. Stuck at Mom's. Feeling under the weather. Which, in New York City, usually means venereal disease. He wonders if it's the same thing here.

Tom has acquired a staggering stock of information. What won't people tell a beautiful man? Especially if he follows What's your rent like— or How much do they pay you over there— or Why Hudson, of all the shitty towns in all the world— with jk it's cool, I know that's an inappropriate question. They answer every time.

Something is happening, when he's working on Tom. He feels

it like electricity, and wonders if this is what Katch meant when he said there was power flowing through Ronan.

He's amassing a staggering dossier of intel, for Attalah. A giant folder of blackmail material.

Because they all send nudes, eventually. Nudes, and sometimes more. It's startling, actually, the alacrity with which boys and girls—but mostly boys—send pictures and videos of themselves performing the most indelicate of acts. Of course they can relock or un-send the photos anytime they want, and there's a degree of comfort in that, the illusion of control, but only because they don't expect the person they're speaking with to be taking screencaps and saving video files just as fast as they can.

Or that he's also looking them up on Facebook. Which—by the way—it proved super-easy to fake a Facebook profile for Tom, complete with posts going back to 2008. They let you edit the date, after all, so you can post wedding photos a week later or upload those sixth-grade slumber party photos you just found and fit them into the right spot on your timeline. Most of his catfish targets he doesn't send friend requests to. That would be weird. But there's an awful lot of information Tom can access, even without being actual friends.

....

LILLY IS ON THE LOOKOUT. Penelope's Quilt's director of community engagement and community building has visited every antique store on Warren Street, an undertaking that has swallowed up most of her day. And turned up nothing. Few of the shop owners she spoke with have heard of this *Jerremy* photographer. A local pastor mentioned him, in an interview for the oral history project Lilly is trying to get off the ground, but even the internet turned up nothing. Apparently only a handful of local old-timers remember him.

But that was what was wonderful about it, what made it so vital and exciting. That's what makes Lilly rub her hands together, stalking up Warren Street for a fifty-years-gone studio photographer who just might be a missing titan of twentieth-century art. The few images she's seen of his were excellent, yes, but quality isn't what compels her. It was the *lore* of it. People knew things about him that weren't on the internet. He existed only in people's minds—and the photographs she knew were out there. What a novel and intriguing concept . . .

The internet has made us expect information to be easy, straightforward, accessible. Pull your pocket computer out and ask it any question, and you can find an answer. And if the answer isn't there—if the question's never even been asked—we don't know what to do. But think of how much knowledge human beings carry around in their heads!

She'd go back to school for it, one of these days. Do a thesis on the memories we cannot share; the knowledge we can never acquire. Or design the app that would make her fucking famous. Ice-BergTip, or maybe icebergtip? ThePastIsPresent?

. . . .

PITY POOR BERGEN, SAILOR. He has spent so long staring into his phone. Flicking his thumb downward every ten or twenty seconds, to refresh the grid of men on his sex app. Torsos in various stages of hairiness and decrepitude; a few faces; a few sunsets or farm silos.

He should be working, but work is slow today. Penelope's Quilt's community projects are at an ebb on Wednesdays.

But then,

One word: *hey*

For a split second he is suspicious. He always is, when somebody above a certain hotness level hollers at him. *He could have anyone he wants—any one of these fit muscled bearded gym boys would be happy to get a* hey *from him, would in fact immediately respond with nude photos of themselves.* In his experience, when someone this hot hits him up, it's because everyone hotter than him has already listened to what the guy wants and said *Oh hell no. You want to chain me to a what? Do what on my chest?* When someone that hot hits him up, he wants Bergen to do unspeakable things. Someone that hot sees Bergen and thinks, *This guy will do anything I ask of him.*

But Bergen lets go of his suspicions immediately, as he always does. Because they're right, those imaginary guys in his head. He'll do anything they ask of him.

This one, for example. Black curly hair, jug-handled ears, a chin you could crack walnuts with. Easily the sexiest thing on offer here—hotter even than that supermodel Quint Whateverhisnameis, who Bergen sees on here all the time and who never returns his taps. Quint is handsome, but this man is dangerous. His scowl sends shivers up Bergen's back. Why is a scowling man so sexy?

Username: Tom Minniq. Age: 29. Height: 5'7". 165 lbs. Body Hair? Hairy. Relationship Status: Single. What I Do: work construction. What I'm Looking For: sex and friends but mostly sex. About me: Hudson native, enjoying all the new fun coming to town. Sex Preferences _____. Safety Practices: _____. Ethnicity: _____.

Hey, Bergen writes back, and when two minutes and fifty-seven seconds go by without a response, he types, You looking?

CHAPTER TWENTY-TWO

RONAN

anal, boring—the brute mechanics of betrayal. Barely worth mentioning. I googled *power of attorney*, spent some time reading up on the basics. Called my father's lawyer. His doctor. Had them come over. Carefully structured it around Margie's work schedule, so she'd never know.

Effortless, all of it. Heart-hurtingly so. My father stared ahead, unseeing, unresponsive. These men who'd known me all my life said kind, sad words, patted me on the shoulder, signed on all the right dotted lines.

Photography was the best way to get my mind off things. Not my own. I'd found a box, in my father's bedroom, while I looked for the deed of sale to the butcher shop. The box was full of postcards, old photos, news clippings, and full-page ads from major papers. Now I sat on the floor at my father's feet, drinking coffee and letting it rile me up inside.

Dinosaurs, in the Seventh Street Park.

A forty-foot-tall T. rex stood in the flatbed of a pickup truck; a brontosaurus sixty feet long was on a trailer attached to the back. Men smiled for photos alongside them.

HUDSON PREPARES FOR THE WORLD'S FAIR, said the text at the bottom of the postcard. In a tiny oval: *Photo by Jerremy*.

The life-size dinosaurs that wowed the world at the fair had been built right here in Hudson. Paid for by Sinclair Oil, constructed by Louis Paul Jonas—who had done some of the most memorable displays at the American Museum of Natural History in New York City. His studio, long since shuttered, still stood out on Miller Road. A triceratops on the lawn was all that was left. Somewhere there's a picture of me on it.

I dressed up as well as I could, including a cardigan I'd bought in the eleventh grade, and headed out. Down Warren Street.

Sunday morning; everyone sleeping in. Pretty soon the street would be packed with pedestrians. Loud with the commentary of strangers: *Isn't it so cute; look how quaint; it's like this whole street has been frozen in time.* But for now—if I closed my eyes and breathed deep—it could have been the Hudson of sixty years ago. My father's city, where dinosaurs stood in the park and trains rode right through the main street in the middle of the day, where crazy people coexisted with the rest of their community, where everyone knew him—the butcher shop prince, who would one day inherit his father's kingdom.

When I left, I disrupted the natural order of things. Broke the chain from father to son. And, sure, the business would have failed anyway. Like everything else on Warren Street that wasn't an antique shop. The few stores that made it through Hudson's long depression would not survive its renaissance. But it wouldn't all have been on Dad. We could have shared that burden, and maybe a smaller share of that crushing weight wouldn't have broken him.

But I couldn't have stayed. Not as who I was. I'd have had to keep myself in some kind of horrible closet. How I made it out at all, without being the victim of a homophobic hate crime, is still a mystery to me.

I had work to do. I was behind schedule with Jark. So far we hadn't found anything, no gaps in his armor or tragic flaws or fatal weaknesses. There was still so much intel to be gotten. And one very big seed to plant.

Across the street, a liquor store. Inside was all smiling sommeliers and artisanal tequilas and bourbon made in barrels built from reclaimed wood—a far cry from the bulletproof-glass-and-lottery-tickets liquor store Hudson used to have on Warren Street. While I stood there, basking in my hatred of it all, I did some googling. Read a dozen interviews with Jark Trowse. Apparently everyone cared what a billionaire had to say. It didn't take me long to see that rye whiskey was his liquor of choice.

As soon as I reached the shelf with the ryes, a wisp of a man appeared beside me. Unsolicited, he started ticking off the merits of each bottle. "Monongahela-style distillation"; "grassiness and spice that linger deep down"; "fruity fudginess." Etc. "Chewable, for sure," he said, discussing one bottle, holding out a hand as if forestalling my inevitable question, like he could see in my eyes how concerned I was about the chewability of my whiskey. I ignored it all and bought the most expensive one, at $215. "Great choice," he said, but not like it was a great choice, like I had failed some kind of test, like I had revealed my passion for whiskeys to be insufficiently all-consuming. "We do have a WhistlePig Boss Hog Black Prince on order but they're *always* backlogged with that one."

"I know," I said. "Why do you think I'm buying this disappointing substitute?"

And then I headed for Jark's.

His house was on Allen Street, a block from the courthouse. Every building on that block looked like something out of *Meet Me in St. Louis*, great gingerbread monstrosities of nineteenth-century wealth; wide, deep porches and Tiffany glass; porticos and gables and other words I never knew before I started researching Hudson home prices—the better to burn them all down. Metaphorically speaking.

These were whaling-boom properties. Jark's house was brick, in a faux-Moorish style with three rounded arches over the entranceway. He'd bought it for four million, five years back.

I rang the doorbell. I waited. No one answered. On the bag the whiskey came in, I wrote: *Jark—came by to see what you were up to, but I guess you were out. Wasn't so sure about leaving this gift unattended in such a seedy neighborhood (lol) but decided to risk it. Thank you for bringing my town back to life.—Ronan*

It cost me a lot, that last line, but I could do it. I set the bottle down and turned to go, and only then did the door open.

"Ronan?" Jark said sleepily.

Had I ever really seen him before? Really looked? Not the campaign poster version, Obama-confident, and not the *Fortune* cover story, shrewd and humble in an utterly fraudulent blend. Here, now, hungover, unprepared, I could see him clearly. Brow permanently furrowed. Hairline receding. Arms skinny.

This thing I felt, it wasn't pity, although it was close. It was kinship. My hairline was receding. My arms were skinny. Two aging gay dudes stood on that porch, slipping into irrelevance. Had been, since we left our twenties. The surface spoiling; a fate worse than death in a community so obsessed with the surface.

"Hey, sorry to bother you," I said, snatching up the bottle again. "Is this a bad time?"

"Not at all," he said. "What's up?"

"Nothing. I just figured you and I never had a chance to really get to know each other. And because my momma raised me right, I never call on anyone without a gift."

"Holy shit, a WhistlePig Fifteen Year Straight!" he exclaimed, taking the bottle from my hands. "That's incredible. Shit, Ronan, I don't know what to say."

"Don't say anything, just pop it open and get two glasses."

"Yes!"

I followed him in. Through a deep foyer, where firewood was stacked three feet high. And then—I saw.

In the center of a soaring open reception room, on a parquet-tile floor, beside a wide central staircase, a woolly mammoth. An ancient skeleton, the brown bones demanding total reverence. Her right front leg raised, head tilted to the side, about to swing her glorious tusks and exterminate an enemy.

It took me a long time to find words. When I did, they were just: "Is that . . ."

"It's real," he said. "I mean, about seventy percent intact. The missing pieces have been filled in with resin composite replicas. Complete skeletons are just not found. I know which bones are replacements, but I don't think anyone else can tell."

It had never even entered my mind that someone could own such a thing. I'd imagined them as something like the Constitution or a national forest—the patrimony of all people, the wellspring of our wonder, something that belonged where anyone could see them.

"How the hell did you get something like this?"

"They come on the market from time to time. There are actually more prehistoric remains in private hands than institutional ones these days. Museums can't compete with oligarchs, I'm afraid. When the Field Museum in Chicago bought Sue the Tyrannosaurus Rex at auction, they had to have support from McDonald's and the Walt Disney Corporation. Way of the world, shitty as it is."

"Way of the world," I whispered. Hating the world. Hating him. Wanting to stand there forever. My attempt to feel like a baller by buying a two-hundred-dollar bottle of whiskey suddenly felt pathetic.

He led me to a kitchen so wide and bright it hurt my eyes. Pulled out two tumblers that had to be over a hundred years old. Survivors of some Western saloon or seaside sailor's bar. Everything Jark owned had pedigree, had texture. What a magical life that of the rich must be. To feel oneself immersed in history all the time. Inseparable from it. In possession of it.

"I always drink the first one neat," he said, pouring the whiskey. "So you can appreciate it in its purest form."

"Sounds great," I said.

Glasses clinked. Hatred had not replaced the surge of kinship I'd felt on the porch. They coexisted, and I decided to ride that contradiction.

We sipped. It burned. It tasted like whiskey.

"It's really chewable," I said. "And I love how the spice lingers."

He nodded gratefully, like a traveler in a foreign land who finally found someone who could speak his language. "People try so many crazy different kinds of barrels these days, but really there's just no substitute for oak. Sometimes simplicity is best."

I left the paper bag on his counter, note side up, where he could find and read it later.

We went to a tile-floored side room where a fire hummed in the fireplace, and sat in brown leather chairs so worn I worried they'd crumble to dust underneath me. Antique maps and a ship's wheel hung on the walls. The ceiling was raw scuffed wood, almost certainly reclaimed from a ship, which explained the air's faint salt tang.

"I'm sorry," I said. "I'm still so bowled over by your mammoth."

"Sometimes I worry it's far too vulgar a display of power," his voice lapsing into a demonic croak to complement the *Exorcist* quote.

"It *is* a lot to process."

"I'm so glad we're friends," Jark said. "I was beginning to be jealous of you. The only person in Hudson with more Instagram followers than me."

"Can't compare our followings," I said. "You value quality. Occasional posts, of special things, and you rarely engage in dialogue. I emphasize quantity. Tons of posts, even of the stupidest shit, and tons of comments on tons of other people's posts. People love that shit. You ask me, that's all anybody wants from social media. A gentle reminder that they do in fact exist."

"You've been studying up on me."

"And you on me."

He raised his glass in acknowledgment. "But you've been quiet lately. No posts at all. Someone like you, with such a big influencer score—if you started hyping up this place, you could really help get Hudson on the map even more."

"It's been a difficult time," I said. "My dad . . ."

I let that sentence expire. But with the whiskey already warming me up inside, and the fire working on the outside, I decided to jump right in. Sincerity was best, when building a bond. "I can't tell you what it's like for me. Coming back here, now. Seeing how much it's changed. Growing up here was so, so hard." I let myself remember bloodied noses, bullies slinging slurs at me. Steve "Stubb" Coffin, the mayor's son, his bizarre obsession with causing me harm. I heard my voice falter. "I never in a million years could have imagined that Hudson would become a safe place for gay people."

"How'd you get out?"

"Very boring, very standard story. Became obsessed with photography. It was my safe space, my only way of asserting control over the world I found so menacing. I coedited a zine with my best friend, actually, and I think that got me into SVA, which was a real long shot application. Moved to New York City. Flunked out, but not because I was fucking around—I was doing actual work, I interned with a photographer and then got hired as her assistant, she liked my stuff and let me use her studio and other resources— helped get my work in front of her clients, who started hiring me for the jobs she couldn't take on—pretty soon I was doing okay for myself." Here I paused, poured myself more whiskey. Wondered how honest I should be. Decided to go all in. The better to wholly hook him. "The fucking around came later. Like apparently every other gay guy in New York City, I started doing a lot of Tina. And fucking a lot of other boys who were into it. Which I guess brings us to the present day."

"You have a bit of a reputation," he said, apologetically. "I guess you know that already. But that's good. Only people who are talked about have reputations. Everyone else is just a hot mess in the privacy of their own irrelevance."

I laughed, sincerely. "Such a poet, Jark. What about you? Any addiction issues, hot-mess skeletons?"

He swirled the last sip of rye around in his glass. "This is going to sound like a cop-out, but my addiction is work. And it's a really dangerous one. Not in the same way as crystal, but still. Dangerous to my health—I get maybe five hours of sleep a night and never remember to drink enough water, and my stress levels would probably kill a man twice my size—and definitely dangerous to my social life. I haven't had a boyfriend in . . . fucking . . . three years? And then it was just a bunch of short-term things."

"That sucks," I said. "I mean, neither have I, but I still have tons of sex. What about you?"

Jark didn't answer right away. I had never seen him on any of the apps. Of course I understood the need to not put all your business out there. No sense saying in a semipublic forum that you preferred getting fucked to fucking, or refused to wear condoms, or what your racial hang-ups were. Especially if you were running for public office. Was there a separate app for superstars and billionaires? If there was, it couldn't have too many offerings in Hudson. "My sex life is another casualty of my work addiction."

Probably he paid for it. Might that be the weak spot I was in search of?

"That's a shame," I said, mock-jocular. Proceeding with extreme caution. "There's no rent boys in Hudson? I wouldn't even know where to look for something like that."

He laughed. "I'm sure there are."

Somehow, we emptied that bottle. Talking about bullshit. Getting drunk; getting ridiculous. No helpful intel emerged, but that was fine. I'd come to deepen my relationship with him, trick him into thinking we were friends, and in that respect the visit was a smash hit.

But here's the thing: I *liked* talking to him. Even if I hated myself for it. That tiny kinship flame kept burning. He and I had so much more in common than me and Attalah, me and Dom, me and Marge or Treenie or my poor half-brain-dead dad. It didn't mean I cared about him.

"I saw in your dossier that Ohrena Shaw is a tenant of yours."

"Yeah," he said, picking up the empty bottle and reading the label. A slight guarded edge to his voice.

"I went to high school with her. We're old friends."

"That's cool," he said, setting it down, along with his guard.

This was it. The most crucial part of our plan so far. Success here meant smooth sailing for the next several steps.

"She's hilarious," I said. "You ever spend any time with her? She should have been a stand-up comedian. Could have been, too, if it wasn't for that husband of hers."

I knew he wanted her out. All the other tenants had accepted buyouts. With her gone, he could do a gut renovation, annex it to one of the Pequod properties. She'd turned him down because she refused to cede an inch to the invaders, but Jark didn't need to know that.

"She told me she wants to move," I said, "but she can't risk a buyout because her husband's sobriety is such a fragile thing. If he had access to a ton of money all of a sudden . . . bad things would happen. And then the money would be gone, and then so would her husband. They've been down similar roads before. And he's abusive, so even if the money was all in her name, she doesn't trust herself to be able to hold out if he threatened to hurt her. Because she knows he will."

"Really . . ." Jark said, drunk eyes wide.

"If she had a house all ready to move into, on the other hand, some asset that couldn't be easily liquidated, they'd be safe."

"Wow," he said. "That's so sad."

"Isn't it? Makes me feel a lot better about being single."

He clinked his empty glass to mine. I could see the ideas vibrate behind his eyes, the well-oiled machinery of his mind chugging down the precise tracks I'd laid out for it.

....

CHAPTER TWENTY-THREE

RONAN

"**H**appy Columbus Day weekend," Marge barked, walking in with two big paper grocery bags. "Prepare to not be able to walk on the fucking street because it's so packed with goddamned tourists."

Shit, I thought, my stomach twisted and my head full of wasps from Jark's rye. Who said expensive liquor doesn't give hangovers? *Please, God, don't let it be Saturday. Don't let me have missed the most important part of our plan, failed to do the thing I needed to do, fucked the whole thing up.*

But my phone assured me it was Friday. And early, still. I might feel like shit, but I'd lost barely any time.

One text message, from Attalah: I hope your boy Tom can deliver tonight.

He will, I typed. If there's one thing I know, it's how easily horny men can be manipulated.

I logged in to Grindr. Tom's inbox was predictably packed. Including one from the night before, from just the man I'd been hoping to hear from. You around? he'd asked, at midnight.

Hey man, I typed. Sorry I missed this. Passed the fuck out after work. How you doing?

The response—Great dude how r u—came almost immediately.

tom.minniq: I'm alright. Going crazy with work and errands and shit

Just Quint: sorry

[two minutes of silence on my end—on Tom's end]

Just Quint: so no time for fun today?

Top Model Quint would never have given a guy who looked like me a second glance or a polite word. But for Tom Minniq he sent over the most explicit imagery imaginable—including several videos where he offered up his orifices to a wide variety of men.

tom.minniq: Probably not :(

tom.minniq: Unless I can clone myself and make the other me go pick up this shit

Just Quint: What shit?

tom.minniq: stuff for my buddy's business. Business cards and buttons and shit. He got it printed up at Staples and I stupidly told him I'd go pick it up for him.

tom.minniq: It's all paid for, I just don't have time to drag my ass all over town getting the stuff and dropping it off downtown. I'm way the hell out in Great Barrington helping out on a roofing gig for a friend of mine and it'd take me two hours with all the driving.

[Forty-nine seconds of silence on my end]

Just Quint: I could go pick it up for you

[Tom's response came with eerie speed, because I'd already typed it and had only been waiting for the offer to arrive to click send]

tom.minniq: holy shit dude thank you

tom.minniq: That'd be amazing

tom.minniq: Gimme your full name and I'll call him, have it added to the order

tom.minniq: You'll need ID to sign for it

Just Quint: yeah man happy to help out

Just Quint: especially if it clears up some space on your schedule so you can come play [winking devil face emoji]

tom.minniq: one of the things is a big tube. Probably too big for a car. You got a pickup truck?

I knew he did. It's why I picked him, out of all the boys who'd gladly have done anything Tom Minniq asked of him.

Just Quint: yup. government-issued-ID name is Quentin Skerping. But don't tell anyone lol. I model under the name Quint Sawyer

tom.minniq: absolutely dude. Maybe this evening. U looking to get fucked?

Just Quint: #always

tom.minniq: dirty slut

tom.minniq: I appreciate a dirty slut

I sent him the location, where the stuff needed to be dropped off. Behind the abandoned taxi-dispatcher stand, across from the train station. Then I lobbed back his winking devil face emoji and logged out.

Marge was in the kitchen, unpacking grocery bags. "Can I give you some cash for that?" I asked, pulling out my wallet.

"Your dad paid," she said, flashing his credit card and putting it down on the counter. "They know me out at ShopRite. I got every receipt in a folder in this drawer, so he can review them. If he ever, you know, can."

"Thanks, Marge," I said. We hugged. Of course she couldn't sense my awkwardness, couldn't tell from that how I'd betrayed my father and sold the building and fucked over our town forever. Could she?

"Hey," my father said, standing in the doorway. My jaw dropped. It wasn't that he was standing there—he could be mobile—but he'd very definitely just said a word.

"Hey, Dad," I said, afraid to speak louder than a whisper.

"Making your coffee, Jim," Marge said, gesturing to the coffee-pot and putting away the groceries like this was super normal.

Dad grunted and went back to the living room.

"Does this happen a lot?" I asked Marge.

"No. Sometimes, but not a lot. Having you here is doing him some good. I knew it would."

She touched me then, an awkward hand on top of my head.

A forgotten bubble of fondness for her swelled inside me, a sense memory of being a little boy at the butcher shop with her massive hand on my head.

"Thanks, Marge. For everything."

When the coffee was ready, I brought two cups out. Sat on the couch. He was sitting in his recliner, but the TV wasn't on. He was watching out the window.

"Here," I said, setting his coffee down on the narrow table between us.

He turned and smiled. The smile was weak but it was there. "Thanks, Ronan."

"How've you been, Dad?"

Nothing.

"I've missed you so much. Dad."

"Me, too. Ronan."

We sat. We sipped coffee. Marge made noise in the kitchen. If I shut my eyes and tuned out everything and tried my best to come unstuck in time, she could have been—

"Mom," I said, opening my eyes. "We never talked about Mom. You never wanted to, at first. And then, neither did I."

Dad stared into his cup.

Here it was. The gulf I'd been skirting since I got there. The pain I'd been hiding from, behind hate. "I want to talk about her now," I said.

"Your mother loves you," he said.

"I know that, Dad." This might be my only chance. He might never be here again. "But why did she . . . do it?"

The question filled the room, like the echo of an explosion. Like we'd both been stunned, deafened, damaged by it.

Dad did not respond. And so, asshole that I am, I repeated it.

"We still get bears," he said, when he spoke again, and already I could hear something missing, something that had been in his voice when he spoke a moment ago and was gone now. "Backyard, sometimes. Wild boars, too. Big nasty things."

Maybe it was true. Behind our house was a scraggle of woodland, and a couple of scrawny dead-end streets, and then the cemetery. But it had no relevance to what we'd been talking about. My dad was gone again. He'd shown up on our doorstep—a miracle, a semi-feral house cat who we thought had run off forever—and I'd scared him away.

"They always unsettled her," he whispered. "The bears."

He'd be back. I told myself that. Let the sweet tang of hope fill my mouth.

"I need you," I said. "I know you can't help me—not right now—but I know you're in there. And I think you can hear me."

Did Dad nod, or was it just my imagination?

"I can't beat them alone."

My phone rang. Dominick. I got up, kissed my father on the forehead, and went into my room.

"Hey," I said.

"How is he?" Dom asked, and the strong, clear sound of his voice went a long way toward diminishing the anger I felt for myself, for bringing up my mother and scaring Dad back into his shell.

"He had a good morning. Talked for the first time since I've been here."

"That's fucking awesome, dude. And you?"

"Hungover," I said, and laughed, and so did he, and the shared sound of it sent a tingle straight to my groin. Which is probably why I said the stupid thing I said next. That, and the fact that asking Dad about my mom had opened the floodgates to introspection I typically avoided. "I have a problem."

I'd never said it before. Not out loud. Not to another person; not without a jokey tone.

"What kind of problem?" he said.

"I'm a drug addict. And a sex addict." *And apparently also addicted to mayhem conspiracy.* "And I do terrible things when I'm in the grip of it. Why am I telling all this to a cop?"

"Because you're an idiot," he said, and laughed, and I wasn't laughing this time, so I could appreciate the sound of his. "And you trust me. And anyway, I already found you collapsed in the street like a fucking drunk, the first night you were back. So I figured you were all kinds of fucked up."

"I love you, Dom," I said, startling myself anew. But unlike with my father, this time once the words were out I felt insanely happy.

"I love you, too, buddy."

"Not like that," I said.

"Not like what? You don't know how I feel. And I don't know how you feel."

"I'm telling you how I feel."

"Yeah, but, here's the thing about being a cop. For me, anyway. You figure out real fast how words are bullshit. Best not to go by them, not really. It's not that people lie, although they do, all the time. The real problem isn't dishonesty. It's ignorance, or confusion. People don't understand themselves at all. Why they do the things they do. What they're really feeling, and where it comes from. So the narratives they construct in their heads, and the way they give voice to those stories, they have a pretty minimal relevance to reality."

"That's deep, dude."

"I'm a deep dude. Don't let the uniform fool you."

I was grinning like a happy idiot schoolboy, there in the darkness of my curtained room. Headache and heartache forgotten by the sound of Dom's voice.

"You got plans tonight?" he asked. "You and my wife masterminding anybody's utter destruction?"

"Nope. Nothing." He made me high. Reckless. "Why? You wanna go out on a date?"

"There's a big fundraiser for Jark Trowse's election campaign to-night, and there's someone I want you to meet. Gay kid, goes to Hudson High. Reminds me a lot of you, back in the day. By which I mean, fucking miserable. Got no friends. Wants to be a photographer. Figured maybe you could take him under your wing."

"Sure," I said. "Okay. I'll see you there."

Who knew whether it was Dom or my dad who made me so happy as I got dressed. Both of them, certainly. But my dad more. I drank glass after glass of water, feeling the ache of my dehydrated head diminish with each passing moment.

He's in there. He's not gone.

I muttered it under my breath, the staccato rhythm of it buoying me up, filling me with a love as high as helium.

I couldn't help the happiness I felt, the hope that he might come back. But I also couldn't help the fear. That he'd find out what I'd done and hate me forever.

And all the air went out of me. And I was suddenly so very small.

No, I thought, grabbing hold of the blade between my ribs. Giv-ing it a twist. *Not this. Not now. There are too many monsters to punish. Too much mischief still to unfold. Tonight we declare war. The whole thing shifts.*

Tomorrow, things get really messy.

CHAPTER TWENTY-FOUR

Searchlights sweep the sky. A step-and-repeat has been set up outside the Elks Lodge, red-carpet-style. On the sheer white backdrop, old-fashioned woodcut whales with the words CITY OF HUDSON around them alternate with the edgy modern logo of Jark's company, and the slogan JARK TROWSE: A MAYOR FOR ALL OF US. People pose. Ronan dutifully does likewise, on his way in. Cameras flash by the dozen. One of the photographers is Vernon Sutphin, the author of a blog that calls itself the *Hudson Gazette* in emulation of an actual (long-dead) Hudson newspaper, who believes (erroneously) that this blog makes him (a) a journalist, and (b) practically a local. Ronan isn't sure who the rest of them are. Probably Jark paid most of them, to give a false sense of paparazzi frenzy. He is on hand, greeting people, popping into the picture with anyone who wants him there. And who doesn't want their picture taken with a famous billionaire and future mayor?

. . . .

ON THIS NIGHT, Zelda Outterson will put more miles on her car than on any other night of her life.

First, she drives down to the abandoned taxi dispatcher stand, where the packages Quint dropped off wait for her between two buildings. Four big heavy boxes, and one massive tube. The tube stays where it is. The boxes she loads into her car. Searchlights make slow circles in the sky, from somewhere to the north. She wonders what the occasion is.

In the past week, she's made nearly a thousand phone calls. Of the three hundred people on the list Attalah gave her, some of them were hard to reach. She was expecting that. When you're struggling, when you probably owe a lot of money, you don't just answer every unknown number whose call comes in. So she left a lot of messages and tried a bunch of times. Many of them are people who she knows.

Some of them said no right off the bat. Some of them took several follow-up conversations. Some never responded at all. Some had had their cell service switched off.

A hundred and eight of them said yes.

So Zelda has a hundred and eight stops to make tonight. At each one, she pulls over and opens up her trunk. From one box, she takes a button. From another, she takes a pamphlet. These go into an unmarked envelope. The envelope goes into the mailbox.

It'll be a busy night, but she should have no trouble getting through it all before the real fun starts at 3:00 A.M.

·······

"RONAN SZEPESSY!" someone says, and a heavy hand clamps down on his shoulder.

"Hey, Mr. Warsaw," Ronan says, acting surprised to see the man with the unlit cigar in his free hand. In truth, he's orchestrated this "surprise" by standing at the makeshift bar pretending to stare into his phone.

"Please, Ronan! Call me Wallace! You're not ten years old anymore."

"I suppose I'm not," Ronan says, laughing loudly. It's the last campaign fundraiser before the election; everyone in the Elks Lodge is drunk and laughing loudly. *They think they have this in the bag. They think nothing can stop their golden boy billionaire candidate.* "How have you been, Wallace?"

"Not as good as you, conquering the world down there in New York City!"

Wallace Warsaw has been the cochair of the Columbia County Chamber of Commerce for as long as anyone can remember. An insufferable blowhard, in Ronan's father's eyes, but like every other business owner on Warren Street, he paid his annual membership dues to the Chamber and went to its seasonal dinners and believed in his heart that the sixth sense for business that had helped Wallace turn his failing father's distribution center into the county's most profitable company would help turn the whole local economy around.

Which, apparently, it has.

"Pretty big deal, getting Jark Trowse to be this year's honoree," Ronan says. "Still, it's a strange choice. An out-of-towner."

Wallace nods, like this is a conversation he's had to have more than once. "Jark's done more for this city than ninety-nine percent of the people who've been here for generations. All the money that's flowing into this city now, we owe this to him—well, to lots of people, but to him most of all—and with him our future will just keep on getting brighter and brighter. The more love we show him, the more love he'll show us."

But who's that money really flowing to? Ronan refrains from asking. Instead he smiles. Waves across the room, to that earnest woman Lilly with the rhinestone glasses. "Wallace, it truly is incredible, what you've done to this place."

. . . .

TREENIE WATCHES RONAN from across the Elks Lodge and knows in her gut that he is up to something.

She couldn't say how she knows it. Sometimes she just knows things. She's blessed with good instincts, that's all. She's a people reader. Served her well in high school, and it's served her well in real estate.

After each new person he's introduced to, he steps to the side and takes out his phone. She can tell what he's doing by the rhythm of his tapping. Looking them up, learning who they are, then tapping out a brief message and clicking send. She sees his face when he's alone, when he's unaware he's being watched, and *that's* the Ronan she remembers from the high school hallway, the one smoldering with quiet rage, sullen hate, the one who dreams of summoning up a flaming scythe and swinging it in a circle and slicing everyone in the room in half horizontally—according to an eleventh-grade English class journal entry she wasn't supposed to read. But then he blinks, takes a couple of deep breaths, and approaches some new circle or triangle of happy partygoers and effortlessly inserts himself into it. She sees how much work it is, to flip that switch inside. Finally, she sees how carefully he orchestrates an "accidental" encounter with Wallace Warsaw. How he texts someone immediately afterward.

Treenie wonders, *What are you up to, Ronan? And what am I going to have to do to stop you?*

. . . .

"HEY," DOM SAYS, finding Ronan alone out on the edge of the Elks Lodge roof. Behind them, in a glass-enclosed room, the party is in full swing. Bright lights. Abundant alcohol. Loud laughter.

"Hey," Ronan says. "When did you get here? I looked for you when I arrived."

"About fifteen minutes ago. Had a visit to make first. Pretty impressive, seeing you operate."

"How so?" Ronan asks, smiling, knowing the answer.

"Acting like you're one of them. The rich artsy New York City guy. They ate it up."

"Glad to hear it."

"Was I mistaken, or did you just get a gallery show?"

Ronan laughs. "You're very attentive. Yeah, a friend of Treenie's has a gallery down by Third Street and offered to do a photography exhibit. *Between Two Worlds*, or some such bullshit."

"I've heard artists complain that it's harder to get a show up here now than it is in New York. Ever since that latest *New York Times* article, all the tastemakers have their eyes on Hudson. And the gallery owners can be extremely picky."

"I guess it's my lucky day, then."

"I almost feel sorry for them," Dom says. "Between you and Attalah, you'll have them skinned alive and turned inside out before they know what happened."

"Where's this friend you wanted me to meet?"

"Wick texted me and said he couldn't come." From his phone, Dom reads out loud: "*I get these very serious depressive episodes and I try to spend them playing video games or listening to loud music with my headphones on, on the floor of my closet under a bunch of clothes. Anyway I'm having one tonight.* This kid's sixteen! He's a trip."

The four circling spotlights converge and disperse, converge and disperse. Scraps of black show between the clouds.

Dom points. "How much do you think it costs to rent those?"

"No idea. But I'll find out for you."

"I know that you will."

"I had a dream last night," Ronan says. "A whale, swimming through the sky."

"Me, too," Dom says.

Sudden, louder laughter from behind them.

They can't see us, Dom thinks, because the mechanics are the same as the two-way mirror at the police station. Bright lights in there, darkness out here. All they'll see is their own reflections. And they'd never even think to try to look past something so fascinating. He stands behind Ronan, wraps his arms around him. Pulls him tight. Kisses the back of his head.

This is wrong, Ronan thinks, but cannot bring himself to say.

"You want to go somewhere?" Dom whispers.

Ronan turns around. "More than anything," he says, but neither one of them budges right away. They hold tight to each other for a very long time.

. . . .

THREE A.M., and Zelda is wearing all black. She parks two blocks away, pulls the black ski mask over her face, and hurries down the hill.

"Hey," says the man who's waiting for her, also wearing all black and a ski mask. He smiles, and by those jacked-up teeth she'd have known it's Rome Byles even if she hadn't been the one to call and ask him to come.

"Thanks for helping out," she says.

"You kidding? What's more fun than breaking the law?"

The crooked-tooth smile is a little bit too wide, and Zelda worries—not for the first time—whether Rome was the right choice for this. True, he had been extremely fond of mischief back when they were teenagers, and, true, his status on the police force meant he'd know better than anyone how to evade capture and throw the rest of the force off the scent when they came sniffing . . . but maybe he enjoyed mischief a little too much. Maybe he took things a little too far. Maybe he enjoyed other people's fear a little bit too much. Not the first time she'd seen a bully or somebody full of unfocused anger gravitate toward the police force.

They walk the half block to the big billboard across from the train station. A smiling blue whale in a darker blue sea, with white words emblazoned over and around it: WELCOME TO HUDSON: A WHALE OF A TOWN. Beneath the billboard, the tools are waiting for them. Rollers on long poles; a bucket where wallpaper powder has already been mixed with water to make glue. They unroll the poster.

"Fucking brilliant," Rome says, seeing it. They turn to look across the street, imagining the hordes of Columbus Day invaders who will stream off the train in the morning to see this message.

....

BERGEN IS PRACTICALLY shaking with anticipation. He's been waiting so long. Thirty minutes—Tom was supposed to have been here twenty minutes ago. He must be insane to be standing here in Prison Alley. It's long after midnight and hardly anyone ever sets foot in the alley even in the middle of the day, but that doesn't change the fact that this is a public place and anyone at all could come along at any moment. At this point, he prays he *is* being catfished. Because if Tom does roll up and drop his pants, he knows he'll do whatever is asked of him. And that's how well-behaved gay boys end up on the sex offenders registry. He asked Tom to come over to his house, even offered to blow him in his pickup truck, but Tom typed back:

I'll fuck you in the alley like the dirty bitch you are

And Bergen became very hard and very scared at the exact same time.

He's not hard anymore. He's ready to go.

Twenty minutes is long enough. If I write back and say I got tired of waiting, I'm not in the wrong at all.

But now! Here he is. Emerging from the shadows between two brick walls, like he was part of the night itself. Jug-handled ears stand out in silhouette, lit from behind by a building's back-door security light.

"Hey," Tom says, lean, hungry, taut with muscle and menace.

All that fear abandons Bergen. "Hey," he says, in a tiny, tiny voice.

Tom reaches out, hooks one hand around Bergen's neck, pulls him close. For a kiss, Bergen thinks, and leans forward, but Tom moves his hand to the top of his head and pushes him to his knees.

Bergen's eyes glaze over, being mere inches from the significant tenting of Tom's pants. But when he reaches out his hand, Tom smacks him in the face and laughs.

"If you want this, I need you to do something for me first."

Anyone could see, by the thirst in Bergen's eyes, that he'd do absolutely anything.

CHAPTER TWENTY-FIVE

T he first train of the day out of New York Penn Station arrives in Hudson at 9:21 A.M. On an ordinary Saturday there are plenty of empty seats—not so many weekenders are eager to get up at 6:00 A.M. on a Saturday to make it to the train station by 7:15—but this is Columbus Day weekend, and it's sold out like every other northbound train.

"We're just pulling into the station now," says a boy who has been on his cell phone for almost the entirety of the two-hour ride—including several long stretches where the train passed through a cell reception dead zone and he just kept saying *Hello? Hello? Can you hear me? Hello?* All around him, fellow passengers exchange murder-plotting glances. Just after Yonkers somebody asked him to lower his voice and he said, *The quiet car is the one behind this. I suggest you go there if the noise is getting to you.*

"Yes, yes, I got it," he says, shuffling down the aisle. "I can read a Google Map, Bergen. I'll walk. See you in twelve minutes according to the map. Holy shit, this fucking town doesn't even have a platform?"

He hangs up and clambers down the steps, refusing the hand the conductor offers and almost falling.

"What the hell?" says the man in front of him, and stops to take a picture.

Across the street is a brand-new billboard. It says ATTENTION: INVADERS FROM NEW YORK CITY in wide block Gothic letters, and YOU ARE HATED in thick playful cursive.

Red letters; white drop shadow. Behind the words there is an angry black sperm whale, on an angry gray sea.

Phone Boy snaps a picture, sends it to his friend Bergen with a message that says *WTF?*

....

I'VE MADE A HUGE MISTAKE, Zelda Outterson thinks, waking up in Rome Byles's bed beside his naked body.

Not the sex. The sex had actually been pretty good, as far as she can recall. Surprisingly. Rome had always seemed like a selfish bastard to her. Not so, in the sack.

No, the mistake was doing drugs with him.

She'd been so good, for so long. She'd made sobriety work for her. Attalah had thrown her a lifeline, getting her this job, and she'd wanted so badly to succeed.

But something about last night had triggered her. The excitement of illegal activity. The thrill of vandalism. It shook her up, reminded her of hungers she'd starved for so long she forgot about them. So when he kissed her, up against the billboard, and then when he said *I wanna fuck you*, she'd nodded, not wanting this newfound buzz to fade. And he'd driven her to his house, way the fuck out in Claverack, because not even Hudson cops could afford to live in Hudson anymore, and she was pretty sure he was on something but she wasn't scared, because he was the law, and the law meant invincibility. And when he snorted something and offered it to her, she snorted it without asking what it was.

Good, right? he'd asked. *I have a great dealer. Her name is the evidence locker.*

She'd watched the whole encounter unfold as if she were an outside observer. As if Good Zelda, the one she'd been for years now, had paused in the middle of walking away, to look back sadly at Bad Zelda's triumphant return. The helpless one, who slept with boys and did drugs because she couldn't stand to be alone.

Who's in the bed with Rome now? she wonders. *Which Zelda?*

"Hey," he says, reaching out to press his thumb against her lips. Horny already.

But not for her, apparently. He reaches under the bed and produces not a condom but a little baggie of crystal. "You wanna?" he asks.

She nods. It isn't a voluntary motion. No thought was involved. It surprises her, that nod, but she knows better than to fight with her body when it gets like this. Because she does. She does wanna. So fucking bad.

·······

BERGEN WRITES A LETTER. Writes it with a pen and paper, because he's not entirely sure how the printer at work works, whether it saves a copy of everything that it prints, whether it could point back to his workstation in the admittedly extremely unlikely case of an investigation. He wouldn't put it past busybody Lilly to periodically peruse the files of the documents people printed.

He prints in block letters. Wears gloves when he does it, when he puts it in the envelope and the envelope in the mailbox of 310 State Street #3.

The text was provided by Tom Minniq, in a direct message in the app.

People like you have no future in this town. Get the fuck out before we have to get you out.

Who is this person—this Heather—and what horrible thing does Tom mean by *People like you?*

Bergen knows it's wrong. He also knows he's weak, he's hungry. He's lonely. And Tom said he'd come see him at home tonight if he did what he asked him to do.

. . . .

TREENIE'S WALKING DOWN Warren Street when she happens to see Ronan scowling into a cup of coffee, in the motorcycle-themed coffee shop that opened up two years ago. Her instinct to say hello is strong, and she has to fight hard to keep from doing so. Instead she goes inside, buys a cup of coffee—keeping her back to him as unostentatiously as possible—and sits down in a corner where she can see him clearly, half hidden by a purely decorative motorcycle.

Ten minutes in, he takes out his phone. Whatever exchange he has is unpleasant. He's scowling even harder when he puts it away.

What are you up to, Ronan?

Eventually he arrives at some decision and gets up. She counts to thirty and then follows him out to the street.

. . . .

PHONE BOY IS ON THE PHONE AGAIN. Bergen assured him the billboard must be some kind of joke, or part of the set of some movie or photo shoot—Hudson has more and more camera crews these days, always making things weird for people. But now, in line at the bakery, the girl behind the counter has a button that is eerily similar.

Red letters; white drop shadow; dark gray backdrop. YOU ARE HATED.

"*Ask her what it's all about,*" Bergen says in his ear. "*I swear I never heard of this before.*"

"What does your button mean?" he asks, when it's his turn to stand before her.

She stares at him and then says, "You're talking to me, or the person you're on the phone with?"

"You," he says, but only because his head's not in the game, the phone call has him distracted—ordinarily no one outsnarks him. "Is it like a band or something?"

She looks down at it. Then she looks up and past him. "No. It's not a band. Help who's next?"

He shuffles awkwardly out of the way of the person behind him in line.

. . . .

SHE'S SURPRISED at how easy it is. TV shows always make it seem so difficult to tail someone. Difficult, and dangerous.

Then again—this is almost too easy. Ronan is oblivious to the world around him. Treenie follows him down Warren Street from half a block behind, but she could have been breathing down his neck and he wouldn't have noticed.

He turns right onto Second Street. Past Rope Alley, past Strawberry Alley.

By now, she knows where he's going. Lets herself fall behind when he heads down the hill. Surrounded by trees; the slope too steep for anything to be built there. And sure enough, he goes to the front door of Dom Morrison's house and rings the bell. Attalah opens it. They speak briefly. Ronan goes inside.

Well, of course. That's where his best friend lives.

There's just one problem: Dom isn't home. His station wagon is gone.

So? How would he know that? Maybe he came looking for his best friend, found out he wasn't home, and decided to wait. Maybe Attalah told him he just went to get a gallon of milk and he'd be right back.

Maybe. Or maybe something else is going on.

Treenie sits down on a bench and watches the Bangladeshis play cricket. She's turned so her back is mostly to the house, but if anyone comes in or out she'll still pick it up in her peripheral vision.

She waits three more hours before getting up and going, one thousand percent convinced that Ronan and Attalah are conspiring.

CHAPTER TWENTY-SIX

RONAN

My father's phone rang, late at night. Once upon a time, it had been my number, too.

"Why'd you come back?" hissed a flat, dead, male voice when I answered.

"Who's this?" I asked.

"You didn't give a shit about your dad for the past fifteen, twenty years," the voice said, and I felt the temperature plummet. "So why the fuck do you care about him now?"

I should have hung up. It would have been so easy. But my finger would not budge and my mouth would not open and it took all of my mental energy to keep from bursting into tears.

"You think we'd forget what a fucking faggot you are?" he said. "We here in this town have a very long memory. And we do not want you here."

"Stubb," I said. "Right? Hudson has a lot of pieces of shit, but I doubt there's any as shitty as you."

"Your own mother didn't want you," he said, his voice so deep it was like it wasn't a human's at all. "She chose death rather than continue looking at you. Why can't you do the same?"

Fifth-grade recess. Bullies stand in a circle around me, hollering insults. A teacher sees it, from her classroom, and comes out and takes me by the hand and drags me to safety. *You don't have to stand there and just take it,* she says, disgusted. If she hadn't rescued me, I might have been there still.

On the internet I could shout down the vilest of trolls, but in the real world I was still the same soft, defenseless grub I'd always been. Anger was a good spur to my eloquence, and so was hatred, but all I felt in the face of this inexplicable hostility was fear.

"Get out now, Ronan," Stubb said, and I was that helpless little fifth-grader again.

That's what stopped me from saying something along the lines of, *I finally figured out why you hate gay people so much, Stubb. You're trying to prove to the world, and yourself, and your dumbass dad, that you're not one of them. But everybody knows you are.* And not saying it probably saved my life.

CHAPTER TWENTY-SEVEN

C alls to make—emails to send—texts to compose.

Attalah stops, standing over the kitchen sink, mug in one hand and dish towel in the other. She takes a breath. She takes two.

There are articles to read. Requests to respond to. Operatives to put in position. Titans of industry to destroy.

To stop—to stand there—to simply breathe—it feels indulgent. Sinful, even. When there is so much work to do.

When hasn't there been so much work to do? Her job, her marriage, her mom's nonprofit, caring for her mother—and now saving the town of Hudson on top of everything else—all of it arduous, elaborate work. When was the last time she dared to stop and just breathe?

College: first year, before pressure from her mom got her to drop art school in favor of a bachelor of science as a stop on the way to a social work degree—a nice, sound, soul-consuming way to be of service to the world. Finals week; she should be studying. She told herself going to the Met was technically art history research, but really all she wanted to do was sit in the Arts of Oceania wing and sketch those magnificent monster masks that have enthralled her since the first time her mom took her there at age ten.

Warthog. Monkey. Cockerel. Unknown ocean deity. Bold lines, big fangs. Glyphs on foreheads: spiders; flames; infinity signs collapsing in on themselves. Names for gods and monsters, never to be spoken by human tongue. Fans of feathers and manes made of spikes. Attalah spent hours sketching. Standing still—her knees and back didn't give her the slightest bit of trouble. A faint voice in the back of her mind—her mother's—said these sacred objects shouldn't be there, they were stolen, but Attalah felt profound reverent happiness to be standing before them.

She knows this can't be true; can't be the last time she had a minute to herself. She must have stopped to breathe since then. Getting ice cream with Dom, watching trash television on the couch—but that's not the same thing, she sees. Taking time to rest between labors is not the same thing as taking time for yourself, any more than stopping to pee is.

She takes out her phone, googles *ceremonial masks of Fiji, Papua New Guinea, Polynesia*. Downloads dozens. Swears she'll find the time to draw them. Soon.

. . . .

MONDAY EVENING; full dark. Ronan opens the back door of the car and lights up a cigarette. Sits. Stands. Bare feet on cold dirt. Naked, and fearless. No one can see them out here. *Private road*, Dom assured him, *no one ever comes out here. And we'd hear a car from far enough away we'd have plenty of time to make ourselves presentable.* Ronan had asked, *What about someone on foot?* And Dom had just laughed.

He's still sprawled half-asleep across the back seat. Their bodies ache in the strangest places. Sex in such a cramped space has its challenges, but they're both impressed with the flexibility and stamina they still retain twenty years later.

"We should tell her," Ronan says.

After a long series of seconds, Dom says, "We should not."

"I don't feel comfortable deceiving her."

"You see? *You* don't feel comfortable. Try not be so selfish, okay? Think about *her* comfort. We have an understanding. She doesn't care what I do. She just doesn't want to know about it. Period."

"You really think she would be fine with it? If she found out?"

"If you think she *wouldn't* be fine with it," Dom asked, "why do you want to tell her?"

Ronan has no answer.

Twigs snap. Something moves through the underbrush.

"What was that?" Ronan asks, pointing into the woods.

Dom sits up, takes out his flashlight, shines it into the dark between the trees. Doesn't see anything. "Probably just a wild pig."

"I didn't know we had those around here."

"We got everything around here," Dom says. "Especially since the Great Hog Rampage a couple years back."

"Excuse me, the what?"

"You didn't hear about it? National news, baby. Back when the slaughterhouse was shutting down. They got lax with the security protocols, and somehow all the cages opened and two thousand pigs got free. Did a ton of damage, too. A thousand of them got killed by hunters in the weeks afterward—the state put a bounty on them—but the rest are still roaming free. Still doing a number on crops and livestock and pets and stuff."

"Wow," Ronan says, and peers into the dark again. Wondering if that's really what was watching them. And what it had seen.

CHAPTER TWENTY-EIGHT

RONAN

"What the hell have you done?"

Katch caught me off guard, sitting in the dark on my pitch-black porch. I stood there, stunned, my postcoital brain too foggy to properly process information, until he sucked smoke from his clove cigarette and the red ember lit his face enough to recognize him.

"Uh . . . nothing," I said. My skin was still aflame from the joy of pressing against Dom's, but I would carry that fire like a secret to my grave.

"Think," Katch said. "Does the name Tom Minniq mean anything to you?"

"Of course," I said. "Part of our plan, mine and Attalah's. An imaginary—"

"Look at this," he said, and held out his cell phone. "Does that look imaginary to you?"

On its screen, footage from a security cam. A man in an alley. Jug-handled ears; lean and hungry and leather-jacketed. A wisp of a hipster twink on his knees in front of him. The man standing turned to look at the camera, locking eyes with Katch and me, and smiled.

No doubt about it, it was Tom Minniq. In the flesh. Somehow.

A shiver climbed slow up my spine.

"I mean, he's probably like you—right? A ghost? Harmless—"

With supernatural speed, Katch was up and out of his seat and across the porch, and my cheek was stinging from a slap I hadn't even seen. "Does that feel harmless? Ghostlike?"

"No," I pouted. "But you and your fucking whale ghosts didn't exactly give me an operating manual, Katch. How was I supposed to know what I could—"

"Because you shouldn't have been able to, Ronan. Something's wrong with you, to be able to do what you're doing."

I shut my eyes and wished I had elected to believe that all these impossible things were mere meth withdrawal symptoms, and got the fuck out of Hudson to go get treatment. "Something's definitely wrong with me."

"They gave Attalah and me power, too, Ronan, but we're not like you. We're not broken inside. We don't carry the same crippling pain" (*blade*) "still stuck inside us. Your hate—it's special. It's helped so much more anger blossom. All that hate, spreading through the city, it comes from you."

I thought of the YOU ARE HATED billboard. I remembered being down in Attalah's dungeon, her eyes wide when I told her my plan: *That's fucked up.* I could taste it on my tongue as clearly as I had then: the sweet drug-tang of hatred. *Was that you—that plan?* I wondered. *Were you feeding on me, and feeding me? Taking my anger and magnifying it, filling me up with monstrous ideas?*

"They're getting stronger every day, Ronan. But still, they're losing. The balance has broken. Which means something way scarier than gentrification could take root."

"What could be worse than everyone I love losing their homes?"

Katch sighed and stood. "Lots of places are under the sway of supernatural beings, Ronan. Some of them are a lot more savage than Hudson. Human sacrifice, mass murder, I don't know, *Children of the Corn*–type shit. 'The Lottery.' *The Wicker Man*. I miss horror movies, dude."

"They don't have horror movies on the other side?"

His eyes glazed over briefly, and he grinned. "They have *everything*. I just . . . I don't know. Time is weird there." Katch shook his head. "Anyway. We don't know what the fuck Tom Minniq is. Not a ghost. Nothing that was ever human. But something that takes on human form, from time to time. And you let it in."

Wind scoured the screened-in porch. "Is there something we can do?"

Katch shook his head. "This was already a delicate operation before you fucked it up. The people we're manipulating—"

"Wait. You can control people?"

"We can *influence* people," Katch said. "But only people who are from here. Of here. We can whisper in their ears. Plant things in their dreams. Get them to do things. If it's something they want to do, it's no problem. If it's something they *don't* want to do, or would never do without our . . . guidance . . . it can get messy. The harder we have to push, the riskier it gets. Sometimes people . . . break."

"What does that mean?"

"It's different for everyone. Suicide, violent rage, complete personality shift . . . depends on who they are and how badly they break. Some people it's like a stroke—their brain stops being able to communicate with the rest of their body. That's why we try very hard not to push people too far."

"Attalah's mom had a stroke," I said. "Did you push *her* too far?"

Katch frowned. "She was on our side, so we thought there was no risk when we tried to make her destroy Pastor Thirza, to stop the Pequod Arms. But apparently . . ." He didn't finish the sentence.

"Are you . . . pushing me?"

Katch laughed and clapped me on the back. "Don't think of it like that. Anyway, you're far too important for us to risk snapping you."

. . . .

STOPPING AT THE IRON HORSE TAVERN was not a wise decision. Also, it was one I had no memory of making. One minute I was walking away from Katch with my head on fire, and the next I was stuck on a bar stool trying to put it out.

Why shouldn't I drink? Why not single-malt scotch? I was all of a sudden an obscenely wealthy man. And all I had to do was betray everything my father believed in. And unleash a hideous monster in the shape of a man. I waved my credit card like a sword that could slay the sea serpents encircling me.

Men and women watched with awe, as I guzzled glass after glass of whiskey. As soon as I got up off the stool I could see from how the room spun that it was too late for me.

Freight train tracks run right through upper Hudson, along Sixth Street, right below the park. Of course I know this. Everybody knows it. In the middle of the day a train rolls through town, bringing traffic to a halt for all of Hudson. This has probably been true since the nineteenth century.

But I guess I forgot. Because coming out of the Iron Horse, I stepped into the street and stumbled on the rails.

Which is why I'm lying here.

But that's cool. Sixth Street is super comfortable.

. . . .

MY MOTHER IS ONE WEEK DEAD.

The doorbell doesn't stop ringing. Neighbors come with casseroles. I never thought I could get sick of Dad's friend Shirl's feta kalamata concoction, but here we are.

It's me who answers the door. Sixteen-Year-Old Me, who smiles and thanks them. Invites them inside. Makes coffee. Tells them Dad just went down for a nap and he's been running himself ragged so I don't want to wake him up but that he's gonna be so, so happy to hear you stopped by, and sorry that he missed you.

This nap of Dad's has been going on for days. He hasn't left his bedroom since the funeral, except for short trips across the hall to the bathroom. The butcher shop is only open because of the efforts of Marge and Kristof, the old Hungarian man who had been sort of a mentor to my dad and still helped out on weekends. Both stepped up in a major way, but they can't do this for long. Kristof is funny and has a ton of amazing Old Country stories, but he's slow as shit now and could barely hold up his end of the work when he had my father standing beside him to do 80 percent of it. Running a business involves making a lot of decision, which is neither of their strong suits. Marge is calling *me* for advice, so you know we're fucked.

The butcher shop was already in a bad place financially. At the funeral someone said, *You know how stressful it can be, to run a failing business*, like no further explanation was needed for why my mom did what she did—

Why she killed herself—

How she could walk three miles down Route 9G and then out onto the Rip Van Winkle Bridge Pedestrian walkway and then—

Why she didn't leave a note—

I open the door to his bedroom, just a crack. The smell of him is overpowering, like cigarettes and body odor and spilled scotch and Stetson cologne distilled and intensified.

And, underneath all that, faint and dying: her. Clean linen; Jean Naté After Bath Splash.

"Dad?" I say to the darkness.

Only silence answers.

Of course he's in there, I tell myself. *He has to be. Where else could he have gone?* But I can't bring myself to flick the light switch.

There's a sound that might be breathing but could also be the crashing of distant waves. A restless sea.

(*dreamsea*)

"Goddammit, Dad."

Maybe later I'll be grateful to him for all of this. Maybe the day will come where I'll think, his breakdown kept me busy. Made me run all the errands. Smile in all the faces. Soak up all the hypocrisy from the people who hated my mother. Gave me something to do with my mind, so I didn't have time to wonder. So I didn't lock myself in my room and go fucking nuts like he did.

Maybe. Maybe later. For now I hate him. For now I gather all my grief and loss and any underlying resentment I might have for her, for what she did, for how she left us, for how she left *me*, and heap it onto the bonfire of my anger at him.

. . . .

STILL LYING in the middle of Sixth Street. My too-warm face feels good against the cold steel rail. How have no cars come, in all this time?

A man stands behind me. Or anyway something in the shape of one. He's been there for a while. He squats down—I smell the sea, I smell rot, like something that clawed its way up out of the muck and took on human form.

"Tom," I whisper.

"You're pathetic," he says, his voice a thrilling, menacing, masculine rumble. Fear and desire harden me, and then—I go away again.

. . . .

MIDNIGHT, and I'm floating on an ocean the temperature of blood.

I always imagined death would be white light, but instead it's black water.

Naked; alone; knowing in my gut that there's no land for a million miles in any direction. Laughing from a happiness deeper than anything I've ever felt before. I'm not afraid. I can tread water forever. All those swimming lessons at Oakdale really did the trick. Overhead the Milky Way arcs at a delirious angle, and the stars are splayed incorrectly across the sky.

Somewhere, I know, I have work to do. Schemes and plans to pull off.

I know all this, but the ache of it is so small it's pleasant, like when your train leaves the station and you remember you forgot to wash the dishes, and you think, *Oh well, I didn't intentionally fail to do it, I am absolved of blame, nothing matters.*

Something massive moves beneath me. I feel it displacing the water, even though it's far below my slowly moving feet. I'm not afraid of it. Emotion comes off it like a smell. I feel love. I feel belonging. I feel connected.

A dark shape moves through the sky. Too fast and solid to be a cloud. A whale, I realize, without immediately also thinking *That's impossible, whales don't fly, there's no such thing as a sky whale* because here (*on the dreamsea*) the boundaries of what's possible are so much wider. It is the twin of the thing swimming beneath me.

I could stay here. Be part of this. Forever.

Except . . . There are so many people to punish. Everyone who hurt my mom, pushed her to do what she did. Everyone who is trying to destroy my town—

I try to bat these thoughts away, to hold tight to the bliss of belonging. But being who we are is a habit. And routines like that are hard to break out of.

CHAPTER TWENTY-NINE

A ttalah stares at her screen and feels suddenly sick.

Time is running out. The polls look terrible. They've only got one weapon, and now is when they need to drop it.

But she can't.

Deploying "Tom Minniq" got them dirt on 250 people. Nudes, screencaps of scandalous chats. In a voter pool this small, 250 people could make a big difference.

The email is all prepared. The images are attached.

If Jark wins, these get exposed. We need you to vote against him, yes, but we need you to do more than that. Do whatever you have to do to make sure everyone you care about votes against him, too. Call your friends and tell them lies about him. Your family. Coworkers. Bribe them if you have to. Because if he wins—or if you tell anyone else about this email—your whole life comes crashing down.

She groans, seeing it on the screen. She can barely recall typing it.

Of course she knows they'd never ever go through with releasing the blackmail material. But even as an empty threat, this is some real criminal shit. The kind of thing you go to jail for decades for. And all it'd take is for one of those people to call the cops, to start a massive investigation.

She knows her neighbors. Plenty of them would roll over on it. Probably most of them. But at least one would fight back hard with everything they've got.

Attalah calls Ronan, but Ronan doesn't answer. She types an email, and then she deletes it. This conversation can't leave any trace.

. . . .

MONDAY MORNING, maybe the worst one of Zelda's life. There had been a time when every Monday hurt worse than the one before, but those days are far behind her. Or so she'd hoped. Now it feels like six years' worth of missed Monday headaches are hitting her at once.

Also, she's pretty sure she has cancer. Above her heart she can feel it, the sense of something beneath the skin. Sharp like a blade broken off between her ribs. Nothing she can make out with her fingers, but nevertheless she knows it's there.

But there's a pleasure in this morning pain, too—the weird galvanic kick she always got from hangovers. They hurt like hell, sure, but they also energized her. The tingling pride of all the bad things she'd done the night before. Her creative gears turning, imagining better bad things ahead. Her hair in a ponytail looped through the back of her baseball cap. Her makeup minimal. Ready for battle.

So by the time her 2:00 P.M. appointment comes in—at 2:37— she's feeling pretty perky.

"Hi, Heather," she says, pretending to look through paperwork.

She'd seen three YOU ARE HATED buttons out in the world already, and gotten a little shiver of pleasure each time. The Chamber of Commerce had replaced the billboard already, sure, but between Staples and Snitko's she had four more posters printed and ready to go. Friday night she'd meet Rome down there again, put another one up. Which would get replaced. And the following weekend they'd do it again, on a Thursday this time. With Rome helping keep the cops off their scent, they'd be able to keep it up until the YOU ARE HATED game moved on into other, more exciting arenas.

Another shiver, remembering Rome. When was the last time she'd met a man so into performing oral sex? They'd spent all Sunday in bed, fucking and doing drugs and talking about all the fun they could have with an underground guerrilla war on the invaders who'd occupied the sovereign nation of Hudson. Attalah's plans are good, sure, but pretty tame in the grand scheme of things. Rome's are balls-to-the-wall crazy shit, and she's down, and she's been thinking up more than a few of her own. She's not sure where they come from, these crazy concepts—like the one she's about to whip out—but she welcomes them, in all their eerie detail.

"How've you been, Heather?"

"You know," Heather says, letting fall the hair she's been chewing. "Things are good."

Things are not good, by the look of things. Or the smell. She's not doing laundry as often as she needs to. Her shoulders are slumped and no matter how many times she tries to uncross her arms they keep on crossing. Heather's mom has her two daughters. Heather's spent two years trying to get them back. Failing just enough drug tests to keep that from happening. Based on her body language today, she knows she's about to fail another one. When she was so fucking close.

Heather loves her girls. Zelda knows this. She'd do anything in her power to get them back. It's just that staying clean is not in her power.

This, though. This will be.

"You still at 310 State?"

"Yeah," Heather says. "For now. My friend's apartment."

"What happened, exactly, at your last address? Your own place. I don't recall."

Zelda recalls. Heather was one of the numbers she called, from Attalah's eviction list. Never got hold of her. Number disconnected.

"Creative differences with my landlord. He got creative with my rent and doubled it, and I wasn't creative enough to come up with that kind of money on any kind of regular basis. Now I think he found where I'm staying, at my friend's house, and started slipping death threats under the door."

"Asshole," Zelda says.

"Exactly," Heather says, with something like gratitude.

Poor Heather. No one ever takes her side.

"Can you shut my door?" Zelda asks.

"Is that allowed? I thought it was some kind of social services rule. Don't wanna risk us deplorables jumping across the table and strangling you when no one can hear or see."

"More of a guideline. And more for the clients' safety than ours. Once upon a time we had a case manager here, a man, and, well, he took some liberties."

"Men always ruin everything for everyone else," Heather says, and leans back to push the door shut. "What's up?"

"When we test your urine today, what are we going to find?"

Heather puts her hands to her face. Presses hard, like she could fold herself up into nothingness. "Nothing good," she says, when she lowers them, and her face is splotched with red.

"This was gonna be it," Zelda says. "Wasn't it?"

Heather nods. Not like this is even something particularly unusual at this point. It's the eighth time she's fumbled the ball at the brink of scoring the point.

"Here," Zelda says, and places a specimen cup on the table between them. Not empty. "That's clean urine, from another client of mine. I had her do two, told her the lab machinery had been getting glitchy. I'm going to submit this as your sample for today, and when the test results come back clean on Thursday, I'm going to mark you down as fully compliant, and recommend resumption of full custody."

Heather's jaw drops. "You're lying."

"I'm not."

"Why would you do something like that? People lose their jobs for shit like that. People go to *jail* for shit like that."

"Not if they do it right. And not if nobody snitches."

"But why?"

"I need your help. I need you to do something for me."

"Anything," Heather says, leaning forward. Flushed; aflame.

"Your old landlord. He owns an antique store. Did you know that?"

"No, but it figures."

"I want you to go in the middle of the night and throw something through the plate-glass window of his store."

Heather laughs. "Are you serious? Shit, I'd do that for the sheer pleasure of it. Getting my girls back'd be icing on the cake."

"I figured."

"But it's not a bomb, is it? Because terrorism becomes some homeland security shit, and if the feds roll in here, they'd have all kinds of crazy technology and who knows what they could turn up. I mean, I know how to be careful, but if they got fucking spy-cam satellite footage of the fucking sidewalk when I do it, and they can, I don't know, rewind it and follow me home or whatever, I don't know about all that."

"Relax," Zelda says, thinking, *This kind of crazy paranoid shit is exactly why some people shouldn't fuck with meth.* "It's not a bomb. It's nothing that would go any higher than Hudson cops, and we know they can barely trace a fucking license plate. I'll mail you a package by the end of the week, with the object and the address and some suggestions for how to do it and not get caught. Not that I think you can't figure that out on your own. It'll be easy. Go by late at night—I got a friend on the force who will be patrolling Warren Street at that time. He'll turn a blind eye to what you do and say he saw someone with a completely different description."

"Is this connected to those YOU ARE HATED buttons?" Heather asks.

"Indeed," Zelda says, producing a fistful. "Give some to your friends."

The rest is details, and gratitude, and paperwork. Heather's crying, she's so happy.

For a second, Zelda's professionalism flickers in her brain. *You're putting two kids in danger. Sending them home with an addict who's currently using—that could go real wrong, real fast.*

But her tracks are covered. Even in the scenarios where terrible things happen, and Heather goes to trial for neglect or endangerment, and she snitches on Zelda and says she knew she wasn't ready to get her kids back, it'll be easy to dismiss as the desperate fiction of a damaged addict failure of a mother. She'll have the clean tests, the paperwork. And Heather's girls are not helpless children. Not anymore. They're thirteen and fifteen. They can fend for themselves if Mommy goes feral.

And anyway it just feels so good, this weird new thing, this tingle. This ache above her heart, between her ribs. This hate.

·······

"YOU SEE IT, don't you?"

Lilly is working from home, since the Penelope's Quilt office has been completely consumed by last-minute campaign work and it is impossible to concentrate on anything else. So she sits on her bed, scouring compact discs full of photographs digitized from negatives found in a State Street attic—when the memory comes to her with a vividness that's almost unsettling. The first words Jark ever said to her: *You see it, don't you?*

Nine P.M. on a Friday night and Lilly was the last one in the office—or so she'd thought, when Jark plopped a chair down beside her desk. Five years ago; six months after she'd started at Penelope's Quilt.

"See . . . what?"

"Hudson." He smiled. Such a smile! Who could say, whether the light that shined out of it had always been there, and is how he *became* such a big deal, or whether becoming such a big deal had filled him up with the kind of confidence that looked like magic, like light. *Or whether it's all in my head*, she'd thought, *the magic light of stardom all in the eyes of the observer*. "You see how special this town is. What it was, what it could be. I'm right, aren't I? I see it in your eyes."

"Yeah," she said, buzzing inside at this kind of attention from the superstar boss she'd barely exchanged eye contact with since she arrived.

"You've been doing a great job on research," he'd said. "But I think it's a waste of your talent, and your passion. I'm creating a new position, and I want you to fill it."

"What's the position?" she asked, even though of course she'd have said yes to whatever he asked.

"Director of Community Engagement and Community Building."

"That's a mouthful," she said. "You probably wanna workshop it a bit with marketing."

"Fuck marketing. What do you say? I want you to lead our efforts to involve community residents and create cultural programming in support of our vision for this city's future. We can make something magnificent out of Hudson. You and me."

She'd felt so seen, after that. So valued. And she'd worked her ass off ever since. She smiles, remembering. Feeling suddenly, superhumanly exhausted.

Looking back now, she figures all Jark saw was a workaholic

with no social life, who was hungry in a way he could exploit. It didn't matter. She *did* love Hudson, and she'd done amazing things since Jark gave her the new gig. She knew she was a small piece of a big machine, and she couldn't take sole credit for all the incredible progress that had been made—the world-famous chefs who opened up Warren Street restaurants; the *New York Times* articles; the references to Hudson on hip mainstream television shows. But she knew she was a part of it. And the two of them were going to make the world see what a special place Hudson was.

She falls asleep at her desk, remembering. In the instant before drifting into dreams, she's dimly conscious of the distant sound of screeching tires and a loud booming crash.

....

JOE ALLEY IS HUDSON'S SHORTEST: three houses deep. Theories abound as to who Joe was or why he got an alley named after him. It branches off Frederick Street, a similarly insignificant thoroughfare situated right where Hudson's urban grid gives way to the curves and hills of the county beyond.

Rich Trappan lives alone in the last house on Joe Alley, the one he grew up in, the one his father left him. An aging, flimsy, single-story structure, built cheap back in the fifties, Hudson's last big boom. A bitch to heat: thin walls with ratty sheets of insulation that do little to hold warmth in. The house, and the recliner he's sitting in, and the failing refrigerator, and everything else in his life he values: it's his father's.

It's lucky Rich doesn't need to pay rent because his employment is intermittent at best. Seasonal work at Wal-Mart; helping out with a buddy's contractor business in summer. One of these days he'll get around to cleaning the place up, building a wall or two to make a second bedroom out of half the living room, start renting it out on Airbnb to these New Yorker assholes who have no problem paying $250 a night for some of Hudson's shittier spots. Of course to do that he'd probably need to stop smoking inside, and deal with some significant plumbing challenges, and, really, who has the time or money or willpower for any of that?

Thursday night is bitter cold, a slice of February in late October, and he's watching television under three blankets. *The Voice* is on. Pretty young creatures shrieking their hearts out. Holding out bloody hands, offering up the desperate dreams they've torn out of themselves. All these shows—*America's Got Talent, American Idol, Top Chef*—the aspiring bakers and acrobats and dancers and models who weep in agony or ecstasy every episode. He doesn't know which he likes more: when their dreams come true or when their dreams are dashed.

His head is cold. He puts the blankets over it and grins at the flatulent smell under there. But then he can't hear the show so well—he's well past due for a checkup, and something is seriously wrong with his ears, but he lacks insurance and anyway if there's something really wrong he doesn't want to know—and he emerges from the safety of the blankets.

He wasn't always like this: some poor sad fuck getting old in a stinking shack. Once upon a time he roamed the night in crowded cars, him and Stubb and a rotating crowd of lesser boys addled by drugs and drink and lust for blood and sex, blasting horror movie soundtracks and the most aggressive hip-hop, striking terror into the hearts of decent citizens lying awake in the dark and praying that they'd pass on by.

Rich hits mute during the commercial break. The wind makes noises like whale cries overhead. The night is still out there. It always has been. Anytime he wants to, he could open that door and step out into it. Why hasn't he?

Brakes screech outside. This is not normal. No one ever goes down Joe Alley. His neighbors are old, infirm creatures. One of them lost her driver's license last year.

Rich listens.

An engine revs. Something big: a pickup truck, probably. It turns. Slides to a stop right in front of his house, shining their brights through his windows. Whoever it is, they know he's in there—because, where else would he be? They know he's terrified.

Rich wants to say something, do something. He can't. As if from a distance, he hears himself fart.

Outside the engine shrieks again. Tires screech. And then: the walls thud.

What the fuck

What the fuck

They just hit my house with their truck

But not hard. Not like they really wanted to break something. Like they were toying with him.

Rich reaches for his cell phone. It's plugged in, on the table, too far away—it's ancient, the battery is always dying on him—and somehow he can't bring himself to budge. Like if he just sits there, very still and very quiet in the safety of his blankets, he'll be fine.

I deserve this, he thinks. *I should tremble in fear, after all the times I made scared old people tremble in fear. This is just karma. Dumb kids fucking around.*

It's not kids, and they're not fucking around. Tires screech again.

The sound is like thunder, striking during the finale of a fireworks show. One big boom and a whole lot of little ones, and then there's a truck in his living room.

Someone just drove a truck through the wall of my house, he thinks, and he still can't bring himself to scramble for his cell phone. Run for another room. Out the back door, into the night.

The driver's side door opens. A man steps out. Wearing a mask on his head: a big blue papier-mâché whale. Behind the man, Rich's roof lurches to the side with a screech.

This whole house is about to collapse on top of me, Rich thinks, and pulls the blanket up over his mouth to keep from screaming.

"You told," the man says, and pulls something very long and sharp from behind his back. A harpoon.

"Told . . . who? What?"

"Told everyone. What we did together. Otherwise why would I have random strangers asking me about it online?"

And then Rich recognizes the voice, even though he probably hasn't heard it in five years. Once, it had been the most important voice on the planet for him. Once they had been best friends. Once they had terrorized the town together. And more than once—many times, in fact—they'd fucked.

"Stubb?" he whispers, and then there is a harpoon in his throat, windpipe pierced, the blade between two vertebrae, spearing him to his father's recliner.

CHAPTER THIRTY

RONAN

Morning hurt.

So much sun came in through my uncurtained window that I felt positively vampiric, about to burst into flames or fade out of existence altogether like a silent movie monster.

Pain. I was made of pain. Probably I had had worse hangovers in my life, but I certainly couldn't remember one right then.

What the fuck had I done last night? I remembered the Iron Horse, the musty smell of it, not like a bar at all but more like a basement (*like a tomb*) where centuries of spilled beer had accreted, and like old wet burned wood. Eyes on me. Smoke and laughter in the crowded bar. I remembered stumbling home, half dragged by someone. And I remembered a whole lot of crazy dreams.

Including Tom Minniq standing over me in the street.

Katch was right. He wasn't a ghost. He was something horrible. Something else was hiding inside that human body. I'd smelled it on him, heard it in his voice—something deep down and dark and ravenous—and been terrified by it even as I was also aroused.

I stumbled to the bathroom. Drank six glasses of water. Turned on the shower as hot as it could get. Stepped inside with all my clothes on, and screamed. My scream became a laugh. My laughter maybe became crying.

. . . .

THOUGHT EXPERIMENT: TRY to remember New York.

The memories were there—I could list them in my mind, the stuff of stories, the building blocks of relationships—but the sense impressions themselves were gone.

Photographs helped, sparked visual resonance, but even that stayed strictly visual.

There had been that one 3:00 A.M. subway ride, stalled forever between stations, a packed car full of people heading home from parties, the woman who projectile vomited and people started screaming and moving away and spraying perfume on it and putting down newspaper and then someone else puked, and then another . . . there had been the man who caught my eye walking home from an event on Central Park West, who bummed a cigarette and then led me into the safe forbidden dark.

I'd told these stories so many times I could conjure them up again, but I couldn't remember the smell of her puke. The taste of him in my mouth. The squish of soft park mud under my knees.

. . . .

"JESUS, RONAN—what the hell happened to your head?"

Attalah pointed at the scrape on my left temple. She'd taken one step inside, so no one would see her speaking with me, but she would come no further.

"I fell," I said. "Had a few too many at the Iron Horse last night."

She opened her mouth like she had something to say, then shut it. Then said it anyway: "You know the Iron Horse has been closed for thirty years, right?"

"Of course," I said. "Did I say Iron Horse? I meant—"

"We can't do this," she interrupted.

"Can't do what?"

She showed me the draft nude-photo-blackmail email on her phone.

"Of course we can," I said, my voice sounding like it was coming from some deep well inside me. *Is this them?* I wondered. *Are they pushing me?* But I knew I had no such excuse. This was all me.

"If just one person snitches—"

"They won't."

I could still smell the rot-and-alcohol reek of Tom Minniq. Where the hell had I been drinking, if not the Iron Horse?

"Pay attention to me, Ronan. This is . . ."

"I know what's at stake," I said, still deep down the well. "And I don't care." Half of me felt like my whale ghost overlords would magically fix everything, keep the matter from coming to light or give the grand jury strokes at the pivotal moment. The other half of me felt like that wouldn't happen, and I'd get caught for sure, but it didn't matter, because I'd take a short walk off the Rip Van Winkle Bridge before they ever came to put the cuffs on me. "Whatever happens, I'll take the fall for it. You gotta believe me on that, Attalah."

"Of course I believe you," she said. "That's not even the issue. This is just—it's *too* wrong. We're not doing it. That's what I came to tell you. Okay?"

I didn't answer, and she didn't wait. I walked out with her, watched her walk down Warren Street.

Blue and red cop car lights strafed the surrounding buildings a couple of blocks away. I wondered whether it was Tom. What he was up to.

CHAPTER THIRTY-ONE

8

"We keep this shit between us," Chief Propst says, scowling down at the bloodshed.

He tells Dom to take the license plates off the truck and orders Officer Van Vleck to hang a tarp over the wide, splintered hole in the wall.

Dom gets it. He doesn't like it, but he gets it. Half of Hudson knows that truck belongs to Steve "Stubby" Coffin, and nobody can know that the mayor's son's truck drove a hole in the wall of the mayor's son's former best friend, who was subsequently murdered. Black boys downstreet don't get the same courtesy, but Dom knows in his gut that the Hudson Police Department's corruption is casual, surface-level stuff. Chief Propst plays the game he has to play, but he's going to get the fucker who did this. Even if that someone is his boss's broken kid.

The smell in the house is scorched toast and blood and shit and beer. The cold calms it down, though, and that's a blessing. Standing there in summertime, the stink would be unbearable.

"Gotta be six hours since this happened," Dom says. "How the hell didn't anyone hear anything?"

No one called it in until morning, when a neighbor on his way to work saw a house with a truck-size hole in the side of it.

Chief Propst curses. He feels it, too, Dom knows. The tingle up the spine. The knowledge something's extremely not right.

"Stubb's in the wind," says Van Vleck, reclipping his radio to his belt. "Officers at his place said the doors were wide open, no sign of him."

In the wind. Such a weird expression. It rubs Dom raw, opens him up to the chill of the wind through the wall, around the edges of the tarp.

What is happening in Hudson?

CHAPTER THIRTY-TWO

RONAN

"Just don't break your neck, kid," said the guy who ran the bowling alley, and just like that, Wick had permission to walk up and down the lane dividers to take pictures. All Dom had had to do was ask nicely. Amazing what a cop in uniform could get. "And don't step off the divider! We just waxed the lanes."

Dom was right—the kid was a trip. In the ten minutes since we'd met, he'd probably uttered a hundred thousand words. About Dom, and how great he was, and about what a shithole Catskill was compared to Hudson, and about my Instagram, which he'd apparently spent an awful lot of time on. Maybe it was just the manic counterpart to the depressive episode he'd described with such eerie self-awareness in a text to Dom, or maybe this was just who he was—either way, I already loved him.

"Remember the light is not so great in here," I said, kicking off my shoes and following him out onto the narrow isthmus between lanes seventeen and eighteen. His excitement was infectious. His skinny little body buzzed. "You'll need a wide aperture and a relatively slow shutter speed."

We'd gone to the Catskill Hoe Bowl for Wick's photo lesson. Attalah was at the counter ordering us burgers and french fries and sodas. A regular All-American family outing: me and my secret gay boyfriend and his wife and the preacher's boy, our surrogate gay son.

"You ready?" Dom asked, holding up his ball at the end of the lane.

"Wait!" Wick said, scrambling to adjust his camera settings.

"With a slow shutter speed, the ball's gonna be a blur," I said.

"Okay!" Wick said.

Dom released: a mighty throw. Wick snapped the shot at the decisive moment, and whooped in delight when the photo showed up on his screen. The ball was a bright green blur, jetting down the center of the shot.

"That's amazing!" I said, rubbing his shoulder. "You're a natural."

"I don't like the way Dom's blurry," he said, pointing to the man in the background, midway through stepping back from his throw.

"So tell him to hold still once he's thrown," I said.

Wick relayed the instructions. The ball clattered back up the ball return. Dom threw, and froze. The shutter snapped. Dom picked up the spare. The photo was perfect.

"You're so good," I said.

"Thanks, Ronan."

"What now?"

"The pins."

"Excellent."

I followed him farther down the lane. Bad classic rock came through the overhead speakers. We couldn't hear anything but ourselves.

Wick said, "Did you know Jark Trowse was sixteen when he started his first website? An e-commerce site for artists to sell their stuff. I'm almost sixteen and I got *zero* good ideas."

I could see it in his eyes, how starstruck he was. "I don't know much about him at all," I said. "And I'm sure you're full of good ideas."

"I met him, once. He came by my mom's church. Got my picture taken with him and everything! He was twenty when he started Penelope's Quilt. Twenty-five when it went public and he became a billionaire. Some people say he's the richest gay man in the world."

"Stop here," I said. "Any closer and you risk getting hit by an errant pin. Photography is about taking risks, but you shouldn't take the risks until you know your basics."

"Sure," he said, and then hollered "Okay!" down to Dom. But Dom couldn't hear. I waved my arms until he saw, and flashed a thumbs-up.

"Use a slightly faster shutter speed," I said. "The pins are gonna move a lot faster than the ball."

Wick nodded and made the adjustment effortlessly. The kid was a quick study. I remembered being that wide-eyed about photography, that eager to learn everything I could. That skinny. That scared, and that happy, sometimes at the same time. That hungry. I wanted to give him a hug.

When the ball hit home, Wick caught it exactly. The pins in his picture were opening outward, like the petals on a flower or the birth of a mushroom cloud. Only a slight dimness marred the photo, a consequence of a shutter speed just slightly too fast for such low lighting. I pointed it out with supreme gentleness, but he looked like he'd been punched in the gut. "It's okay," I said, touching one shoulder as gently as I could, for fear of snapping him. "You did amazing." I wondered what kind of criticism he was used to getting, that even such a small piece of it could deflate him so quickly. "Let's try it again with a different—"

"No," he said, stepping off the divider onto the forbidden lane, almost slipping on the waxed surface. He walked around me, got back on the lane divider, walked to where Dom and Attalah were eating all the french fries.

I followed. We sat down, and I could see by the way he drank his soda that he was sulking.

"Wick did great," I said. "Show them your photos."

"Later," Wick said.

"Hudson used to have a bowling alley," Attalah said. "Where the Walgreens is now."

Wick shrugged, uninterested in ancient Hudson history. But his anger ebbed, as we sat and ate and no one pressured him to cheer up or chat or anything.

"They're trying to make an art museum, for local artists," he said, when the french fries were all gone.

"Who is?" Dom asked.

"Jark Trowse. Part of the Pequod Arms. Maybe you could get your photography in there, Ronan."

"You and me both," I said. And at that, he smiled. It was a radiant smile. Its rareness made it more so, and also sadder. "Which reminds me. I got these for you, Wick. They're some of my favorite artists. You should learn about what you love—what speaks to your soul—because that will teach you what kind of artist you need to be."

I handed him five photography books, huge and heavy. Richard Avedon, Gordon Parks, Dorothea Lange, Diane Arbus, Sebastião Salgado.

"Holy shit!" Wick exclaimed, and then covered his mouth with his hand. "I'm so sorry!"

"No one here gives a shit," Attalah said, in a stage whisper, and we all laughed, and watched Wick tear off the plastic and dive on in.

Dom and I bowled a game, while Wick devoured the art and Attalah worked on a folder full of papers she'd brought. Every four or five minutes she took out her phone and sent off a quick message. Getting people to place public calls for a postponement of the election, citing fear over what happened to Rich Trappan. Facebook posts; Instagram comments. That afternoon we'd brainstormed some samples to send people: *I don't feel safe in my own town anymore and that's not the way it's supposed to be. Bad enough they've been pushing us out, now they're murdering us.* Etc.

"Poor kid," Dom said softly to me.

"His wounds do seem pretty deep."

"Deeper than yours were at that age? In Hudson?"

"You can't really compare," I said. "I had a thick invisible armor called white privilege to protect me. He's dealing with a whole set of other shit, on top of the shit I survived."

"Hudson High has a Gay-Straight Alliance now," Dom said. "Couple years ago, two boys were the Homecoming Couple. Things are a thousand times better for boys like him, but that doesn't mean they're easy." He picked up his bright green ball but then just stood there.

"What?" I said, finally.

"I mean . . . shouldn't a boy like him—a boy like you—have a chance to grow up with as few scars as possible?"

"Of course," I said. "That's not even a question."

"What I'm saying is . . . Hudson's transformation is changing things. Five years from now, boys like Wick—or like Katch—will only have to deal with the same old bullshit adolescent agony as everyone else."

"I see," I said.

"If you stop it—things will go backward."

"You don't know that." He stared at me until I had to nod, conceding the point. "I can't accept that the only way to make things better in some ways is to make them so much worse in others. Why can we only have music and culture and gay rights by gentrifying the city past all recognition, driving out the people who made this city in the first place?"

Dom shrugged. "It's like God or the Easter Bunny or fascism. Whether they're real or not has nothing to do with what you want or accept. You and Attalah need to really think about what you're doing, and what the consequences might be. This whole YOU ARE HATED thing? You're playing with fire."

"Thing about fire is, you can't burn down the bad guys' house without it."

"Fire doesn't care what it burns," Dom said. "It just wants to burn."

He held a straight face until we both broke out in giggles. We played the rest of our game like that, laughing often and talking shit, serious subjects left behind.

"Any favorites so far?" I asked Wick, when Dom had soundly beaten me and we went to rejoin the rest of our magnificent momentary family.

"I love these," he said, flipping back and forth between spreads in Avedon's *In the American West*. In one, a boy held up a beheaded rattlesnake, split down the middle with its guts arcing elegantly. In another, a slaughterhouse worker held a bloody severed calf head over his own. Dead blank eyes stared out accusingly.

"You like the gruesome stuff," Dom said.

"My mom won't let me watch horror movies," he said, smiling gleefully. "I love this shit."

"Look at that kid's expression," I said, pointing to rattlesnake boy. "He's proud and he's scared at the same time. That's what makes the photograph great. We know so much about this boy, who he is on the inside, based just on what Avedon captured of his outside."

"Totally," Wick said, touching the boy's face so reverently I could see that he did indeed get it. We watched him turn the pages, eyes widening at each new marvel.

But even in that blissful moment, I couldn't keep my mind off what was happening. *Your hate helped immensely*, Katch had said. *You've helped so much more anger blossom.* We'd given it life, Attalah and I, fed it on our hate, and now it was feeding our hate back to us and to everyone else in town.

Wick said: "I was born for this, you know. My mom named me

Jeremy, after that mysterious Hudson photographer from the fifties. Jerremy with two Rs. She always said she felt a special kinship with his work."

"I didn't know you had a first name," Dom said, laughing. "Jeremy Bentwick. That doesn't seem like you at all."

The kid laughed, too. "Why do you think I go by Wick?"

"You should practice portraits," I said. "Telling a story with nothing but a human face is half of the fun of photography."

"Let's do it!" he said. "Who's my first victim?"

We three parental substitutes exchanged glances. In that instant Wick could have captured a brilliant portrait of any one of us. Equal parts embarrassed and proud.

"Do me," Attalah said, standing. "These two boys are too pretty. Anybody can take a good picture of someone handsome."

Dom booed. "I accept your compliment, but I do not accept the implication that you're any less gorgeous than us two beautiful boys."

"Try the arcade," I said, pointing to a nook of brightly strobing colors. "Dramatic lighting."

They went. Dom and I drank sodas. Our shoulders touched and everything was beautiful and I should have known, then, that nothing this nice could last for long.

CHAPTER THIRTY-THREE

T his is so fucking not good," Chief Propst says, when Dom walks into the station. At first he thinks it's being said to him, but no, the chief's been saying it over and over again all day.

Word spread through the force fast, about what happened at Historical Materialism. Dom pours himself some coffee, sits down at his desk. Officer Van Vleck is typing under a blue tarp, from where the station ceiling's leaking.

"The fucking mayor is on his way," says the chief. The six-foot-six man has never seemed so small. He holds his hat over his stomach like a shield. Freshly shaved cheeks shine.

Dom reads the report. A rock through the window of the Warren Street store, and then a series of big paper bags stapled shut, all of which burst open on impact. Splattering rancid meat all over the walls and floor and countless priceless antiques. In the pictures it looks like more than one murder went down in there. The stink, to hear Chief Propst tell it, made eyes water and stomachs reject their contents.

Rome Byles had been out on patrol that night. He was on the scene within three minutes, drawn by the siren that went off when the window broke, and says he saw someone fleeing the scene. Young, white, male, hooded black sweat suit. A little red wagon was left behind, complete with meat ooze, but there are no fingerprints on it.

"So fucking not good. We got an election coming up, and Winter Fest right after that."

Dom drinks his coffee, does some paperwork, gracefully exits before Mayor Coffin can arrive.

No wonder the mayor's taking this seriously, Dom thinks, heading down to Second Street. *The new arrivals got spooked bad enough by that billboard; this is going to make them lose their minds. They'll be seeing hostile natives hiding behind every bush. And calling us about every loiterer and slammed door.*

. . . .

WHEN THE COPS HAVE GONE, and the CLOSED sign is hung on the door and the door is locked, Rob Creighton is alone inside Historical Materialism with the stink of death and a hundred ruined artifacts. The bottoms of his shoes are gummed with soft rotten fat. Flies buzz. Maggots from the meat already emerged from their pupae. There's only a quarter of a bottle of bleach left, in the closet in the back of his store. *I'll have to go out and get more. I'll have to venture into this city that hates me.*

Wind whistles through the huge wound in his plate-glass storefront. Locals gawk, across the street. He sees his old tenant Heather, looking meek and helpless as ever. He wishes he had curtains. When he moved in he'd inquired about getting a steel gate installed, but all the other store owners said it would be "an egregious violation of aesthetic norms."

We're all undefended, he thinks, looking up and then down Warren Street. *Our precious aesthetic norms might just get us all killed.*

. . . .

HEATHER GETS BACK to the couch she's crashing on, and sits to savor the throb in her chest. Hate; pride; anger; ecstasy—all given physical form, it feels like, a sweet jagged pleasurable lump (*blade*) (*tumor*) of it. The stink of rotting meat is still on her fingertips. It seeped through the work gloves, and she is glad that it did.

I did that.

She shuffles through photos on her phone. Two girls, getting older fast. She has so few pictures of them.

You see, girls? Your grandmother says I'm not strong enough to do what I need to do to get you back, but look how strong I am. Look what I can do. What laws I can break. What fear I can strike in the hearts of evildoers.

She'd stopped by the store that day. So had half of Hudson, seemed like, a whole crowd of them standing on the sidewalk, so she wasn't worried about showing her face at the scene of her crime. She saw it, the fear on the face of the man who ran it. So much fear, on so many faces.

In her purse is a fake lipstick tube, hollowed out for holding drugs. In the tube is a sweet huge chunk of crystal. Some sexy little Latin or Arab guy with a bad whale tattoo down at the Half Moon had just handed her a baggie of it the night before, said she looked like she could use a pick-me-up.

She pulls out the lipstick, tips the meth out onto the table. Looks at it. Puts it back in the tube. Looks at her photos some more.

....

FROM THE *HUDSON GAZETTE*:

Photographic It Boy Ronan Szepessy, long the darling of the darker edge of the New York City editorial scene, has come home. Twenty years ago the Hudson native fled from a very different city, one where being an artist and openly gay were not realistic life choices.

"Growing up here gave me some pretty deep wounds," Ronan told me recently. "I dealt with a ton of homophobic violence, both physical and emotional. And I guess you could say that every photo I've ever taken has been an attempt to stitch those wounds closed."

For all its pain, this healing process has richly rewarded Ronan. He's shot for some of the biggest new names in fashion, and his work has been in ads and editorials for everything from Vogue to Paper to BuzzFeed. Equal parts crime scene and sex scene, a Ronan Szepessy image oozes a studied, nostalgic sort of sleaze.

"Coming home to Hudson has taught me so much about who I am as an artist," Ronan says. "This is the landscape of my dreams—and my photography. All at once I could see that I'd spent the past two decades trying to get back here, reconstruct it out of whatever raw materials were around me."

Voluptuous bodies lay sprawled in narrow alleys. Bootlegger molls leer from high windows. Figures grapple in front of a rickety line of buildings, the whole picture so unsaturated it could be in black and white. Some of it is trickery

and aftereffects—he didn't rent Ford Model T's and artfully arrange them in the background—but it's a testament to the strength of Ronan's compelling, incantatory vision (and his skill with Photoshop) that the extraneous elements only enhance the spell these images cast.

Now Ronan will have his first major gallery exhibition, a retrospective covering his entire career, right here in Hudson.

"Walker Evans photographed Hudson. Abraham Lincoln's funeral train passed through Hudson. History is alive here. It's not some dead thing on a shelf, or under glass in an antique store. That's what I've been trying to capture, in every photo I took. No matter how far I fled, my art kept bringing me back here. In a sense, I never left. In a sense, I'll never leave."

And Ronan believes the time is right for his unique perspective.

"I hope I can be a bridge," he says. "Between the old Hudson and the new. With all the animosity bubbling up to the surface lately, I think we need to have a serious conversation about who we are and what this city really is. I hope my art can help that along."

"Ghosts of Home" opens December 22nd at the Volker Gallery, 557 Warren Street.

. . . .

DOM IS AT work; Ronan is otherwise engaged. Attalah opens the bottom drawer of her dresser, pulls out the sketchbook.

Once upon a time, she went through one of these every six months. Drawings poured from her pen like water from a faucet. Then a pad would last her a year; then two years. This one she hasn't cracked open in five.

The pencil stuck between its pages needs no sharpening. She sets it down on the bed, sets herself down beside it. Takes out her phone, summons up a formidable horned tusked warthog demon mask fashioned by the Bamana people of Mali.

The doorbell rings. Attalah ignores it.

She deserves a moment to herself. But so much is happening. Just last night she had Rudy Snitko on her doorstep, telling her he's gotten twenty different Hudson contractors to commit to a non-participation pact—carpenters and landscapers and plumbers and painters determined not to do any work for any of the invaders. To her great shock, Ronan even got his shit together enough to set everything up for Ohrena to have her big moment with Jark.

And the person at the door won't stop. And really she shouldn't be ignoring it—for all she knows it could be another aggrieved Hudsonian, with another new wrinkle, another brilliant plan to help fight back.

Her mother had always said it, remembering her own community organizing glory days, and Attalah had tried hard to believe it but had never quite been able to: people are incredible, once they figure out how powerful they are. Another thing she always said was: *This stuff works best when it's a little bit out of your control. That's what Dr. King used to say. In the beginning you might need to manipulate people, but once they get going, they'll start manipulating you.*

So she puts back the sketchbook.

"Treenie," she says, when she opens the door, and the smile she'd worked up fades fast.

Because whatever Treenie came for, it wasn't to help save Hudson. She'd made too much money helping suck it dry.

"Attalah."

Five silent seconds pass, so Attalah says, "What can I do for you?"

"Can I come in? It's cold out."

She shrugs and steps inside. Treenie follows. She smells like clean sweat, like she's been jogging. Her hair is in a ponytail. She's always been *almost* a pretty woman. Attalah doesn't ask her to sit down, offer any hot or cold beverages.

"Isn't it crazy?" Treenie says, shutting the front door and leaning her back against it. "What's happening around town?"

"What, exactly?"

"You know. All this new . . . I guess *hate* is the only word for it. That billboard. The buttons. And now it's escalated to violence. You heard about Historical Materialism?"

"Is it new, though? This . . . hate. Or has it always been here? Just . . . under the surface?"

Treenie folds her arms across her chest. "That's a fascinating question, Attalah. I wonder."

Attalah thinks: *Of course she suspects I'm involved. I've been the face of the resistance for years now. But she's just here on a hunch, on a hope. Trying to feel me out, provoke me into revealing something. She can't possibly have any evidence. I've been too careful.*

And then: *I've been careful. But has everyone?*

"Was that all you came for, Treenie? To talk about buttons?"

"If it's been here all along, under the surface, like you say, what do you think could have brought it to the surface?"

"No idea."

"This isn't accidental. Someone's behind it."

"Interesting theory."

Treenie smiles and takes a step forward. Attalah doesn't like the new look on her face—eager, hungry—but she won't take a step back.

"It's not a theory," Treenie says. "It's happening. I know it is. You and Ronan Szepessy. You're behind it all."

Attalah laughs. "You're an idiot, Treenie. You were in high school, and you are now. Back then you liked to think that getting so many people to fall in line behind you meant you were smart—and now you probably think because you've made so much money, that's just more proof of how smart you are. But any idiot can make a lot of money, if all they want to do in life is to make a lot of money."

"Deflect all you want. I know it's true. I knew he was up to something, even before all this started. Why else would he have come home? Certainly not because he gave a shit about his father. So I've been following him. And the other day he came over here and stayed for hours."

"So? He and my husband were best friends in high school. They've been reconnecting lately. They played fucking Super Mario Bros 3, for Christ's sake."

"But Dom wasn't home. You were here alone."

"He was waiting for Dom, then. And he got tired of waiting. And later he came back, and they played fucking Super Mario Bros 3. I'm sorry I don't have time-stamped video footage to try to satisfy this grand jury you've got going on in your delusional head."

Treenie flashes that grin again, the one she'd wanted to punch in high school and wants to punch now. "How are you doing it, exactly? What kind of schemes are you two orchestrating?"

Attalah grins back. "I didn't have anything else planned today. Stay as long as you want, and spout whatever crazy bullshit makes you happy."

"It's okay. Of course I know you won't tell me. That's not why I came here. I wanted to tell *you* something, actually."

"Be my guest."

"Ronan Szepessy is fucking your husband."

Attalah works hard to keep her face from doing anything. "Was there anything else you wanted to share?"

"No, just that."

"Well, it's been great catching up. Glad to hear you finally developed an imagination. I always like a good story."

"Do you want details? I have them. You can ask your husband, if you want. Like I said, I've been keeping tabs on Ronan. I followed them to Livingston, after Dom picked Ronan up in his squad car. They drove down a private road, parked near the river, got in the back seat. Etc."

Here, anger ekes in. Attalah feels it. Knows it's wrong to let Treenie get to her. Tries to stop from saying anything. Can't. "I know this will be difficult for you to understand, Treenie. Because you haven't had a serious boyfriend since Scott Plass in goddamn tenth grade. You have no idea how marriages work, and you definitely don't know the first fucking thing about me and my husband."

"I figured you probably knew all this already. Once I saw it, I figured, this has to be some freaky open marriage shit she and Dom have got going on. And it's a shame, because if I'd known he wasn't fully off the market . . . but then again you and I are apparently not really his type."

"You're a disgusting little troll," Attalah says, smiling. She won't tell Treenie to get out. She'll stand there with a smile on her face for as long as she has to, until Treenie turns tail and flees.

CHAPTER THIRTY-FOUR

RONAN

"Something's not right," Dom said.

"Nothing's right," I said. "But what specific not-right thing were you thinking of?"

He groaned and sat up. There in the dark, on a back road in the back seat of a car again, we weren't forty-year-old men anymore. We were kids, teenagers, trying our hardest to find a safe place in a world full of monsters. Reveling in the freedom of love and sex, sure, but also: scared shitless. "It sounds crazy, every time I try to say it."

"Um . . . have you met me? I'm fucking nuts. Tell me your craziest thought and I'll show you one crazier."

Dom stayed silent. I reached for his hand. He grasped mine gratefully. I pressed the other one against the small of his back.

"It's just that . . . things keep happening. That don't make any sense. People behaving irrationally, even for people. It's like the whole town's gone crazy. Like something got into the water supply. Or . . ."

Or there are whale ghosts in all our heads, whispering in our ears and deforming our dreams until we do terrible things.

And also I might have accidentally tapped into their power and

*summoned up a demon who looks like a sexy man and is bent on blood-
shed and destruction.*

Dom's back went goose-bumpy beneath my fingers. Like the
thoughts went from my mind to his. His voice was no more than a
whisper when he said: "Do you believe in the supernatural?"

"I do," I said. "And I think it's here."

Dom looked relieved that I didn't try to talk him out of it. Like
if he had been coughing up blood for weeks, and trying to pretend
it was nothing, and he'd idly said *Maybe I should see a doctor for
this*, without knowing whether he wanted to hear *Nah, I'm sure it's
nothing, don't worry* or *Oh yeah you definitely need to take that seriously.* "It's crazy, though," he said. "Right? It has to be. I know that.
But things have been happening, and there's just no non-crazy explanation."

Dogs barked, somewhere in the distance. I wanted to tell him
everything. Katch, the whales, Tom Minniq. How the blade between my ribs had opened up a hole, and my hate and rage had let
them all in. But I couldn't. Dom knew in his cop's gut that something was rotten, but he'd never follow me down the rabbit hole
of whale ghosts I'd fallen into.

I said: "To me the question isn't: why is it happening? It's: what
can we do about it?"

"In the horror movies, you gotta find the body of the girl who
fell down the well, or Freddy Krueger, and give it a proper burial or
say a prayer or set it on fire or *something.*"

"There's a lot of horror movies. Many of them contradict one
another. As monster destruction instruction manuals, I think their
helpfulness is minimal."

"Plus Freddy Krueger keeps coming back."

"Still," I said, remembering Katch's words: *We're losing. Our
wards are being broken one by one.* So, supernatural entities could
be destroyed. Time and money had been destroying it, but with everything I'd set in motion I didn't think we could afford to sit back

and wait and hope. "There's got to be a way to . . . stop it. Whatever the hell *it* is."

"Yeah," Dom said.

He lay back down. We spooned together and it didn't matter if the world outside that car was on fire and ghosts were murdering people.

CHAPTER THIRTY-FIVE

RONAN

Y ou," Marge said when I came out of my bedroom in the morning. My mouth was a dry foul ruin, my eyes still sealed with sleep crust—and there she sat, on the couch beside my father, her back to me—smoking.

She'd been there for more than one cigarette, by the smell of it. Smoke made the air thick, bright with late-morning sun.

"Marge?" I said, because what else could I say? "Why are you smoking inside? You know my father—"

"Oh!" she exclaimed, standing up, whirling around, and I could see now that not only was she furious—she'd been crying. And I knew exactly what was happening. And there was nothing to do but let it happen. "*Now* you care about your father's wishes. *Now* you worry about what he wants."

"Marge," I said.

She waited. I had no more.

"You thought no one would find out? You thought no one would fight you on this?"

"My father's not getting any better," I said. "And he has expenses and obligations that you know nothing about. Decisions need to be made, Marge, and I'm sorry you can't see that."

She laughed. "You stupid little shit. You should be ashamed to come up in this house and try to play the dutiful son. With me, of all people, who's been wiping his fucking ass for you for years."

"You know how much I appreciate you," I said. "Me and him both. It's just—"

"It's just that all that money was too good to keep turning down. So you had to get a power of attorney so you could seize control of everything he owns and sell the building against his wishes. Are you going to try and deny it?"

My father sat there, watching the dead television. *What channel is it tuned to—what long-canceled or still-to-be-developed show is he watching?* I wondered, idly, sloppily staving off panic with non sequiturs.

"You're taking advantage of a sick man, and he still has a lot of friends in this town. We might not win, but you can bet your fucking ass we're going to fight you."

"Marge," I said.

You've got it all wrong. I'm not on their side. I'm not trying to get rich by helping them out. I'm trying to destroy them. We're on the same side here.

But I couldn't say any of that. Because Marge had a big mouth and liked to drink and had tons of friends, and I couldn't trust her to keep it secret. Within a day the town would be abuzz with rumors of what I was up to.

And anyway, a very public fight with them will only increase my standing with Jark and the other invaders.

So I didn't say anything at all.

Anger had been the only thing keeping her hurt at bay, and now that she could see I wouldn't be baited into a battle, the sadness came crashing in. "Your father"—and her voice broke—"your father is a fucking saint, and I have worried myself sick trying to take care of him. While you've been off god knows where doing god knows what with—"

She stopped that sentence, but I knew where it had been going. Would have been easy enough to pick up on it, draw out the homophobia she was clearly holding back, get her to say something awful, use it to discredit her in the ugly fight that was coming. But I loved her too much, for how much she loved my father. For everything she'd done for him. She was human—she was a Hudsonian—and so there was hate inextricably woven into her DNA, homophobia and racism, and I wished I didn't but I did still love her. I wouldn't hurt her any more than I had to. Marge was not my enemy, even if she believed she was.

"All these years, he's defended you. Told us we were all wrong about you, that you were a good boy who loved him and this town and that you'd find your way back one of these days. And now—this is how you repay him?"

All I wanted to do was brush my teeth and wash my face and get back into bed and die. But I couldn't do any of those things. I had to stand there and take it.

"I've been blinded, too," she said. "That's my fault. I've still seen you as that little boy who used to come into the meat market and who thought his father was great God almighty. Do you remember how you used to climb up on the conveyor belt at the cash register, and even though your mother had told me a thousand times not to, I turned it on so you could run in place?" Before I could comment, commiserate, come in for a hug, she continued: "That's the Ronan I've wanted to believe in. But you're not that little boy anymore. You're something else. Something awful."

She heaved herself up from the couch. The door slammed.

Cold wind brushed my bare feet, slit my femoral arteries open. Blood rushed out of me like a stuck sink suddenly unclogged. In seconds, I was empty.

She was wrong about me. But she also wasn't wrong. That's why it hurt so bad.

One lesson I could learn from Katch, or the thing that wore Katch's body now. Act like a person, and it's easy to convince people that you are one. Including maybe hopefully myself. So I took out my phone and started doing dumb shit on it, just like real people did.

It had been a while. I'd been so busy with our monstrous machinations, I'd almost forgotten the sweet bliss of social media shit-talking. Shouting at strangers. Sending ambiguous GIFs. Heaping praise on people I had no real respect for.

Automation took over, tapping from Twitter to Facebook to email to texts, the complex incantation rituals we use to summon up ourselves. Before long I remembered precisely who I was and what I was doing.

I opened Grindr. Sure enough, Tom's inbox was packed. Pleas for sex. Gratitude from boys and men he'd been with in the last few days. An unceasing line of strangers sharing their secret selves.

What were the rules of Tom Minniq? Was his physiology human, now that he'd been summoned up into what looked an awful lot like a human body (and was solid enough to satisfy discerning sexual partners)? How long did it take him, after orgasm, to be able to have sex again? He could be a top or a bottom depending on the situation—whatever would make his latest mate happy—but how malleable was he? Did he have a big dick for a size queen and a more modest one for timid virgins? Could he be in more than one place at the same time? Was there a body somewhere—maybe down a well—I could give a decent burial to?

The more I read of his hundreds of conversations, the more disturbed I was.

Do you know WB_Uncut? he'd asked HudsonHiker. He's got some kind of sick STD situation going on. Like, bleeding sores.

Do you know HudsonHiker? he'd asked WB_Uncut. He's a fucking asshole. Last night we hooked up, and I made him wear a condom, even though he really didn't want to . . . and halfway through I noticed something was different. The motherfucker stealthed me, took the condom off and then came in my ass.

To Antiqueen, he'd said: Do you know SixthAndState? He lives in the apartment below me, and this morning I heard him on the phone, and I swear to god he said "no one knows it was you, I paid the cops to say he saw someone running away from Historical Materialism who matched a completely different description, and you'll get your cash at the end of the week like we said."

To SixthAndState, he'd said: Do you know Antiqueen? I don't know what you did to piss him off, but he's telling everyone you showed him a snuff film you had downloaded to your phone. Really disgusting stuff, something to do with a deep fryer.

It went on like this. Across forty conversations, in the past day alone. Harsh, hateful stuff. Brilliantly orchestrated, too—way better than anything I could have accomplished. Scrolling back through a couple of the conversations, some of them going back weeks now, I could watch in awe as he drew them out. Locals, invaders; he expertly assessed their fears and insecurities and every soft weak spot, and then handed it over on a silver platter to some perfectly matched opposite. Every bit as skillfully as he'd drawn out each one's filthiest kink. He even leavened out his lies with actual gossip—like how he told everyone about the mayor's son's secret boyfriend.

I opened up Tinder and found more of the same. He told women about men who he professed to be friends with, who'd confessed to all kinds of crimes to him. He provided screencaps of men's profiles. My brother on the PD told me Sal M got arrested for sexual assault but his dad intimidated the girl until he got the charges dropped. Bobby O. forced my sister to get an abortion. To this day he denies it.

Whatever he was setting in motion, I wouldn't be able to control it. These people all knew each other. They'd seen each other's faces, in person or on the app. They'd run into each other all the time. One woman, he gave her a recipe for a tasteless poison that would induce extreme diarrhea. Sooner or later, something ugly would happen. Probably lots of somethings.

Why did this scare me so much? Tom was doing what I wanted. So what if he was doing it too well?

Back in my bedroom, at the bottom of my backpack, where I always kept it in case of an emergency, I found my old phone. Opened it up, and logged in to my own Grindr account. And then I clicked on Browse Nearby.

Sure enough, the nearest man to me was Tom Minniq. <25—less than twenty-five feet away.

Horror movie lines flashed through my mind: *The calls are coming from inside the house.*

Would he listen to me if I told him to stop? Could I control him? Was he grateful to me for giving him life, bringing him into this world? But since when were sons grateful to their fathers for bringing them into this world? And I wasn't his father, more like his Dr. Frankenstein—and we all know how well that worked out for the doctor.

It's Ronan, I messaged him. We need to meet.

. . . .

"RONAN!" TREENIE CRIED, waving her arms in the air like somehow I'd miss her.

"Hi," I said. A drafty second-story Warren Street studio space, converted into Jark's campaign headquarters, currently home to seven volunteers doing phone banking. One of whom was Jark himself, making his own calls—ostentatiously egalitarian. "Cool if I help out?"

"Of course," she said, hugging me. Smiling. Oblivious.

This idiot has no idea how close we are to destroying everything she's built.

She produced a spreadsheet page. "This is from the county Democratic Party logs—it's so late in the game at this point that we're focused on calling our Yeses, to remind them about the election and thank them for their support, and ask for them to commit to call their friends to see if anyone needs help getting to the polls.

We're still leading by a lot, but this whole YOU ARE HATED thing has caused a slight dip at the polls."

Such chumps, I thought, *to let any stranger with secret hostile motives walk in and get the keys to the campaign car like this.* I sat down and read the script and reached for the phone.

But maybe they weren't. There wasn't much harm I could do them, there in that crowded room. Anything off-script, they'd hear. Maybe I could walk out with the page of Yeses, call them all to ask them not to. That was just one of hundreds of pages.

The worst I could do was drag my feet, and that's what I did.

"Hey, Ronan," Jark said, standing up, giving me a hug. "Thanks so much for helping out."

"You know it," I said. "Although I have to imagine all of this is pro forma at this point. Right? Your lead is so significant . . ."

He laughed, sage and wise. "Many a political campaign has been lost by a candidate who was so confident of victory that they slacked off while their opponent was pushing themselves full steam ahead."

"Good point," I said, clapping him on the back, sidling into the empty seat next to him. "You must be feeling pretty good, though."

"Cautiously optimistic," he said, his smile appropriately, performatively humble.

This was a start-up billionaire, a Silicon Valley brigand. Small-town upstate politics was child's play to him.

. . . .

THIS DREAM IS NOT A DREAM. It's a thing that happened. Somehow, I am seeing it. Somehow, I am sitting in Wallace Warsaw's office down at the Hudson Chamber of Commerce, an unseen observer.

"Jim doesn't know I'm here," my mother says. "You won't tell him I came by, will you?"

"Of course," Wallace says.

"The bank turned us down for this loan, and there's no reason for it," my mother says. "We really need your help, Wallace. If you talk to them . . ."

By her short spiky haircut I know when this happened. She got it all chopped off, just a couple weeks before she died. The day I came home from school and saw her sitting at the kitchen table I was super excited, seeing its edgy transgressive boyishness as a mark of solidarity with my own secret sexual transgressiveness. But then she died, and I could see it for what it was: someone desperately rattling the bars of her cage, who probably already knew that the only way out was to leap straight to her death.

Wallace Warsaw says, "I'm so sorry, Hild."

"The butcher shop will close without it. You know that. Just like the Jersey Bakery did. Just like—"

"We have to look toward the future, Hild. Hudson has been dead a long time. Butcher shops and bakeries are not sustainable. The margin of profit is so small. The tax benefit to the town is negligible. We're working with the banks to come up with better overall portfolio goals. There's a plan in place."

"So it was you," she says. "You got the bank to turn down our loan."

"Not me personally, and not your loan specifically, no. But, yes, the Chamber has been meeting with political and business leaders, as well as our local lending institutions, to develop a strategic plan for revitalizing Hudson. And part of that involves setting priorities for how our limited resources can best be leveraged."

"Let me guess," she says. "Those three antique stores that just opened on Warren Street are the tip of the iceberg."

"Arts and antiques are a major area of strategic focus, yes."

"You fucking son of a bitch," my mother whispers.

"That's totally uncalled for," he says, as if her vulgarity is the real crime, as if what he's been doing is merely *strategic leveraging*. Setting *portfolio goals*. I find myself immensely frustrated that I am not physically present, and therefore cannot seize one of the antique harpoons off the wall and ram it through his neck.

"What you're doing is fucking evil," she says, getting up. "Who the hell are you to decide whose business lives and dies?"

He shrugs, looks out the window, like, *You just can't reason with some people.*

"Fuck your *plan in place*, Wallace, and fuck you, too."

She storms out. I have enough presence of mind to briefly wonder, *Is this real? Can I trust this? Am I being pushed?* And then that presence of mind is washed away in a flood of sweet cold blue hate.

CHAPTER THIRTY-SIX

S omeone is whispering, in the hallway behind Attalah's office. CPS is an old building, built as a school before the fifties. Weird tiles—smooth and brown, not stone, not marble— conduct sound strangely. Strange echoes are not unusual. Words get crumpled, twisted—impossible to make out what's being said—but tone of voice always comes through loud and clear, and whoever is speaking, hers is hushed and urgent and a little bit angry. CPS has seen more than its share of angry parents exploding after a meeting did not go so well, so Attalah gets up and goes in that direction almost without thinking about it. In her hand, she carries the small air horn they all have in their desks.

"No, *you* listen," the woman is saying. "I already told you what to use, and I told you how to make it. I'd fucking make it myself if I didn't have *a fucking job* over here."

Silence. Whoever she is, she's on a cell phone.

"We already had this conversation, Paula. I told you, I chose this for a reason. It won't kill anyone. It'll give them the shits, and that's *all*. And if you can't do it I'll find someone else who can, and the deal is off, and your sister will have custody of your kids until they're not fucking kids anymore."

Attalah doesn't need to stick her head around the corner now to know that it's Zelda. And that she's talking to Paula Dinehart, a woman on her caseload who should under no circumstances be allowed to reunite with her children until she's completed six months of addiction treatment, including a minimum of two weeks inpatient, all of which she has steadfastly refused to do.

"I don't want any goddamn excuses. Just get it done."

There's a curse, and then a long measured exhale. Attalah debates scurrying off. Not because she's scared, but because she's baffled. The pieces of what she's just heard: they refuse to come together in her mind. Mercifully, the full magnitude of what is happening escapes her for a few more sweet moments. And then, in her instant of indecision, Zelda comes around the corner.

Neither one of them says anything, not for a while.

"Hey, Attalah," Zelda finally says, rubbing at the bottom of her nose. "What's up?"

And Attalah gets it. Not only what she's just overheard, but the bigger picture. Something is very wrong with Zelda Outterson. Her eyes twitch. Her lips are ragged.

"What was that all about?" Attalah asks.

"That?" Zelda looked behind her, like *that* was something physical, like the empty hallway was proof of her innocence. "Nothing."

"To me, it sounded like you were having a conversation with one of our clients, on your personal cell phone, in the hallway, so no one could hear you."

"No," Zelda said.

"That wasn't Paula Dinehart?"

"It was, but—it wasn't about anything CPS related."

Attalah looks her up and down. Zelda is on drugs. That much is clear from the look of her. And it's not the harmless bloodshot eye of someone who smokes a joint to help them get through the day. Zelda is strung out in a serious way. And that makes her a liability. Only Attalah's own myopic focus on the schemes at hand—and her anxiety over the revelation about Dom and Ronan—and her anger at herself, for not seeing it herself, for giving that asshole Treenie Lazzarra the satisfaction of telling her—could possibly explain how she missed it until this moment. "A personal call."

"Yeah," Zelda says, nodding too fast; she's an utter amateur at all of this.

A terrifying dilemma, how to proceed from here. What she *should* do is check it now, nip it in the bud, curse Zelda out and make it excruciatingly clear that she needs to get her shit together or get the fuck fired.

But Zelda has something on her. It isn't much—that she asked Zelda to participate in some very low-level illegal activity—but if Zelda got mad at her, and if Zelda felt like she had nothing to lose, she could make some noise about it and get Attalah investigated by internal affairs. It might be enough to get her fired. And even if it wasn't, it'd establish a paper trail pointing back to her. Documentation that she helped orchestrate at least part of what was unfolding in Hudson. And depending on how the next few weeks went down, that might be enough to get her locked up.

So, instead, Attalah takes a gentle approach. Even though it makes her deeply uncomfortable. "Are you okay, Zelda? You look tired."

"I'm fine, thanks."

"Are you up to something? With the YOU ARE HATED stuff?"

Here, Zelda smiles. "Some exciting things are happening, that's all. People are talking. Stuff is in the works."

"And you've been . . ." *blackmailing our vulnerable, damaged clients into doing terrible things in exchange for access to children they shouldn't be anywhere near?*

"Talking to people," Zelda says. "That's all. Lots of people are talking to each other, finally. For years we've all pretended nothing's happening, or there's nothing we can do about it, and those days are over."

She stares at Attalah, a hard square look like *Thanks to you.*

"I'm happy about that," Attalah says. "You know I want them out as bad as anyone. But there are limits, Zelda. Putting up billboards and wearing buttons is one thing, but we can't break the law in serious—"

"Fuck the law," Zelda snaps. Finger joints pop as her hands make fists. "Who is the law there to protect? Why does the law say that I'm not allowed to write GO HOME YOU ARE NOT WANTED HERE on the side of my new landlord's car, but he's allowed to evict my downstairs neighbors? Which one is worse, Attalah? Which act is more violent? Any set of laws that says it's okay to throw a family with kids out into the street in the middle of winter is not worth my respect. Or my obedience."

"I agree," Attalah says, because of course she does.

"I should probably get back to work," Zelda says, her voice dismissive, as if already the power dynamic has shifted, as if Attalah is no longer the supervisor here. "Heather is my next client, and if she shows up on time for once, and I'm not there, she'll storm out of here and it'll be a miracle if we see her again before Thanksgiving."

"Of course," Attalah says. "But you'd tell me, wouldn't you? If anything big was going to pop off? After all . . ."

. . . *I started it*

. . . *It was all my idea*

. . . *Whatever happens, it's all on me*

But Attalah can't find a safe way to end the sentence.

"Of course," Zelda says, and hurries out of the hallway.

⋯⋯⋯

"I'M SORRY, ATTALAH, but I think you know that's way above my pay grade."

The Columbia County Board of Elections has its office in the same building as Child Protective Services, so Attalah doesn't even need to put her coat on to go file a formal request for a postponement of the election.

"People are scared," she says. "Someone drove a truck into someone's house and then stabbed them to death. We've got a murderer on the loose, and I've got people saying they're afraid to go outside. Talking about going to stay with family until they catch the guy."

Susan Greckle frowns in feigned frustration. "I hear that, Attalah, I really do. But it's not my call to make. Only the Common Council can decide to postpone an election, and good luck getting those assholes to agree on anything." She hands her a flyer. "Are you coming to Winter Fest?"

Everyone on the Common Council is in Jark's pocket in one way or another—either they're partnering with him on real estate deals or they got donations from him for their own election campaigns . . . With him ahead in the polls—but the YOU ARE HATED *shit starting to chip away at his lead—a delay would only help his opponent, so they'd never do it.*

"Will you at least file the paperwork?" Attalah asks. "There's gotta be a form I can fill out, something you can submit to them."

"Of course," Susan says, relieved to have it out of her hands. She opens a filing cabinet drawer and roots around for the forms at the back that hardly anyone ever asks for.

Attalah takes it to the end of the counter and starts to fill it out. She knew it'd be a long shot. But their situation is too precarious, their larger victory too uncertain, to keep from taking a single shot.

· · · · · · ·

THE FRIDAY 9:05 P.M. train from New York Penn Station had been sold out, and it's a weirdly warm night, and no taxis are in sight, so the scene at the station is a big, happy, milling crowd. They are weekenders, after all, with a whole weekend ahead of them! What brunches they will have; what antiquing they will engage in! The world is their oyster.

Several people see the naked man and don't bat an eyelash. Same way they do when they see someone eating out of the trash, or beating their kid, or puking. They are New Yorkers, after all. Public nudity is unusual but not inconceivable. And anyway, some of them have been warned. *This place has so much character; These people are real characters; You definitely see some characters up in Hudson!* Et cetera. Here is real life, which is what they'd come for.

Only when he screams "Look at me" do they dare to do so.

What they see: a man with no clothes on, forty going on seventy, possibly handsome once, his whole body sagging and full of folds now. Soaking wet, they think, except for a couple of people standing very close, who smell the sharp reek of gasoline and step back.

"Look at me," he says again. "We burn for you."

The ticket taker recognizes him. "Stubby?" he calls in the instant before the mayor's son lights a match and sets himself on fire.

....

JARK TROWSE IS TRYING TO HAVE FUN. Even having fun takes care, planning, strategy. It's essential to make even his fun functional.

Hence, the Helsinki. Hudson's biggest spot for live music and expensive drinks. A spot at the bar, front and center, where everyone can see him. A bright salmon shirt. His customary round of drinks on the house.

He's taking a break from working on his speech. Not the one he gives when he wins the election; that one's been written for weeks. But Winter Fest is just a couple of weeks after that—and with it the groundbreaking at the Pequod Arms construction sites—and he still hasn't found the right note to strike. He wants humility, respect for Hudson's specialness—but he also wants to assert himself. Lay claim to its future; ensure that everyone knows he is the engine that powers this ship.

By the standards of Renaissance Hudson, the Helsinki is downright historic. Almost twenty years old, part of the first wave of Culture to come feed on Hudson's carcass. Masterminded by a "California producer and visionary"—well connected, wealthy, able to bribe and cajole famous musician friends into coming up for impromptu shows in the sticks. Some big-deal chef to come cook "elevated soul food" (Jark wondered if what made it "elevated" were the extremely high prices or the fact that the chef was Caucasian). At the Helsinki, upper-tier locals rubbed elbows with big-deal new arrivals. Everyone spent too much money, drank too much, descended together into a shared buzz.

Down the bar, Jark spies Rick Edgley. The big burly locksmith had worked on his office and his home—Jark was a firm believer in hiring locals for any work whatsoever—buying goodwill one contractor gig at a time. The fact that Edgley was adorable, in a bald bearded pugilistic daddy kind of way, only increased the pleasure of his company. Jark shifts stools to sit beside him.

"Hey, Rick!" he says. They shake hands, exchange hellos. To the bartender, Jark says, "Two more of what he's having."

"You don't have to do that," Rick says, wounded pride edging into his voice. So hard to tell where largesse will be met with gratitude and where hostility.

"You can get the next round," Jark says. The bartender brings over two bottles of beer. His name is Joe Davoli, a local Italian boy whose troubled brother owns the failing pizza place on Eighth Street. Thanks to his friends on the Chamber of Commerce, Jark knows exactly how well every business in town is doing. "You just looked a little glum tonight is all."

"That obvious?" Rick says, laughing, rubbing the back of his head. "Yeah, it's been a tough week. I got a little too big for my locksmith britches, I guess. Decided to try to play real estate mogul."

"The real estate game is tough," Jark says. "People think it's easy."

"Amen, brother. Anyway I bought this house out by Claverack, fixed it up, figured I'd flip it. Like I got any goddamn idea what the fuck I'm doing. Fully furnished, ready to move in. I had someone all set to buy, and that just fell through."

They sip. The wheels turn, in Jark's mind. "Fully furnished, you say? Ready to move in? How much do you want for it?"

Rick names a price.

"That's high," Jark says. "No wonder you're having a hard time finding a buyer."

"I know, I know," Rick says. "But my dumb ass spent too much. I lower the price any, my profit margin gets shredded."

"Sorry, man. You got pictures?"

Of course Rick does. He shows him, on his phone, and Jark assures him that it's a damn lovely house and someone will be damn lucky to end up in it.

They drain their drinks. Discuss other things. Drink other drinks. Order Cajun truffle fries, which they both agree are not so great.

"You know Ohrena Shaw?" Jark says, after carefully biding his time—because it's one of his gifts that no matter how drunk he gets, his timing remains impeccable.

"Course."

"She's a tenant of mine. Looking to move out, but hasn't been able to find the right place. Yours looks perfect."

Rick laughs. "Just between you and me, Mister Trowse, but Ohrena Shaw'd never in a million years be able to afford it."

"Call me Jark, please. And actually I was preparing to make her a buyout offer. I want her building for the Pequod Arms project, but I didn't want to just boot her out."

"That's a damn nice offer, Mister—Jark. But Ohrena would never in a million years accept charity like that from you. Trust me on that. Me and her go way back."

Jark nods. More drinks come. More truffle fries, too, because they're drunk enough that anything salty and greasy would be great.

"Maybe I could talk to her, Jark. Tell her I talked to you, and we worked something out where you'd stand the loan for her mortgage, she can keep on paying you the same amount she's paying in rent but it'll actually go to pay off the loan at a reduced rate . . . Something like that. I don't know anything about the legalese that'd be involved—maybe this is all fucking crazy—and maybe you wouldn't be interested in something this shady—but—"

"I'm very interested," Jark says, and then has to repeat it over the sound of the firetruck screaming past. The amount he'd make if he could get her out of that building is thirteen times what he'd spend paying cash for that house. "Interested enough that we can figure out how to make the legalese work if we have to. Talk to her first. Find out what she'd be comfortable with. We'll go from there."

Jark is drunk. He knows this; takes a moment to compliment himself on being such an expert negotiator even while intoxicated.

"You got yourself a deal, Jark. You're a hell of a good guy. She deserves something this nice, after all she's been through with that piece of shit husband of hers."

Rick sticks out his hand. They shake. Then they hug. For the first time, Jark notices his ears: how both are battered and bent. He actually *had* been a pugilist. Mixed martial arts. Something. It should scare him, he knows, but instead it makes him like him more.

． ． ． ． ． ． ．

SOMETIMES SIMPLICITY IS BEST. Classics are classic for a reason, after all. No sense reinventing the wheel when you want to scare someone.

And anyway everyone forgets, in this age of email and cell phone calls you can silence with a finger, the profound psychological power of a ringing telephone. How something so banal can suddenly become so terrifying, after the sun sets. So invasive.

Zelda sends lists, to people who responded positively to her initial YOU ARE HATED entreaties. Names and phone numbers. Some guy on Tinder sent it to her, a little hottie with jug-handled ears who started a convo by saying he liked her profile pic—a close-up of a YOU ARE HATED button. Said he'd been collecting info on the new arrivals for a long time. Waiting for someone who would know what to do with it.

She gives her pupils no specific instructions, other than *scare the shit out of them*. Creativity is important, is something she wants to cultivate in her apprentice (*offspring*) terrorists. She knows they are full of great ideas. She believes in them.

Connor keeps it simple. Sometimes he just screams when someone answers. A blood-curdling shriek of anger or pain or fear. Other times he'll start right in with threats and profanity, bellowed in a low monster voice.

Sally is more of an artist with it. She starts out all business, sounding like it's a real call. A kind voice from the doctor's office, a Quinnipiac poll. Something believable, something that won't make the person hang up right away. And then a couple of sentences in she'll start to turn it around, following *Do you ever wonder what it would feel like if someone slid a knife into the meat of your thigh and dragged it all the way down to your feet?* or *That dog I hear barking in the background, do you ever worry you'll come home to find it gutted with its entrails ripped out and the body cavity stuffed with screws and nails and broken glass?* In a voice as sweet and slick as honey.

All night long Zelda's chest has been throbbing, a jagged something pressing up against her heart. She likes the throb of it. It tastes sweet, like hatred. It means her pupils are hard at work. Phones are ringing all over town. Distant sirens sound. People are lying in bed, shivering from fear. Telling themselves everything will be all right. Knowing it won't.

. . . .

TREENIE HEARS IT on her police scanner, the one she made her father get her way back when, so she could hear about every arrest
and ambulance call and arrive at school well armed with gossip and
inside intel.

*We've got a fire down at the Hudson train station. Reports of nude
white male. Apparent suicide situation.*

It's Stubby, says the cop who calls it in. *Steve. Steve Coffin. It's the
mayor's son.*

"What the fuck, Steve," she whispers, shivering. She knew the boy
wasn't well—everyone did, even back in high school when he was just
one more bully—but there had been something, even then, in his
eyes, in the veins in his neck, that let you know there was something
far scarier than standard adolescent anger going on under there.

Setting yourself on fire in a public place—that's a political act.
Or at least: it'd be easy to spin it that way.

Treenie puts her coat on, pockets a handful of YOU ARE HATED
buttons. She snatched them up from a bowl in the ladies' room at
the Plaza Diner, without knowing why, and she congratulates herself now. A skilled operative anticipates opportunities well before
they arrive.

She knows where Steve Coffin lives. And she knows, from listening to the police scanner, that the cops have been looking for him
since his truck ended up in Rich Trappan's living rom. A poorly kept
secret, that one. Cops talk. She's heard it from three other people.

She'll go to his house, which if she knows the skill level of Hudson cops—and she absolutely does—will be poorly secured if it's
secured at all. She'll plant those buttons. She'll call Vernon from the
Hudson Gazette, and tell him that the man who's been terrorizing
Hudson was One Of Them. She'll discredit the movement. They'll
all move on from this obnoxious interlude and get back to the business of making Hudson big again.

CHAPTER THIRTY-SEVEN

RONAN

The whole town buzzed with word of what the mayor's son did. You could smell the excitement in the air—and also the actual stink of burning flesh. Gawkers thronged the train station, took pictures of the blackened spot on the ground.

Attalah filed a second motion to postpone the election, but we knew it was futile. We made phone calls, got people to commit to sign affidavits maintaining that they had stayed home from fear, calling on the board of elections to decertify the election and call for a second one, but we didn't have much hope for that, either.

Fear did not, in fact, hurt voter turnout. Nor did the end of the Coffin mayoralty or the superstar candidate give a boost. The Columbia County Board of Elections would later report a total number of votes that was statistically equivalent to the last three mayoral elections.

Attalah voted at St. Mary's Academy.

Dom voted at the Hudson Central Fire Station, on North Seventh Street, on his lunch break.

I didn't vote. I wasn't registered in Hudson. I wasn't registered anywhere.

....

I WATCHED THE POLLING SITES. Tried to place each voter who walked in and out—old Hudson? New Hudson? Sometimes it was harder to tell than I'd ever have admitted.

I walked Warren Street. Every antique store I entered, the staff was on me immediately. Smiling, *Let me know if there's anything I can help you with*, but nervous, and never letting me out of their sight, just as they hovered near anyone else who entered. I took great pleasure in each new entrance.

I scoured every shop for weapons. Some ancient object invested with supernatural power. Something that could kill Tom and set my city free from the madness that was swallowing it whole.

"Everybody's on high alert today," I said to one chubby boy who backed off slightly when he saw how my clothes said *Hipster* instead of *Hudsonian*.

"Yeah," he said. "With what happened at Historical Materialism—and that horrible tragedy down at the train station—to say nothing of what's been going on all over town . . ."

"Going on?" I asked, all innocence.

"There's been a lot of anger stirred up, among the locals. A few of them have been . . . acting out. And there are these YOU ARE HATED buttons."

"Hated, wow," I said, smiling flirtatiously, fingering telephones. "Such a strong word. Why do they hate you?"

"Who knows?" he said. I had seen him on Grindr. He'd told Tom Minniq some of his deepest, sickest secrets. "Most of them are homophobic, and they say we're all a bunch of immoral gays and liberals."

"Is that it, though?" I asked.

"What do you mean?" His smile was suspicious.

"I mean, is that why they hate you? Or is it because you've stolen all their stuff and transformed their town into something they don't recognize or feel welcome in?"

Dangerous stuff, playing devil's advocate this openly. All I really came for was a weapon. Something old, something magic.

Also, a month before, there had been harpoons on the wall of every antique shop. Now, when I needed one, there were none.

"Change happens," he said. "What can you do?"

His innocence was unfeigned, his stance unassailable. He felt entitled to this place.

"This space we're standing in, it used to be a bakery. I'd buy apple turnovers for fifty cents, on Saturday mornings on my way to work at my father's butcher shop two blocks down. And now it sells doorknobs and glasses that cost hundreds of dollars. And now you're working here, all by yourself, in a place that used to employ ten people at a time. So you don't think people have a good reason to hate?"

"I understand their anger," he said. "But it's not like I did anything to anyone. I need a job and a place to live as much as they do."

Realization hit me, wet and rough upside the head. How hard our brains work, to keep the sense of self intact. How they will filter out anything that threatens to shine a light on how we are horrible. I could practically hear the unspoken mantra playing out in his head—the same one playing in mine. *I am a good person. I do my best, and sometimes I fail, but I would never willingly hurt someone. If harm is caused by my actions, like if I buy the cheaper bag of rice at the grocery store and keep peasant workers enslaved, the blame belongs to the systems I am a helpless pawn of. If someone hates me, it's because something is wrong with them.*

It'd take a lot more than a billboard to break all that.

I picked up a phone receiver; heavy black Bakelite. I held it to my ear. No dial tone, of course. No Tom. I debated buying one, leaving it unplugged, waiting for him to call. Then I debated smacking Smug Antique Shop Boy in the face with it as hard as I could. Neither course of action made any sense. But neither did anything else lately.

"You coming to Winter Fest?" he asked, sounding apologetic, like he had broken the Customer Service Prime Directive by not agreeing with everything I said. "Big deal. Party in the streets."

"Wouldn't miss it," I said, and swam deeper into the store. Past flags with fewer than fifty stars, and framed photographs of generals and well-dressed families. Newspapers and *Life* magazines from the day we landed on the moon, the night when Sputnik hit the sky, the time we dropped atomic bombs on crowded cities. Antique stores were like little museums, where the past was for purchase. Where anyone with a ton of money could pick up a piece of history and walk out with it. Put it on their mantel. Proclaim their ownership of it. So poor people could watch through the windows with hungry eyes.

Excuse me, sir, you wouldn't happen to have a whale-blood-rusted ghost-killing harpoon for sale here, would you?

My cell phone rang.

"Hello?" I asked.

"Ronan?" The voice was fragile, cracking. Wind laughed at it in the background.

"Wick? Are you okay?"

"It's my mom," he said, and I could hear how he'd been crying. "She's . . . I don't even know. But I'm scared."

She found out, I thought. *That Wick is gay. She found out and she did or said something awful.* "I'll come get you. Okay? Where are you?"

"Outside. Prison Alley, between Fifth and Sixth."

"I'm on Warren," I said. "By Third. Stay there, okay? I'll be right there."

I hurried out of the store, avoiding eye contact with Shop Boy. At the bottom of Warren Street, blood orange sunset clouds were climbing over the Catskill Mountains. The day had gotten ten degrees colder since I'd started hate-shopping. On the radio, Miss Jackson had said it might snow tonight. I walked east up Warren, turned north onto Fourth, and then headed up the alley.

"Here," a voice called, and I looked up to see Wick standing two stories up on a set of back stairs. He wasn't wearing enough layers.

"Uh . . . is that your house?"

"No," he said, climbing higher. "You coming?"

I looked up the alley and down it. Genteel scheming was one thing; trespassing was a different sort of crime altogether. "Come on!" he called, annoyed at my hesitation.

Fuck it. You're damned already. And if it's the criminal justice system you're afraid of, you should have thought of that before you started manipulating and framing people.

Four stories up, I stepped onto the roof. Wick stood at the far edge, looking down onto Warren Street.

"Why are we up here?" I asked.

"I like it here," he said, wiping his eyes. "I come here a lot. You can basically run from roof to roof as much as you want, and no one else is ever up here to fuck with you."

I looked in both directions and saw that he was right. The roofs of the buildings on that block made a more or less unbroken pathway, a second sidewalk.

"What's going on?" I said, going to him. "You said your mom . . ."

He turned and grabbed me, hugged me tight. He cried, and I let him. I smelled his shampoo. I wanted to put him in my pocket and keep him safe from every awful thing in the world.

"Something's wrong with her," he said, finally, and sat down on the roof. I sat down beside him. We were facing west, watching where the light faded out of the sky. Behind us was a peaked set of windows, through which bright warm light spilled out of someone's bedroom or studio. "I came home, and the whole church smelled like gasoline. And she was standing there in the center of the sanctuary, with a cigarette lighter in her hand. She'd doused the whole place."

"Shit," I said. That was not at all what I'd been expecting to hear.

"It's like she . . . snapped." Here he broke down again. I put an arm around him, said *It's okay* several times, even though I knew he knew there was no way I could know that.

"It sounds like a psychiatric breakdown of some kind," I said, speaking from experience, remembering my own mom screaming about monsters. Remembering, too, Katch saying: *The harder we have to push, the riskier it gets. Sometimes people . . . break.* Was this on me, too? I'd let these monsters loose on our town, and now a whole lot of people were . . . breaking. "Has she had a history of mental illness?"

"Well, she's a drug addict," he said, laughing sourly. "Painkillers. So maybe she's in withdrawal or got a bad batch or something? But I think it's more than that. I asked her what was up, and she said she received some very interesting information. And she finally realized how widespread the rot was. And I think—I'm afraid—what if she means me?"

"You mean what if she knows you're gay?"

As soon as I said it, I was sorry. He'd never told me he was. Maybe I was way off base, or maybe he wasn't ready to accept it and would react with defensive anger.

Or run for the edge of the building and leap.

Leap like my mom leapt off the Rip Van Winkle Bridge.

But he didn't say or do anything, not for a while, and when he did do something, it was a nod. "Yeah. What if someone told her that, and it caused her to lose her damn mind? She's a pastor. The most moral person on State Street, for fuck's sake. It might be enough to make her burn the damn building down. With me inside of it, for all I know. I don't know. So I ran."

"Your mom loves you," I said. "Whatever else she's got going on—addiction, ignorance, hate—it might get in the way, but not forever. The love is what's forever."

He shrugged. He wasn't comforted. He knew I could very well be wrong.

"Do you need a place to stay tonight?" I asked.

"No," he said. "I already talked to my friend Audrea. She said her mom said I could stay with them."

"Okay," I said. When we were done here, I would call Dom. Have him swing by, see if Pastor Thirza was still contemplating arson, and if he could talk her out of it if so.

"I should go," he said, standing up, and I could see the pain still smeared across his face.

"Are you sure?" My father's forever medicine flashed in my mind, the only remedy he could offer when someone was in distress. "Are you hungry? When was the last time you ate? Let's get a hot meal—maybe at Pizza Pit?"

"Pizza Pit," he said, smirking. "You know that shit's been closed since I was like six."

And he turned and ran west along the rooftops. I pulled myself up—pausing for the pain in my kneecaps to die down—cursing my age and wondering what the fuck I'd been eating, all those times in the past couple weeks I thought I was at the Pizza Pit.

"Don't worry about him," said a voice from the dark.

I looked around, a slow careful circuit of the rooftops around me, and saw no one. It's true that there was very little light up there, but there was some. Enough to know I was alone. And that when the voice said, "He'll be safe," and I turned back around, the short curly-headed man behind me hadn't been there a moment before.

"Hello again, Tom."

"Hey," he said, gruff and caustic, snapping his fingers to light the match he'd held between them. He raised the little flame to the cigarette between his lips, and I could see his demon-handsome face. "How you been?"

"Pretty good," I said, caught between horror and amusement, with amusement winning out. The absurd hilarity of it. "A little heartbroken. My only child, and you never call, you never write."

"I been busy," he said. Below one rolled-up sleeve, I could see the tattoo on his forearm, the same thing I saw on Katch's: a crude infinity sign collapsing in on itself:

"I guess you have," I said.

"I got your message. You wanted to talk?"

"What are you up to, Tom? I've seen the messages you've been sending—really vicious stuff. Some of this stuff is getting out of hand."

He breathed out blue smoke. And then he laughed. "I knew this would happen. I knew you wouldn't be able to handle it. What needs to happen."

"It's not about what I can handle," I said. "We have a plan. You're jeopardizing it."

He laughed harder. Stepped closer. His smell was cigarettes and body odor and clove oil and dead flowers. Desire and revulsion made my elbows ache. "You're so stupid. I remember being as stupid as you are now, but that was a long time ago." Here his voice flanged, flattened, acquired an echo. A deeper one, just beneath his own, that came from the air around him instead of his body. "We know all about your plan, Ronan. What you've got up your sleeve for Jark. Ohrena Shaw, Rich Edgley—you really think that'll be enough to stop them? All of them? I think you know that won't be enough. But you don't need to worry. We have a plan of our own. Harrow their souls, just like you wanted. And when we're done with them, you'll see—they'll run screaming away from this town, every single fucking one of them. If they're lucky enough to be able to. And we can have it back."

Something animal throbbed in his last few words. Something guttural.

"You're getting some funny ideas in your head," Tom said.

"How do you know what's in my head?"

"You think you can stop us. But I'm not a girl who fell down a well. You can't just say a prayer over some bones and be done with it."

It took me a second to recover from that. "What the hell are you?"

"You wanna see?" he asked, eyes wild and gleaming, and then Katch's frigid wind was on me again.

. . . .

NIGHT; A BEACH. Palm trees. Somewhere in Polynesia; tall-masted European ships anchored in the harbor. "Follow me," Tom said, and I went after him into a long high-ceilinged building with a palm-frond roof, open on all sides. Long tables piled high with food: islanders on one side, white sailors on the other.

"First contact," Tom whispered. "No Europeans had ever visited this island before."

"That's you," I said, pointing to one jug-handle-eared European.

"That's not me," he said. "Not yet."

More wind, and then it was almost dawn. Natives and Europeans alike lay sprawled about, over-feasted and asleep. The man who would become Tom wakes up, wanders stealthily through the incapacitated crowd. Searching for something to steal. Well fed, but still lean and hungry.

We followed him out. Down the beach. Into home after home, until he comes to a structure built of blackened wood.

"They were warned not to venture into that building," Tom says, one firm hand on the back of my neck, and even in this reverie I can smell him, the musk of the man and the something-else of the monster.

The space inside was small; the sailor couldn't even stand up straight. A couple dozen hideous masks filled one wall.

"Those masks were reserved for the gods," Tom said. "No human could ever touch them, let alone put one on."

The jug-handled sailor let his fingers graze the forbidden masks. Finally he selected one: a boar, with scythe tusks and fearsome eyes.

"No," I said, reaching out, as if I could stop something that happened maybe two centuries ago.

The sailor put on the mask.

"The god entered him," Tom said. "Well, *god* is probably not the right word. But neither is demon. Imagine something in between."

The mask fell. The man looked the same. Until he smiled.

"That," Tom said. "*That's* me."

The wind picked up again, whisking us through a sort of time-travel montage. Tom in the ship, poisoning water supplies. Tom in London and Macau and a hundred other ports, murdering drunken European sailors. On distant ships, cutting anchor when it lay harbored during a storm. A chain of violence down the decades.

More wind, and we were back in Prison Alley—but ages ago. Three men had him pinned down in the dirt.

"Just my luck I got caught in Hudson, trying to drug a particularly pretty sailor so I could have my way with him—how was I supposed to know he had a whole posse?"

They beat Tom mercilessly, and even took to stabbing him dozens of times, but the boar-deity thing inside of him kept the body alive. Finally they chained him up and hacked him apart, threw him into the most-recently-dug ditch where whale entrails were rotting. In the morning, men came to fill in the pit where Tom would wait in the earth for a hundred and sixty years for me.

. . . .

ONCE AGAIN WE were four stories over Warren Street, but back in the present.

"I don't care what the fuck kind of colonizer-pillager-plus-island-chaos monster you are," I said. "I'm not going to let you hurt the people I care about."

"Let?" Tom laughed.

"I'll stop you if I have to."

"You?" he asked, his voice dilated back down again. "Stop me? How would you do that, Ronan? Someone so weak, against someone so strong? You love a lot of people in this town," Tom said, with a prizefighter's smile on his face. "We could break them all, as easy as thinking about it."

"I gave you life," I said.

His hand grazed my cheek. Rough, calloused fingers, triggering traitorous lust. He smiled, seeing my heart, my sick needs. And then he pulled his hand away and punched me in the mouth. Hard. Hard enough to knock me backward, drop to one knee. I yelped, a high, weak, ignominious sound. It had been a long time since I'd been punched in the face. Stubby Coffin was probably the last person to do so.

"You didn't give me anything," Tom said, stepping closer, pressing his thumb against my chin. "All you did was let me out. And you can't stop me."

CHAPTER THIRTY-EIGHT

The nave of Grace Abounding Church smells so strongly it makes him wince. Bleach, and soap, and, yes, the faintest whiff of gasoline.

"Hello?" Dom calls.

No answer. He walks down the center aisle, which is still wet.

"Pastor Thirza?"

Maybe Wick misunderstood. Maybe she spilled some gasoline (*but why had there been gasoline in the church in the first place?*), and now she had cleaned it up. And, yeah, maybe she was acting weird. People did that sometimes, especially if they were addicted to painkillers. Or maybe Ronan had misunderstood what Wick said. Maybe this was all a big awful game of telephone.

It wasn't a game what the mayor's son did down at the train station, sailor. Or what he did to his former best friend.

Something is happening here. Something you should be way more scared of than you are.

On top of terrified, Dom feels guilty. If she did have a psychotic break, or if she had frightened Wick into running away, he can't shake the fear that it's his fault. Confronting her, in retrospect, had not been smart. His entire pursuit of whatever weird imaginary thing he thinks had happened to Ossie—none of it was smart. And for what? He's gotten no answers. Only more shit that doesn't make sense. Right now he needs to be doing his job. Mayor's son set himself on fire; borderline-terrorist attacks on antique shops; now Rick Edgley's spent the whole damn day down at the station making crazy claims. Real problems are popping up all around him. No sense hunting for imaginary ones.

He'd feel a lot better if Wick would answer his phone. But Wick won't, no matter how many times he calls.

· · · · · · ·

"HEY, LILLY," Bergen says, in her face before she's even hung her coat up.

"What," she says.

"Did . . . anyone tell you about Jark?"

"What about him?" she says, exasperated. Exhausted from a day of monitoring polling sites. "And who would have told me? You saw me walk in that door like thirty seconds ago."

"The mayor came by. They went into Jark's office, but they were only in there for a minute and a half. And then they left together."

"So? You know the two of them are friends. They were probably going to get a drink together, before the potluck."

"Mayor looked scared as shit. And when Jark left with him, so did he."

"Cut the shit," she snaps. "Whatever absurd story you and the other gossips in this office are imagining here, keep it to your damn selves."

"Sorry," he says. "Did you vote?"

"Go, Bergen," she hisses, and Bergen slinks away.

· · · · · · ·

"**YOU GUYS HAVE** the worst fucking coffee," Mayor Coffin says, throwing the one-sip-short-of-full Styrofoam cup in the trash. "How do you drink shit that strong?"

Chief Propst groans. "Had I known you'd be joining me, I would have sent out for some of that civet shit coffee they sell for thirty dollars a cup at that damn patisserie you like so much."

"You know this is ridiculous," the mayor says, staring through the silvered glass at the interrogation room. Jark sits there, sporting the kind of fake earnestness most Silicon Valley CEOs practice for the congressional inquiry they pray never comes. Probably there's someone who trains them on stuff like that.

Mayor Coffin is on autopilot. He's been mayor for so long, it's effortless. Hugging people he hates, agreeing wholeheartedly with deranged proposals—dishonesty and dissembling are so essential to the game that he can stand here now and smile and nod and say actual sentences even though his son had just died in a horrific public suicide after driving a truck through the wall of his best friend's home and stabbing him to death with a harpoon. He knows no one will mention it.

"Man like him, he wouldn't be so fucking stupid."

Chief Propst laughs. "It's ridiculous, except we have the word of the victim that Rick assaulted her and told her to take Jark's buyout and get the fuck out of her apartment, corroborated by *the confession of the perpetrator* that Jark paid him to threaten her into moving out. And we have a third-party witness who can confirm that she overheard Jark and Rick down at the Helsinki the other night, discussing threatening Ohrena."

"Still," the mayor says. "You know something doesn't add up."

"I know a couple of things. I know we have enough to arrest him right now. And probably the judge will set bail, which, no matter what it is, he'll be able to pay it. And I know he can afford the kind of obscenely expensive lawyers—like, O.J.-level stuff—

who will dance circles around anything the district attorney can do, and probably get him off. All that—it's not my problem. Not my job."

"*And* you know something doesn't add up. Look around you, Chief. A whole lot of people hate him right now. Who's to say that Rick and Ohrena and whoever your goddamn witness is aren't all collaborating on some kind of conspiracy?"

"What do you want from me, Nate? You want me to let him go because he's rich?"

"Sorry," the mayor says, going up to the glass. "You know that's not what I'm saying. I'm just . . ."

No need to end that sentence. They're both just . . . a lot of things. Confused and scared, mostly.

"How about this?" Mayor Coffin says. "It's election night. If he spends it in jail, it'll cast a cloud over his whole term. We need stability moving forward if we're gonna get over all this . . . whatever the hell is going on. Let him go, celebrate with his people. Ask him a couple of softball questions now. Tell him we're still in the early stages of an investigation. Thank him for his time. As a favor to me. The last one I ever call in."

Chief Propst puts his face in his hands. "He'll know we arrested Rick. If he's guilty, and he runs, I'm finished. The town is already out for newcomer blood, and it won't take long for folks to figure out I decided not to make an arrest when I had everything I needed to do so."

"You know he won't run. That's an innocent man right there, I'm sure of it. And our next mayor. He wouldn't throw everything away for some trumped-up—"

A single angry laugh interrupts the mayor. "Is it so hard for you to believe that these people who are so used to getting what they want would break the law when there's no other way to get it? I know you've drunk an awful lot of their Kool-Aid—and taken an awful lot of their money—but they've already hurt a ton of people here in Hudson, legally. So I don't put it past them, hurting people illegally."

"*These people*," the mayor says, stirred to anger, struggling to keep it under control. "You sound an awful lot like one of those YOU ARE HATED thugs right now, Earl."

"It is what it is, Nate."

"Look," Mayor Coffin says, smiling, switching tactics. "Even if he *is* guilty, he could defeat this easily. And he knows it. And he has too much at stake in this town to run. And he's too used to being in the public eye to spend the rest of his life in hiding."

"But if he does, I'm throwing you under the bus."

"Sounds like a deal," Mayor Coffin says, sticking out his hand. They shake. Then they look through the glass, both of them baffled, both of them seeing this as the tip of some horrific iceberg beyond comprehension.

. . . .

"YOU'RE LOOKING FOR THIS, aren't you?"

Zelda whirls around, surprised by the voice in the mostly empty CPS parking lot on Rope Alley.

The man who stands beside her car is beautiful, and terrifying. Lithe, limber, hungry-looking. Jug-handled ears. She knows him from Tinder: his smile unspools something inside of her. But the twinge of lust she feels for him is dwarfed by the one she gets when she sees the little plastic baggie between two of his fingers.

"I heard about you," he says, tossing it to her. She catches it with a skill she didn't know she had.

"What'd you hear?" She clenches it in her fist, ecstasy already filling her up.

"How hungry you are," the demon-handsome man says. "How full of great ideas. I've got one of my own. I thought you might like it."

He puts a brown paper bag on the hood of her car and stalks off into the alley darkness. She hollers at him to wait—even turns on her cell phone's flashlight function and hurries after him—but he's already gone. So she returns and looks into the bag, where dozens of brand-new paintbrushes await. And a note. With a plan. And a very long list of addresses.

CHAPTER THIRTY-NINE

RONAN

Thick snow, painting the whole town white. Whales swimming through the sky. Shattering clouds with every sweep of their massive tails.

"You've got to get out of here," someone said, his mouth mere feet from my ear, his voice a whisper that echoed so loud I came awake with a shout. Into utter darkness—but cold dark, not the warm dark of our living room. My father laughed, beside me, like someone laughing in a dream. We were on the front porch in almost total darkness, curtains drawn, the smallest sliver of streetlight coming in through the screen door. We sat side by side on the porch swing.

"Jesus, Dad," I said. "How did you—"

"You've got to get out of here," my father said.

Was it him? Could I trust this?

But I was awake. I knew it for certain. "How are you here right now?"

"Only for a moment," my father said. "I fought so hard to get here, and I can't stay long. But I had to tell you: go back. To the city. You've got to. *This place—it's feeding on you. It needs you.*"

"Needs me for what? What is it going to do?"

"I don't know," he said. His hand groped for mine. I clasped it tightly, gratefully. As in the dream, I was wearing my nicest suit. My neck was raw, freshly shaven. Judging by how dark it was, I'd already missed the election watch party I'd promised Jark I'd come to.

"I can't leave you," I said.

"*Now* you can't leave me," he said, and laughed, and I laughed, too.

"I'm sorry I left you for so long," I said. "I really am. I was an idiot. I was lost, and miserable, and I blamed this place. But wherever I went, I was just as unhappy."

He heard me. I know he did.

"I'm sorry I couldn't keep you safe," he said. "From this place. From everyone who hurt you here. From what happened to your mother."

His voice came close, but he did not cry. And here, finally, the last of the walls I'd built around my heart came tumbling down. I saw their construction, brick by brick so slow I never even saw I was doing it, how I'd steeled myself against the homesickness and hurt of not having him around, how I'd pulled up bulkheads to shield myself from the scorn of my classmates, the homophobia of my neighbors, and never saw, until now, how much I was hurting myself by doing so.

My father said, "I think we'd both do things differently, if we could. But we can't. All we can do is try to keep things from getting worse."

I squeezed his hand. This meant something.

"I started something terrible, Dad. I need to stop it. I don't know how I'm going to do that, but I have to. Otherwise—"

Otherwise the ghost or monster that I unleashed will suck this city dry of all its hate and fear and anger and use it to shatter our souls.

Otherwise a whole lot of people are going to die.

Otherwise Hudson burns.

"You can't stop them," he said. "Don't try. Just get out."

Sudden light filled the darkened porch. My phone, left faceup on the table in front of us. An incoming call from Dom. In that harsh glow, I watched my father's face slacken.

Fuck, I thought. *You scared him away.*

I answered and held the phone to my ear. "What the hell, Dom?"

"Ronan?" he said, and his voice sounded so fragile, all my anger evaporated.

"Yeah," I said. "Everything okay?"

"Can you come to the hospital?" he asked, and I could hear that he'd been crying.

"Of course," I said, because Columbia-Greene was a block away from me. "What happened?"

"It's Wick," Dom said. "Fucking goddamn Christ."

"Is he okay?"

"Wick's dead, Ronan."

CHAPTER FORTY

They sit, the three of them. Dom in the middle, Attalah and Ronan on either side. Holding hands. Staring at the floor, or sometimes the ceiling.

What time is it? Dom wonders. In the grim, bleary-eyed, backstage warren of an emergency room, it is always two in the morning. But now he thinks it is *actually* two in the morning. But he is also afraid to look. Or move. Or say anything. Like if he waits long enough, the ice will freeze around him and he'll be able to climb up onto something solid again. Instead of drowning in the black waters of despair.

At five P.M., someone driving across from Catskill saw a pedestrian climb up onto the guardrail of the Rip Van Winkle Bridge. She slowed fast, already rolling down the window, but before she could shout *Wait!* the person had stepped into space. By five-ten, an ambulance was on the scene. Five-twenty and the police rescue boat had been dispatched, heading for beneath the bridge. By five-forty, the fallen pedestrian had been hauled on board. Five-fifty and all resuscitation attempts were suspended. Jeremy Bentwick, identified from the learner's permit in his pocket, was pronounced dead.

He's back there, somewhere. His body. Being probed and examined. No helpful information will come of that. Only ugly answers to questions no one actually asked. Did the impact kill him? Did he drown? Was he on drugs when he jumped? Wick's phone is down at the police station, being scoured for signs. He'd left it unlocked, which they said was a hopeful sign that maybe he wanted them to find something there. A note, maybe. Typed or handwritten . . . or recorded on video, a jerky dim selfie shot while he walked out onto the bridge. A sad list of lonesome grievances; an angry series of shrieked accusations at everyone who ever harmed or failed him.

Dom groans, imagining every horrific thing that could be found on the phone. What did it matter if he left a note or not? Wick was dead. A sad, beautiful, talented creature was gone forever.

We've been here before, Dom thinks. *Me and Ronan, together.* He remembers holding his best friend's hand the night his mother died. The ER looked a lot different back then. Twenty years; three big renovations ago. And back then it was Ronan who needed love and support. Now they all do, Dom knows, but he feels like he needs it the most.

"I'm going to be sick," he whispers.

"You picked the right place for it," Ronan says.

Attalah rubs Dom's back, whispers, *Shhhhhh.* He lowers his head, lets it hang between his knees. The pain of it is unfair, disproportionate. He'd only known Wick for a couple of weeks. How dare it hurt this much?

This is why I never wanted kids, he thinks, like another answer to a question he'd never asked. *I'm like my dad. I love too hard for a world this full of hurt.*

Dom lowers his head, presses his knees together against his temples, wonders if it's possible to crush one's own head. Decides to try. Is unsuccessful.

. . . .

ATTALAH CAN'T HEAR her, from way across the emergency room, but she can sure as hell read Pastor Thirza's lips. What else could she possibly want to know?

Where is my son?

"Dom," she says, nudging her husband awake.

"Fuck," he says, rising fast, hurrying to her.

For eight hours, they've been looking for her. At her home, at the church. Calling up friends and family and parishioners. The most likely explanation is that she was out cold somewhere, in her bed or office, buried under six feet of opioid bliss, unable to hear or respond to phone calls or door knocks. But Attalah can't shake the image of her wandering the streets and woods and walking the freight train tracks, holding aloft a lantern, repeating the question she's now asking Dom.

Where is my son?

Whoever found her, they already told her. Whatever storms of pain and grief took hold of her when she found out, they've subsided now, leaving a puffy face, red eyes, and utter numbness.

Attalah has never seen her out in public without her wig before. Baldness makes her seem taller, somehow, even without the extra inches her hair provided. She wears a small hat. Ultramarine. Askew. All wrong. She embraces Dom, who has started to cry again, and it's like she's the one comforting him. She whispers something in his ear.

Attalah can hear Wick's voice, quavery and uncertain, taking photos of her at the Hoe-Bowl arcade. *You're so lucky to have found a guy as good as Dom.* His face transformed by flashing game lights. Mauve, then teal, then bright sky blue.

That remembered voice is what does it. What breaks something loose inside her.

Did you ever leave Hudson? he'd asked her. *I want to go to college for photography. I want to go away and never return.*

Dom sits back down beside her. A heavy sound; a tree falling in the forest. When did he get so big? So old? When did she? She holds out her hand and he takes it. Ronan is asleep. Somewhere nearby, someone cries out in pain.

They watch Pastor Thirza move through the emergency room—which is weirdly overcrowded tonight—opening doors, pulling back curtains and dividers, intruding on surgeries and lifting sheets, saying her son's name like a mantra, in a low voice respectful of this space hallowed by so much suffering.

. . . .

NO WONDER the emergency room feels so full: half of Hudson seems to be sick. Explosive diarrhea.

Paula Dinehart has never liked her job at the motorcycle-themed café. The owner is an asshole, and the pay is crap. And the coffee is too expensive for anybody she knows, anyone who actually comes from here. So only pieces of shit ever shop there. So when that sexy guy she'd been chatting up on Tinder appeared on her doorstep the night before with a stack of DVDs—Oscar screeners, all the ones she'd been wanting to see, half of them still in theaters—and a vial of clear liquid, and some simple instructions, she was elated. Easy to slip it into the carafe of filter coffee that morning, the soy milk, the half-and-half, dab a dot into every mug so that the espresso drinks will get some, too.

It didn't take long to start to work. Some of these hipster freelancers, who buy one cup and plant themselves in a corner with a laptop for the rest of the day—one by one they rush to the bathroom, and stay in there for a long, long time, and then skedaddle. She doesn't mind how often she has to replace the roll of toilet paper, or how bad the smell is. They are suffering way worse than she is, that is for damn sure.

And Paula is not the only one who got handed such a vial.

By 10:00 P.M., almost everyone who went to the Jark Trowse

election watch party is feeling the pain as well. Jark Trowse, Mayor Coffin, Police Chief Propst.

....

"**HE WON**," Dom says, holding up his phone to show a Facebook post.

"Of course he did," Attalah says.

They sit, staring at the floor. Smelling the stink of voided bowels. Hearing a mother call out her dead son's name. Not giving a shit about any of the schemes and hate that have consumed them for the past month.

"It doesn't matter," Ronan says.

"Nothing does," Attalah says. They all know she doesn't mean it, but they also know that self-pity and hopelessness are as valid and transitory as grief.

....

WEDNESDAY MORNING, sick as a dog, and Jark is nevertheless still hard at work.

Because there are photos on social media to be Liked, and thank-you emails to be sent, and Pequod Arms preparations to be finalized. Winter Fest is just a couple of days away. The Ferris wheel is on order. Food vendors getting locked down. The Pickle Guys causing problems. Nothing he can't handle.

Diarrhea-addled Jark canceled or postponed all of his planned postelection events. The press conference; the symbolic photo of him and Mayor Coffin. But that doesn't mean he isn't working. He's just doing it from the toilet.

Working so hard, in fact, that he keeps forgetting—and then remembering: *I fucking won. I'm a fucking mayor.*

Trawling the Hudson Community Board on Facebook for any

early-riser posts about the election, he sees a picture of a skinny, unsmiling, young Black man, and the words RIP WICK.

The face is familiar. He met this boy, once. Backtracking through his tagged photos—before the deluge of the last twelve hours—he finds it. A photo of the two of them, posted by Wick, where he's smiling to beat the band.

SO CRAZY that I got to meet Jark Trowse tonight! This guy lives the life I want. #goals

Jark remembers seeing the photo the next day, but not meeting the boy. In a church, apparently, based on the backdrop. Flipping back to the community board, he finds three comments on the RIP WICK post, from three separate users:

How did he die?

Suicide I heard

It's none of our business respect his family and their privacy

And maybe it's the abject physical misery he's in, and maybe it's the lack of sleep or the emotional high he's still riding from the night before, but Jark starts to cry.

He does a quick trip through Wick's posts. Finds out a few key facts. Downloads the photo of the two of them. Prepares to share it to his own Instagram. Spends an exorbitant amount of time puzzling out the caption. These three sentences take him eighteen minutes:

So sad to learn that we lost Jeremy "Wick" Bentwick last night. I didn't know Wick well, but he was clearly a luminous soul who infected everyone he encountered with joy and laughter. He aspired to be an artist, and like most great artists he must have had some real darkness in him, but I'm sick at the loss of all the light he could have brought into the world.

He smiles, impressed with himself—*I'm going to make a hell of a mayor*—and taps POST. And empties his bowels again.

CHAPTER FORTY-ONE

RONAN

At least there was YouTube.

We'd spent three hours on the massive brown corduroy couch in Dom and Attalah's living room, tumbling deeper down a rabbit hole, using our phones to cast onto their giant wall-mounted panel television. Mostly old music videos from the eighties and nineties. That helped. Sometimes Dom got into it. He liked Lil' Kim and REM. He made requests. The video for "Losing My Religion" prompted him to ask for the trailer for *The Cell*, starring Jennifer Lopez, which had been directed by the same guy as that video, and then the rabbit hole shifted to nineties movie trailers.

It was after midnight. I prayed we'd never run out of videos. Because every time one ended, in that slim pair of seconds while the next one loaded, the pain came flooding in. And it hurt so fucking bad.

The pain, and the remembering. Wick's awkwardness, his energy, his joy to have someone to talk to. His pain.

Attalah and I were on Dom detail. Trying to keep him from starting to cry again. He was so, so upset. So were we, but Dom's grief was a raw live thing, a terrifying animal. He was his father's son. A profoundly decent man. Too decent for a world like ours.

Caring for him helped us, too. His grief was so much purer than ours. Focusing on it meant we could forget how all of our schemes and plans were falling apart. We'd lost Wick, yes, but we'd also lost the election. We'd lost Hudson.

"This asshole," Attalah said, holding up her tablet so we could see a post Jark did, reposting a photo of him and Wick. "How much you wanna bet he'd never have known who Wick was if Wick hadn't tagged that photo and fanboyed out about Jark?"

I went to the kitchen, inspected the cabinets.

"Cool if I make chocolate chip cookies?" I asked. "You have all the ingredients."

"That'd be amazing," Attalah called.

I thought of my dad, as I wielded the wooden spoon and whipped together the butter and the brown sugar and the white. It was his instinct that had brought me to the kitchen. His drive to care for people by feeding them.

We'd had a moment, last night. Him and me, on the porch, in the dark, talking for the first time. And maybe some of him rubbed off on me. Maybe we'd bonded, on some deep ghost level. Maybe he'd help make me more whole. Maybe I'd help wake him the fuck up for real.

Maybe he'll help me kill Tom Minniq. Maybe he knows how.

"Hey," Dom said, standing in the doorway.

"Hey," I said, and handed him a teaspoon, because I'd been prepared for this moment. "You want some cookie dough?"

"Damn right I do," he said.

It wasn't planned out. Had I given it any real thought, I'd have known this was not the time to talk about it.

"I was thinking about your dad today," I said, avoiding looking at him. "He loved my dad's cooking. Or at least he always said he did. Sorry. I'm sorry to bring it up. We don't have to talk about it if you don't want to."

"No," he said. "I like talking about him. No one ever wants to. They're afraid I'll start crying. Which, to be fair, I do do pretty often."

"How did it happen?"

"Emphysema attack. Three years ago. While he was driving. He always had too much stress in his life. Always took on too much. He was like your dad, really. They both cared so much about the people in this town that . . ."

". . . it killed them," I said.

"Your dad's not dead."

"But it broke him all the same."

Dom nodded. "Good cookie dough. Not enough salt, though. You need that, to balance out the sweetness."

I disagreed—I'd added just the right amount of salt—but I sprinkled more in all the same.

"You two," he said. "You have to stop all this."

"Hand me the tinfoil," I said, and then spread it out on the cookie sheet, and then sprayed it with Pam, and then started placing spoonfuls of cookie dough.

"Don't pretend like you didn't hear me, Ronan."

"The thing is, though," and I spooned out four more cookies while figuring out how to proceed, "I'm trying. And I don't think we *can* stop this. It's so much bigger than us, now. Half the stuff that's happening, I have no fucking idea what it is or who is doing it or why."

"You have to try," he said. "I talked to Attalah about it, and she told me to stop worrying, everything is going to be fine. But you— you know I'm right. Don't you? This is out of control, and it's getting ugly, and it's going to get a lot uglier if you don't do something."

I nodded. "I just . . . I don't . . ."

"You have to try."

I opened the oven door. Held my face close to the heat. Let it blast me. I took my time sliding the cookie sheet in.

"If you don't," he said, coming closer, his voice dropping, "I'm going to tell her. About us."

"Why would you do that? Because before, when *I* wanted to tell her, you kept talking about her feelings this, your arrangement that . . ."

"The two of you, you're toxic together. I don't pretend to know what's going on here—and, yeah, I know that it's not all under your control anymore—but I know for damn sure that it all started when the two of you sat down together and got to work."

"So you're going to tell your wife we're sleeping together . . . why? To break us up?"

"Something like that. I know there would be consequences. I just . . ."

"You're not thinking straight, Dom. I don't know if it's Wick or what, but you need to take a minute and think about what you're saying."

"I've been thinking about this for a while."

And then: Attalah wailed.

"What the hell?" Dom said as we hurried back into the living room.

She sat on the couch. On the television screen, the trailer for *The Sixth Sense* was on pause. Bruce Willis's face frozen in the moment of final horrified comprehension. Attalah's expression had been turned to stone in a corollary anguish. She held her tablet on her lap. It cast shifting light and shadow onto her face.

"Someone sent me this on Facebook Messenger," she croaked. "It's apparently everywhere."

A voice on the video hissed, *Shut the fuck up.*

"What is it?" Dom asked, sitting down beside her, and I watched his face crumple up into simultaneous fury and agony.

Attalah turned it around, so I could see.

I started to say, *Don't.* I started to turn away. To shield my eyes with my arm—to do anything to avoid seeing what she had seen, being harrowed by what had harrowed her—but I wasn't strong enough not to look.

idnight, and someone is leaning on Jark's doorbell. Hard.

He's awake. His diarrhea is not better, and he's been un-able to sleep for fear of fouling his bed. So he's been sitting on his screened-in veranda, taking a break from celebratory emails and responses to the congratulations flowing in from locals and Silicon Valley colleagues and celebrities alike. Listening to the rain, reading books, hydrating, trying not to freak out. His phone has been shut off for hours. A common step, for times when stress threatens to overwhelm him. Something his guru recommended.

The doorbell chimes, over and over.

Passing the mammoth, he sees bright blue and red lights flash-ing outside. And the little mouse nibble of fear he felt earlier, when the mayor showed up at his office all smiling and apologetic to take him to the police station for some questions—is now a gaping shark bite splitting him down the middle. Intestines unfurl in the dark sea around him. Cold water floods his internal organs.

They've come to arrest me. I don't know why and I don't know what to do about it but I know that's why they're here.

Like any self-respecting billionaire, Jark has a go bag hidden in his house. Cash and passports; credit cards under other names, backed up by actual bank accounts. For six seconds he stands there, in the shadow of his skeleton, and debates making a break for it. Grabbing the bag, running out the back . . . into what? A freezing downpour; a tiny town where the whole police force is apparently right outside his door? Even if they didn't have the place surrounded, even if they didn't tackle him before he takes his third step across the backyard, he wouldn't last fifteen minutes out there.

But it's a stupid instinct. He didn't do anything wrong. Whatever it is, he can fight it. He can afford to win.

He opens the front door, to find the outgoing mayor with his thumb on the doorbell, and a dozen cops standing behind him. Is this some weird hazing ritual, a good-natured passing of the baton?

"Nate," he says, smiling, but the mayor doesn't smile back.

The man looks like shit. Pale and wan and soaking wet. Probably he has diarrhea, too. Chief Propst looks angry, and the cops look even angrier.

"Jark Trowse, you're under arrest." The chief's voice is flat, emotionless. Cold.

Jark turns to the mayor, looking for the friendly man he's known for years now. "Nate, come on. What's this all about?"

"For the statutory rape of Jeremy Bentwick," continues the chief. "And for filming the incident without the knowledge or the consent of the subject. And for sharing that recording on the internet, which constitutes distribution of child pornography." He speaks slowly, like Jark might be dumb. Like he had been completely wrong about who he believed Jark was. Like they all were. Like he hates himself for it. "You have the right to remain silent. Do you understand?"

Jark doesn't understand. He doesn't understand anything.

"Anything you say can and will be used against you in a court of law. Do. You. Understand."

Jark is wearing his pajamas. They put the cuffs on him.

"You have the right to an attorney."

He knows he should at least ask if he can put on his jacket—a pair of shoes, even—but all of this is so far beyond the scope of what he thought life could ever hand him that he is completely unable to formulate a sentence. When they lead him out into the rain, he feels as cold and dead inside as Chief Propst's voice.

PART III

CHAPTER FORTY-THREE

RONAN

We ate all the chocolate chip cookies. They didn't help. We knew they wouldn't, but we kept on eating.

We slept. Sometimes separately, sometimes all at once. We were exhausted and sick and the world was too awful to stay awake in. Sprawled on the floor, on the couch, wherever we could fling ourselves.

We tried not to think about it. To unsee what we'd seen on that video. To unhear what we'd heard.

We made phone calls. Attalah called her boss and begged for a personal day. She got it, of course. Everyone in Hudson was just as sick at heart as we were. Worse, in lots of cases—apparently some ugly bug was going around. Dom had the day off, but he called some of his friends on the force to confirm that, yes, Jark had been arrested, and, no, there was no further evidence. Like a note in Wick's handwriting that said Jark was to blame for his suicide.

Not that anyone needed such a note. Everyone knew he was. The whole town tingled with rage.

Astonishing, how fast he'd vanished from everyone's social media feeds. All those dozens of election-day photos and congratulatory posts, all those sycophants both local and imported who couldn't get enough of Jark—now they were scrubbing every trace of him.

The one picture that remained, of course, was the one Jark posted late last night. The one Wick had shared, originally, of the two of them at his mom's church. *That* photo had hundreds of comments on it. The kindest of them encouraged Jark to kill himself.

Hudson's new mayor was a monster. They'd chosen him as their leader. This was who and what they were. No wonder the whole town had an existential hangover.

My own words played back to me: *I want them broken. I want to harrow them down to their very souls.*

Wasn't that what happened? Tom/Katch gave me what I asked for. And considering how many times I've read "The Monkey's Paw," I really should have done a better job of anticipating how getting what I wanted would harrow me even harder.

To each other, we barely spoke. Dom was baffled. This video—this revelation—it did not jell with the world he wanted so badly to believe in. Not that he was naive. As a police officer, he'd come across far more heinous instances of interpersonal cruelty and violence. But he'd kept enough of his faith in humanity that each new atrocity was a shock to his system.

I didn't know Attalah nearly as well, in spite of all we'd done together lately, but I could tell by the set of her jaw and the way she stared out the window and into the future that her fury was already evolving into action. A plan.

"I should go," I said, hating saying it.

"No, no," they both said, each explaining how I was welcome to stay. I was loath to leave their side, but I'd intruded enough on their intimacy. I loved them both, and I loved what they were together. I felt icky, a parasite on their love. A barnacle on the hull of their invincible battleship.

Twilight. The rain had stopped. Curtains were drawn; doors were locked tight. Everyone was alone with their outrage. Hudson was a hermit crab that had withdrawn into its shell.

Walking south on Second Street, up the steep block that fell away to a ravine on either side, where the rain still fell from the trees and the air smelled like rot and wilderness, I heard a voice say: "Why so glum, glummy?"

Katch sat on the guardrail, bone dry and smiling. He stood, and then stepped up to stand on the rail.

"You don't know?"

"Oh," he said. "That."

I didn't stop walking. "Yeah, *that*. A little thing like a monster abusing a boy we cared about, who killed himself as a result."

Walking on the guardrail, balancing somehow on a narrow band of metal, Katch hurried along beside me. "It wasn't real, if that helps."

At this, I stopped.

"What?"

"The video. It never happened. No one hurt Wick. Not like that, anyway."

I stared at him. I wanted so badly for that to be true. Which was reason enough to be suspicious. "I don't believe you."

"We've shown you things that weren't real before."

And it was true. Tom Minniq had all kinds of incriminating but utterly false footage and photography, which he'd shared with people on Tinder and Grindr to stir them up. This thirty-second clip wouldn't be such a big leap beyond that.

"Why would you do something like that?" I asked, feeling tears blur my vision. "I'm not saying I believe you. But . . . why?"

Katch laughed. His voice was louder than I'd heard it before. He stood up straighter. Whatever he was, in addition to being Katch, it was strong now. Unafraid.

"Tom is effective. He has plans. A way to *really* turn the tide. Not that little shit you were working on. Framing one man for something he'd never be convicted of. This—this will completely change the conversation."

I turned and kept walking. We reached the top of the hill. The guardrail ended. Katch hopped down.

"And Wick's death? Did you have anything to do with that?"

"You people are so silly," Katch said. "So shortsighted. You think death is this big thing."

"Isn't it? Isn't it *the biggest* thing?"

"It's just another day." He extended his arm and curled his hand in. Two lit cigarettes appeared there.

"You're getting cocky."

He nodded and offered me one. I took it. It tasted like cloves and wet pine and I suddenly felt very close to throwing up. Katch raised a hand and pointed two fingers at the sky. "Want to see me split the clouds?"

"Stop trying to distract me. You *did* have something to do with him dying."

Katch shrugged, then closed his eyes, then flinched. "I can't tell. Tom doesn't want me to see what he's up to."

"Tom's dangerous," I said. "You know this. Can you help me stop him?"

Katch went paler than I'd have thought a ghost could get.

"You're scared of him, too."

Had Wick snapped? These monsters I'd let in—had they pushed him and broken him? Was that on me, too? We reached Warren Street. The holiday decorations were up. Strings of white lights spiraling around every tree. Doubled in the wet streets. Empty sidewalks. "So why'd you appear to me tonight?"

"You're having doubts. Aren't you?"

"You just killed a fucking kid!" I yelled, and prayed no one was sitting at one of the windows of the building we were walking by. What would they see beside me, I wondered, if they looked out right now? Katch, real as you or me? Or nothingness? When he spoke, would they hear only the wind? Faraway whale cries? "You *possibly* killed a kid," I said, voice lower, "and you *possibly* created a video of him being sexually assaulted, and you *definitely* posted it up on the internet for his mother and the whole world to see! Of course

I'm having doubts about working with someone—something—that would do *any* of those things."

Katch groaned. "Wick is better off, trust me. And to answer your question, the reason I appeared to you tonight is to warn you. Any doubts you're having? Keep them to yourself. Don't get in my way, Ronan. We can do a lot more tricks than I could when we first met."

Katch clapped his hands together. All up and down Warren Street, the white lights on the Christmas trees went out. Deep blue twilight remained, punctured by occasional lights from storefronts and high windows. One breath, two breaths. Three. He clapped his hands again, and the rest of the electricity died as well. Windows went dark; streetlights ebbed. In an adjacent building someone shouted *What the fuuuuuuuuuck* in the inimitable despair of the video gamer who's had the plug pulled on her at the pivotal moment. Thunder boomed, a question or a command. The ground trembled in answer. Katch laughed, then snapped his fingers, and the city blazed back to light and life.

CHAPTER FORTY-FOUR

Zelda is double-high, climbing the steps to work Tuesday morning. There's the actual high, of some good meth her little mystery man handed off, the kind that slides into your bloodstream slow and easy, raising the pulse without sending it through the roof, just enough to make you hyperaware and alert and aglow. She took some before her morning coffee and she's hard into that sweet post-buzz phase where she's the smartest person on the planet and pity the fools who try to start a conversation with her because they will be *destroyed* by some Wu-Tang level verbal assassin stuff.

And then there's the figurative high, the euphoria of conquest, of bliss, of *You were right, Zelda*, all the people who wouldn't take her calls before but they're sending text messages now, since they saw that sick fucking video, asking what they can do to help. Last night she got word that a very important package was delivered by the pharmacist over at Walgreens. Confronted with real monstrosity, Hudson is awake. And ready to fuck shit up.

So she isn't surprised to find Attalah sitting in her office when she arrives. She saw it in her eyes the other day, the curiosity, the hunger to know what she was up to, but her professionalism prevented her from stepping up her game. From seeing what Zelda saw: that the half-assed measures Attalah had taken weren't going to be nearly enough. Now, though. Now she's ready.

"You gave Heather back her kids," Attalah says. Her dreads are coiled up in a wrap, which is what she does when she doesn't have time to do them right. "Because she did something for you. Right?"

Zelda is smart enough not to answer. High enough to know not to smile. Holy fuck, why isn't everybody on meth all the time? It makes you so much better at absolutely everything. Politicians needed it. Lawyers. CEOs. Anybody whose job involved outthinking someone. She could outthink anyone right now.

"It just clicked," Attalah says. "She came by last week, even though she'd been in the week before. I figured maybe the situation had been such that you needed her to come in for something else, but, no. I checked her file. There's nothing. Just a passed drug test, and a recommendation for reunification. What was it?"

Zelda sits down behind her desk. There's bliss in not answering right away. Like being close to orgasm but holding off, wanting to ride the ecstasy of the moment a little further.

"It was the rotten meat," Attalah says. "Through the window of the antique store. Wasn't it?"

Zelda grins. No reason to be cagey about it. Maybe Attalah's recording all this but probably not. She'd know that whoever heard that recording would hear some things about her they wouldn't like. "You're smart, A. Brains like that, you could be a real help to what we're doing."

"What you're doing is what I started," Attalah says, smiling, but a smile that's clearly a cover for some other facial expression.

You're playing checkers and I'm playing chess, Zelda wants to scream, but instead she just smiles, too. "Well, you might have started it, but we're the ones who are going to finish it. All that shit with the buttons and the billboards—that was cute for phase one. But we're looking at phases five through fifty right about now. It's cool, though, don't get me wrong. We need lots of help. You down? To help?"

"I am," Attalah says. "What can I do?" Her face is steely but also angry, and not at her—Zelda knows exactly what is happening. Her rage at the invaders has eclipsed everything else. She's angry enough, now. Everyone is, since that video started circulating.

"You got any idea where we can get a pig?" Zelda asks. "Or . . . just a bunch of pig's blood?"

. . . .

JOHN HA HAS only been interning at the Hudson Walgreens for a short while, so he's not familiar with the protocol for reporting stolen medication. And pharmacy school up in Albany is so grueling. When he discovers there are three bottles of Rohypnol missing from the shelf, he tells his supervisor, and then he forgets it ever happened. He doesn't notice how unshocked Mrs. Slauson is, by the news.

. . . .

LILLY SCROLLS THROUGH her Instagram history until she finds it, and when she finds it she feels physically sick.

First week on the job, five-years-ago Lilly a little slimmer and her hair a little longer—back before she'd bought her beloved rhinestone cat-eye glasses—sitting at her desk, whose signature heap of chaotic paperwork is still in its larval stage. Jark Trowse standing behind her, one hand on her shoulder. Both of them smiling to beat the band. A proud moment, back when it happened. She'd never gotten more likes and more comments on a photo, before or since. Everyone had been impressed. Even her dad, who resolutely refused to understand what it was that Penelope's Quilt did, no matter how many times she explained it.

You rock star

Omg I can't believe you know him

First step: become friends with a billionaire; Next step: become a billionaire

Reading through the comments, she can feel the thrill of power and success she felt back when she first saw them, and that thrill makes her even sicker.

He was a monster, the whole time. I fell for it. We all fell for it.

She deletes the photo, but deletion feels insufficient.

I helped him. His whole greedy sick rapacious enterprise—I worked my ass off helping him build it.

"I'm going for a walk," she tells Bergen, who looks shocked to be the one working hard while she fucks off.

The sweet river stink of Hudson usually makes her smile, fills her chest, buoys her up. Not today. Today it further unsettles her stomach.

They're so linked: the love she feels for Hudson, the love she feels for Jark. The pride in who she is, it's so bound up in this place, this job. *All of this is mine*, she'd think, sometimes, this spooky weird lonely kingdom frozen in time by the river, this flashback to eighty years ago. While her friends wasted their lives on the hamster wheel of Brooklyn, still in the Matrix, she'd popped the red pill and awakened in the grit and back-alley mud of reality.

But Hudson isn't hers. And the city Jark wanted to make, the one she was helping him build—it wasn't real. It wasn't love or appreciation, like he said. It was conquest, invasion, exploitation, corruption. A car slows to a stop at the red light on Columbia and Fourth Street, and the driver turns to look at her.

Lilly gets it, then. All in a flash: enlightenment beamed telepathically by the hate in a stranger's eyes. She knows what this woman sees, when she sees her standing on the doorstep of Penelope's Quilt. A hipster invader who works for the pedophile monster.

A no-longer-twentysomething who still dresses like she's trying to find herself. Lilly's glasses have never felt so wrong on her face. She takes them off, puts them in her pocket, but can't bring herself to turn and walk away from this stranger's withering stare.

....

THE MAYOR PICKS UP, midway through the first ring. Anyone who owns any real estate in Hudson, Mayor Coffin always takes their calls. Those are his donors, after all. He knows where his bread is buttered. "Hi, Treenie," he says, sounding like shit.

"Nate," she says, remembering his son just in time. "I'm so sorry for your loss. How are you doing?"

"You know," he says. "Getting through it."

"Anything I can do?"

"Put me out of my misery."

Outside her office, people hurry by. Looking scared, looking angry. "Sorry, bud. You gotta be mayor for a little while longer. We really need one, right now. Do we even know what happens, if our newly elected mayor isn't able to take office because he's come down with a slight case of life in prison?"

"Trust me, I've been familiarizing myself with the nuances of the Hudson City Charter more in the past twenty-four hours than in my whole time in office up to now. Common Council has to select someone to fill the seat until a special election can take place."

"Is that going to be you?"

"God, I hope not. But, yeah, probably." He sounds more human than he's ever sounded before, and Treenie remembers: he didn't only lose his son. He banked everything on Jark Trowse. Gave him tons of cushy deals over the years, then handpicked him as his successor. A politician leaving office thinks of little else than his legacy, and now his was going to be drinking the Kool-Aid of a perverted monster. Like that British politician whose name Treenie couldn't recall, whose chumminess with the Third Reich became his only historical importance.

"He fooled all of us, Nate. And we've all been fucked by what he did. Don't take it personally."

"You know how many death threats have been called in to Penelope's Quilt since yesterday? A fucking hundred. More, probably, in the time we've been talking. Any kid, and it would have been bad. But the pastor's kid?" He clucks his tongue, like, *Duh, Jark, pick better targets for your child sex needs.* "At any rate. Is this strictly a condolence call, Treenie, or was there something I could help you with?"

"People are saying the Pequod Arms is dead now," she says, "but that's not true. Not by a long shot. All the signatures are in place. Equipment secured, for the groundbreaking after the Winter Fest. But we're vulnerable to a reconfiguration. Investors asking for terms to be reexamined. And we can't let any of that happen. You know that, right, Nate?"

"Of course. I want the project to happen as bad as anyone, obviously."

"Why did you take Jark to the police station on Tuesday afternoon?"

The mayor sighs. "How did you know about that?"

"It's a small town. You thought something like that wouldn't be noticed? Talked about? People are saying you knew about the tape, before it went public."

They're not, but it wouldn't take much to get them started.

"Fuck, Treenie, you know I didn't."

"So tell me what was up. Let's make sure these vile rumors get nipped in the bud."

Mayor Coffin's voice gets high, the way it does when he's upset, which is often. "Ah, fuck, Treenie, are you fucking kidding me right now?"

"Relax. Hardly anyone knows about your little trip to the police station, and then him walking out of there a free man. But something was up, even before all this broke."

"Stupid shit. Weird, but stupid. Ohrena Shaw said that Rick Edgley assaulted her, threatened to *fuck her up worse* if she didn't move out of the apartment where she lived. In a building Jark Trowse owned. One that's part of the Pequod Arms. Crazy, we thought, but when they went to talk to Rick? He confessed, and said he was acting on Jark's orders. And a witness heard the two of them talking about it at Helsinki a couple of nights before."

Silence.

"Who's the witness?" Treenie says. "Because to be honest, it sounds like bullshit to me. Skilled bullshit, but bullshit all the same. Rick and Ohrena are both friends of Attalah Morrison's. She could have—"

"Chief wouldn't tell me who the witness was, and to be honest, I didn't want to know. I agree, I think it's bullshit. At the time, I figured it would all fall apart in a day or two. Which I guess it has, since all this shit came out."

"Have the cops talked to Attalah?"

"No, not to my knowledge—nor to any of the other hundred and fifty people Rick and Ohrena have as friends in common."

"Don't joke. Someone is behind all of this YOU ARE HATED shit. Maybe more than one person. Am I wrong?"

"I don't know what's going on here," Mayor Coffin says, and she can hear the politician's effortless evasiveness take charge. "The police are working on it. That's all I know. I have to trust to the common decency of my fellow Hudsonians that this will all get sorted out."

"At least tell me that the chief is exploring the roots of this conspiracy. Not running around putting out fires while ignoring the woman with the metaphorical can of gasoline and the matches, like Hudson cops have always done."

"This town was already a powder keg," the mayor says, not answering. "Jark might have just provided the spark. That rhymes, but I didn't mean it to."

"I know, Nate. Don't worry—no one who knows you would ever accuse you of having a poetic bone in your body."

"And I appreciate that."

"And I appreciate your time, Mayor. Do let me know if there's anything I can do for you."

"Fucking harpoon me and put me out of my fucking misery."

Treenie hangs up. Night is taking back Warren Street. Rain makes the streets shine, like the river is rising to swallow them all.

....

HEATHER WAKES UP WET with (*seawater*) sweat, disoriented, confused. She looks for the starry sky and the gentle waves but finds only bare wide windows with amber light bleeding in from the street.

It's always this way, when she wakes up. Even after all these years away from it, she looks for the seascape that was painted on her childhood bedroom walls. Bright stars; calm waters.

You're not at home. You're crashing with a friend on State Street— for now—but it's like the fifth friend you've crashed with since getting evicted and you know how this goes, how there's always a ticking clock, a matter of time before your welcome gets worn out and you gotta move on, and that's another friend you can scratch off the list of your friends.

This is not your city anymore. It hasn't been, since your father lost the scrapyard to tax foreclosure.

She takes out her phone, cycles through the photos of her girls. Soon she'll have them back. Soon everything will be okay.

....

NO ONE SEES THEM. It's an accomplishment, really. To visit so many places—to engage in so many tiny acts of vandalism—and to never be noticed. It feels eerie even to them.

Ten teams of three, evenly distributed across the city. Each with a small map of five blocks, and a list of addresses. And a bucket of pig's blood. One team member to do the thing, two more for standing lookout in both directions. A couple of times a late-night pedestrian or passing car requires them to shift into the "cover story stance"—three friends stumbling home drunk, and lost—but no one even looks closely enough to notice that it's strange how they all wear black nondescript baggy clothes, let alone wonder why one of them is carrying a bucket and a paintbrush.

Two hours is all it takes.

CHAPTER FORTY-FIVE

RONAN

Whatever had happened, there on the freezing cold porch, that allowed my father to speak—the next couple days went by without a sign of it showing itself again. And other than waiting for it, hoping for it, I did precious little. I stayed inside. I ate ice cream. I drank coffee. I wanted a drink. I wanted to get high.

I wanted to not feel so sick all the time. So frightened, of what we'd unleashed. So furious with myself.

We helped kill him.

We started this thing, and we have to stop it.

I could see it all so clearly, now. My own motivations most of all. I'd told myself—told Dom and Attalah—that I was trying to save people from getting thrown out of their homes—and that was true. But it wasn't the whole truth. It wasn't even the main truth. The truth, the bloody blade-pierced heart of it, was that I felt like I'd been robbed of something I was entitled to. I was the Butcher Shop Prince, after all. My father *was* this town. It should have been mine, and instead it had been stolen.

I was a small, greedy, sick, wounded, petulant child, and look what my smallness had done.

I did research. Mythology, folklore. Ghosts, and how to kill them. Gods and how to appease them.

I eavesdropped on panicky conversations, in the private Facebook groups of locals and transplants. I logged in to Grindr and Tinder and watched as Tom continued to arouse and enrage his hundreds of targets. And that was just the stuff I could see, the messages he sent as himself, which of course I could see because so far it hadn't occurred to him to change the password. Nineteenth-century sailor ghosts are not remarkably good at the nuances of online security practices, apparently. But who was to say what else they were up to, Tom and Katch and their god whale ghost masters? What inflammatory messages they'd be sending under other aliases, or on other apps, or from the log-ins of actual humans?

I looked at train tickets back to New York City. I drafted emails to my old clients, asking if they had any upcoming needs, and did not send them.

I ignored Attalah. I even ignored Dom.

By Thursday morning I was too creeped out, too confused, and, yes, afraid, and I decided to unplug. To go for a run. To buy overpriced pastries at one of the new bakeries I'd been avoiding. To go to the Hudson Library and find a couple dozen big books of photography, and hide in a corner and look at black-and-white brilliance.

So it was a surprise when my phone buzzed in my pocket: an email arrived with a link to an article that had just come out:

UPSTATE, A WAR OF WORDS BECOMES AN OUTRIGHT WAR—THE NEW YORK TIMES

Recent hostilities between long-term residents and newer arrivals in the sleepy hipster mecca of Hudson, New York, reached a new level of menace on Wednesday, when hundreds of transplants to the city awoke to find their front doors smeared with pig's blood.

"As far as we can tell, none of the doors of native Hudsonians were marked," said Hudson Police Department Chief Earl Propst. "And as far as we can tell, every home where a more recent arrival was staying was marked with blood. Sometimes multiple marks on one door. One for every New Yorker who was there that night. Even Airbnbs that are owned by native Hudsonians, but where a non-local was staying. It's terrifying, really, to think of how someone could have all that information."

In the fifteen years since new money started flowing to this depressed Rust Belt city, hit hard by economic decline like so many other industrial cities around the country, animosity between the new and the old has been set to a low simmer. But in the past two months this conflict was turned up to a rolling boil—most recently crystallizing around the revelation that famed billionaire Jark Trowse, one of the architects of the Hudson Renaissance and a candidate for mayor, had had sex with a minor, and recorded a video of it, and posted the video online . . . the day after he was elected. The boy, the son of one of Hudson's best-loved religious leaders, committed suicide. This just days after the son of the outgoing mayor took his own life via a very public self-immolation at a crowded train station.

And with the ominous biblical appearance of blood smeared on doors, many of the people who helped build the New Hudson are suddenly afraid that resentment will soon lead to violence.

"What this says to me is, we know who you are, and we know where you are," said Giulia Varese, the famed "East Coast Garden Queen" of the popular television series by that name. "And we want you to be afraid." Until recently, Ms. Varese was one of Hudson's biggest boosters. Now, she says, she's already looking at properties across the river in the Catskills . . .

Mostly, I was exhilarated at the thought of all that blood on the doors. But I was also angry—that Attalah could have cut me out of something like this, that the proceedings were so far out of my hands—and afraid. Because what if it wasn't Attalah? Or what if Katch's whale ghost god monsters were influencing her now, and other people as well? What else might they have up their whale sleeves?

What other loved ones of mine will they snap?

Dom was right. Somehow, I had to stop them. Even if it meant going up against Attalah. For days I'd been trying not to admit that to myself. The only thing scarier than the thought of what they'd do to me if I tried was the thought of what they'd do to everyone around me if I didn't.

I put the books back. I headed home. I needed a shower before I could go confront Attalah.

I could feel it, now. Walking up Warren Street. The hate in the air. The fear. It thrummed like faraway thunder slowly unfurling, or a train whistle just far enough away to be audible only on a sub-conscious level. Everyone avoided eye contact, except for the people who held it for too long, and smiled like they were formulating un-pleasant plans for you. I looked for the blood, but of course it had already been scrubbed clean.

After Eighth Street, Warren gets weirdly quiet. For its last two blocks there are hardly any businesses, and the residences are stately old trophy homes not exactly popping with activity. I was relieved to be away from all that festering animosity—but I was also unsettled, to be away from watchful eyes. *Strangers keep you safe*, a junky told me once, pretty kid I was photographing down on the Bowery, for some awful clothing line that only hired "gritty-looking" nonpro-fessional models . . . and didn't last more than five seasons. *That's why we sleep in public places like Penn Station, even though that comes with the risk of cops fucking with you. Because it's worse other places, where no one can see. Friend of mine, his father was sleeping in an underpass when someone dumped gasoline on him and set him on fire.*

I took out my phone. What are phones for, if not to provide an illusory sense of safety? Of connection? An escape from the horrors of the real world, whether they're mild boredom or the fear of im-minent violence?

We should meet, I texted Attalah. You around in about an hour?

At the top of Warren Street, off to the right, there's a Car Care Center. Cars in need of care cram their little strip of land and overflow onto the street around it. When I'd been younger and their business was better, it had been a point of conflict between my father and the guy who ran it. After my mom died, my dad didn't give a shit how close those crummy cars got to our front lawn.

So I didn't think anything of it, walking between a bunch of broken-down cars on one side and a tall raggedy hedge on the other. Both had always been there.

"Hey," came someone's bark, so close I flinched.

Five people stepped out from between parked cars. Three men and two women, if I had to guess. And I did have to guess, because they wore black baggy nondescript clothes . . . and whales on their heads. Blue smiling papier-mâché sperm whales, oversize and cartoonish, except where some of them had been smeared with what I hoped was red paint and worried was not.

Also, they carried harpoons. And all you had to do was look at them to know they weren't papier-mâché, weren't fake. As close as these whale-headed marauders were standing, they could all five have run me through without taking a single step forward.

"Can I help you fine folks?" I said, one hand on my phone in my pocket.

They stepped forward. Made a circle around me. And I didn't budge. Didn't try to run or eyeball which one was weakest and surprise them with a kick to the balls and make a break for it. There was no fight in me. No flight.

One of them raised his harpoon. Pointed it at my face, mere inches from my eyes. I could smell the vanilla-petroleum tang of WD-40 on it.

So at least now I knew what it was like, for all those whales murdered for their blubber across the long decades of the whale oil trade. To be staring down the barrel of a bunch of cruel sharp metal blades perfectly engineered to cleave the blubber and pierce the inner organs.

I knew them. I had to. I went to school with them, probably. My father had given them slices of bologna when they were wide-eyed happy children who came to the butcher shop with their parents. Whatever they had come to do, I couldn't stop them.

"Do it if you're gonna do it," I said, and shut my eyes. I wouldn't beg. Not because I was proud or unafraid, but because right about then death didn't seem so bad. As a matter of fact, it sounded fantastic. An easy out from the stress and sadness I'd been suffering from since approximately forever . . . to say nothing of the hate I'd helped unleash. A just and fitting punishment, the kind that wiped slates clean in Hollywood movies.

A whistling noise jolted my eyes open—the blade whipped back. Somebody laughed. If they'd come to deliver a message, other than stark intimidation, they left without delivering it.

CHAPTER FORTY-SIX

When Lilly gets a text from Bergen, she is almost surprised that it makes her happy. Like, she's been missing him. Somehow.

Is it true you're going to see Jark today?

I am, she types. He's asked most of the department heads to come visit him. Now it's my turn.

They've all been working from home, since Jark's arrest. With all the death threats aimed at Penelope's Quilt, and the delivery of a big box with BOMB written all over it—although it turned out to just have rotten meat inside it—the board said it was better for everyone to stay in their homes where (hopefully) no one knows who they are.

Bergen types: You need to tell him to watch out. I had a dream. But not a dream. Where something awful happens to him. Happened. Will happen.

Lilly: A dream

Bergen: But not a dream. Tell him to watch out. What he thinks are dreams might not be. And vice versa. Tell him that?

Sure thing, she writes, wishing to cut short this session.

Oh good, she thinks. *It's not that I missed Bergen. It's that I missed the thrill of hating him.*

Lilly gets back into bed. She has work to do. So much work. Instead she takes a nap. Almost immediately she is floating beneath a sky full of stars, on a sea that stretches as far as the night.

．．．．．．．

THE POSTS GO UP AT 3:00 P.M. Hundreds of photographs, across multiple social media networks.

Disgusting stuff. Everything anyone ever shared with Tom Minniq on a sex app. All of the actual photographs, and countless fakes. Inflammatory images, expertly constructed for maximum rage. Cheating spouses in the throes of passion. Naughty nudes of the most proper people. Locals and newcomers alike.

Most come down within an hour or so, flagged as inappropriate by humans or by bots, but the damage is almost always already done. The people who needed to see them already saw. Lots of them downloaded copies. Plenty get mysteriously emailed as well, for the folks who aren't on social media.

．．．．．．．

THREE-THIRTY, and Lilly sits down across from Jark.

He isn't at the Hudson Jail. Security concerns prompted Chief Propst to move him to an undisclosed location. Fears of riots, assassination attempts. Even most of the other cops don't know where he is. The chief knows better than to assume anyone on the force would respect the law more than their own anger. So Lilly had to get the address from Jark's lawyer, which is how she is here—at the Hudson Library, which before being a library had been a mental institution and before that a foundlings' home, and both of those establishments had been in need of a cell in the basement for their most recalcitrant occupants. The library had used it for storage, but it had been easy enough to clear out the stuff and return it to its former function.

"Hey, Jark," she says, after two cops check her against a list and run her ID and lead her down to a low-ceilinged room. Smelling like mold and (*seawater?*) rotting books. Lit by a single standing lamp, whose cord trails out the door to an extension cord. A testament to the slipshod nature of the HPD's ability to handle this situation: the cord is an obvious suicide risk, but it was either that or let him sit in the dark.

"Hi, Lilly," he says, his voice low, his posture poor, the circles beneath his eyes immense. His cheeks are ragged with stubble. She's never seen them other than clean-shaven. "How's everybody doing?"

"We're pretty well fucked," she says. "I guess you know all that."

He nods. "Word is, the board is going to vote to remove me. And they've hired big-deal image consultants to consider a rebranding. Renaming. Whatever. They always said Penelope's Quilt was too complicated, we should just cut all that shit out and be a faster, better Etsy, and now they'll finally get to dumb it down the way they always wanted. What I meant was, how is everyone's morale?"

"That's the question I was answering."

Jark nods.

Disgust and anger war inside of her—but even here, even now, she is afraid of him. Years of working for him, and the big-boss billionaire is still in her head, even if he's not in the flesh. Even if now she knows what a monster he is.

"I've asked the board to allocate five million dollars to your department, under your control, to finance the completion of several projects that would open us up to potential lawsuits if we abandoned them. That part's not true, not entirely, but they don't need to know that."

At this, her jaw drops.

"They've said yes. It's already been set up. You'll be able to spend it however you want, although all of your expenditures will be tracked and subject to review by my lawyer. I'm going to beat this. It's bullshit, and I'll beat it in court. But that may take a while. In the meantime, I need the project to move forward. Bribe whoever you have to. Winter Fest has to go off without a hitch."

Can't he see it's finished? That it's all over for the Pequod Arms? How can he seriously think he'll beat this?

The best she can do is ask, "Why do you care so much about stupid Winter Fest?"

"Because it's a distraction. Keep all our enemies focused on that— meanwhile I got ten bulldozers lined up to start construction the next morning at multiple sites. Once the ground is broken, phase five will be a cinch."

Of course she nods. Smiles. Thinks: *You got our enemies focused on the Winter Fest, all right. So focused that we might all end up dead.* Thinks: *We're screwed, but I gotta do what I can do before the money all gets locked up . . . and before the blood starts flowing in the streets.*

And with five million dollars, maybe, just maybe, somehow, I can repair some of the damage that's been done. And stop the blood from flowing in the first place.

Five minutes later, she is walking back to her car. She doesn't notice the blue van parked down the block, where someone sits watching for her, just like she didn't notice them when they followed her to this facility.

. . . .

FOUR-FOURTEEN, and Officer Van Vleck gets fired. For sending dick pics to Rebecca, who works dispatch down at the police station. Which he swears he did not do, but he can't deny that's him in the pictures. Yes, he took them, yes he had them in a locked album on his online dating profile, so somebody must have hacked his phone—remotely, he hasn't had it out of his sight for days—and no, he doesn't know whether such a thing is possible, because he doesn't know anything about hacking, but it must be possible, because it happened.

He cries, and Chief Propst changes his dismissal to indefinite suspension without pay, pending an investigation—which is really just a deferral of the firing, to get him out of his office.

Four-thirty, and Bergen's mother deletes the email her son sent her, with the video attachment, the one she only saw three seconds of—proud of herself, at first, because she only recently mastered the occult art of downloading and viewing attachments—and then, horrified—because someone had filmed her son performing oral sex on him. A mistake on Bergen's part, surely. He meant to send it to someone else. This is just how kids are, these days. She saw something about it on a talk show. With their cell phones and their social media, making sex tapes as routinely and cheerfully as her generation went to the roller rink. She will never speak of this to anyone, least of all her son.

Four-fifty-seven and Lettie creates a brand-new email address, HudsonNeedsToKnowTheTruthAboutPastorRoss@gmail. First name Concerned; last name Jehovah's Witness. She attaches the fifteen obscene photographs that arrived via WhatsApp from the pastor, along with a sixteenth—a screencap of the text message that accompanied them, Why don't you get your ass over here and help me out with all this. She copies and pastes five hundred email addresses from the "To" field of the last church newsletter. Pastor Ross never did get the whole concept of a BCC.

Five-twenty, and sixteen-year-old Kenny Paddock comes home from football practice, walks in his front door, catches an aluminum baseball bat to the stomach. His fourteen-year-old brother Donnie swung it, and he swings it again, hitting Kenny in the side, screaming. Kicking. Because who else but his big brother could have filmed him masturbating, and logged in to Facebook as Donnie and posted it to his own page?

Later, at the hospital, Donnie wants to ask the doctor to take a look at his ribs—see if she can figure out what this weird jagged thing beneath his skin is, lodged between two ribs, and why it hurts so bad—but decides to stay quiet about it. He's already in enough trouble when his father finds out what he did to Kenny. If it turns out he's got something wrong with him, the kind of something that costs money to fix, it'll be so much worse for him.

. . . .

NINE-FIFTEEN P.M., and Eddie Roraback wakes up with the worst headache he's ever had in his life. The owner of Town & Country Realty just got over a nasty case of explosive diarrhea picked up at the election night party, so he assumes it's some lingering consequence of that. Dehydration—even though he's been trying his hardest to drink lots of water—but why is his mouth so dry?—and why was he asleep at his kitchen table?—and why the hell can't he remember anything that happened that day, not since going to breakfast at the fancy restaurant that used to be the Columbia Diner, where he and most of the realtors in Hudson met to try to figure out what the fuck to do to survive the present storm—but he doesn't remember what they decided, doesn't remember much at all—

And why is there . . . is that hair? . . . all over his kitchen table. Dirty blond, short and thin. Like his own.

In dawning horror, he raises his hands to feel his head—where all his hair has been shaved off. Wind licks the side of his face, from the broken window of his back door.

Someone drugged me. Then they broke into my home while I was unconscious, and cut off all my hair. But who would do such a thing, and why?

There's a printout, a black-and-white photo of three miserable women in a public square, weeping as all their hair is cut off. Surrounded by jeering, laughing neighbors. A headline explains: *Resis-*

tance Fighters Shave the Heads of French Women Who Collaborated with German Occupiers during World War Two. There's also a button: YOU ARE HATED.

Later he'll call his colleagues, learn that the same thing happened to four of them. One of them will drive up to Albany Medical—because Columbia-Greene couldn't get a goddamn pregnancy test right—and in two days they'll get the results, traces of Rohypnol in their system—they'd been roofied—and they'll call the cops. By then the cops will be too busy.

CHAPTER FORTY-SEVEN

RONAN

Rain was falling when I left the house, and by the time I got down to the river it had turned to snow. It cast a hush across the city, the river and the valley sitting in silence. At the boat launch I sat on the metal guardrail and watched the water. Most of the boats had already been taken out, dragged to dry dock. Dom's was still there.

My father hadn't been in the living room when I left. I knocked on his bedroom door and he didn't answer. I decided to let him sleep.

I sat for a long time, in the snow. Trains passed, heading north to Canada or south to New York City. On my phone I'd called up the schedule, even selected a ticket on the 5:34 P.M. back to the city. Entered my credit card number. But I couldn't click Buy. I couldn't go. Not alone.

Evening; the sky and the water and the Catskills all deep shades of blue slowly blackening. No wind. The snow fell heavy and straight and deliberate. Clump flakes, widely spaced. I wondered which of the sixty words for snow this one was. My father and mother and I used to come here, after going out to eat. We ate out a lot. Most of the restaurants in town bought meat from my dad, and half of them owed him money at any given moment. Business was shit for everyone. My dad made the most of it. And afterward we'd come here, breathe the fresh air, go for a little walk along the edge of the water. For as long as I was small enough, he'd hoist me up onto his shoulders. I could see so much more that way.

They came easier, now. The memories of him. And of my mom.

A truck came, with a flat pronged trailer behind. I knew it would. Who knows how. I knew it would come, and I knew they would both be inside. Maybe that was more of Hudson's metaphysical caul in action.

"Ronan?" Dom said, getting out once he'd backed the car into place at the water's edge. The trailer was mostly submerged.

"Hey," I said.

Attalah exited the car as well, and took his place behind the wheel. "Hello, Ronan," she said, and then rolled down the window to give Dom a thumbs-up.

I watched them work. They did this together every year. The banal, beautiful details of dry docking. Dom walked down to the boat, got in, started her up. Attalah got out and double-checked the trailer hitch. My throat hurt, watching. Seeing the well-oiled machine that they were. How their love had bonded them into something new.

Love could do that. It always did. It had bonded me and Dom, all those years ago, and we'd rebuilt that bond these last few months, but we'd never achieve something like what they had. What my parents had, down here in this very spot, holding hands and watching me run screaming after seagulls. Give love enough time, and it could weave people into a quilt as big as a city. With a hundred thousand threads. One for each of us.

That's what the whales had done, here in Hudson. They'd knotted us all up together into something that could keep us safe, even if it also kept us stunted.

The ache in my throat evolved, while I watched. As Dom drove the boat toward the trailer. As it slid neatly into place in the cleft of its prong. As he stepped down into the water, knee-high rubber boots keeping him dry, and began to loop and knot the ropes that bound the boat to the trailer. I realized: *I love them.* Above all things—above the town, above my pain and hurt over what had been done to it, above my hate, above my need for revenge for the people who'd lost their homes and the people who'd lost their minds. Above my need to punish people for what happened to my mom.

Dom walked out of the water. Went to the driver's door. Put his hand on the handle to let Attalah out.

I got up. I walked over. The three of us looked at each other without speaking. They were scared of me. I knew that. I was half crazy; I was an addict; I was accountable to nothing but my own savage inexplicable self. I had intruded upon their happiness. I was a threat to them. But I loved them. And I would do anything to keep them safe.

"We have to go," I said at last.

"Just stop, Ronan," Attalah said, still sitting behind the wheel.

"I'm serious. We have to leave here. Something really bad is going to happen."

"Something bad," Attalah said, and smirked. "What the fuck did you think would happen, when you released all those goddamn naked pictures?"

"That wasn't me," I said. "I know it sounds crazy but it wasn't me."

"Who was it?"

But I couldn't say it was Tom Minniq. Dom might be open to seeing the possibility of supernatural intervention here in Hudson, but I knew damn sure Attalah wasn't.

"I don't know. I got hacked. I . . ." I let my voice trail off.

Dom's lips pressed tight together. He was trying not to say something. But I saw it in his eyes. Their fear; their comprehension. Still beautiful; still wide and round and brown-by-gold, but broken now. The tiniest of cracks in his unbreakable confidence in the world's essential goodness. Dom had come undocked. He knew.

He believed. "I think Ronan might be right," he said, at last. "We have to leave here."

"I've got money," I said. "Jark's last check cleared, before they froze his assets. We could get adjoining suites at the fucking Waldorf-Astoria for a goddamn year. Or, you know, if you'd rather, you guys can stay there, and I can go back to my apartment and leave you alone. Whatever you want. But for the next couple of weeks, at least, if not months, I think—"

"Stop," Attalah said, and I heard an anger there I'd never heard before. By the look on Dom's face, I doubted he'd heard it too many times himself. "Both of you, just stop. We're not leaving. You can go if you want to, Ronan—I think it'd be best for all of us if you did. But we're not."

My hand moved to my throat, as if she'd punched it. "Please, Attalah. You can't mean—"

"You're goddamn right I mean it," she said, and got out of the truck. Slammed the door. "You've done enough damage. I don't know what kind of hurt feelings or lingering adolescent trauma motivated you to get involved here—and I am grateful to you for your help in getting this all started—but it's bigger than you, and it's bigger than me, and I'm not going to let your weakness or your selfishness or *whatever*—"

"Hey," Dom said, putting a hand on her arm. "Come on now. There's no need to get personal. Ronan's right. Things are happening that are scary as hell, and I'm actually actively frightened. I want us to go. To get the hell out. Before . . . I don't know. Before things get really ugly."

She took hold of his hand and lifted it off of her arm. Pushed it back at him, like a gift refused. "You think I don't know? Are you really that naive?"

"I'm sure you know all about what's coming," Dom said. "Because I'm sure you're involved. Okay? Of course I know that, Attalah. That's the biggest reason why I want us to get the fuck out of here. I can't lose y—"

"No, Dom," she said, and looked from him to me to him to me. "I'm not talking about any of that."

Dom physically flinched. He got it several milliseconds before I did. "Honey . . ."

"You think I don't know that you two are fucking?"

Dom took a step back. Like now it was him she'd punched, with words.

Sweet-smelling diesel billowed out of the muffler. In the cab of the truck, the radio was playing. Miss Jackson introduced "One Is the Loneliest Number."

"Attalah," I said. "I am so, so sorry."

She opened the driver's-side door and got inside. Dom looked at me. He was crying.

I took a step back.

They weren't mine. I loved them more than anything, but they were theirs. I wasn't worthy of what they had. There was no place for me. It'd been a mistake to believe there could be. A crime, to try to make one.

"We're not going anywhere," Attalah said.

A train whistle sounded, far behind us. The southbound from Albany. The 5:34. I watched it come, a tiny light in the blue distance getting bigger. I watched it wail past us, a clanking metal whale swimming through the dark.

$\mathcal{O}$

For two weeks, Morse Saulpaugh has been saving up dead rats. Only the biggest and goriest corpses will do.

In his job as an exterminator, he sees dozens of them every day. Finds them in traps, or dead of poison. Hudson has always had an astonishingly large rat problem, for a city its size. Morse has friends in the business down in Poughkeepsie, and they're shocked by what he describes. His previous boss blamed bootlegger tunnels—old Hudson lore, allegedly connecting key buildings all over town, a secret rat kingdom. No one's ever seen these tunnels, but still.

So. Rat corpses. He's got some good ones. And before dawn— dressed in black—he places them all up and down the 600 block of Union Street—the fanciest block of the most expensive street in Hudson. He puts rats in mailboxes. On car seats (and isn't it amazing, how in this day and age so many people still leave their cars unlocked?). He walks right up onto porches and opens screen doors and wedges a body in place, so when they open their front doors to go to work in the morning a big dead stinky rat will roll over onto their feet.

He couldn't say for sure why he does it. Most of his business is with the new arrivals. He's never had any particular ill will toward them, no more than the standard hate he harbors for all humanity in general. Something is just in the air. Something exciting, inspiring, invigorating.

He hides his rats, and he parks his car, and he watches. Smokes cigarettes, lighting one off the other.

Here's the thing: no one does not scream. Even the boldest and bravest cry out in terror or shock at the sight of a big bloody possum-size rat. Down the block some fucking New Yorker fruitcake opens his car door, wails in fright, staggers backward, falls on his ass.

Morse laughs, but the laugh collapses into a cough, and the cough fucking hurts. His emphysema has been getting so much worse lately. Something is pressing down on his lungs. Something big, and jagged. He can feel it with his fingers. Poking out between his ribs in six different places. He never heard of lung cancer being hard and pointy, but what the fuck else could it be?

....

ALMOST MIDNIGHT, by the time Treenie parks in the municipal lot. Her workday ran way long, running around trying to calm people down. The ones who want to sell, who she visited in person to try to talk them out of it, but also a ton of calls from panicky home owners already feeling the burn of fucking Attalah's fucking non-cooperation movement shit, who suddenly can't find anyone to put heating oil in their boilers or figure out why their HVAC isn't working. The last one stood her up; some guy she doesn't even remember selling to, who hit her up on Facebook Messenger and then totally ghosted. So she's exhausted *and* annoyed.

Force of habit that she parks in the lot. This late at night there'd be plenty of on-street parking. But during the day there never is, so she always parks in the lot, which is why even now, so late at night, that's where she goes. And regrets it, as soon as she hears her own car door slam behind her. The lot is empty. The spire of St. John's Lutheran Evangelical looms up above her. Prison Alley is long and hungry-looking. And the narrow walkway that leads to Warren Street, passing between Mane Street Hair Salon and the Department of Motor Vehicles, has never been so dark. A lesser woman would get back in her car, drive around to park on the street. But Treenie could never admit that kind of weakness to herself. Instead, she puts her keys between her fingers and marches forward.

During the day the walkway smells like fresh clean clothes. But now the laundromat is shut down for the day, and the only smell is distant wood smoke on the cold night air.

Treenie walks fast. On her right, halfway there, is a little nook with a set of benches and a sycamore tree. In high school she used to party there sometimes. It was a safe, dark nook to get up to no good in. Now someone is sleeping there. That happens, sometimes, these past few years. It never did back when she was young. People with nowhere else to go at night.

That's how you know we're a real city now, she thinks, and feels awful for it. *We have homeless people.*

Two of them, by the look of it. Maybe three. Huddled together for warmth, and safety. Sympathy slows her down—probably she knows them, probably she went to school with them. It's happened before. Heather Scutt was sleeping on that bench once. Poor sick Heather. Treenie went to visit her in the morning, with two cups of coffee. And took her down to Social Services to see if there was anything they could do for her.

There wasn't.

"Treenie Lazzarra," someone says, a deep voice, a woman's, trying to sound like a male's.

She looks up, cursing herself for letting her attention waver. Three figures step off the Warren Street sidewalk and onto the walkway. Wearing black, with—what is that on their heads? Some big oblong ovals, which make them look like they have freakishly large craniums.

Behind her, the people get up off the benches. There were indeed three of them. And they are also all dressed in black, and wearing shit on their heads. Except these ones are close enough that she can see what they are: blue smiling whales. Clumsy and dented and very clearly homemade.

Also, they're holding harpoons. All six of them are. And she's trapped between them.

"Shit," she says.

Overhead, there are lights in second- and third-story windows. If she screamed, would anyone care? Would they call the cops? Or were they in on it? Was everyone part of the great big YOU ARE HATED conspiracy?

"Your last appointment stood you up," says another whale person.

"That was you," she says.

They all laugh. They all come closer.

"I'm not scared of you," she says, and she's surprised to find that she's really not.

"We don't need you to be scared," says the woman trying to sound like a man, who has stepped forward from the rest. She's wearing red All-Stars, Treenie notices. It's the only detail she can see on any of them. Already she's preparing for the statement she'll make to the police, when these fucking assholes finish trying to freak her out and run away like the cowards that they are. "We just need you to be dead. You fucking collaborator."

Another whale person—a man, and a chubby one, to judge by his body—hoists his harpoon. All six of them step forward, closing the distance between them all. She's in harpoon-stabbing range for the chubby man now, and still she's not afraid.

"Are you a whale, or are you a whaler?" Treenie asks. "You're mixing your metaphors. And you're not gonna do shit. So why don't you just run along home?"

But then the man thrusts his harpoon forward and stabs her in the leg. The kind of cut that's meant to scare, and wound, but not kill. And Treenie does feel fear, but only for a second.

For Treenie is a true child of Hudson. She combines both Town & Country, just like the name of the oldest realty spot on Warren Street. *Town* in that she owns a pistol, carries it with her everywhere. And *Country* in that she used to go hunting with her father and her brothers, and she has pretty solid aim.

The gun is in her pocket. She pulls it out, swift and steady and unhurried, thumbing off the safety. She shoots the chubby man in the head, and shoots twice more at the whalers behind him. One drops. The other runs. It's the one in the red sneakers, and this upsets her more than being stabbed, the fact that this bitch got away.

From behind her, someone throws a harpoon. She feels it hit her in the side, but her adrenaline is thumping now. That old cheerleader energy that let her power through practice sessions when she knew her knees were already on their way out.

Treenie swings around. They're already running. She shoots three shots. One yelps, hit, but keeps running. One falls to the ground, holding his stomach. Screaming. His whale mask rolls off when he hits the sidewalk. She recognizes him. Of course she does. Couple years older than her. His sister was in her high school class. Can't remember her name, or his, and that's a bad sign. Maybe it's the animal frenzy that's taken over her body, and maybe the wound in her side is more serious than she thought. She debates picking up one of the dropped harpoons and jamming it down his wide red screaming mouth, but decides it'll be much better if the cops get to take a crack at him. Find out who his accomplices were. Who that bitch in the red shoes is. *Death is too good for you*, Treenie debates saying, liking the badass sound of it in her head, and then she passes out.

. . . .

GUNSHOTS WAKE LILLY UP. They wake up half of Hudson, but most people roll over and go back to sleep. Lilly can't. Because she has been having the most horrific nightmares of drifting on a midnight ocean (*dreamsea*) for hours now. Bright indifferent stars; calm waters.

And also, because someone is in her apartment.

In her room, in fact. It's totally dark, with her blackout curtains on—lately it's been harder and harder to sleep at all—but she can hear them. Scratching. Five fingers, clawing at the walls. Right next to her bed. If Lilly moved her leg the slightest bit to the left, she'd touch them.

What the fuck

What the fuck

What the absolute fuck

Maybe if I lie here and don't say or do a thing they'll leave

But she knows better. She knows that won't work, just like she knows this is not a dream. She knows all kinds of things, now. *It's Hudson,* she thinks. *Hudson has gotten inside of me and I am a part of it now, even if—or maybe because—it also wants to destroy me. And that person in the room is clawing away at the wallpaper and their fingernails are long and sharp and they are giving off a smell like the inside of a long-abandoned warehouse but also like rotting flowers and sour alcohol and they have come for me.*

"You're awake," comes a woman's voice.

As quietly as possible, Lilly reaches for her phone. Finds it. Squeezes the side to turn it on.

Its light barely makes a difference. She can just make out the shape of a woman, tall and thin and skittish, and see what's on the wall where she's scratched away almost all of the wallpaper.

A painting, of a night sea. Indifferent stars. Precisely what she'd been dreaming of.

"This is my home," the woman says. "This was my bedroom, when I was a little girl. These were my walls. I still come here when I dream."

"How did you get in here?" Lilly asks, her own voice startling her. She didn't mean to be so loud. She'd underestimated the silence.

"No door is closed to me," she says, and turns away from the wall for the first time.

Her eyes are wild. Her face is haggard. Lilly can see all that, even in such little light. She picks up Lilly's cat-eye glasses from the bedside table and wrinkles her nose. Then she puts them on.

"My father lost the house," she whispers. "Couldn't pay his mortgage anymore, when our business died. Forced to sell it. New guy kept us on for a while, but once my father died he jacked up the rent. Said he had to." She laughs. "Sure. He *had to* kick us the hell out so he could rent it to little asshole rich kids like you."

Lilly hears sirens. Responding to the gunshots, most likely. Certainly not coming to rescue her. She is on her own. Alone with a crazy person with a chip on her shoulder.

"I'm sorry," Lilly says. "I'm really sorry that happened to you. But I'm not a rich kid. I'm just—"

"If you can pay fifteen hundred dollars a month for an apartment I couldn't pay five hundred for, you're a damn sight richer than me, kid."

Lilly stops. Knows this is true.

The woman takes off the glasses. Puts them back where she found them. Sits down on the bed beside her. Springs creak. Lilly draws her legs in, pulls herself up into a seated fetal position. Anything to get away from this woman. She can smell death wafting out of her pores, the fermented stink of an alcoholic who's spent decades pickling herself.

"Have you ever been evicted?" the woman asks.

"No." A whisper; a tiny one.

"It hurts so bad. You can't imagine. Before my father died, I couldn't imagine how much that would hurt. I thought I was ready for it, but it split me open from the inside. Have you had a parent die?"

Another tiny "no."

"It's not the same, of course. Getting evicted. But it's not that different." She leans forward, puts her face near Lilly's. "I wish I could make you feel it." But her voice isn't unkind.

"What's your name?" Lilly whispers. Police procedures ring in her head: *humanize yourself to your hostage takers.* "I'm Lilly."

"Heather," she says. "Heather Scutt. My father used to own—"

"Scutt's Scrapyard," Lilly says.

"That's right," Heather says, pleased. "Everybody knew him."

"What do you want?" Lilly asks.

"I want my room back," Heather says. "I came here planning to take it."

Lilly thinks of the blood on the doors, the locks that don't keep out marauders. They were fools to come here, all of them. Criminally arrogant, ignorant, to have believed they could claim it for themselves. This town was not just a jumble of streets, old homes, wood and stone and soil and shrubs. It was something more. Something (*monstrous*) alive. It would never belong to them. And it would destroy them all before it let them change it.

"I want my home," Heather says, and Lilly's never heard a voice so full of hurt and fear. "But I can't have that."

A train whistle wails. More sirens.

"That's the ambulance," Heather says. "In school they used to teach us the difference between the different sirens. Did you know that when the fire alarms go off, the rhythm of the blasts tells you where in town the fire is happening? Used to be all the young men were in the volunteer fire corps, so when the alarm went off they could take off running in the right direction."

"I didn't know that," Lilly says, wondering how that's possible— one more thing that every Hudson local knew by heart, that she'd never even imagined. *Hudson past and Hudson present, two separate planets,* she thinks, wondering if it was possible to bridge that gulf. Again she thinks of the app or grad student thesis she dreams of one day making. *The PastIsAPresent; PastIsPresent.* Panicky brains make the strangest leaps.

"All four ambulances," Heather says, and Lilly swears she can hear fear in her voice. "Never heard that before. Something really bad must have happened."

"Do you want to turn on the radio?" Lilly says.

"No," Heather says, a little girl afraid in the dark. Just like her. "Whatever it is, I don't want to know."

The sirens diminish slightly, heading downstreet.

"Something really bad is coming," Heather says. "Or it's already here, and it's just getting started. I'm so scared, Lilly."

"Me too, Heather."

Heather's hand fumbles in the bedsheets. Lilly reaches out and grabs it. The fingers are freezing, dry and old. They clasp hands, hold tight.

CHAPTER FORTY-NINE

WINTER FEST WILL PROCEED, AGAINST OBJECTIONS—THE HUDSON GAZETTE [EXCERPT]

Mayor Nathan Coffin announced this morning on WRGB—and on Twitter—that this evening's Winter Fest will take place as planned.

The controversial decision came after days of demands from both sides of the recent war over Hudson's future that the event be canceled or postponed until cooler heads could prevail.

"We've beefed up the security and scaled back the venue," he said, "in anticipation of smaller crowds, and in the hopes of better ensuring the safety of all concerned, we'll gather at the Hudson boat launch."

Responses to the announcement ranged from celebratory to antagonistic, with some Twitter users saying "Goddamn right, we're not going to let a bunch of thugs ruin our good time," and others tweeting at the mayor "DIE YOU FAT FUCKING SELL-OUT WHALE."

. . . .

Wallace Warsaw works his contacts, struggling—after all that's happened—to summon the stern clout he used to carry. To cajole, to browbeat, to plead when he has to. Whatever it takes to get people there.

Treenie Lazzarra posts from her hospital bed, blitzing social media to beg people to turn out. I'm stuck in this hospital bed with a damn harpoon wound, so there'll be no Winter Fest for me. Doctor's orders. But I implore the rest of you, don't let them take this away from us. And don't let them try to tell you this is an Old-Hudson-vs-New-Hudson thing. It was never about old vs. new. If it was, I wouldn't have gotten stabbed—my family's been in Hudson three generations. No, this is about the people who want to keep Hudson for themselves, even if it means staying a depressed miserable middle-of-nowhere, and those who want to actually build a future. Together. We've worked hard to turn this [. . .]

． ． ． ． ． ． ．

ZELDA IS MAKING TURN-OUT CALLS, too, but to a much smaller set of people. These are not random seat fillers, a wide net intended to swell the crowd. Everyone Zelda calls has a very specific task to accomplish tonight. She doesn't look up when someone knocks at the door of her office down at CPS. "Come in," she barks.

"You got a minute?" Attalah asks, sticking her head in the door.

"Of course," she says, but still doesn't look up. Hopes that this will convey that she doesn't have a minute, has barely thirty seconds for whatever foolishness she's come for.

"You doing okay?" Attalah asks, sitting down across the desk from Zelda. "You look" (*like shit*) (*like you haven't slept in days and are fiending for some kind of drug that does terrible things to your skin and eyes*) "tired."

"You don't look so hot yourself," Zelda says, finally taking in the lack of makeup on Attalah's face, the slightly-less-than-immaculate clothes she's wearing. Attalah's off days look a damn sight better than most people's on days.

"Been going through a tough patch in my personal life. Just between us. Some super upsetting stuff has been happening. I'll leave it at that."

"I hear you," Zelda says, turning off her computer screen, leaning back. She wonders if Attalah knows she knows exactly what she's talking about. If she's aware what the Hudson rumor mill is handing around, about Attalah's choir-boy husband. She permits herself a moment of unclenching. A deep breath, even.

"What have you got planned for tonight?"

Zelda smiles. "Don't worry about it, Attalah. We got this under control."

"I don't doubt it. And I want to help."

"I don't think you do," Zelda says, reveling in this rare instant of superiority. Of power. Nothing ever made her feel powerful before, outside of bed or substance abuse. "I know you, Attalah. You talk a good game, about fighting the power and all that shit, but at the end of the day all you want is to make the machine run a little nicer. You don't want to break the damn machine in half. That's what we're going to do tonight."

"You *don't* know me," Attalah says, her voice dropping dangerously. "And you don't know *anything* about this machine you're talking about, if you think I don't want to fucking break it in half. Hard as you've had it in life, you haven't seen the tip of the iceberg of how it chews people up and spits them out. I'm not trying to say that Black people are the only ones getting fucked over by it. I'm saying no one has been fucked over as hard as we have. And whatever you're going through, little miss middle-class third-generation Irish daughter gone wrong, you never had to see your sister slowly wasting away over a fry vat at McDonald's because she couldn't go to college and that was the best she could do. You never saw your brother behind bars. Or your aunt's foot amputated because she didn't get the care for her diabetes she should have. Have you?"

Zelda shakes her head *no*.

"And you damn sure never had to know in your heart that the man you love most in the world is broken inside, because his dad raised him to believe that the best way for a Black man in this world to survive is to make his own needs less important than those of the white people around him, so he'd betray his marital vows just because his best friend needed him to."

Silence. So deep it seems like they can hear the hammering down at the waterfront. The Ferris wheel being assembled.

"So I want to know what you've got planned for tonight, and I want to help. I want to break the fucking machine into a thousand fucking pieces."

Zelda smiles. "Okay. Okay. Sorry, I just had to check. You know how it is."

"Of course," Attalah says, also smiling.

Zelda leans across the table and starts to talk.

. . . .

"I DON'T UNDERSTAND," weeps the man in the hospital bed. "I don't know how this could have happened."

"It's okay, Rudy," Dom says, rubbing his foot beneath the sheet. "Just tell me about that evening."

"That's the thing," he says. "It's all like a dream. The harpoon in my hand, the whale mask on my head, the fact that I'm fucking standing in the alleyway threatening Treenie Lazzarra, who was my sister's best fucking friend in high school . . . I don't remember how any of that happened. Just pieces. Moments. But, like, weird moments. Stuff that doesn't make sense. Like I was on a boat, like I was drowning. You know me, Dom. I'd never . . ."

Classic dissociative state, Dom thinks. Cop training comes back. Psych 101. *The brain, unable to process a traumatic event—or, the sense of self unable to accept its own culpability in that event, clouds the memories until they no longer make sense.*

Either that, or the monsters made him do it, too.

"We need to know who you were with," Dom says. "That's all.

Because they're probably planning to hurt more people, and I know you don't want that."

Rudy starts crying again. Dom comes around to hold his hand.

"We only wanted to scare her. That's what we said. I know that much. I never . . . I wouldn't have . . ."

"Who's *we*, Rudy?"

"I got some kind of crazy tumor," Rudy said, tapping at his chest. "I thought I was imagining it but the doctors saw it on the X-ray. They tried to take a piece to biopsy it and they said it's made of fucking metal, like old shrapnel, except I was never in a goddamn war, never got shot, wounded"—and here his voice rises to a shriek—"So how the hell did it get under my skin, Dom?"

Oh good, Dom thinks. *He's lost his fucking mind.*

. . . .

"WE'RE NOT GOING to hurt the four of them," Zelda says, at last. "We just want to humiliate them. Make an example of them. It'll be unpleasant, for sure, but we mean them no harm."

She leans back. Puts her feet up on the desk. Red Converse All-Stars.

Attalah doesn't say anything at first. Then she grins. "You have no idea how excellent that sounds to me. How can I help?"

. . . .

LILLY'S PHONE KEEPS PINGING. Assembly of the Ferris wheel is all finished; all ten bulldozers have been dropped off at the construction sites; enough gasoline cannisters to power a fleet of band saws and jackhammers and forklifts. Come Monday morning, the Pequod Arms will be under way. And unstoppable.

None of that feels real.

Two dirty mugs sit on her kitchen table. They feel real.

Lilly made hot chocolate, for her and Heather. They sat in the dark until the sun started to rise, and then Lilly got up and went to the kitchen. She'd briefly entertained the idea of calling the cops to report the woman for breaking and entering. She was crazy, yes, but who could blame her? Lilly had never really thought about it before: how traumatic an eviction would be. She can't imagine what something like that would do to her.

So Lilly made Heather hot chocolate instead of calling the cops on her. And sat with her, and talked. And thought. And planned. Read a ton of stuff, online, about evictions. And alternatives. By daylight Heather looked even more worn and frayed than she had seemed in the dark. A lot sadder. Like she'd come to some decision, and it was nothing good.

．．．．．．．

OFFICER PADDOCK IS ALONE on guard duty inside the old library when they come. His partner has the car; is making a run to Bagel Tyme. He's surprised that they got past the high-tech lock on the back door, but only for a second. Of course they got in. All the members of the board of directors of the library have key cards. *Chief Propst probably miscalculated. He would have known that they'd have keys, but must have figured they're all upstanding citizens, pillars of the community, and they'd never be a party to any vigilante murder nonsense.*

All of this is happening at a glossy black-and-white slow-mo remove. The people with whales on their heads pointing harpoons at his belly, they can't be real. Can't be serious.

One of them says, "You know why we're here, Joe."

"I guess I do."

"You gonna let us take him?" says another, a woman. "Or are you going to die to protect a fucking pedophile rapist?"

"Well, when you put it like that," Officer Paddock says.

In the movies, the cops who fold like cowards always ask to get beat up a little, a black eye or flesh wound to show they tried their hardest to do their jobs. Officer Paddock doesn't much feel like any of that. He hands them the keys and steps aside. Two go downstairs to grab Jark Trowse. Two remain to keep their harpoons aimed for his soft and squishy parts, in case he gets any funny ideas about calling for help. Once they've gotten what they want, one will remain behind for ten minutes to make sure he doesn't summon the cavalry.

It's unnecessary, all of it. Joe Paddock has never been one for funny ideas.

....

IT'S PURE DUMB LUCK that Attalah stops by the office of UPLIFT Hudson on her way to her first Zelda errand. She rarely does these days. The staff she hired runs the arts programming, the youth work. She just needed something familiar, something stable.

"Mrs. Morrison?" asks an eager but wild-eyed young white woman as soon as she walks in the door.

"Yes?"

"My name's Lilly, and I work for Penelope's Quilt. I know that doesn't exactly predispose you toward kindness toward me, but—there's something we'd like to offer you."

Pure dumb luck, too, for this lost little girl, that Attalah says yes. Leads her into her office. She hadn't planned on it. Wouldn't normally. Doesn't want any of the things that Penelope's Quilt has tried to offer her over the years. Mountains of money; a big brand-new space. *We want to be good neighbors,* said the guy they used to send—this girl's boss, probably, a white man with soft hands, who believed his good intentions made up for all the damage he caused. She never took any of it, no matter how badly she needed the resources. Once she did, she'd be hooked. Unable to say a single bad word about them, ever again. It'd have been different if she could have used that money to meaningfully fight to protect her people, stop the displacement. But no. They were too smart for that.

So whatever this girl has come to offer? It isn't anything Attalah wants.

Except information. The company's back is up against the wall. Whatever she came for, whatever she needs—she'll probably spill plenty, without even meaning to.

"What can I do for you, Lilly?" Attalah asks once they are sitting down in her office. "It's a busy day for me, as I imagine it is for you. Big plans for this evening."

"Yes," Lilly says, not taking the bait. "I'm sorry. I'll make this quick. We're in a weird position over at Penelope's Quilt these days. With J—with our CEO in jail, the board of directors is trying to steer the ship, but our CEO always kept them in the dark about day-to-day operations—didn't want them interfering in the work too much. He still doesn't. So he has given a ton of power and resources to a bunch of the department heads. And, well, some of us—mostly just me—we want to do something with that money that's actually helpful to Hudson."

Attalah smirks. "Like what? A scholarship in your name? New books for the library?"

"This is going to sound crazy," Lilly says. "And I haven't thought it through, not really. And I don't have a ton of time before the board figures out what's up and moves to regulate the resources I'm sitting on. Two, three days tops. So what I'm asking is for you to sign on to something super vague and full of kinks to be worked out."

"Tell me." Attalah has to fight to keep a dismissive edge out of her voice.

"I want to establish Hudson as an Eviction Free Zone, calling for a moratorium on police involvement in execution of eviction proceedings and asking landlords to sign a pledge. Penelope's Quilt owns five buildings around town, and we'd sign the no-evictions pledge and work to get our friends and donors to sign on, too. I know it sounds crazy, but it's been done in other cities. I think it's the only way that we who've helped displace so many people can start to help heal Hudson." Attalah starts to say something dismissive, and Lilly adds: "Also, I have five million dollars that I want to put into a fund for low-income tenants who are in rent arrears, and for legal representation in eviction proceedings. I hoped your organization could administer it."

Attalah keeps her face expressionless. What she's offering—that could change everything. Assuming this girl even knew what she was talking about. Assuming they didn't snatch this ball out of her hands the next morning and fire her just for thinking of such a thing.

Lilly puts a five-million-dollar check down on the table, made out to UPLIFT Hudson.

"Tell me more," Attalah says, stealing a quick glance at the clock.

. . . .

HIS FIRST THOUGHT WAS, *They murdered my dog.*

Rob Creighton came out back and found his beloved rescue pit bull Bethesda covered in blood. Fresh off the trauma of a rancid meat terrorist attack on his antique store, along with seven others, it really wasn't an unreasonable assumption.

But, no. Bethesda was fine. Pleased as punch with herself. She had just been having some fun with the giant dead rat someone tossed over the fence into his backyard, that's all.

They want me to have a nervous breakdown, Rob thinks. *But I will not.*

He goes and gets the gun he's never shot in his life, never even loaded, just keeps around to potentially scare someone should the need ever arise. He swings by Wal-Mart on the way to Winter Fest for bullets.

All over Hudson, similar decisions are being arrived at. All together, eighteen ordinary otherwise-innocent citizens put weapons in their pockets or purses or backpacks when they head out to Winter Fest.

....

THREE HUNDRED HARPOONS are heaped in the back of a truck.

Ten bulldozers are parked in construction sites around the city. Six canisters of gasoline at each site as well.

Fifty-seven people are waiting to spring into action. Staring at the clock. Watching the sun set. Checking their cell phones every five minutes.

CHAPTER FIFTY

RONAN

I slept for fifteen hours after leaving Dom and Attalah down at the boat launch. After Attalah took my heart in her hands and ripped it in half.

Not that she was wrong. That's why the breaking hurt so bad. Why I slept for so long. Why I would have slept forever if I could, or stopped breathing altogether.

My ticket was bought. By 7:00 P.M. Winter Fest would be under way, and I'd be on a southbound train speeding under the Rip Van Winkle Bridge, returning to my real life. For a glorious couple of months I'd been able to convince myself that *this* was my real life, *this* was my place, but that couldn't be true. Attalah was right. Someone as twisted up inside as me could do nothing but damage here. My accidental white savior act had ruined everything. I'd had a dream that I belonged somewhere, and it was a wonderful dream. But now I had to wake up.

I packed. The suits and nice shirts I'd bought—I left them on the floor. They belonged to that other Ronan, the one who could move in the same circles as the obscenely rich. Who could smile in their faces, shake their hands, drink their single-malt scotch. Trick them. Manipulate them. Make them fall screaming into his traps.

My father still wasn't in his recliner. I made coffee, enough for two. Set out our mugs.

Could you break a power of attorney? Or sign it over to someone else? I'd give it to Margie if I could. Hand her a chunk of Jark's blood money. Too late to get the butcher shop back; too late to stop the Renaissance from snapping the spine of whatever was left of the Old Hudson. I'd have to live with that. Another thing Attalah was right about: even if the Pequod Arms were folded forever, we couldn't stop what was coming. Not without horrific violence, or unthinkable effort exerted by both sides.

"Dad?" I asked, knocking on his bedroom door.

No answer. I pressed my ear to the door.

Wind whistled. I dropped to my knees, pressed my fingers to the floor. Freezing.

I jumped up, tried the door. Locked.

"Dad!" I cried, and pounded hard against it.

Here's a thing I never thought I could do: break down a door. But I did it. Rammed my body into it as hard as I could, three or four times. Fucked my shoulder up something fierce. Door didn't budge. So I got a hammer and broke the doorknob off, then hammered the lock all the way out. Door swung in.

Window wide open. Drift of snow on the sill. So cold in there I could see my breath.

"Dad?" I whispered, waiting for my eyes to adjust, knowing he wasn't there.

His bed was made. The way *he* used to make it—folded corners, turned-down bedspread—not the simple spread sheet and flattened spread that Marge favored. I checked in the closet, and under the bed, but he wasn't anywhere.

I called Margie. It went to voice mail. I hung up.

Beeps from the kitchen: the coffee was ready. I poured myself a mug—my father's—and plopped myself down in his recliner. Sat there in despair for ninety seconds and then dialed her number again.

Margie, please, I said in my message. Call me back? It's Ronan. Whatever you did with my dad—I just, I need to know he's okay. Okay? Just call me to tell me he's okay.

I was halfway through that pot of coffee when the doorbell rang. I leapt up, ran to it. Yanked it open, all eager idiot optimism, so that my right shoulder screeched in agony.

"Hi, Ronan," Attalah said.

"What's up?" I asked—suspicious, hopeful.

"Can I come in?" she asked. "I wanted to tell you something."

"Sure," I said, stepping aside. "Did you want coffee? I just made some."

"No, thank you," she said, her heavy body pressing against mine as she navigated the narrow space. "I'm sorry, Ronan. I'm so sorry."

"Oh, Attalah," I said, but I only had a split second for euphoria— *Everything is okay! She forgives me! We can be a family again! I'll never touch her husband again but the three of us will be best friends and we'll go bowling and on photo shoots and to the diner and we'll fight the power and be together forever here in our city, our home, our life*— astonishing how many words a desperate human brain can manage in a split second—before I saw that she wasn't sorry for what she'd said down at the waterfront. She was sorry for what she was doing now, pushing me hard against the door and clamping a wet hand-kerchief to my mouth. *Tastes like bitter fruit*, I thought, and then I didn't think anything.

CHAPTER FIFTY-ONE

The night smells like cotton candy no one wanted. Carnival food stalls line the back of the boat launch parking lot, all of them looking lonely. Fried Oreos; bright red candy apples. All for the kids who hadn't come. *Somebody should probably have called these vendors up a couple of days ago,* Lilly thinks, *scaled it back. Paid them a kill fee and told them not to come.* But what did it matter, really? More of Jark's money pissed away. Who cares? And do carnies even have kill fees?

The night is cold. Snow comes and goes. The Ferris wheel is still dark, looming ten stories high in the night beside her. Music blares through shitty speakers, old holiday hits, Black musicians exploited by white producers.

Lilly accidentally makes eye contact with a woman working one of the food stalls. And so, out of pity, she buys a candy apple. Dark red coating, peanut-studded. She doesn't intend to eat it. Still has some residual fear, from a prepubescent Coney Island trip where her mother told her *Don't eat those, they sit there for months and the coating is hard as glass and you'll crack your teeth and the shards will cut your gums to ribbons.*

She takes a bite. The coating is soft, the flesh firm. It is delicious. For a moment she feels like she's gotten away with something, and then she snaps back to the moment. She can't let down her guard; can't pretend like they're out of the woods. Winter Fest only formally started five minutes before. So much could go wrong.

. . . .

"HUDSON POLICE DEPARTMENT," Rebecca says, caught off guard by the call. Almost an hour since the last one.

She should be happy, to have had so few calls tonight. She's been praying for a quiet night, throughout these past couple weeks of nonstop fuckery.

Instead, she's afraid.

"Hey, Rebecca," says a familiar voice.

"Hey, Attalah. What's happening?"

"Not a whole lot."

Rebecca hears wind whistling in the background. "Surprised you're not down at the Winter Fest," she says. "You're not scared, are you? You wouldn't be the only one. Tons of my friends won't go because they're convinced some damn lunatic will start shooting people. Or, I don't know, stabbing people with harpoons."

"What's the word from the officers down that way?" Attalah asks. "I'm heading there shortly."

"All quiet on the western front."

"That's good. Listen, Rebecca. I need you to do me a huge favor. It's kind of an emergency."

"Of course," Rebecca says. "Whatever I can do."

"I know this is going to breach six hundred different kinds of protocol, but you have to trust me that this is the best thing to do."

"Sure," Rebecca says, eying the dispatch board uncertainly.

"I need you to radio Dom for me. Okay?"

"Why don't you call him?" Rebecca says.

"We kind of had a fight. He's mad at me, and when he gets mad at me he stops taking my calls. And, honestly, every second counts right now. I need you to radio Dom and tell him to go to the Rip Van Winkle Bridge. Park his car on the Hudson side, without turning on the lights or sirens or anything. There's a jumper, out on the pedestrian walkway."

"Why don't we send an ambulance?" Rebecca asks. "If someone is experiencing a psychiatric emergency, we should send some trained professionals. Dom is a great detective, but he's no therapist. And in a situation like—"

"It's someone he knows," Attalah says. "Someone who trusts Dom, who would *not* trust a stranger. Even a trained mental health professional. Especially if they rolled up with flashing ambulance lights. So please, radio Dom and tell him to do this. And to hurry. And don't tell him I told you to call, or he'll think it's some weird scheme of mine, and he won't do it. You know Dom, when he's faced with conflict he shuts down. That's why he won't take my calls, and that's why he won't go if he knows I told you to tell him. But trust me, Rebecca, this is life or death we're talking about."

"I don't know," she said. "Chief Propst wants all hands on deck down there."

"I know the chief doesn't want his officers ignoring valid emergency responses. That's why you're there, isn't it? You have to trust me that that's what this is."

Rebecca has always been a little bit afraid of Attalah. She can't say why. Always assumed it was a tiny sliver of racism on her part, some vestigial fear of a strong Black woman, and so she's always gone out of her way to ignore that fear. Which is what she does now, as she says, *Yes, Attalah, I'll do it, no, Attalah, I trust you, no need to thank me, talk to you soon.*

....

HEATHER SHIVERS, alone in the dark at the top of the Ferris wheel. The pods are heated—this is an all-four-seasons kind of Ferris wheel, and whoever imagined that such a thing could exist?—but she has the windows open. She likes the wind. It keeps her present. Alert. Awake. Grounded. Even this high up.

She's alone, but not. Because there he is, all of a sudden, knocking on the door of her little pod. A man she met in a dream, who then turned up on Tinder.

"Hey, girl," he says, reaching in the open window to open the door when she doesn't move.

"Hi, Tom," she whispers.

He hands her a book of matches. "Are you ready?"

Heather nods. She looks out at them: the lights of her city. So many. While she sits here in the dark.

Tom's hand is on her face. His smell is strong—marine, mammalian—but overpowered by the stink of hay. Hay is packed tight into the seat she sits on, the walls of the pod. Into all of them. Sheaves of hay soaked with gasoline are strapped to all the struts with duct tape.

She takes his hand off her face. He grunts and then gets up. Opens the door. "Don't get cold feet on me now, Heather. You can do it. You can set the fire that burns them all out. But a fire like that? It needs a very special sort of kindling."

. . . .

"WAIT FOR IT," Zelda says. "You know the signal."

The man beside her grunts and sends a group text with those words.

Snow, intermittent up 'til now, begins to fall in earnest. The temperature's dropping, and Zelda loves it. Whatever the hell drug that Tom guy gave her, it's cranked up all her physical sensations and made her hyperaware. Not like meth does; not even like ecstasy. More like fear. But a fear that exhilarates.

She's parked on the sidewalk in front of Historical Materialism.

Behind the wheel of one of ten bulldozers, evenly spaced around the city. When she sees the signal, she'll rev the engine and drive the bulldozer straight through the plate-glass windows of the store. She'll back up and drive through again if she has to. Whatever it takes to completely compromise the structural integrity of the building.

Every dozer has two occupants. One to drive it, the second to step through the breach and place the gas canister and light the Molotov cocktail strapped to the side. For every dozer there are two lookout cars, one at either end of the block. They'll lean on the horn if a cop on foot comes near, and if a cop car approaches they'll move to intercept. Block the street. Buy the dozer teams some time. Sixteen minutes, she estimates, will be enough to completely destroy thirty businesses and homes. Twenty-eight minutes and every antique store on Warren Street will be gone. By that time she imagines the cops will be able to overcome the limited defenses they've put up and start shutting them down one by one, and the exponential destruction rate will slow down. But she might be wrong. The cops might not have the means to stop them at all. They might get to reduce every nonlocal business and million-dollar home to rubble.

The bulldozer has a radio. Apparently even construction workers need some music sometimes. Zelda switches it on. Rides the tingle, the electric thrum of anticipation.

"*This song goes out to all the lovely people shivering in the cold down at the Hudson boat launch*," Miss Jackson says, her voice sweet and happy. "I've Got My Love to Keep Me Warm" comes on, Billie Holiday sounding like love and warmth herself.

....

"**THIS SONG GOES OUT** *to all the lovely people shivering in the cold down at the Hudson boat launch*," says a man's voice through the speakers, sounding sad and robotic. "I've Got My Love to Keep Me

Warm" comes on, Dean Martin monotonous as cold and loneliness personified.

She's not sure why or when it started, but Lilly is afraid. The sugar buzz of the candy apple has worn off. Her teeth are chattering.

The crowd has gotten a little bigger, and that's a good thing. But then again, an awful lot of them are wearing clothes that are baggy and dark and nondescript.

Probably she's just being paranoid. This is Hudson, after all. Not exactly a fashion capital. Baggy and nondescript has always been pretty standard. Same as it would be in any town where Wal-Mart was the place most folks went for clothes.

She prays it made a difference, her trip to UPLIFT Hudson. Her offer to Attalah. She'd accepted, hadn't she? That had to count for something.

But wouldn't you? Lilly thinks. *Wouldn't you say yes and smile in the face of the naive little girl who came knocking? If only to buy yourself some time to . . . to . . .*

Well, Lilly can't really think of what Attalah might be buying time for, what diabolical schemes might be moving forward behind the scenes even now.

Whatever happens, we deserve it.

She can't get her night with Heather Scutt out of her head. How broken the woman was. How afraid. She'd never gotten it, before that moment. The depth of the violence of what they'd done in Hudson. Even with the best intentions.

I stole her home. I didn't mean to, but I did.

At least it's started to snow for real. Snow and thunderstorms still make her feel like a child again. Full of wonder and awe at what nature can do. She watches how it turns each streetlamp into a cone of drifting orange flakes.

Pretty soon the mayor will get up there and make a speech. He's running a little late already. Any minute now.

CHAPTER FIFTY-TWO

RONAN

The sea today has turned to blood. It billows in the water, turns the churning whitecaps pink.

Blood-drenched men move all around me. Heaving, cutting, sawing, stripping. Flaying. Metal knives as long as swords. I stand on the deck, blinking in the bright harsh hot sun. A moment ago I was somewhere far away, very cold but not drenched in blood. My hands are deep red; my body is black with it.

I sense it, off to the right. Lashed to starboard. I refuse to look, but its black bulk looms heavy in my mind. Rolling slowly, as the diabolical instruments slowly strip it of its blubber.

This is where we came from, says a voice in my ear, part Katch and part whale cry, and then I'm not on the ocean anymore. I'm standing in Hudson, still covered in black dried blood. White snow is everywhere, except where bright red blood spatters it. Giant metal pots billow black smoke. Two whale carcasses loll in the shallow water. Men carry strips of blubber to the blackened pots. Barrels await. Blood seeps into the soil.

This is what you are. What we are.

"Why would you want to protect us?" I ask. "After we did all this to you?"

Protect you, says the voice, and I think it laughs, but it's hard to say with a whale cry. Maybe there's some sadness in there, too. Some rage.

Human words are such imprecise instruments, the voice continues. *Like everything you make. Protection is only one piece of what we have built, here in Hudson. We are bound up together. All of us. The murderers and the murdered. The small and the large. We protect you, yes, for all time we protect you, and we fill you up with magic, but we punish you as well.*

Again the scene shifts: darkened bedrooms; sleeping shapes writhing inside of nightmares. They feed us on their dreams, but we feed them on our nightmares. We feed off of each other. Parasite-on-parasite symbiosis.

A man stands there, leaning against the railing. He sees me looking and smiles. Waves. A woman is with him. She sees me, too. I have never seen a smile so huge.

I gasp: "Mom?"

········

I SAID IT AGAIN, softer this time. But my mother wasn't there.

Neither was my father. Just a cold wind, its bite a welcome jolt, and the smell of water.

My head still spun, emerging slowly from a short chemical slumber. I shut my eyes and the dizziness subsided slightly.

"You're awake," came a garbled voice, from across a great distance. "I'm sorry."

"You said that before," I said to Attalah. "Where are we? And why am I here?"

"It'll all be clear soon enough."

A sharp updraft struck my face. Snow, carried on a harsh wind. The kind of wind that whistles through the wide-open spaces where there are no trees or hills or buildings to impede it. The kind of wind that howls through the Hudson Valley in winter.

All my dizziness ebbed away. I was awake. I was present. My hands were cuffed behind my back. My shoulder felt like a truck had hit it.

I was kneeling on the pedestrian walkway of the Rip Van Winkle Bridge. Staring down into the same dizzying dark, the same twenty-story fall that swallowed up my mother.

A train whistle wailed. Southbound—funny how I could tell the difference by how the sound Dopplered. The train I should have been on. I watched it from the bridge, a long narrow line of light moving through the dark, and remembered looking up at the bridge from the train on the night I arrived.

I watched it abandon me. Everything felt so flimsy. Like a dream I knew I was about to wake up from.

CHAPTER FIFTY-THREE

Heather lights a match, then puts it out. She is so cold. But not in a hurry to set herself on fire just yet.

This is not like the Ferris wheel at the Columbia County Fair every summer. This one is special. So much bigger. She can see so far. All the lights of her city, spread out in an orderly grid getting smaller as it moves away from her. Past that, even, to the darkening countryside beyond. The wide black rift of the river. The dark cloud-shapes in the sky, swimming against the wind. The lights of the Rip Van Winkle Bridge to the south. Albany's dull glow, beyond the horizon to the north. The snow falling faster now. Heather can see far enough to wonder: is there or isn't there a place for me in this town?

....

MISS JACKSON FADES OUT. A cheer rises up from the tiny crowd. Everybody knows that when the music stops, the show begins.

Rick Edgley shifts his weight from foot to foot. Uncertain; anxious; freezing cold. Snow is beginning to accumulate on his boots. His blue whale mask is in a plastic grocery store bag between them. He has his orders but doesn't know much beyond them. Attalah told him what to do.

He hasn't felt so good since what went down with Ohrena. He let Attalah talk him into something he felt awful about. Sure, it might have helped save his town, and that made it a good thing, but it also showed him how he was maybe not such a good person, and didn't that count for something, too? What did it matter if they saved their town, if they became monsters in the process? Was it better to be good and homeless or bad and housed?

Plus, he was out on bond. Awaiting a trial date. Ohrena swore up and down she'd recant before it came to that, even if it meant the cops turned around and charged her with filing a false police report . . . but he was still in the position of having his fate in the hands of someone else, and that was never a position he wanted to be in. He remembers fights that went the distance, the agony of waiting for the judges' decision, and this is like that, except, it could go on for months.

"Ladies and gentlemen!" shouts Mayor Coffin into the mic. Wallace Warsaw stands behind him, the next to speak. Two sellout sons of bitches. But also, men he's known his whole life.

"The Ferris wheel!" someone shouts. Rick's muscles tense. The signal involves the Ferris wheel.

Spotlights shift. Screams start.

Jark Trowse is strapped to the center of the Ferris wheel. Drugged; asleep. Bleeding.

That's not the signal. What is Attalah up to here?

"Everyone, please be calm!" the mayor squawks. "I assure you Chief Propst and his—"

With a sharp static squeal, the microphone cuts out.

. . . .

"**SOMEBODY HELP HIM!**" someone cries. Police officers scramble. The chief barks orders.

Lilly is giddy with fear and cold. Excited, even. Almost. Euphoric at the violence she can smell in the air. For days now she's been worried about a sudden explosion of violence. When you've been so twisted up with waiting for something horrible, there's a delirious pleasure when it finally comes.

"Put the music back on!" she hears the mayor shout, unamplified. But something is wrong with the speakers, and she can hear the music but only very faintly.

"Kill that goddamn spotlight," a cop shouts, running toward it.

Everyone else is staring at the center of the wheel, where her boss is bound by ropes. And also maybe dead. Hopefully dead. Hopefully there's no further awfulness in store for him. Either way, Lilly can't bear to look at him.

Which is why she's the only one to see a figure climbing down from the Ferris wheel. A woman, slim and nimble, swinging hand over hand around the spaces between pods.

"Hey, Heather," Lilly whispers, knowing she can't hear her.

She waves, when Heather gets to the ground, knowing Heather won't see it.

All of which is why Lilly misses it.

Someone next to her shrieks. The general sounds of a low-level panic are suddenly escalated. Screams crowd the air. Wails. Everyone is wailing, it seems.

Lilly turns around. The mayor is still standing on the platform. One hand on a mic that no longer works. Looking down with deep confusion at the harpoon through his stomach.

· · · · · · · ·

SOMEHOW DOM IS NOT SURPRISED when he sees who's standing there at the center of the pedestrian walkway. He knew something was off when Rebecca called to dispatch him. He could hear it in her voice. That there was more to the call, something she wasn't telling him. *Like maybe, your wife is the potential jumper.* He walks faster, slipping slightly on the snow that's accumulating on the sidewalk.

"Attalah!" he calls, thinking: *She can't jump. I'll die if she jumps.*

But then he gets closer and sees the figure at her feet. Kneeling. Handcuffed.

"You came," she says, smiling. He can't read her smile. He has no idea who she is right now.

He remembers Rudy in the hospital bed, baffled by what he'd become.

"What the hell are you doing, Attalah?"

"I had to," she says.

"Why is Ronan handcuffed?"

"I'm sorry," she says.

"She keeps saying that," Ronan says, and Dom is now close enough to see the blood on the side of his face.

"What did you do to him?"

"He fell," she says. "I chloroformed him, and he struggled, and he fell and hit his head. I'm sorry. I didn't mean to."

"I'm fine," Ronan says. "For now. Who knows what the hell she's got up her sleeve."

"I just saved your lives, assholes," Attalah says.

"Saved us from what?" Dom asks. The wind is so strong and so cold out there that he has trouble standing up straight.

"Wait," she says. "Any second now."

"This is crazy," Dom says, unholstering his radio, ready to phone in—what? My wife kidnapped my best friend and gay lover and is going to make him walk the plank? My wife is part of some horrific plan that almost certainly involves mass murder and destruction?

"There," she says, pointing north, toward Hudson, and Dom turns to see a massive ring of fire kindle in the darkness. The Ferris wheel, blossoming into flames. He hears what might be human screams, carried south on the wind, or might just be the wind shrieking through the metal girders of the bridge.

"They snapped," Ronan says. "A whole lot of people . . . they broke."

. . . .

"PEOPLE OF HUDSON!" a woman cries, whale-headed, microphone in hand. The speakers are working again. Even from here, across the parking lot, she can feel the heat from the burning Ferris wheel.

Some people are fleeing. Some are putting on whale masks.

Wallace Warsaw steps forward, says, "Now you listen to me, missy," and then there is a harsh shout from nearby and suddenly he has a harpoon through him, too. This guy's aim is a lot cleaner than that of whoever speared the mayor. The mayor is gurgling on the ground, gut split open, very much alive and wishing he wasn't. Wallace Warsaw got his through the neck and is dead a matter of seconds after he hits the snowy ground.

"People of Hudson," the woman says, and almost gasps with joy, with power and energy. "Tonight is the night when we take back our town!"

Cheers. Well over half the crowd is wearing whale masks by now.

"They tried to take what is ours, but we will not let them."

Baleful, bloodthirsty shouts.

"They tried to build something new on our ashes," she cries, wondering where it came from, this sudden eloquence, this long-sought clarity. *From the blade between your ribs, sailor,* says a voice from somewhere inside her, and she sees that this is true, that the jagged shape beneath her skin is one point in a web that ties her together with everyone else in Hudson. "But it's they who will burn. Like good vultures, they saw us as a beautiful carcass they could feast on. They came for our old buildings, our antiques. Let's see how much they like this town when we've destroyed all of that."

Distant explosions.

Jark Trowse is awake, alive, burning at the center of a circle of fire. His screams echo across the parking lot.

CHAPTER FIFTY-FOUR

RONAN

He came, I thought, heart swooning, when I watched Dom cross the bridge to where we were. Low clouds swept across the bridge, moving south with the wind, swallowing up and spitting out the welcome sight of him.

"Attalah, what are you talking about?"

"They were going to kidnap Ronan, same way they kidnapped Jark Trowse," she said. "They had something planned for both of them, and Wallace and the mayor. They said they wouldn't hurt them—just humiliate the hell out of them—but I don't believe that at all."

"Who's they?"

"The motherfuckers in whale masks," I whispered, and Attalah nodded.

"I went along with them, but only to find out what I needed to know. I had to say some pretty fucked-up shit to convince them, honestly." If there was more to it, if she'd been on board for a while and then had a change of heart, I respected her too much to press for more information.

"Who are they?" Dom asked.

"There's a lot of them," she said. "But Zelda was the main one pulling the strings."

"Zelda?" Dom asked. "Mousy little Zelda who needed to take a ton of speed before she could even look somebody in the eye without having an anxiety attack?"

"No," Attalah said. "It's another Zelda now. She's . . . different."

She hasn't been herself lately, I thought, echoing Norman Bates. *She's fallen in with a bad crowd. Under the influence. Ghosts, monsters, whale god spirits. That sort of thing.*

I wasn't scared of the dark beneath us anymore. We were together. What on earth could I possibly need beyond the three of us? And what could hurt me as long as they loved me?

"Attalah," Dom said, his voice low, anxious—clearly not sharing my sudden sense of utter peace. "What do they have planned?"

"There's nothing you can do about it," she said, stooping to uncuff me. This time she wasn't the only one to struggle, standing up straight. My knees ached; my thighs burned.

"What. Do. They. Have. Planned?"

"They're going to destroy a whole lot of shit, that's what," she said. "They've got bombs and bulldozers and fucking harpoons, and depending on how crazy they are they'll either bulldoze a building or two, or they'll burn Warren Street to the ground. Me, I think they're way closer to crazy than not. And there's not a goddamn thing you can do to stop them. But I know you, Dom. I know you'd try, anyway, and you'd get yourself killed in the process. That's why I had Rebecca help me get you out here. Where you're safe from them and safe from yourself."

He turned and looked south. The city lights, the burning wheel—clouds came so thick and low and fast now that we could only see them in tiny glimmers. But the pain on his face, I could see that clear as day. He loved Hudson too much to let it die. He cursed, under his breath, and turned to go.

"Dom," Attalah and I said at the exact same time. He didn't stop.

A cloud came, then, so thick I couldn't see the people standing at arm's reach. And when it dispersed, I wasn't on the bridge anymore.

Warren Street, burning. Antique stores engulfed; millions of dollars of irreplaceable artifacts reduced to ash.

Warren Street, bare, burned. A month or a year or a century from now. Dead terrain, covered in snow.

Warren Street, bare, before it was a street at all. Five centuries ago, or possibly a thousand. Dead land under snow, sloping down to a river.

Between the two of them, you couldn't tell the difference.

"Scary stuff, isn't it?" Katch sat on the railing beside me.

"Can't we do something?" I asked.

"No," Katch said. Sounding sad; sounding scared. "We pushed too many people too far. Tom did, mostly. But me, too, a little. What happens now is out of our control."

Wick stood in the middle of the bridge as well. So did my father. In the distance, on the pedestrian walkway, was a woman. Too far away for me to see who she was, but didn't I know? Couldn't I guess? Hadn't she always been here, waiting for me?

They twitched. They jerked. As Hudson suffered, so did they. When it died, so would they.

Tom wasn't trying to save Hudson. He was going to burn it down.

We were between gusts of snow. No cars crossed the bridge. Even the clouds around us were frozen in place. Dom stayed still, mid-step. Attalah's mouth was open, another word stopped on its way out.

Oh good, I thought. *Time has stopped. How nice.*

"What can we do?" I asked Katch.

"Nothing," Tom said, standing on the railing beside where Katch sat. Grinning. Hungry.

"That can't be true," Dom said, turning back toward me. Toward Tom.

"You can see him?" I asked, startled. "Hear him?"

Dom nodded.

He believes. Attalah doesn't.

Again the scene shifted. The Hudson boat launch. Ferris wheel flames frozen in place but still giving off heat. Bloodshot eyes; raised weapons.

"They let me in," Tom said, "they opened their hearts to me. Their hate fed me. Now I feed them. I can show them anything now. Instead of their mother they'll see the bully who beat them up in high school, maybe, and instead of open arms they'll see raised weapons. Or they'll see nothing at all."

Cops stood at ease, blind to what was unfolding around them. One looked out at the water, a mouthful of cigarette smoke standing still in the air in front of him, while a screaming woman stabbed a harpoon into a man's open mouth beside him.

I called out into the cloud mist. "Can you see this, Dom?"

"I see it," he said, his voice inches from my ear but also echoing from endless miles away.

"We're dying," Wick said, and then it was just me and Dom and Wick and Attalah at the bowling alley. Dom tried to give the boy a hug, and he pushed him away. "Do something, Dom," he begged, his voice weak as wind. Dying with the town.

You humans are so shortsighted, Katch had said. *Wick is better off, trust me.*

The whales had built a safe place for souls to stay, here in Hudson. Where they'd be protected—and punished—and together, forever. But if they ceased to be, so would Wick. So would Katch and (*my mother*) (*my father*) (*Dom's father*) everyone else we had ever lost.

"You have to help us," said my father.

How could I stop him? Where did his strength come from? But I was worried I already knew the answer.

Your hate helped immensely, Katch had said. *You've helped so much more anger blossom.*

All that hate, spreading through the city, it comes from you.

You're far too important for us to risk snapping you.

This place—it's feeding on you, my father had said. *It needs you.*

Attalah helped Katch crystallize, but she hadn't been able to feed him what he needed. She wasn't toxic enough. Her heart wasn't overflowing with hate and rage and sadness.

For that, they needed me. My pain. My weakness. I'd fed them, and I'd let Tom in.

My father said, "You have to go, Ronan."

I touched my chest. The blade between my ribs was bigger now, a knotted vein of metal with new sharp metastases—extending through me, into the hearts of others. A toxic tree that had sprouted from the soil of my shattered heart. The roots had burrowed deep into the dirt, branched off into a hundred new directions, piercing the hearts of hundreds of others, but the taproot, the one all the others broke off of—that was me.

"I know what to do," I said to Dom, even if I didn't *know*, not really. I had hope, not knowledge, but hope would have to be enough. "How to stop all this."

CHAPTER FIFTY-FIVE

What are you talking about?" Dom asks.

"I love you," Ronan says, stepping closer, like he's going in for a kiss, but then he hugs him hard instead.

"You're scaring me," Dom says, hugging back. Not intending to ever let go.

"I love you both," Ronan says. "If there was a way that we could all three survive, *and* save the town, and the people we love, I'd take it. But I don't think there is."

"Fuck the town," Dom said. "It's just buildings, streets. It's home, and I love it, but it's just . . ."

"It's not," I said. "I can't explain it, but there's so much more to this place. Someday you'll see it for yourself. They've created something, a safe place beyond the reach of time and death, but that's been under attack for so long it's about to get washed away. The thing that's threatening us—ultimately, its power comes from me, Dom. I let it in. I gave it life. It's grown out of control, but it's all rooted in me."

"You're not making any sense."

"You know I am," Ronan says. "We can't kill them, but without me—they'll be crippled. All these people under its control, they'll be freed."

"Shut up with that *without me* shit. You're not going anywhere."

"Let go of me, Dom. Don't make it any harder for me to . . ."

"I love you, too, Ronan. We both do. We love you and we need you and this town needs you."

Slowly, almost imperceptibly, the snowflakes around them have begun to fall again.

"We've been stuck here, inside a single moment," Ronan says. "Katch" (*the whales*) "did that, I think. To buy us time. But pretty soon that moment will come to an end, and the killing will resume. The destruction. Hudson will burn to the ground."

"This can't be real," Dom whispers, his head lodged in the crook of Ronan's neck. Suddenly he is the one being held up, not the one doing the holding.

Wind picks up. Its wail grows louder.

"I always thought I was the strong one," Dom says.

"You are," says Ronan, inhaling the sweet spice smell of Dom for the last time. "You always were. It took a hell of a long time, but a little of your strength finally rubbed off on me."

"There's got to be another way."

"You've seen what I've seen. You know there's not."

Dom lets go. Ronan steps back. Climbs up onto the railing of the pedestrian walkway.

"No," Katch says, eyes widening in fear.

"Stop," Tom says, standing there beside him, and unleashes a torrent of high-volume profanity. Most of it isn't even human words. He reaches out for Ronan and then pulls his hand back. Afraid to even try.

Wick smiles. So does Jim Szepessy.

"You'll tell Attalah?" Ronan asks. "That I love her?"

Tom goes rigid, frozen in fear. In the knowledge that he can't stop this. Wolf howls and angry bellows echo in the wind.

"She already knows," Dom says, one hand still extended to grab hold of Ronan and hold him there forever. "But I'll tell her anyway."

Ronan takes one small step into the darkness.

Dom lunges forward. His fingers close on empty air. A wailing fills it up—his own, astonishing in its volume, its violence.

A squall of snow sweeps up, like Dom's pained cry given physical form. It washes over the bridge, a tsunami of fog and cold. When it's gone, time has slipped back into its old familiar groove. Cars crossing the bridge. The red lights of radio towers flashing in the distance.

Dom and Attalah are alone.

"Oh my God," Attalah says, and her hands fly to her face. To grab hold of the scream that wants to come. To stop it in its place.

"What did you see?" Dom asks.

Wick squats on the railing, watching. And a woman Dom hasn't seen in twenty years.

"I saw him jump. I saw—" Attalah pauses, turns to look around. Shakes her head. "I must have . . . I don't know what I saw."

Dom hugs her. He's crying. "You and me both," he says.

CHAPTER FIFTY-SIX

RONAN

L ove is harder than hate," Pastor Thirza said, looking past the packed house. Every pew occupied; a bigger turnout than Grace Abounding had seen in years, if ever. "When I decided that would be the subject for my next sermon—when I put it up on the sign outside—I don't think I'd really thought it through. Those were dark days for me, I don't mind telling you now. I had a lot of crazy thoughts running around in my head. *Love is harder than hate*, that was one of them."

Behind her, a line of easels holding framed photographs five feet tall. Everybody who died in the final days of the Late Unpleasantness. Mayor Coffin; Wallace Warsaw. Jark. A man I didn't know, part of the crew that tried to threaten Treenie Lazzarra and got shot for it. Five more unfamiliar faces, harpooned or shot down at the boat launch. One of Tom's conquests, some schmendrick whose screen name was *Bergen_Street*. I don't even know how or when that happened.

Me. My father.

Dom found him in the snow, behind our house, when he went to tell him about my own death.

I watched them weep. Watched them mourn us. Watched them

sit together, hands clasped or hands pressed together in prayer. Trying together to process what had happened to them.

Margie sat in the front row. Her eyes never left the photo of my father. I'd always imagined maybe she'd been a little bit in love with him, but now I knew that wasn't true. She admired him, that's all. She believed he was the only truly good person she knew. Incorrectly, of course. He wasn't truly good, but neither was anyone else in her life. Humans are so shortsighted while they're still alive.

She was a Catholic, but she came anyway. So did the Ukrainian Orthodox and everyone else. In a little while Rabbi Morris Freinberg from Congregation Anshe Emeth would say a few words, followed by an imam from the Islamic Society. With how many faiths and their followers were packed into the relatively close confines of Grace Abounding, the event should have been held at the much larger Episcopal or Lutheran church, or maybe St. Mary's—but all the other faith leaders deferred to Pastor Thirza in her time of grief.

"At the beginning," she said, "all I meant was, love is *stronger* than hate. Like a diamond is harder than an emerald. There was so much hate in Hudson, so much simmering anger, and I thought that I could remind people that hate was not the answer, that love would triumph."

She was a handsome woman, without her wig. Sobriety agreed with her. Wick's death had helped her kick the habit. The physical pain of going cold turkey had been a welcome distraction from emotional anguish.

"But now I'm not so sure. I've been tested, along with all of you. For the first time, I knew true hate. And what I realized was, *hate is easy.*"

"I know that's right," said a woman somewhere in the room.

"Hate is easy. Sounds sinful to say it, doesn't it? But it is. I know that now, and I suspect that some of you do, too. Am I wrong?"

"You're not wrong," a man said.

"Bad things happen to us. To people we love. People hurt us, sometimes without meaning to. Cancer hurts us. Evictions hurt us. *God* hurts us. That's what we think, isn't it? That's what it feels like. God lets terrible things happen. Oh, sure, we try to tell ourselves He must have a good reason—a plan—but we know we'll never know it. And the knowing it's part of a plan doesn't make it hurt any less. So it's easy to turn to hate, when the rug gets pulled out from under you. When what you love most in the world is taken away. Hate is easy in times like that."

Dom and Attalah sat toward the back. Their fingers laced together. Clenched tight. They couldn't see me, didn't know I was there.

"But love? Love is hard."

. . . .

"WELCOME," SHE SAID, ushering the woman in. "I'm so glad you came. My name's Lilly."

"I'm Ohrena," she said, entering uncertainly. "My friend Lettie did this thing, and she said it helped her out a lot, but she couldn't explain it super well. Might be I'm just kind of ignorant, though."

"It's a bit of a strange concept," Lilly said. "*Hudson: Past and Present* is an interactive experience, a living history machine, an opportunity for people to share their experiences and their knowledge. The idea is, Hudson belongs to all of us, and if we're going to be able to move forward from all this hell we've been through lately, we need to be able to talk about it openly. Can I get you a cup of coffee? Tea?"

Ohrena asked for coffee, black. Lilly made two.

Calling it a Truth and Reconciliation Commission would have been too much. She'd tried, but Attalah shot her down. *Let's try not to make people think too much about genocide or apartheid, okay?* But the principle was the same. Both sides of a conflict sat down to engage in open dialogue, so as to better understand what happened and help survivors on both sides move toward healing, and forge a path forward that was just and fair for all sides.

"I'm going to set you up in this pod here. This tablet will ask you a couple of basic questions, about who you are and what time period you're talking about, and then you're good to go. As you talk, the software will recognize key phrases and names and they'll pop up on the screen. You can reject them if they're incorrect, or verify them if they're right, or ignore them altogether. Whatever's easiest for you. But the more we can make your testimony accessible and cross-connected, the better. So that if people a hundred years from now want to know about the Winter Fest Fire, or the Diamond Street Whorehouses, or Mayor Coffin, or Walker Evans, they can click on it and get all the different stories that people have told about it. Understand?"

"I think so," Ohrena said, chewing her lip. Intimidated by all the elaborate tech Penelope's Quilt paid for.

"You look like you have questions," Lilly said, sitting down.

"My friend, Lettie? She came because her sister committed suicide, because someone was threatening her, because she was an obstacle to something they were trying to do. And she said it was really great to be able to tell that story. But a lot of people, they're not so innocent. If someone were to confess to a crime here, could they get in trouble for that?"

"Well, we can't guarantee immunity or anything like that. And if someone's actions caused harm or defamation to another individual, they still retain the right to sue. So a civil action is always a possibility. But as for criminal prosecution—we're working closely with the Hudson Police Department, and their main priority is healing Hudson—not mass arrests that'll only further traumatize our communities. So for most crimes other than physical assault committed in the process of what some people are calling the Hudson Renaissance Resistance, they're offering participation in our project as an acceptable pretrial alternative, with immunity from arrest if all sides are satisfied with the results of the dialogue."

Ohrena nodded.

"Here's a couple you can take a look at," Lilly said, queueing them up on the tablet.

Quint, discussing being beaten by Hudson cops. A mom describing the shelter where she went with her kids, after her sister had to kick her out to make room for their mom, whose building got bought and torn down. A high school Italian teacher, talking about the two old ladies who used to live above the Silver Dollar, sisters, wearing filthy fur coats from September to May.

"Everyone's story matters," Lilly said. "*Hudson: Past and Present* is a way for all of us to tell our stories, and listen to both sides, and get a better understanding of history and how we relate to it. Last week we did an amazing interview between a woman who'd been evicted and the guy who threw her out. Powerful stuff. They were both crying by the end of it, and he signed the Eviction Free Zone pledge the next day. But you can tell a nice happy story about being a kid in Hudson if that's what you want. You have any other questions?"

"No, ma'am," Ohrena said.

"Just call me Lilly," she said, clicking their mugs together in a mock toast.

. . . .

"LOVE IS HARD," Pastor Thirza repeated. "It's hard to love someone who is flawed, or sick, or so twisted up inside that they hurt the people they care about. It's hard to love a God who lets bad things happen to us. It's hard to love the people who push us out of our homes. Hard to love the people who hate us."

Behind her, on the wall, another framed photograph, thirty years old or so. Four little girls, all African American. One of them, the eagle-eyed will observe, is Pastor Thirza herself. Down in the lower-right-hand corner is a tiny oval with the word *Jerremy* inside it.

Attalah had been there, the day that Lilly gifted it to her, after finding it in an attic crate somewhere. The pastor had wept. Said, *I always felt drawn to his work, I don't know why. And now I find he took a photograph of me?* And the woman had pointed to that younger Thirza, the one smiling suspiciously at the photographer, and asked, *Do you remember that day? Do you remember what he looked like?* And Pastor Thirza had paused a moment before shaking her head *No*, and when she did so she had the strangest secret look on her face, like whatever was making her smile was hers to hold on to.

Which is what she looked like now, standing at the front of her church, bringing her sermon to a close.

"But hard as it is, love is the way forward, beloveds. Trust and believe that. When we love, we let God's light shine through us. We are most fully ourselves when we hold tight to the people who make us who we are. We exist in community. Not *E pluribus unum*—from many, one—but simply one. We were never *many*. The divisions between us, they were never real. Illusions, nothing more. I'm here to tell you what God says, and that's this: love your neighbor as yourself, because your neighbor *is* yourself."

. . . .

AS A VIOLENCE-RACKED TOWN FORGES ITS FUTURE, A PIECE OF ITS PAST RESURFACES—THE NEW YORK TIMES [EXCERPT]

Hudson, NY.—For years, the 1950s-era photographer who signed his work only as 'Jerremy' was a subject of much conjecture here in his upstate home. Some say he was nothing more than a small-town studio portraitist, whose struggling business lasted less than a decade and who left behind only a handful of pedestrian images more valuable as history than as art. Others believe he is a forgotten American master, a peer of Dorothea Lange with a splash of Weegee's lurid DNA and Henri Cartier-Bresson's knack for catching the decisive moment, whose sympathetic invasive eye prefigured Diane Arbus and Nan Goldin.

And now, with hundreds of his photographs suddenly coming to light, the latter camp appears to have triumphed.

Little is known about Jerremy—that he was a man, and that he was black, are long-held assumptions with no real evidence behind them. And while these new images shine a dazzling light on his incredible artistic genius (which can be seen in great detail in this weekend's Arts and Leisure section, and on our website), they cast little illumination on the man behind them.

Still, they are a welcome discovery for a town struggling to reconnect with its illustrious history after a period of unrest that culminated in mass arson and mass murder a month ago. With alleged ringleader Zelda Outterson awaiting trial for two dozen charges ranging from manslaughter to kidnapping to conspiracy to commit arson—but resolutely refusing to name any of her co-conspirators . . . [. . .]

. . . .

DOM AND ATTALAH STAYED, long after the service was finished. Through interminable remarks from well over a dozen different speakers. Through the long shuffle out. The sound of a hundred different good-byes: high fives and handshakes and hugs and cheek kisses echoing around them. Until no one else was left.

"Hey, honey," Hazel said, emerging from the back a half hour later. "Thanks for waiting. That was a tough one, for Thirza, and she needed some talking-to after it was over. Sort of an informal prayer circle. Or NA meeting."

Laughing, Attalah rose to embrace her mother. They spent a long time hugging. Attalah was loath to let her mother go, lately. She'd spent so long thinking she'd lost her, she was still suspicious of the good right feeling of having her back.

"She okay?" Dom asked.

"She is now. Amazing what a little prayer can do."

Anyone with eyes could look at Attalah as she stared at her mother and know what she is thinking. *It's a miracle. They told me she'd never move or speak again, and here she is acting like she never had a stroke.*

Dom's face was harder to read, but I know how to do it.

Ronan did this. I don't know how it works, but I know that when he died, he broke the hold that thing had on Hazel. Her and half the town, practically.

Arm in arm in arm, they walked out into the sunlight. Laughed, as one, at how it hurt their eyes.

"Hey, Heather," Attalah said, seeing Heather Scutt standing around on the sidewalk. Puffy-eyed from crying, but who wasn't today? "Where are you off to?"

She shrugged. "No particular place to be."

"You want to come with me and my mom? We're going to a meeting of Our Future. Have you heard about that?"

Heather shook her head, looking vaguely alarmed.

"It's a bunch of different people who have a stake in Hudson's future, trying to work together to make sure that no one gets left behind."

"Oh," Heather said, frowning deeper, "that doesn't really sound like my kind of scene. I don't think I'd have much to offer in the way of . . ." She trailed off, but of course Attalah would not let her off so easily.

"You have as much a right as anyone to decide what our future looks like. Your family's scrapyard was an important part of this city's economy for, what, thirty years?"

"Thirty-seven it was open."

"Exactly. But more important, you were born here and raised here. Hudson is yours. Ours. Just come to the meeting, okay? Maybe you'll find it boring as hell, or hate having to talk to a bunch of businessmen and gentrifiers, and run screaming out the door halfway through. If that urge hits you, go right ahead. I wouldn't be one bit mad at you. I get the urge myself, several times a meeting."

Heather smirked but then frowned again.

"There's free coffee and cookies," Attalah said, hoping to seal the deal.

Dom said, "I'd go, just for the coffee, if I didn't have somewhere else to be."

Everyone laughed. Finally, Heather nodded. Smiled. Said, "Okay. Let's do it. Where are we going?"

. . . .

"I DON'T KNOW why you insist on coming here," Dom said, sitting down on a stool at the counter.

"I like the ambience," I said.

He saw an expensive Hudson Renaissance restaurant: square card-stock menus, and ten-dollar milkshakes. Obscenely costly reproduction wallpaper. I saw the gritty fluorescent-lit Columbia Diner my father and I used to come to, on the way down to work at the butcher shop. A heavy old Greek behind the cash register, instead of a bearded young thing with rectangular spectacles. Crow Man perched on a stool nearby, making cawing noises. Bowl of pee-flecked mints at the counter. Factory workers coming off a twelve-hour shift. Filthy mirror across from me, giving me back myself.

"Two coffees," Dom told the counter man. To me, he said, "Where's Wick?"

"Last I checked he was in the 1930s, going through film from a shoot he did, of bootleggers' molls getting dressed up before a movie premiere. Before that he did some great shots at this creepy children's masquerade on ice from the winter of 1957, down at Oakdale Pond. Kids bundled up but wearing homemade monster masks. Real nightmare fuel."

"I'm still not sure I understand how y'all are time travelers now."

"We're not time travelers. It's just . . ." Katch's words seemed best to describe the indescribable. So I repeated them: "Time is weird here. We exist outside of time as you know it, so we hop around. We can't always control where . . . I mean, when, we end up." I elected not to tell him that this was part of the supernatural caul that cloaked Hudson. He'd figure it out soon enough, when he died and ended up with us. "Tell Lilly to check a filing cabinet in the fourth-floor storage of the Child Protective Services."

"I'll do that," he said. "You hear Aperture's looking at doing a monograph? Getting included in that MoMA show really put him on the map. Kid's making a real name for himself. Shame he had to be dead to do it. You done good, Ronan."

"I haven't done much. Kid has an incredible eye and a hell of a heart. I'm just trying to help him trust them. You're the one helping his work be 'discovered.'"

"Don't think I didn't notice that extra R in his name. That's you, isn't it?"

"His idea," I said. "An homage, he says. I'm not completely comfortable with it." I sipped my coffee, cheap old grounds the way I remembered them. A pyramid of tiny cereal boxes stood beside the coffeepot, just like I remembered. "How are you, Dom? Things seem good around town. Never would have imagined I'd see the day when Attalah voluntarily sat down to a meeting with Treenie Lazzarra and Pastor Thirza and some woman from Penelope's Quilt who looks like she still gets carded at bars. Let alone meeting with them once a week for months."

He exhaled, heavily. "Things are okay. A damn sight better than they were a little while ago, but still pretty fucked. Not everybody's all peace-and-love-and-kumbaya-and-let's-come-together-to-build-a-future-for-all-of-us. A lot of greedy bastards are . . . still greedy bastards. There's lawsuits, and we're still seeing fights break out over all the shit that went down. Last week a wife shot her husband because of a photo of him fucking her sister, which both swear wasn't real. He'll be fine. She said she knew how to shoot to wound, so the first one was a warning. Dude didn't want an order of protection, if you can believe that."

"Don't forget all that priceless architecture Zelda and Co knocked over," I said. "Eleven buildings total, homes and businesses. 'An inestimable loss,' according to the *New York Times*."

"How could I forget."

I put my hand on his. I could feel his heat, but I knew he could not feel mine.

"I miss you," I said.

"I'm right here," he said, eyes electric on mine.

"I'm not," I said.

Dom nodded, turned away. I'd seen the way his eyes got wet, though. "I wish you were, though."

"It's fascinating, where I am," I said. "And there's some good people, who I enjoy talking to. People like your dad. And also I've been carrying on a very scandalous affair with a notorious and flamboyant gangster in 1927. I'm serious about the scandal part—there's an oblique reference to it in the *New York Post* society pages for October second of that year. Look it up."

I wondered how much longer he'd be able to see me for. He couldn't see Wick, who was scrutinizing negatives at the booth at the end, looking up occasionally to smile at us. Would the day come when all of these conversations would come to seem like weird dreams to Dom?

The whales were still there. I saw them sometimes, swimming through the sky. So was Tom Minniq. Still sort of a demon, but diminished now. Small enough to exist in stasis.

"I love you, Ronan," he said.

"I love you, too."

In the filthy mirror, I could see my mother and father crossing through the Sixth Street Park. Coming my way.

"What would it look like to all these people," he asked, "if I kissed you right now?"

"As far as I can tell, people try real hard not to see any evidence of the . . . other side? So, probably by some magical coincidence, absolutely no one would happen to be looking in this direction when you did."

He leaned forward, kissed me soft and gentle on the lips. Wick laughed. No one else saw.

"Fate is a fucking nasty son of a bitch," Dom said, getting up to go. "For you of all people, who ran screaming away from Hudson the first chance he got, to be trapped here for all eternity."

"It's not so bad," was all I said. I'd already tried to tell him what I'd learned. More than once. And I failed, every time.

It's okay to love something that you hate.

Just like it's okay to hate something that you love.

And we all have to learn to love the cages we're in, because we carry them with us wherever we go.

ACKNOWLEDGMENTS

First off, I must acknowledge that the Hudson of this book—while deeply rooted in my own experience growing up there—is not the Hudson of reality. No character in this book maps onto anyone in real life. No business mentioned in these pages is intended to mirror any actual establishment, even if they share the same name (except for the Pizza Pit, which really did make the best pizza on the planet, and which really has been gone for decades).

I do owe some huge debts of gratitude to real people in the real Hudson, however.

The Hudson Area Library is a magnificent community resource, and the staff was incredibly helpful in the course of researching this book—particularly when it came to accessing the archives in the History Room. Big gratitude to Brenda Shufelt, Emily Chameides, and Brigitte Gfeller. It is true that I've taken some dramatic liberties with my representation of how whaling happened in Hudson, but that's not due to any deficiency in the archives—when the stories I'd heard as a kid conflicted with the actual history . . . I went with the stories I'd heard as a kid.

Amber Kline gave me invaluable insight into the incredible work of the Columbia County Department of Social Services.

The team of Kelley Drahushuk and Alan Coon have built a magnificent space for local artists at the Spotty Dog, one of my favorite bookstores on the planet. I'm profoundly grateful to them, as I am to all independent booksellers everywhere.

Giovanni di Mola was generous with his time, and helped me understand the perspectives of some of the first-wave artist arrivals who set the stage for Hudson's transformation. The blogs of Sam Pratt and Carole Osterink were similarly helpful.

My mother, Deborah Miller, gave me free room and board when I needed to come up to Hudson to do research and reacquaint myself with the local ghosts. She also taught me how to be a writer.

I owe Seth Fishman so much that it's hard not to sound repetitious about it, but one thing worth calling out here is that when I went to him and said, "Everybody says the smart career move is to stick to one genre, but I have a creepy supernatural thriller I really, really wanna write," he said what he's always said: "Write what you want to write and let me worry about everything else."

Zachary Wagman made this book sparkle, knowing exactly how to slash and burn and streamline to bring the edgy thriller pacing to the forefront. Reading through the galleys for last-pass copyedits, I kept thinking, *Damn, Zack, this thing is really humming!*

The Ecco team of Sara Birmingham and Martin Wilson and Co. have always made me feel confident that my work will get the support it needs to reach the people it needs to reach.

The gentrification of Hudson is real—but so is the resistance. I salute the folks who've been fighting to keep low-income residents in their homes and preserve some of what has always made the city special—they'd never make any of the mistakes made by the 1,000 percent–fictional resistance in these pages.

Ronan Szepessy is an only child, and maybe if he had an awesome sibling like my sister, Sarah, he would have turned out better. But having her as a cheerleader and friend when I was a lonely, bullied, miserable teenager made a huge difference, and I owe her much more than I can ever give back.

Finally—and forever—I must acknowledge Juancy Rodriguez, my husband and my hero, without whom none of this would have happened.